VENGEFUL

THE GABRIEL SERIES - BOOK THREE

DAVID HICKSON

AEON BOOKS

First is a Judge

ONE

J ustice Francois Rousseau – as a man of the law – might have been expected by most people to speak the truth.

But I am not like most people, which was why I had broken into his house this Sunday morning to ask my questions in person. And I was finding that Justice Rousseau was reluctant to speak anything, let alone the truth.

"Disappeared?" he said, in a voice tight with anger.

"She disappeared," I confirmed.

Justice Rousseau grunted. He was a short man with a balding head, wisps of grey hair straggling in all the wrong directions because he had woken unexpectedly upon discovering that there was an intruder in his house, and had not taken the time to comb his hair into place. The body beneath the head was substantial, and although he had his back to me, he contrived to have his heavy shoulders broadcast his sense of superiority.

I had asked my questions about the missing journalist gently, almost kindly, but he had not taken it at all well. He stood in a gesture of dismissal and gazed out through the tinted glass wall at the infinity pool, which reflected the azure sky above a sleepy Johannesburg.

"What does this journalist have to do with me?" he asked, his eyes still fixed on the view offered by his modern monstrosity of a mansion, which was perched high on Northcliff Ridge. Beyond the carefully tended garden, we could glimpse buildings between the trees of the world's largest man-made forest that sheltered the sprawling metropolis of the business capital of South Africa.

"I believe she came to see you," I said. "Interviewed you, perhaps?"

"*Believe!*" scoffed Justice Rousseau. "*Perhaps!* What would she have come to see me about?"

We had gone through his sneering rejection of the idea that he knew anything about Sandy or her disappearance, and then he had played the outright denial card. Now we were doing the harder 'why me' stuff. This was harder, because Justice Rousseau knew very well why him. I had already explained that his name was on a list of men that the journalist had been investigating before her disappearance.

"She came to see you about the girls," I said.

Justice Rousseau turned, his silk dressing gown fluttering open beneath his corpulent belly, revealing for an unfortunate moment his shrivelled manhood. The silk gown was black with yellow and orange dragons, a Japanese kimono made for a less substantial person. His face, now that I could see it clearly, was not the most attractive I have encountered. A pockmarked ball of greasy clay with a bulbous nose pinned on the front and two small seashell ears below the halfway level.

"Those girls are here of their own free will."

He gave a twitch of the head to indicate the three young women lounging in the early morning sun beside the pool. Three slender beauties who represented the range of ethnic diversity in the country, from the pale-skinned descendant of European colonists, to the sculpted dark chocolate of the Masai warrior. The cultural link was a toffee-brown girl of mixed race. I had noticed, when waiting for Justice Rousseau to join me, that there was a distinct lack of clothing between the three young girls. Only a couple of thongs, a modest set of briefs, and they all seemed to have forgotten to pack anything to wear on the upper part of their bodies. Which was probably how Justice Rousseau liked his girls to dress on the morning after a night of satisfying his appetites.

"It is not those girls that I am speaking about," I said.

Justice Rousseau considered me, his capillary-veined nose scrunched up as if I had a foul smell, although I was fairly clean this morning, and fully clothed, which he was not. But that was my fault. I had bypassed his security by arriving shortly after dawn with the team of garden workers, and had surprised him with my presence when he had stumbled into his entertainment room, pulling the inade-quate kimono about his naked body, just moments after being woken by the strains of 'Parigi, o cara' from Verdi's *La Traviata*, which I had found in his wall of musical entertain-ment. I had increased the volume a little more than might have been necessary because I had grown weary of waiting for him. We had been building to the second chorus when Justice Rousseau stumbled through to find me enjoying the view from the embrace of his reindeer-leather couch.

"Do you know who I am?" he asked now, avoiding the

question that would clarify which girls I was speaking about, and choosing instead a return to aggression. "How dare you threaten me?"

"I know who you are, Justice Rousseau."

He was one of the most senior judges in the country, a man who had built an impeccable career over the past forty years, starting way back in the apartheid years.

"I also know about a club you belong to."

"Club?" said Justice Rousseau, and his tongue came out of his mouth like a deep sea creature emerging from a cave. It squeezed itself across his upper lip, and then retreated, leaving the lips damp enough for the denials that he would need to make.

"One which provides young girls to men with particular appetites. The club that you are a founding member of."

"I have no idea what you are saying. I haven't founded any clubs."

But if he had ever been a convincing liar, it was a skill that he had lost as his sense of his own importance had grown to match his swelling body.

"Admittedly, your name is not to be found on the club documents," I said. "But I suspect that is because of the nature of its activities."

"Who the hell are you?" said Justice Rousseau.

"Gabriel," I said. I had told him before, but that had been when he was recovering from the shock of finding me in his entertainment room so early on a Sunday morning. "Like the angel," I added.

"Angel?" he said, as if I had insulted him.

"The Archangel Gabriel."

"You with the police?"

"No, I'm not with the police."

"You're with one of those new military outfits, aren't you?"

"Not any longer."

"What is that accent?" Justice Rousseau's nose wrinkled again with displeasure. "Is it British?"

"I was raised in Britain, but my father is Canadian – my presence in this country is owed to my mother."

"Your mother?"

"She was South African," I explained, and brought us back on topic by adding, "She was not one of the girls you trafficked."

Justice Rousseau drew in breath as if he was about to start shouting.

"Get out," he said as a feeble start, then his voice rose to a shout as he repeated, "Get out!"

"If you are quite sure you cannot tell me anything about what happened to the journalist."

"I'm calling security," said Justice Rousseau.

"I wanted to give you the chance to speak off the record. Unofficially, before the law gets involved."

"I am the law!" declared Justice Rousseau. He strode across the deep pile carpet of his entertainment room, his silk kimono opening regrettably in the rush, and he pressed a button on an intercom in the wall. His eyes stayed on me, a moment of panic appearing behind them as it occurred to him that I might have gained entrance to his property by disabling his security with extreme violence. But his press of the button was responded to a moment later by the squawking of a man's voice.

"There's a man in my house," complained Justice Rousseau, the tension squeezing his voice several tones higher. "Come and remove him. Now."

The intercom uttered a surprised squawk, and Justice Rousseau gave me a look of cruel satisfaction.

"They are armed," he said.

"I don't doubt it," I replied. "I am not."

Justice Rousseau's eyes narrowed, as if he might better spot hidden weapons in that way. But only a fool would break into a house with armed security carrying a weapon. He stayed with his back against the wall beside the intercom, his false bravado dissipating.

We stood in silence for a moment, and then I said: "Is this considered art?"

I indicated the framed illustrations of exotic sexual poses and moody erotic photography that adorned the walls of his entertainment chamber. "Or is it simply pornography?"

Justice Rousseau's tongue came out of its cave again and licked his upper lip, but he did not deign to reply. There was no time anyway, because a door opened at the far end of the room, beyond the grand piano, and a security guard followed his Sig Sauer through the opening.

"This the man, boss?" he asked, unnecessarily, it seemed to me. I raised my hands to identify myself as the man to be removed.

"You can tell your coloured journalist," spat Justice Rousseau, his confidence restored by the presence of his armed protection, "that if she has accusations to make, she will need to make them personally, not send some out-of-work gun-for-hire."

I said nothing in response to that. When I reached the door, I turned back to find his frightened eyes on me, gave him a farewell nod, and left the room.

Justice Rousseau might not have answered my questions, but his fear provided me with answers more clearly than any words could have. And he had – unintentionally – spoken a word of truth in that last moment. Because I had not mentioned the colour of Sandy's skin, and there was no way he could know she was of mixed race, unless he knew who she was, and perhaps also knew what had happened to her.

TWO

The disappearance of Sandy had not been a dramatic affair. It had occurred some months ago when she failed to return from a trip on which she had been investigating a story that involved human trafficking.

The police suggested I fill out several forms and make a sworn statement about her failure to return. They opened a missing person case and looked regretful as they squeezed the file into a cabinet that was bursting with other files. The police officer who helped me fill out the forms didn't look at all accusatory. He gave the impression of a man experienced in the matter of relationships that had turned sour, even to the point of one party needing to disappear entirely. He had rested a reassuring hand on my shoulder and told me he believed me when I said Sandy had not been desperate to escape.

However, when Sandy's clothes and belongings disappeared from my apartment several days later, the police didn't agree that there was anything sinister in that, and without regret, they closed the missing person case.

Because what kind of missing person collects their own clothes?

My efforts to find Sandy over the following months had proved fruitless, until a small department of military intelligence offered me what they called a 'ten-figure remuneration' for a minor job they wanted me to do for them. The ten figures were the digits of a phone number Sandy had called. She had called it several times, but only one time of interest to me – after her disappearance.

Which was why, four days before Justice Rousseau's denials that he knew a journalist called Sandy, I had set off in a rental car for a three-hour journey in an easterly direction from Cape Town, to the address of a building which held the telephone that bore the number of my ten-figure reward.

———

As I drove through the outskirts of Cape Town, I passed a team of soldiers mounting a shiny aluminium pod beside the road. These ribbed metal boxes had become a familiar sight since the declaration of a State of Emergency. They sprang up unexpectedly and squatted like alien craft, their generators humming, cold halogen lamps buzzing through the rain as they transformed into operating centres beside which the army conducted road blocks and harassed the citizens in a show of military force that reminded us, lest we forget, that the country was teetering towards civil war.

An hour further into my journey, I was stopped at one of these roadblocks. The rain was coming down hard, so the cold-eyed military policeman didn't spend too long comparing my fake ID photo with my face. The picture was genuine enough, if a little old and blurred. It was the name that bore no relation to reality. The man scanned the ID card with a glowing reader wrapped in plastic to protect it from the rain, then waved me through impatiently. I didn't make any jokes about weapons in the trunk of my rental car, and I tried not to show enthusiasm as I accelerated away from him. As it happened, I did have a licence for my Glock 9 mm pistol, which was the only weapon I had with me.

In any case, weapons were not the only thing they were searching for. I knew that well enough.

Although weapons, explosives and even propaganda were the declared reason for the roadblocks, they were also looking for something else. One occupant of each of these alien pods was not a soldier at all, but a member of a private security company, and tucked into his, or sometimes her, breast pocket was a collection of photographs. Blurred and indistinct photographs of the suspected members of what the media were calling the 'Gold Heist Gang': three men and a woman who had robbed a prominent and wealthy member of South African society of some gold. Riaan 'BB' Breytenbach, chairperson of the South African Gold Mining Conglomerate, had suffered an unfortunate accident on his game farm a couple of months ago when a man wearing the uniform of his private security had shot him three times. He had lost his left leg as a result, but he had survived the incident, and had recently been discharged from hospital.

While recovering in his hospital bed, BB had reported that a few London Good Delivery bars of gold were missing from his private game farm. Only a few, because it was illegal to store large amounts of gold on private property. As each bar was worth three quarters of a million dollars, he had been motivated to support the government's initiative to control the traffic of illegal weapons across the country and he had partly financed the roadblocks. In every road-block, he posted a member of his small army of private security, allegedly to keep an eye on the way in which his money was being spent. These black-uniformed security guards ensured everyone looked after their new silver spaceships, polished all the shiny bits and didn't break any of the windows – and referred to their photographs of the Heist Gang whenever someone fitting the description of a gang member passed through the roadblock.

The roadblocks had succeeded in finding many weapons, a large quantity of illegal drugs and reams of anti-government literature, but they had located none of the Gold Heist Gang, and had not recovered a single Good Delivery bar. And so Breytenbach had pumped more money into the system, making it almost impossible to travel anywhere without being stopped, searched and generally harassed.

Three hours from Cape Town, I reached the point where the highway twists through a couple of hills and crosses a languid river. Signs encourage drivers to reduce speed as they pass the outskirts of a small town called Heidelberg. I turned off the highway and took the straight stretch of road directly into the heart of the town, nestling between the hills. The ubiquitous Dutch Reformed church presided over the inhabitants from its neatly trimmed patch of lawn, the whitewashed spires glowing dully in the over-cast gloom of the afternoon when I arrived, as they stretched up to get closer to the heavens. Across the road, cowering under the church's reprimanding glare, I found the Heidelberg Inn.

The inn is the second oldest building in town, because the Afrikaans farmers had recognised the need for providing refreshment as a close second to their spiritual needs, and had staggered across the road after building the church to create the inn. No reaching for the skies here; it was a squat and faintly castellated building dedicated to matters of a more earthly nature. Thirty years ago a misguided hotel manager had painted the building a deep purple in contrast to the ethereal white of the church, a move that had shocked everyone so much that they had done nothing to the building since, although the purple had faded over the years of blistering Cape summer sunshine, and the paint had peeled in places.

The grand old inn occupied an entire block, and behind it, sheltering from the pious glare of the church were the small cottages of the original inhabitants, who had named the town after the German branch of their Christian religion, and whose needs were fulfilled by a place for worship, a place for drinking, and simple homes with little more than a bed, a table for eating, and a patch of land for growing vegetables – water provided by the river at the foot of the patch.

The address I had was for one of these small boxes huddled behind the inn. Neatly trimmed grass with a paved path which led to the freshly painted front door, and a window to each side like a child's drawing. All that was missing was smoke coiling up from the chimney. I wondered who lurked behind the door, and my hand hesitated a moment before knocking. Who was the one person that had meant enough to Sandy that she had broken her complete separation from everyone and everything? In that moment I wondered whether I really did want to know who it was. Because the police officer who had rejected my missing person claim had not been entirely wrong – my relationship with Sandy had changed in the weeks before she disappeared – not soured particularly, but it had lost its verve, the passion had faded. Was I doing the right thing now, in trying to find her?

But it was a fleeting hesitation, and my knuckles were already banging on the wood. The sound of the knock rang with the hollowness of an empty house. But I stood there for a full minute, then knocked again. Still no response. I turned away from the door and discovered an old man in a crumpled felt hat and the khaki uniform of the Afrikaans farmer standing beside my car and watching me. He leaned on a gnarled stick and considered me through narrow eyes.

"You'll not find him there," he said in Afrikaans, as if the idea was a ridiculous one. "You selling insurance?"

I doubted I looked much like an insurance salesman. I had sustained some physical damage in the final moments of my job for the Department – a grazed cheek and a partially blackened eye – and hours in the rental car had done little for my general presentation. But I smiled at the obvious mistake.

"Friend of the family," I said.

"That so?" He sucked his teeth, then used his tongue to demonstrate the way in which his dentures could be made to perform a somersault without leaving his mouth. It wasn't a particularly pleasing display, but I kept smiling as he decided whether to take our conversation any further.

"He'll be in the bar then, won't he?" he said, once his dentures had returned to base with a nasty sucking sound.

"Of course," I said, as if I should have realised that, and felt an uncomfortable shiver. The thought that this person – so special to Sandy that he had been the only person she had called after disappearing – was sitting in a bar in the middle of the afternoon was not encouraging.

"Where else?" said the man ominously, and he gave a twitch of the head to indicate the hulking purple inn behind him.

THREE

The arched oak doors of the Heidelberg Inn gave onto a warm entrance hall with dark wooden panelling, deep pile Persian rugs over polished terracotta, a central table with flowers beneath a ceiling fan that drooped like a palm tree out of season, and a stern lady trapped behind a reception desk who was reading a glossy magazine through half-moon spectacles. She looked up at me by moving her eyes over the half-moons like a chameleon while her head remained static. I had already seen the door leading to the bar and pointed at it so that she wouldn't have to move any other parts of her body in that creepy way, and she gave me the sort of understanding smile that teetotallers give you when they catch you shaking as you reach for the bottle.

There was only one customer in the bar, but he pretty much filled the place. There must have been two hundred kilograms of him; he'd surpassed the maximum size offered in khaki shirts, so bits of the two hundred kilograms were in evidence where the buttons had popped. I took a moment to take in his full glory, and his pink eyes gazed back at me with disinterest.

Was this the person Sandy had phoned? Sandy, who had persuaded me to put down my gun and take up a camera, who had won awards for her journalism, who had the fiercest sense of independence and pride of anyone I had ever met. I couldn't imagine that this immense and inebriated man was the person she had called. But then, many things that Sandy had done were hard to imagine.

An elderly barman stood behind the counter, working his way through a platoon of glasses that were steaming gently, giving them a polish with a dishcloth bearing the embroidered logo of the inn. He was a tall man with chiselled cheeks and heavy-framed spectacles, not as old as I had initially thought, which was a trick of the tight curls of prematurely white hair against his dark skin. He focused on the glass he was polishing as I settled onto a stool at the bar counter, holding it up to the light in the tradition of barmen around the world. Satisfied with the state of the glass, he gave a slight grunt of approval and placed it into a rack above the counter.

"What can I do you for?" he asked in a deep baritone, and only then did he look at me, his unusually light hazel eyes emphasised by the heavy frames of his spectacles. The bar wobbled on its foundations – they were Sandy's eyes. The hazel colour, the small flecks of lighter yellow, even the lively humour that lay behind them.

I asked for a whisky. The barman said he had a good Scottish single malt and poured me a double, all the while watching me with Sandy's eyes because my own had betrayed my surprise. He placed the glass on a card mat and positioned a trio of snacks beside it.

"Dreadful business," I said, because the television in the corner was playing the report of the Afrikaans socialite who had been killed in a failed bombing attempt at a sports stadium a few days before.

"Hard to believe," he agreed in a non-committal manner.

Having thus dealt with current affairs, I took a taste of the single malt.

"Passing through?" he asked, and pulled the dishcloth from his shoulder and resumed the glass polishing routine, but his eyes stayed on me.

"No," I admitted. "I came here to find you."

He showed no surprise; held the glass up and squinted at it.

"You're her soldier," he said, after a pause. It wasn't a question.

"I was."

He slid the glass with care along the metal rails of the rack above the bar, then returned the dishcloth to his shoulder, and took two paces to stand before me at the end of the bar, his back to the bottles, and folded his arms.

"She said you were a good man," he said, and glanced over at the sumo wrestler in the corner, who showed no sign of needing any service, and frankly only minimal signs of the persistence of life. Having established that we had a few minutes to ourselves, the barman turned back and settled Sandy's eyes on me.

"She didn't tell you she'd found her father?" he said. "Did she tell you I was dead?"

"No, she never said that. Only that she had been raised by her great-aunt. And that you had not been around."

"Was not given the chance," he said without bitterness. "They gave her a good life, no doubt of that. But not a life with space for an impecunious room service waiter."

Not even one that used words like 'impecunious' I

thought, but said nothing. He was a man of contrasts – his manner spoke of a life in the service of others, pouring them drinks, cleaning up their spills, perhaps delivering trays of food to their love nests, and yet he struck me as a man who read books late into the night. He had Sandy's pale eyes, but darker skin than hers. Another contrast – caught between the two races that had mixed higher up the family tree. As chance or genetics would have it, he appeared more African than European, but his daughter had drawn the other card.

"When a woman dies in childbirth," he said, "you cannot blame the child, can you? If someone must be blamed, it is the man who planted the seed in the first place." He smiled regretfully and removed his glasses to give them a polish with the dishcloth, then put them back again, and focused on me as if to read something on my face. "They needed someone to blame. You've met them, I'm sure; a matriarchy, strong women, all of them."

"They took Sandy away from you?"

"I had a few hours with her, here and there. But what can a man do in those circumstances? We have none of the tools. I was young, I was naïve, I had lost the woman I loved, I was confused." He removed the glasses again and blinked at me. "They closed the door on me, took her into their witch's coven, and told me not to upset her. Some days they would let me in, allow me to visit my daughter, give me a few minutes of gazing on her, let her little hands grab at my fat fingers. But most days they wouldn't. The time is not right, she's sleeping, she's eating, she's feeling ill, come back next week, next month, next year, or better yet, come back never." Although his words were harsh, he spoke without rancour, as if he was justifying their actions. "Five years I loitered outside that brothel of theirs, like a man without a soul."

He laughed suddenly, put the spectacles back on and brought the dishcloth back into his hands and ready for action.

"You know about her family business?" he said with sudden concern.

I did know about her family business – for three generations Sandy's family had run a brothel. A famous, or perhaps notorious, brothel that had played a part in the history of the vibrant mixed community of an area called District Six. Inclusive of all races, religions and cultures, it stood for everything that was anathema to apartheid. That was probably why the government sent bulldozers in to raze it to the ground.

"Of course you know," he said. "Why am I telling you this nonsense?" He stepped away to pick up another glass. "Everything okay there, Mister Du Preez?" he called to the sumo wrestler in the farmer's suit. The man nodded and opened his mouth to speak but only produced a juicy cough that rattled about his chest, as if he was underwater and struggling to surface. The cough reached a climax with a strangled gasp. He cleared his throat and swallowed with a nasty gulp.

"*Alles goed,*" he said finally, which didn't seem the truth, but Sandy's father accepted it.

"Sandy found you?" I prompted after a moment's pause.

"There was no keeping the truth from her, was there? That's the one thing those brothel madams didn't account for." The bitterness surfaced finally, and the glass that he was polishing took the brunt of it. "No keeping secrets from my Sandy," he said, and placed the cracked glass on the counter away from the others.

"Although she was good at keeping her own."

"She was that," he agreed, then suddenly thrust his hand out towards me. "My name is Benjamin," he said.

I smiled at that. "Ben," I said. "I'm just plain Ben."

I wondered whether Sandy had ever mulled over the coincidence of our similar names, and I almost said something to Benjamin. But who knew what Sandy had ever thought? The way one gets past the voluntary disappearance of someone is by refusing to indulge those kinds of thoughts. At least that was how I did it.

"I wanted to ask you about the phone call Sandy made to you," I said.

"That last call," said Benjamin, and he picked up another glass and started polishing it. He was silent for so long that I thought he would not answer me. Then he said: "She used to call me every month, on a Saturday. First Saturday of the month. 'Happy New Month, father.' Like clockwork. And twice a year she would visit. A few days was all we needed to fill those missing years. Isn't that strange? We would walk, talk, cook, eat. But then she missed a call. Suddenly, just like that."

He raised the glass for an inspection, then gingerly slid it along the rails to join the others. Stepped away from me to collect another one, then stepped back, his focus on the glass.

"She told me about you. Working for the secret government departments we're not meant to know about. The ones that spy on our every move. I was sure you knew all about her calls to me, and I told her as much, but she laughed and said she had her secrets." He noticed an invisible spot, which he rubbed angrily.

"I only learnt about the calls a few days ago," I said.

He didn't seem to have heard me.

"She didn't call on her usual Saturday, or the next," he said. "It had happened again."

He stared at the glass as if trying to remember what he was doing with it, his eyes magnified by the thick lenses of his spectacles.

"Again?" I said.

He looked up at me.

"Sandy is not my only child. She has a half sister. Thirteen years younger than her. Thirteen years and one week exactly. We used to laugh about that. My birthday is only a week before her sister's. We had blood in common and also our stars. Isn't that what they say, that your birth can foretell your life?"

"What was it that happened again?"

"I never believed in that astrology nonsense, but it was something that bound us. We needed all the help we could get in trying to belong."

Benjamin polished the glass. I waited.

"Her sister had a different mother, of course, who survived the planting of my seed, but who didn't have it in her nature to stay with me or her daughter. Went to visit family in the Transkei one summer when our daughter was only three years old. Said she'd be back, but ..." he shrugged, then smiled and his hollow cheeks lifted. But Sandy's sad eyes were unmoved. "It's my curse," he continued. "I know that now, but didn't know it then. I built a wall around myself and the baby I still had. Bricked up the doors, barred the windows, I would not let her go."

"It didn't work?"

"Never does, does it? It's what all the books say, and all the wise men. If you love something, you must let it go. Build a cage, and the bird will fly."

"And she flew?"

"Not long after Sandy found me, her sister fell in with a bad lot. She was slipping down the slope, and I knew it. Sandy scolded me. Do something about it, Father, she would say. But nothing I did seemed to work. Or perhaps it worked in reverse, my fumbling effort pushed her further away."

From the corner of the bar, came the sound of the sumo wrestler struggling to overcome another respiratory problem. Benjamin took a fresh tumbler, a bottle of water, and some rum over to him. The man survived the attack. Benjamin returned to his post behind the bar.

"Pushed her where?" I asked.

Benjamin shook his head. "There was no *where*. No here, no there. One day she was here, the next she wasn't."

"And the bad lot she fell in with? They didn't know where she was?"

"Drifters, nobodies, all I knew of them was their nicknames, not a single real name between them. The police accepted the forms I filled in with my blood and tears and put her photograph at the bottom of the pile. Do you have any idea how many people go missing every year?"

I had a vague idea, garnered from Sandy's passion for the research she did on what she called 'her girls'. She had mentioned numbers, and quoted statistics that turned every conversation we had on the subject into a display of bad temper on her part because it made her so angry.

"Perhaps you do," said Benjamin when I failed to reply. "The police certainly didn't. Just a huge pile of photographs of other people's children. Each one stapled to a form and pushed to the bottom of the pile." He looked up at me, and I realised now where Sandy's passion for the story had started. I had played those last weeks over and over in my mind in my search for sense and reason. And here was the only reason she needed.

"Sandy followed her sister," I said. "That's what happened to her, isn't it?"

"Amanda," said Benjamin, pronouncing the name in the Afrikaans way with three flat As. "That was her sister's name. She had my pale eyes, like Sandy. Even paler. Her friends used to tease her about her golden eyes."

"Did Sandy discover what happened to her?"

Benjamin nodded.

"In that last call to me she explained what had happened."

Benjamin looked down at his hands, which were fidgeting as if they were trying to unpick the dishcloth.

"Can I ask you a question, Ben?" He didn't look up.

"Of course."

"How long did it take you to forgive her? Sandy." He looked up at me now. "For doing what she did."

"Is that what I'm meant to be doing, forgiving her?"

He nodded, as if that was an answer.

"She called to tell me she had found Amanda," he said.

I could guess the rest, but Benjamin needed to say it.

"There was no mistake about it. She met with others who were with her when she died. No mistake at all."

A spluttering sound from the sumo wrestler's corner signalled his need for some more refreshment. Benjamin was there in moments with water for health, and rum for the soul.

———

Benjamin and I talked for another hour. He was a gentle and kind man, who seemed to have suffered the many injustices of his life with a calm stoicism. I could see much of Sandy in him, the quiet but intense passion; the solid core of moral integrity; the absolute knowing of the difference between right and wrong, which contrasted with my immersion in the murky, grey areas where I found it difficult to distinguish the two. Sandy had such clarity that she had been my rudder when we had been together and kept me on what she called the 'straight and narrow'. It occurred to me, talking with her father, that I had drifted so far from the straight and narrow I don't think I would have recognised it if I stumbled across it again.

Benjamin told me about Sandy's discovery of the depths to which Amanda had sunk. About her arrest for prostitution, the drug addiction that he had spent so long denying. And about the three-month prison sentence for solicitation.

"She served her sentence? Or disappeared before?"

"It was after prison," said Benjamin. "Do you know the authorities don't tell the family when a prisoner is coming out? I didn't even know when Amanda was being released."

"You didn't see her after that?"

"Walked straight into the hands of traffickers. That's what they were, according to Sandy. Human traffickers."

When I held out my hand to Benjamin as I took my leave, he held it in both of his and told me to return when I could. "Sandy said goodbye to me," he said. "On that last call – when she told me Amanda was dead. It was more than I deserved. More than I'd had before, and more than anyone else had, I know that. 'Goodbye', she said, 'and don't follow me. If anyone follows me, I am done for.'" His hands held mine in a firm grasp and his eyes tried to see inside my head. "I believe she is still alive, Ben, but I don't want you getting any foolish ideas about going after her. Because I think it is the kind of thing you might be inclined to do. I know you were a soldier. Promise me that you won't go after her, promise me that."

I made the promise, and spent most of the three-hour drive back to Cape Town wondering whether it was one I could keep.

FOUR

Khanyisile Gabuza of the Department called me as I struggled along a country road in heavy rain to avoid roadblocks on my way back into the city.

"Where are you?" she asked, and I could imagine the bared teeth of what she thought was a friendly smile, which she tried to project down the phone line.

"In my car," I said.

Khanyi sighed. "Father thinks you're up to no good."

"Does he?"

Don Fehrson, the elderly leader of the Department, had attended Bible college in his youth, some time in the Dark Ages, and might even have been ordained as a priest, although there were few people alive who remembered that far back. It was apparently for this reason that Fehrson encouraged his staff to address him as 'Father', although I suspected it was his way of overcoming the stain of his despotic past. 'Father' Fehrson was well past retirement age, and the methods he had used to outlast his peers and survive so long in the secret corridors of state security were rumoured to be of a dubious nature.

"We received an alert on that identity you stole from us," said Khanyi.

"Identity?"

"Freddy Moss," she said. "The identity you took from the seventh floor."

"You've tagged that?"

"You said you'd misplaced it. Or it was stolen in that business at the rugby grounds.

"But it turned up?"

"Someone using the identity passed through a road-block on the N2 heading out of Cape Town."

"Goodness," I said.

"Father wants you to bring it back."

"I've misplaced it. How can I bring it back?"

"He says you're up to no good."

"Does he?"

"He's concerned for you, Gabriel."

"You can tell him I'm fine, thank you, Khanyi."

Khanyi sighed. "Father wants to see you."

"Because of the missing identity?"

"No, on another matter."

There was a note in Khanyi's voice that I did not like; it had the ring of someone in authority about to ask something of me, something potentially life-threatening.

"Want to discuss it over the phone?" I suggested.

"No. Father wants to see you," repeated Khanyi, as if she'd run out of her prepared lines.

"I'll pop around some time and we can drink some of the Department coffee."

Khanyi made a dismissive sound. She knew my opinion of the dishwater the Department served under the guise of coffee.

"You still in Caledon, Gabriel?"

"Certainly not."

Which was true, because I was just entering Franschhoek, a small town on the outskirts of Cape Town.

"That man Breytenbach has been speaking with Father," said Khanyi.

"Has he? The gold mining Breytenbach?"

"You know very well which Breytenbach I mean. The one who lost all that gold."

"I thought it was only a few bars."

"More than a few bars, Gabriel, you know that."

"Why has he been speaking with Fehrson?"

"Why don't you come in for that coffee and Father can tell you all about it?"

"I look forward to it."

"We've got our eye on you, Gabriel. Be careful what you get up to."

And she ended the call.

———

I called Tannie Sara to rid myself of the bitter aftertaste of my call with Khanyi. Tannie is Afrikaans for 'aunt' and is also used to address women in an informally respectful way. Tannie Sara was Sandy's great-aunt, but she had stepped in to be a mother to Sandy and had raised her from the age of three when Sandy's grandmother, Tannie Sara's estranged sister, had died of grief a few short years after Sandy's own mother had died giving birth to Sandy.

Tannie Sara's late sister would have been mortified at the thought of her granddaughter being raised by a member of the family she had forsworn on moral grounds. But Sandy couldn't have wished for a better childhood; Tannie Sara had never failed to provide her with boundless love, despite the demands of managing the family business.

When she answered my call, Tannie Sara complained how long it had been since my previous call and said that she would be delighted to see me, of course she would. Neither of us mentioned Sandy. But I could tell that she heard something in my voice, and would probably fortify herself with a sherry in preparation for the news I was bringing about her beloved niece. Tannie Sara was one of the strongest women I knew, but also one of the most vulnerable, and Sandy's disappearance had taken a dreadful toll on her.

District Six House had established new premises in Green Point after the government razed the old ones to the ground with their bulldozers. The tax documents described the Green Point establishment as a guest house, and it did have beds, and there were guests, but the primary service it offered involved shorter-term stays with less emphasis on the warm embrace of the comfortable decor, and more emphasis on the human embrace of the employees. And in Tannie Sara's defence, the term 'brothel' was not one of the options on the tax forms.

The House was in a tiny cobbled street that headed up the slope of the mountain from the main road, but ran out of steam after only a couple of hundred metres, leaving in its wake a double row of semi-detached Victorian houses, which gazed across the cobbles at each other, and determinedly avoided looking down the hill and out to sea.

Tannie Sara insisted on several hugs, and she held on tight and wiped away her tears before they could smudge her mascara. She had been a beauty queen many years ago, and despite her substantially increased girth and additional sixty years, was still one, in my opinion, although she struggled to see it in the mirror when applying her make-up and always ended up overdoing it. She held my arms and pulled back to inspect me, then nodded with satisfaction.

"You need a drink," she said, "I've already had a small sherry myself."

"Why don't you have another," I suggested. "And make it a whisky for me."

"Single malt, on the rocks," she said, releasing me and wiping her eyes again. "I never forget these things, not when it comes to family."

The front room, which Tannie Sara called the day lounge, had a crackling fire, which we had to ourselves because her other guests were upstairs amusing themselves as best they could, given the poor weather. I stood in front of the fire and admired the wall of photographs showing the history of the establishment, while Tannie poured our drinks with a heavy hand.

The photographs were arranged in chronological order, starting when District Six had been only a few city blocks on the windswept and less desirable flank of Devil's Peak, overlooking Cape Town city centre. It was populated originally by freed slaves, and became a cultural centre for the burgeoning mixed-race population produced by the many cultures that met at the southern tip of Africa. The sixth municipal district of Cape Town developed a unique community where a new people forged their own identity and culture. The brothel had been the brainchild of Tannie Sara's strong-willed and ardently feminist grandmother, who headed up their matriarchal family and who had raised Tannie Sara. The photographs showed her as a stern woman, standing straight and proud on the top step of a handful of stone stairs leading up to the old house. She had recognised the opportunity presented by the powerful sex appeal of young, coffee-skinned beauties with few career options on the one hand, and the insatiable appetite of the men who wielded power within the divided country on the other. Exhibiting an impressive business acumen, she had created the 'House', which provided refreshing drinks, spicy Asian dishes, and additional spicy entertainment in the upstairs rooms for those guests who needed a little something extra.

Tannie Sara handed me a tumbler of whisky, then dropped into an armchair with an audible sigh. She sipped at her sherry, then placed the glass on a table beside the chair, laced her fingers together, and looked up at me.

"Is it bad news, *skattie*?" she said, using the Afrikaans term of endearment she had adopted in the time we'd spent together – trying to understand what had happened – in mutual bereavement after Sandy's disappearance.

"Not bad news, Tannie, surprising news."

Tannie Sara reached for her sherry and took another tiny sip as if she wanted to delay the surprising news.

"You shouldn't be doing this, *skattie*," she scolded. "You know you shouldn't. It's time you stop chasing her. You've got yourself that nice new girl now, is her name Robyn?"

"Robyn, yes."

I had told Tannie Sara about my nascent relationship with Robyn. I had even introduced them over an afternoon tea, and Tannie Sara had given her approval.

"That nice new girl Robyn has kicked me out," I said.

"What did you do, *skattie*?"

"I think the word she used was 'closure'."

Tannie Sara nodded and sipped her sherry.

"She'll wait," she declared. "I can read girls like a book. That girl will wait for you."

"If she doesn't drink herself to death first."

"Oh, that's her problem, is it?" Tannie Sara placed her sherry back on the table. "I knew there was something."

"It's one of Robyn's problems."

Tannie Sara drew a deep breath.

"I'm ready, *skattie*," she said. "Ready for the surprising news."

"Did you know that Sandy found her father?"

Tannie Sara didn't seem to react. She sat absolutely still in her armchair, like a stone Buddha.

"I didn't know," she said.

But then two tears appeared in her eyes, and spilt out, leaving dark trails of mascara down her cheeks.

"My sister wouldn't let him near Sandy. She said he was worthless and no good." Tannie Sara sighed, reached for her sherry, and took a sip. "When my sister passed, I made no effort to change that." Another sip of sherry. "I regret that now, regret what we did to her father."

She sipped at her sherry again, but discovered the glass was empty. I went over to the gilded drinks tray and poured her another.

"I should have said that to Sandy," she said. "That's what I regret the most. Not that I didn't try to undo the damage my sister had done, but that I never spoke to Sandy about her father."

"She had a sister as well," I said, and Tannie Sara looked up at me with surprise. "Half-sister, different mother of course."

Tannie Sara sipped again at her sherry, and another two tears rolled down her cheeks.

"The things we didn't know," she said, then pulled a tissue from between her breasts and dabbed at her cheeks.

"Did Sandy ask you anything about trafficking?" I asked, "in the last few months?"

"Trafficking, *skattie*?"

"Young girls being drawn into prostitution, being sold."

"I know what trafficking is," she said bitterly. "You're not going to do this to me too, are you?"

"Do what, Tannie?"

"My girls choose to do what they do. They are career girls, you know that. They make good money, they wear Prada, prance about in Jimmy Choo, take holidays in Greece. There's nothing shameful; don't start flinging about your big words, Benny. There's no trafficking here."

Tannie Sara wiped at her eyes again. She had stopped worrying about preserving the mascara, and looked back up at me with eyes surrounded by dark smudges.

"Is that what Sandy suggested?"

Tannie Sara buried her face in the damp tissue and gave a quiet sob, her great shoulders heaving up and down. I waited a moment, then went to her and placed a hand on her shoulder.

"Sandy would never think you were involved in that, Tannie," I said. "She knew your business was different."

She looked up at me, her face a mess of dark streaks.

"I should have said I would take them, *skattie*, but I'm not a rescue centre, am I? I'm a business, not a charity."

"Take who?"

"The girls she wanted me to take in."

"Girls that had been trafficked?"

Tannie Sara applied the tissue again and spread her mascara further.

"There were two of them. I said to her: 'What are you doing messing with girls?' Do you think she would answer me?"

"I don't."

"That's when she started about the trafficking. It made

me angry, *skattie*. 'I'll not have anything to do with those girls', is what I told her. They're the damaged ones, the drug addicts, the ones who won't make it. My clients don't want that kind of girl, do they?"

Tannie Sara looked at me with her panda eyes.

"I said no," she said, and two further tears rolled down her cheeks. "It's why she left, *skattie*, I know it is. It's why she left."

"No, it isn't. Her leaving had nothing to do with you or your house. She went to find her sister."

Tannie Sara sniffed and used the crumbling tissue to wipe her cheeks again.

"Did you suggest where Sandy could take the girls you wouldn't accept?"

She nodded and applied the tissues again.

"When she wouldn't stop pestering me about it. A private house called Pandora; appointment only. They take all types. Run by a woman called Lee, half Chinese, I think. I told her to take them there. I didn't want to end up in one of her newspaper articles, did I? She said she wasn't going to write about it, but I knew it would end up in the papers somehow. And she didn't want you to know about it. I knew she'd become ashamed of it all. Ashamed of me, of my business."

"She was never ashamed of you, Tannie, never."

Tannie Sara took a deep breath, which she let out in a heavy sigh. "You think her sister is one of the girls she wanted me to take?"

"I think she might have been."

"I should have taken them."

"Sandy should have told you the truth."

"Go to Pandora, *skattie*. Go find her sister, maybe she can tell you where Sandy has run off to."

"Her sister isn't there. Not anymore. She's dead."

Tannie Sara gazed at me with her Panda bear eyes, and I could see her adding that fact to the tally of her guilt. She leaned forward in the armchair and started struggling to her feet. I helped her up.

"I'll get the card for Pandora. I keep them in the back office."

She crossed the room with her slow, rolling gait, as if the past few minutes had worsened the pain in her hips. She paused at the door and turned back to me.

"You know what they say about dancing with the devil, *skattie*." She hesitated, so I shook my head. "The devil won't change into an angel, but he will change you into a devil. They say that the girls who come into the business through drugs, trafficking ... It's a one-way street. There's no way out for them. I tried explaining that to Sandy, but I didn't know it was her own sister she was trying to help."

She turned and left the room. The heat from the fire was causing steam to rise from my trousers. Tannie Sara's stern old grandmother gazed down at me from the photos on the mantelpiece. She stood in the central photograph with a bevy of young beauties arranged around her, like a group of nurses gathered about the matron of an old-fashioned hospital. But with too much flesh, not enough clothing, and smiles on the faces that hinted at a shared secret. Before them were a few small children, smiling cheerfully, a little out of focus. One of them was Tannie Sara. Dressed in her Sunday best and forcing a grin so large that it closed her eyes. Her almost identical sister stood beside her. They both grew taller and more elegant as the pictures stepped through the years. A photo of Tannie Sara giving a regal wave with the sash over her shoulder, when she had been declared the Queen of District Six, riding in a horse-drawn cart, petals in her hair, her sister looking glum in the background. Then Tannie Sara was standing beside her grandmother, who seemed to shrink with each year as Tannie Sara grew in height and girth. The sister too grew, but as Tannie Sara widened and strengthened, she became narrow and frail. Other young girls sprouted on the steps in front of District Six House, like the staggered frames of a flip-book animation. Tannie Sara's sister rested a proprietorial hand on a fragile girl, and the two of them moved steadily to the side of the group of constantly changing seductresses, the physical distance a manifestation of the separation that Tannie Sara's sister and niece had created between themselves and the family business. In the final frames they stood to the side, the mother's hands always resting on her daughter's shoulders. Then in the next photo Tannie Sara's sister stood before an empty space, her face looking as if all the strings had been cut, her hair turned grey and in her arms a baby.

That baby was the end of the matriarchal line. That baby was Sandy.

FIVE

That evening I returned to a warehouse at the end of an outer jetty of the Cape Town docks that had been my home for the past few weeks. I was looking forward to a quiet, solitary evening, but as I pushed open the rusty door, I discovered I was not alone.

The warehouse was a vast echoing space, large enough to play a game of football in, if it hadn't been for the hulking shells of old ships abandoned by the previous tenants. When I had first taken occupation the place had been littered with old paint cans and rusty tools that had spilt from their toolboxes and lay scattered about the floor as if the shipbuilders had departed in a hurry. But Robyn and I had cleared away the junk and imposed a little order on the space. A collection of broken deck chairs huddled beside the rusted hull of the Anna-Marie, which had been a fishing trawler in her youth, and now served as a lounge or a briefing centre, as occasion demanded. Sleeping quarters were in the small rooms at the back. The centre of the warehouse was occupied by a working kitchen that Captain Steven Chandler had some Italian fitters install. Chandler had been my captain when I served with the special forces, and he too had been discharged. He had recently included me in a small squad of misfits he had put together, and it was his idea that I should move into the warehouse because of the heightened risk that my identity had been compromised.

The kitchen comprised a wooden island with gas plates, an eye-level oven and a range of free-standing drawers which opened on luxuriously smooth runners. It gave the impression of a film set, particularly when all the lights were on, as they were tonight. The bulky ships receded into shadows where one expected to find crew members sneaking a cigarette between takes.

And playing the lead role tonight was Captain Steven Chandler himself, standing in the brightly lit kitchen with a wooden spoon in one hand and a striped apron over his regulation black uniform. He had just opened the oven door when I arrived and the steam cleared to reveal him. The highest rank Chandler had achieved in the British Special Forces was captain, but we called him 'Colonel' because of the respect that we had for our leader. He was over six foot of finely toned physique, clothed in paramilitary garb that fit him like the skin of a panther. His face was lean, sharp cheekbones and lines etched into it from many years of active service. His white hair was cropped short like a skull-cap, his eyes were grey and seemed cold at first glance, but when you looked into them as I had done in some of the most terrifying moments of my life, you saw the warmth of the man inside.

"Where is Robyn?" he asked.

"She moved out," I said. "A few days ago."

"Why?"

Chandler closed the oven door and turned to face me,

his eyes probing me as if everything depended on my answer to that question. I could have replied that it was none of his business, but of course her irrational behaviour was his business: Robyn was a founding member of the team; she had worked with Chandler before I joined them, when I had been working for the Department and living with Sandy.

"You know how vulnerable she is," said Chandler, not waiting for my reply. "She needs to be watched. How could you let her walk out?"

"How could I stop her? I'm not her keeper."

"She's drinking – we cannot afford that now."

"She hasn't spoken to you?"

"She hasn't."

Chandler's face was tight with irritation. The oven behind him started beeping and he swung back to it as if he was about to punish it for interrupting. But he grabbed some oven mitts, opened the door, and removed a steaming dish.

It was worrying that Robyn hadn't called Chandler. He had become like a father to her when he had supported her through her grief after the death of her fiancé, Brian, who had been a good friend of mine and a comrade of ours. In turn, Robyn had helped Chandler to build a new life outside the British army after his discharge. It was a life that applied his military skills and training in a very different way.

"You seen the news?" asked Chandler, dropping the subject of Robyn for the moment. "Our friend BB made an announcement."

"About what?"

"Best you see for yourself. You got a device to connect with the outside world?"

He looked around the warehouse as if finding it hard to

believe that someone could live in such a way. I refrained from pointing out that it had been his idea that I take refuge here, and fetched a laptop from the sleeping quarters.

It didn't take long to find the announcement. Riaan 'BB' Breytenbach was standing on a raised platform in one of the plush meeting rooms of the Gold Mining Conglomerate of South Africa. The podium was raised because BB was not as tall as he liked the world to think he was. The room was filled with assorted media hounds who had been treated to a lavish breakfast by the looks of it, and were checking to make sure all the bottles of champagne were really empty as Breytenbach held his hand in the air and waited for silence.

His was a face familiar to most South Africans, not only because he was one of the country's wealthiest bachelors, but also because of his extraordinarily brave survival of the daring heist that had been performed on his private game farm. The bravery of that survival was purely the spin that the Gold Mining Conglomerate's media relations department had put on it – they had painted the picture of an innocent hero with nothing but an old Winchester shotgun to defend himself against a cruel gang of heist criminals.

The truth of the matter had been a little different, but that hadn't stopped Breytenbach from rising to the status of hero – and he made a fitting hero. He had film star good looks and an even tan from the golf course, which had paled only a little during his time in hospital. He also had an artificial leg which served as the perfect reminder to his fellow citizens of his battle against the criminal forces that were threatening to overwhelm the country, having been deprived of the real one by the devilish criminals who had stolen gold bars from him. His impassioned speeches about his efforts to bring the 'Gold Heist Gang' to justice and have them pay for their crime had become popular media events.

"Skip past this bit," said Chandler, looking over my shoulder. "I'm sure you've seen it all before. He's got some funny pictures coming up. Skip to them."

I skipped ahead, and some faces popped up in rapid succession. I went back and played them at normal speed. They were an artist's impression of four people. A man with brown hair, an unremarkable face and heavy-framed spectacles; a woman with a thin face, black eyes and short tousled hair; an older man with a skullcap of white hair; and a black man with big drooping jowls and small eyes.

"New pictures," said Chandler. "And he's offering a reward. A million US each."

"They're better than those blurred photographs," I said. "But still not very good."

"Of course not. BB was so busy trying to shoot off that old Winchester, you think he bothered looking at anybody?"

"A million US? Dead? Or alive?"

"Alive," said Chandler. "He wants them alive, doesn't he? Wants to know where they've hidden his gold."

"It must be a relief for them," I said. "Life insurance of a million dollars."

"A relief indeed," agreed Chandler, and he smiled for the first time. "The food's ready. Let's eat."

————

Chandler had cooked an Italian pasta dish. The recipe, he told me, came from a man he had fought with in the Pathfinders in Kuwait. Chandler had always taken an interest in cooking, and enjoyed producing quality food in difficult conditions, such as over a campfire on an active mission. Since his discharge, the interest had developed into a passion that sometimes verged on obsession.

I told him about the call I had received from Khanyi, and he shook his head with derision. He had little respect for the Department.

"Let them play their game, but tread carefully," he advised.

"What is their game? They can get hold of me whenever they like. Why bother with the cat-and-mouse nonsense?"

Chandler took another mouthful and chewed thoughtfully.

"Perhaps it's not you they want," he said eventually. "They've already got you. It's your new friends they're interested in."

"You think so? For what?"

"What do we do best?"

"You and me? Or all four of us?"

"That's a good question." Chandler turned his head to the side as if he was listening for something. "It's stopped raining?"

"Stopped when I arrived. If it was still raining, we wouldn't be able to hear ourselves over the racket it makes on the steel roof."

"Let's take a walk," he suggested.

The rain had stopped, but the broken surface of the quay was so flooded that we had to pick our way using the higher ridges of tar as stepping stones. Eventually we gave up and splashed through the potholes. We took our regular walk back towards the start of our quay, which was one of the original structures built in the late 1800s. It provided the harbour with protection against the cold Benguela current carrying water up from the South Pole.

We turned and walked down the quay adjacent to ours. This one was still operational, and served medium-sized cargo ships, brought into the docks by pilots who would manoeuvre the enormous vessels alongside so that they could be offloaded by a team of crane operators and officious men in hard hats. But the dock was deserted this evening. There was only one hulking ship, the offloading completed, and a few crew members smoking on deck and watching the city settle into the night.

A pair of headlights bounced over the rough surface of the quay towards us. A vehicle moving slowly, as if it was looking for something. I pulled Chandler over to the narrow strip between the cranes and the water where we hesitated under cover of one of the hauling machines. The vehicle was an open-topped jeep. Two men wearing black military-style outfits, scanned the area lazily. The passenger held a Vektor R5 automatic casually on his knee.

"Breytenbach's goons," I whispered.

Breytenbach's private security outfit were the only ones who carried R5s and wore those all-black uniforms. The two men were doing a useless job of searching the quay, if that was what they were doing. They glanced around but were blinded by the reflection of their own headlights and didn't even notice us behind the bulky machinery.

When they had passed and the sound of their jeep had faded into the night, Chandler and I continued a couple of hundred metres down the quay, where we stopped. I lit a cigarette, and we looked up at the crane beside us. There were seven cranes that lined the edge of the quay, huge steel structures that reached ten storeys into the air and could lift forty tonnes each. Their legs rested on widely spaced tracks and could be coupled to the immense, grey machines that pushed them up and down the edge of the quay. The crane beside us had a new set of counterweights hanging in a steel cage, large slabs of concrete stacked one above the other.

Chandler squinted up at the counterweights.

"Holding up okay," he said.

"Not for much longer. We're going to have to move them."

"And soon," agreed Chandler. "Breytenbach knows his gold is here somewhere. That's why his black-suited goons are searching the docks. My ears on the ground tell me he's figured out it came down with that wildlife and believes it hasn't been driven out of here. I didn't realise they'd started the search already."

"They've been running haphazard searches for a few days."

"It will work against him," said Chandler. "He might as well be using a loudhailer to tell everyone he's lost his gold here."

"But they'll not find it," I said, more to reassure myself than because it was fact.

"Maybe not. But they will find our warehouse, you can be sure of that."

"We'll have to move out then, before they do."

"It's our only option."

"And we'll need to clear the gold out first. How long do you think we have?"

"A few days, a week at the most."

"Will your man be ready?"

"In five days he'll be floating offshore. International waters where we won't be bothered. We can take it out to him."

I finished my cigarette and tossed the stub into the sea.

"Breytenbach is somehow involved in the game the Department are playing," I said.

Chandler's eyes narrowed. He knew Breytenbach as well as I did, if not better, because he'd been our captain when our squad had been sent to one of Breytenbach's gold mines for our final posting. Supposedly to help Breytenbach and his cohorts defend against terrorists from the Congo who were stealing gold from them. But it turned out that the gold was not being stolen by the terrorists after all. Unfortunately, by the time we discovered that detail we had already killed most of them.

"That's interesting," said Chandler. "You should be careful of those government goons, Angel. I don't like the sound of them joining forces with Breytenbach."

"Will do," I said, and took a last look up at the blocks of concrete in which we had hidden Breytenbach's gold bars. Khanyi was right about my knowing that there were more than a few of them. I had counted them – there were one hundred and twenty.

"I'd better find Robyn," I said.

"You had," said Chandler. "Bring her back, even if she's too drunk to stand up on her own. We need to do this together."

SIX

"You probably think about a box, don't you?" said Madame Lee, in a voice that sounded like she was crushing rocks in the back of her throat. She hadn't removed the ivory cigarette holder that drooped from the corner of her mouth like a permanent growth and which bounced up and down as she spoke, leaving a trail of smoke like an aeroplane writing messages in the sky. She pursed her lips now and sucked on the cigarette, then opened her mouth again like a huge frog, wisps of smoke emerging from between her teeth. The impression of a frog was enhanced by the thick spectacles which caused the wide Asian eyes to bulge.

I admitted I had thought of a box.

"Mistranslation," said Madame Lee. "It was a jar, not a box. A stone jar, and it contained all the evils of the world. Well, what did you men expect? She was the first woman, wasn't she?"

"Was she?"

"Pandora," said Madame Lee, after sucking some more smoke in to fuel the gravel machine, "means 'all gifts' in Greek. She was the first woman, commissioned by Zeus to punish Prometheus for providing men with the gift of fire. That's what women are – a punishment wrought upon men."

Madame Lee sucked on her cigarette and did the frog face again.

"But a divine punishment," I said, "which makes it easier to bear."

Madame Lee's mouth opened and a cloud of smoke came out to the sound of an animal bark.

"And didn't Hope remain behind in Pandora's jar after she had unleashed the evils upon the world?"

"You're a classical scholar," said Madame Lee, showing no surprise.

"I read about it on the back of a breakfast cereal box. It's why we keep wanting to open Pandora's box – to find that hope."

"Which is why you're here," said Madame Lee, returning to business with a bump. "You want to open the box."

"I do."

"What's your taste?" asked Madame Lee.

"A friend of mine spoke of a girl he liked here. A couple of months back it would have been."

"Did he," said Madame Lee, forgetting to add the question mark. "You'll have to provide more detail than that. We have many girls, and cater for a wide range of tastes."

"A young girl," I said, "coloured, with light, almost golden eyes."

Madame Lee sucked on the cigarette, then allowed the smoke to drift through her teeth.

"I don't have a girl with golden eyes," she said without regret, "but we have other coloured girls. You like them coloured?"

"I do."

"Mulatto then," she said and held up a hand with knobbly knuckle joints and used a finger from the other hand to bend back an index finger which bore a large ruby. "Girl," she said, bending a second finger back. "You like a bit of pain?"

"I prefer the pleasure."

"Like to give pain?"

"Not particularly. My friend said the girl with the golden eyes had a friend here. Arrived at the same time as her. Perhaps if the golden-eyed girl is no longer here, her friend might be?"

Madame Lee toyed with the third finger, and her eyes narrowed to see me better through the smoke.

"We don't like history," she said. "At Pandora you start afresh, you find yourself a new girl, or boy, or whatever you want, we don't like emotional baggage or over-specific requests."

"No history," I said. "Just that she sounded like my kind of girl."

Madame Lee took an extended draught of the cigarette, and her face swelled a little as if she might burst, but then smoke found its way out through her teeth and the crisis passed.

"We do a line-up," she explained, "and we pay in advance. No discounts, no refunds."

"I understand," I said, and the third finger was released in order to press a button on her mahogany desk. It was a heavy finger, weighed down by a diamond large enough to have been stolen from a museum, and it rested on the button for a few seconds.

Madame Lee and I sat in silence for a minute, then the door behind me opened soundlessly, allowing a small draft of air in to snatch at the haze of smoke around us and swirl it about.

"Take Mister Moss to the front room," Madame Lee said to the bodybuilder dressed in black silk who appeared beside me. His skin was so dark that it was only possible to tell he was looking at me when his teeth glimmered through the haze as he gave me a discreet smile to show that he made no judgement on men who needed to be taken to the front room.

———

The front room of Pandora was fitted out like the drawing room of an English country manor, complete with a small bar containing a smiling, bald barman who provided me with a whisky while I waited for my line-up. He placed my credit card on a silver tray in case it would be needed to pay in advance for further services without the possibility of a refund, and encouraged me to enjoy the view of the gardens through the wide bay window so that I didn't feel I was required to explain myself to him.

The gardens were worth enjoying. Rolling, green lawns with carefully tended flower beds, some of which contrived to add a little colour despite the season. Beyond the lawns, the serried rows of Groot Constantia vineyards were etched onto the valley floor, waiting hopefully for the heavy clouds above them to burst.

Four young women arrived for my consideration, ushered into the room one at a time by the bodybuilder with the white teeth. The first to arrive was coy, fluttering her eyelashes and smiling at me from a lowered face as if she was drinking from a non-existent straw and auditioning for a role in Lolita. She took a mineral water from the barman, perched on a stool and was toying with her glass when the second candidate arrived. Number two's approach was more brash, a knowing pout and eyes that implied she knew my darkest secrets. Her mineral water provided her with something to tap with her long, sparkling fingernails while the three of us engaged in conversation about the weather. Number three was a sporty variation in case I turned out to be the fun-loving, energetic type of customer, despite appearances to the contrary. She wore a small amount of Lycra stretched over a lithe body, had glittering eyes and laughed at everything anyone said, whether it was intended to be amusing or not.

The fourth possibility was quiet and withdrawn, wearing an emerald silk dress with a high collar in the Chinese style. Her hair was tightly curled African, trimmed very short, so that she cut an androgynous figure. She was the only one of the four who did not smile at me, and when the bodybuilder announced that my lineup was now complete and that if I struggled with making my decision I could always choose a combination for a special price, she alone did not giggle.

None of the four had golden eyes.

The bodybuilder left me to make my choice, and instead of starting with small talk I broached the subject of the girl with the golden eyes. I explained that she might have been brought to Pandora at the same time as another girl, and that she might have had a troubled past. Numbers one, two and three shook their heads and looked confused, but number four kept her green eyes steady on me and said she might remember a girl with light eyes, but probably did not.

"She is no longer here at Pandora," I said, to help jog her memory.

"No," said number four. "She isn't here."

Number three laughed at that, in case it was amusing. Number one fluttered her eyelashes, and number two pouted because I was not being much fun.

"But you did meet her when she was here?" I asked.

"I don't think so," said number four, but her eyes said she had. They held mine with a steady gaze. The pupils were tiny pin-pricks in pools of green – she was high on something.

"Have you made your choice?" asked number two suddenly, and number three laughed again. "You're staring at Leilah like it's love at first sight."

I said that I had made my choice, and number four stood and smoothed her silk dress over her narrow hips.

"Madame Lee doesn't like men like you," warned number two.

"Like me?"

"Men who want to talk, who aren't here for the tits and ass. Are you a policeman?"

"No, I'm not."

"A private dick then?"

"Not that either," I said.

"You look after yourself, Leilah," said number two, "you know the old dragon won't like it."

"I always look after myself," said Leilah. "Don't you girls know a soldier when you see one?" She turned to me. "Come on, soldier-boy," she said, and led me out of the room.

She still hadn't smiled.

———

Leilah led me through a maze of carpeted corridors and up two flights of stairs to a room with a four-poster bed with dark sheets and a mountain of pillows, on top of which sat a disgruntled teddy bear. A sash window was wide open, allowing an icy wind to sweep into the room and play games with the heavy drapes.

"I need the fresh air," explained Leilah. She turned to me and placed a hand on my chest and looked up at me with her solemn green eyes. "Could you?" she said, turning her face to the side and touching the nape of her neck where the silk dress had a zip fastener.

"Your friend was right about my wanting to talk," I said. "That's all I need; to talk."

"I like to talk too, but Madame Lee has her rules. Customers want their money back if we keep our clothes on. Please undo the zip."

I unzipped the dress, and Leilah shrugged it off so that it slid to the floor. She stepped out of the dress and turned to face me, her eyes on mine to assess my reaction. The first thing I noticed was the scar. It ran across her neck in a thick line, as if she was a rag doll whose head someone had tried to remove. She was an attractive woman, with a face that could have been beautiful if it had not been so hard, and an elegant, long-limbed body, although she was too thin and altogether too vulnerable in her black lace underwear. Her face relaxed as she saw me accept the scar, and for the first time she gave a small smile.

"I was right about you being a soldier, wasn't I?"

"What gave me away?"

"Your eyes – you've got the eyes of a killer – an official one. Licensed to kill."

She stooped to pick up the dress and held it up against her.

"Could you close the window, soldier-boy? I like the fresh air, but it's going to get cold if you're just going to stand there and waggle your tongue."

I closed the sash window and then Leilah insisted I unclasp her bra and sit in a low-slung armchair. She sat in my lap and picked up my hand and used a painted nail to trace the lines on it as if she was going to read my future.

"You are a killer, aren't you?" she said. "I'm never wrong about that. I can see things about people, like an aura around you, and yours is stained with blood."

She took my hand and placed it on her small breast, cupping it with my fingers.

"Look as if you mean it," she said. "We need to keep Dragon Lee happy."

"Is she a dragon?"

"She breathes fire, and sits on her hoard of gold. Isn't that what dragons do?"

Leilah tilted her head back and closed her eyes. She opened her mouth and gave a sigh, as if the slight pressure of my hand was giving her a disproportionate amount of pleasure. It was a convincing display.

"That one's for the camera behind the mirror," she said. "But there's no microphone, so you can tell me why you're interested in the girl with the golden eyes."

"She's been missing for some time. I'm trying to find her."

"She a friend of yours?"

"No, not a friend."

"Well, you won't find her."

"Why not?"

"Because your girl with the golden eyes is dead."

"I see. And do you know how she died?"

Leilah nodded and brought her face close to mine. "I

know how she died, soldier-boy. She lost the game, and I had to watch them kill her, didn't I?"

"What game?"

Leilah smiled, a strangely mesmerising smile with not one iota of joy.

"The game of life, the game of death. Whatever you want to call it."

"Who is they? Who killed her?"

Leilah took a deep breath as if she was about to make an announcement, but then she pursed her lips and blew minty breath into my face.

"What do you want with the golden-eyed girl, soldier-boy? What did she do that I cannot do?"

"I am trying to find someone else," I said. "Someone who wanted to help the golden girl, but failed."

"Wanted to help her? Why?"

"They were sisters."

Leilah stopped the gyrating movement of her hips and pulled back from me.

"You want the golden-eyed girl, or her sister?"

"You know the sister?"

"Yes, I do. Natasha saved my life."

"Natasha?"

Leilah's eyes narrowed. "Does Manda have more than one sister? Natasha was the sister who saved my life."

"And how did she do that?"

Leilah lifted herself off my lap and took up a pose against a post of the bed – one leg raised to point its narrow knee at me, her arms held high to lift her breasts.

"Natasha was an angel sent from heaven," she said. "She came down to hell, where she saved me. Then she hunted the devils, didn't she?"

"The devils?"

"She said she would hunt them all down. She even found one of them. Gave me the name of the devil."

"Perhaps you should tell me what happened, from the beginning?"

"You want it from the very beginning – with all the dirty bits?"

"Let's start with the highlights."

"We'll start in prison then – that was a highlight. Manda and I were in together for three months. We rode there from the courthouse with a bunch of other girls. I'd been doing too much tik. I kept some of the money I made from my tricks to myself, and Thabo, my main man, wasn't any too happy, so he checked me in for some rehab – that's what he called it – and Manda was there with me in the truck, coming down and shaking 'cos she'd been too high. She was just a baby – only fourteen, fifteen maybe?"

"Wait a moment," I said. "Manda, short for Amanda: the girl with the eyes?"

Leilah nodded.

"Tik? What is that?"

"Crystal meth – we call it tik. We all do it, but Manda did too much of it."

"And Thabo, your main man?"

"My dealer, my pimp, my main man. He was my protection, but when I broke the rules he let them take me in for some rehab behind bars."

"And after prison?"

"The friends of the devils were there to meet us when we came out. But you are skipping the best bits, soldier-boy."

"What were the best bits?"

"When they seduced us with their little messages."

"What messages?"

"Letters, phone calls. They even sent us little bits of money, enough to buy ourselves cigarettes, not enough to buy our way out of trouble."

"Who sent the messages?"

Leilah made a sound like she was blowing a feather off her lips.

"They said they were our friends, wanted to help us. That they understood us."

"Didn't the prison warders block those messages?"

Leilah blew another feather.

"Of course they did, but the warders were on the side of the police and the magistrates. What did they know? The harder they tried to stop the messages the more we wanted to hear from the people who said they were our friends."

"And they were the ones there to meet you when you'd served your time and came out?"

Leilah nodded and changed her pose with a different leg up and a hand pulling at her panties.

"Of course they were there. They pay the prison warders for the tip-off."

"What about your family?"

She gave a small laugh. "I had a mother, but she killed herself with booze. There was a man, not my father, who preferred me to my mother, and who hit me when I said no. So he doesn't count."

"Alright, so your new friends met you and Manda outside the prison. What happened then?"

"They had a big van, one of those family cars with ten seats that they could load girls into. Tinted windows and free tik for the ride. They parked outside the gate, and the guards knew them and waved, and grinned at them."

"You went with them?"

"What else should I do? Sure, I had a choice – get in the

van and take a hit of tik, or stand on the street corner and wait for some stranger to come along and shove his beer bottle up my fanny, after he broke the top off. I don't come from your world, where your sweet mother comes along and takes you for ice-creams so you feel better."

"And the place they took you?"

Leilah said nothing for a moment. Her green eyes turned into deep pools, and two perfect tears rolled down her cheeks.

"Come and lie with me," she said, after wiping angrily at the tears. "Do you mind the teddy bear?"

I didn't mind the teddy bear. Leilah arranged the mountain of pillows around us like we were lying in a small cave, and she insisted on removing my shirt. She ran a delicate finger over the scars on my chest.

"Bullets?" she said.

"Shrapnel: little pieces of metal, screws and nails that are built into the homemade bombs and mines the gooks build."

"What gooks? Terrorists?"

"These were in the Congo. Allied Democratic Forces was what they called themselves."

"You were lucky they didn't go deeper. This one is right over your heart. I can feel it beating."

"We weren't all so lucky."

Leilah looked up at me and kept her finger running along the scars. I could see the thoughts being marshaled as she considered telling more of her story.

"You have your own scars," I said.

"We all do. That's what life is, isn't it? One scar after another." She let her breath out in a long sigh. "They sucked my life from me. That's what they did in the place they took us to. It was worse than prison – too much tik and booze. There was a big red couch with broken springs, and a crappy widescreen TV. That's what I remember, having my life sucked out of me on that couch in that room. More than my life, they sucked my soul dry. We were the dog shit on their shoes. We were their slaves."

"How did you get out?"

"Natasha found me, didn't she?"

"You and Manda?"

"No, Manda was dead. Didn't I tell you she was dead? I watched her die."

"You met her sister after she died?"

"Her name was not Natasha, was it?"

"Her name is Sandy."

Leilah's green eyes looked into mine as she considered this. Her hand kept moving gently over the scars on my chest. There was something bothering me about her story, but I couldn't figure out what it was. Something to do with the sequence of events and Manda dying before Sandy appeared.

"You've watched friends of yours die?" she asked. "The ones who were not so lucky with the bits of metal in the bomb?"

"Not really. Those deaths come quickly. I couldn't say I watched. But I've been there when friends of mine have died."

I thought for a moment of Brian's eyes as he turned to look at me and Chandler after we heard the clumsy trigger the ADF had rigged. A tripwire with a spring-loaded device that was armed when Brian caught the wire with his boot. We all heard the sound of it arming over the whimpering of the little boy he had been wanting to comfort, pinned to the ground with a bayonet beside the body of his dead father.

"Manda took ten minutes to die," said Leilah. "That's

what my friend said, ten minutes, but to me it felt like hours."

"In the room with the red couch?"

"No, this room had a golden couch with thin legs and little feet on them like a lion's paws. Fancy chairs, and a nice carpet that was rolled up because they didn't want Manda's blood all over it. It was a party in a party room with pretty pictures of naked women – they didn't want to spoil it with blood."

"You were at a party?"

Leilah closed her eyes, and I thought for a moment that she had decided to feign sleep, but then she said, "It was a special party. A big job for us, they said, a lot of money. There were three of us girls."

Her eyes were still closed, and her hand continued to feel its way around my scars as if she were trying to read a Braille message on my chest.

"Three of us went in, two came out," she said in a voice without breath.

"The game?" I said. "Is that what you meant by the game?"

Leilah opened her eyes and looked at me. There was a wall of stone now behind her green eyes.

"It was their game, not ours."

"These were the same people that sent you messages and took you away after your time in jail? Your friends? It was their game?"

"No, we had no friends, soldier-boy. These were a different level of monster. Fat and old and evil. They wore masks, you know those masks you see in the movies? With the hooked nose, and the holes their nasty eyes could look out of. They had wrinkly skin, and tired, limp cocks. It was their party, and their game – we only learnt the rules of the game after Manda had lost. They'd given us a whole truck-load of shit before it started, so our heads were in the clouds, you know what I mean?"

"You were high."

"Not just high, we were higher than ever. They had coke, tik and E. Fancy paintings on the walls, glass tables, big cushions, soft carpets rolled up, and we left our heads up in the clouds and our bodies went down to hell. The windows were closed, they had cigars they smoked, and while Manda dripped her blood all over the floor, I couldn't breathe. They fucked her while she died. Did I say that? Their cocks went harder, they took it in turns, and we watched."

Leilah rolled away from me on the bed and scattered pillows onto the floor as she flailed her arms up and down like she was trying to shake herself free of the memory. She placed her hands on her breasts and made as if she was going to tear her chest open.

"Can you open the window, soldier-boy? I can't breathe, I need some air."

I opened the window and a blast of icy air burst into the room. In the distance the clouds had succumbed and trailed patches of rain over the vineyards. Leilah lay on the bed, taking huge gulps of air, and started to cry. I looked out over the trimmed lawns and Leilah said I should light a cigarette because she wanted some, but I ended up smoking most of it as I watched the rain shift like a lace curtain over the vineyards.

———

Natasha, whom I knew as Sandy, had arrived at the hell-hole with the red couch months after Manda had died.

Leilah had recognised the golden eyes, and knew immediately that there was a connection with Manda, but her keepers had already long forgotten about Manda and made no connection between them.

"How did she arrive?" I asked.

"What do you mean, how? She arrived in a car."

"But under what pretence?"

"Pretence?"

"Did she say she was looking for her sister?"

"She knew her sister was dead, but she didn't know how. That came later, when we told her how it happened, after the transfer."

"Transfer?"

"Natasha bought us, didn't I say that? She bought us from the monsters. She arrived in her car, paid them with a big bundle of cash, and drove away with us like we were household appliances she'd picked up at the store."

"Did she bring you here?"

"No, she wanted us to work for her, didn't she?"

The heavy drapes beside the windows billowed into the room suddenly, as if someone was trying to get through them. I felt the slipping sensation again, of things not making sense, but I still couldn't put my finger on what it was. The thought that Sandy would buy women to 'work' for her seemed absurd.

"Just you, or were there others?"

"Two of us. Flossie and me."

"And this was the work you did?" I said, gesturing vaguely around the room, encompassing the bed, the low-slung armchair, our mutual state of semi-nudity.

"Yes," said Leilah, "but classy, not dog-shit-on-the-shoe work. Natasha found us top clients, the very top."

Leilah wanted another cigarette. She watched me curiously as I lit it in a cupped hand to protect from the gale coming in through the window.

"What's your name, soldier-boy?" she asked.

"Gabriel," I said.

"There was an angel, wasn't there? An angel Gabriel?"

"He was an archangel, one of the big ones. But there's nothing angelic about me."

"I can see that. Didn't I tell you I can see your aura?"

"Tell me how you came here," I said. "To Pandora."

"Natasha arranged that we would come here when we were done with her. She knows the business. Her family have their own house, did you know that?"

"Yes, I knew that."

"She wanted us to join the family house, but I think she argued with her family. So she arranged for us to come here."

"Why did you stop working for Natasha?"

Leilah shrugged, took the cigarette from my hand and sucked at it like it was a straw.

"We didn't stop. We came to Pandora, didn't we?"

"You know what I mean."

Leilah looked at me as she blew smoke into the cold wind.

"We helped her find one of the men who killed Manda. That was all she needed. Then our job was done."

"And the other girl, Flossie – did I meet her in the front room?"

"No, she's gone back to the street, back to Thabo."

"And what did Natasha say she was going to do with the men who killed Amanda?"

"She said nothing."

"You saw her after you came here?"

Leilah handed the cigarette back to me and shook her head.

"She said we would not see each other again. That she was going back to her other life. What did you say her name was?"

"Sandy."

"But she didn't go back to that life?"

"She didn't."

Leilah turned to look out at the vineyards. She was leaning up against me at the window in a pose that she had explained the Dragon would appreciate as being post coital. She laid a hand again on my chest and felt the ridges of the scars.

"Why have you waited so long to look for her?" she asked. "It's been months."

"I didn't know where to start. And besides, I wasn't sure she wanted to be found."

Leilah took the cigarette from me again. She sucked at it, then flicked it out the window.

"Why did you stay on here at Pandora?" I asked.

"Because Pandora is heaven. I have died and now I have come to heaven."

She smiled, and for the first time I glimpsed something approaching joy in her face.

"I'm good at what I do," she said. "You don't know what you've missed, Angel Gabriel. And Pandora is good to me – I have a life, I have more money than my drunk mother ever dreamed of. This is the life your Sandy gave me, and I will never let it go."

As we shared a last cigarette together and Leilah's fragile body warmed me against the icy wind, I realised what had been bothering me. Sandy's father had told me she had called him weeks after staging her disappearance in order to tell him that her sister had died, but Leilah's story implied she had discovered that truth earlier, before her decision to assume a new identity and rescue Leilah and her friend, a process that had taken several months. And if that was the case, why had she phoned her father? And what did she have to say to him?

Someone was not telling the truth.

SEVEN

That afternoon I drove past Robyn's apartment block, then I took various routes that allowed me to circle past it several times. I took note of the cars parked outside the block, but only one of them was occupied, and it had moved away on my fourth loop, so I parked in a position that gave me a view of her windows and waited. The windows were closed, and the blinds were drawn. It was still raining; the street was deserted and there was no sign of life.

After fifteen minutes of watching the window, I climbed out of the car and dashed through the rain. I took the stairs out of habit and reached the third floor a little out of breath. I listened at the door first, but there was no sound from within, and so I rang the doorbell, then knocked. There was no answer. Robyn was either not there, or was there, but not conscious. I considered picking the lock, but the elevator door pinged, and Robyn's neighbour appeared, a youthful man with a pink face who worked for a bank in the city.

"Looking for Robyn?" he asked, then without waiting

for a reply, said, "Not seen her for weeks. I think she's left town or something."

"Damn," I said. "Just my luck. I should have called first."

And we shared the regretful smiles of two men who have let a beautiful woman slip through their fingers.

———

Back at the warehouse I opened the enormous doors that let onto a slipway, and sat at the entrance to smoke and watch the sea beat itself against the dock and try to climb ashore. The afternoon's rainstorm had dissipated into a fleet of low-hanging clouds that hovered out at sea, as if they were planning a fresh invasion. The last light of the day still lingered on the horizon beyond them.

There were only a few places that Robyn could have gone, and I ran through them in my mind. There was a girlfriend she hardly ever saw, a rehab centre she spoke fondly of, and my own apartment: the most foolish place to hide, because we knew that Breytenbach had men watching it. The ringing of my phone interrupted my ruminations.

"Well?" said Bill when I answered. "Who is it? I thought you were going to call me?"

"Sorry," I said, and lit another cigarette. "I've been busy."

"Working?" asked Bill suspiciously. Bill Pinter was a history lecturer at the University of Cape Town and his appreciation of the country's history had instilled in him a scepticism for government departments. Ironically, his scepticism was something we shared.

"No, I haven't worked for weeks," I said.

"Who was it? Who did Sandy call?"

Bill had been Sandy's closest friend. He was an over-sized man, both in terms of his physical presence – with a substantial belly and extra chins – and in terms of his personality. The world, according to Bill, was more dramatic, more desperate and more extraordinary than anyone else's world.

"Her father," I said. "Did you know her father was still alive?"

Bill was silent for a moment. His heavy breaths came over the line and it occurred to me that I should probably have softened the blow. Bill might be loud and bigger than life, but a lot of that was sheer bluster.

"Shall I come around?" I suggested.

"Sure," he said. "I'll cook."

————

Bill Pinter's house was what estate agency crooks would call a homestead, because it had fruit trees on the land below the terrace, neatly pruned and maintained so as not to obscure the view of Hout Bay's quaint harbour and the sea beyond. Not pruned by Bill, he assured me, because he was not built along the lines of a person who could climb ladders.

The house was elegant in a simple country-kitchen way, but it was not expansive. Bill just about fitted himself into it, and there was space for a large variety of female companions, who squeezed into the small space left by Bill's personality. The terracotta tiled floor was heated, and a fire crackled in the grate to help things along, because Bill had the French doors open so that we could see the masts of the yachts below.

"I thought her father was dead," he said, looking at me

through spectacles misted from the steam. His brown hair was forming untidy tufts because of the way he had been running his hands through it as part of the creative cooking process. "Died years ago when she was little more than a baby. She was raised by her aunt – or great-aunt?"

"Tannie Sara is her great-aunt. Her mother was Tannie Sara's niece, who died giving birth to Sandy."

"That's right, I remember now."

Bill pronounced the lamb ready, removed his apron, and rolled up his sleeves. We sat at the table before the open doors, warmed on one side by the fire, and cooled on the other by the breeze coming off the sea.

"You know she never introduced us?" said Bill, his vast face drooping. "I met none of her family."

"I didn't know that."

When Sandy had disappeared, I had lost a lover and partner, but Bill had lost a friend. Sometimes I forgot that. Before her disappearance, Sandy had been the only thing that Bill and I had in common, but the shared disaster of her disappearance had drawn us together. We had been united in the struggle to understand what she had done and why. At first we had both been convinced that something dreadful had happened to her – an accident or a brutal crime. But when her clothes and belongings were removed from my apartment, our sense of dread turned to confusion and dismay.

It was Bill who received the handwritten note posted two weeks after her disappearance. I remembered the evening he had read it out to me, doing his best to keep his emotions in check, although his powerful bass voice betrayed him and wavered as he read the words aloud.

In the days, then weeks that followed, we had become friends.

"Of course, I knew about her family and what they did," he said. "Was she ashamed of them, do you think?"

"Not ashamed." I thought back to the times I had spent with Sandy and her aunt. "She was proud of her family. Perhaps the fact she was proud of them was what shamed her."

"She needn't have been," said Bill. "It was a different time. Brothels fifty years ago were not what they are today. Nowadays they are places of shame – scarcely legal, bent lawyers on the payroll, huge bribes to the police, dark rooms hidden behind heavy security."

"It was different fifty years ago?"

"You must remember the political situation when Sandy's family started their brothel. Did you know District Six House is a celebrated part of the history of District Six? You go to the museum today and there are old black and white photos from the fifties with the women standing proudly on the steps. Those are Sandy's great-great-grandmothers and aunts."

"I've seen some of those photos, on the walls of the new place in Greenpoint."

"They had to find new premises when the government bulldozed the whole suburb. You know they did that? Literally razed the entire area to the ground."

"They have photos of that too."

"District Six House was a place of empowerment. Sandy's great-great-grandmother was entrepreneurial. She empowered women to fight against the apartheid regime. She believed in the power of women, and if that meant exchanging sexual favours in return for the kind of income beyond the wildest dreams of the poverty-stricken workers squeezed into those tiny houses in District Six, then for her it was an opportunity to uplift her people."

Bill laid his cutlery aside and produced a huge handkerchief from a pocket, which he held at the ready.

"The people labelled 'coloured' during the apartheid years are a fiercely proud community, but they have a humility learnt from years of being considered second-class citizens. Sandy should have been proud of her family."

The handkerchief swooped in, and Bill blew his nose like a trumpet.

"It's the season," he said. "All this alternating from hot to cold. I just don't know where we are. Think I'm getting a cold."

He held the handkerchief ready and fixed me with an accusatory stare.

"Do you really think you should stir things up, Gabriel? You're putting her at risk."

"If she was ever at risk, Bill, that time has passed."

Bill studied me for a moment through the lenses of his spectacles. What he saw didn't seem to convince him.

"I know you think you're this super-spy, Gabriel, with all your secret service work, but you've got the army written all over you. If Sandy's investigating something to do with human trafficking, you should stay well clear of it."

"I don't think Sandy is investigating anything anymore, Bill. That's what I'm saying."

Bill tucked his handkerchief away and turned his attention back to the meal. After all these months, the possibility that Sandy was no longer alive was still not something we discussed.

———

Bill took his life into his hands by proposing that we enjoy our coffees on the terrace. He donned a thick woollen sweater, hand-knitted by one of his earnest fans, with a roll neck to keep the chins warm. He held his handkerchief in one hand and his milky coffee in the other, and gazed out over the moonlit bay with the expectant pose of someone about to sneeze.

"This young prostitute," he said. "Has it occurred to you she might be making the whole thing up? Is there a word of truth in any of it?"

"It has occurred to me, and yes – I believe there are some words of truth."

Bill looked out over the bay. A string of three fishing boats were heading out for the midnight cod haul, their lights played hide and seek with the moon.

"And is it possible that Sandy's father, who must be terribly bereaved, has embellished his own version of the story?"

"It's possible," I said.

"Don't take this the wrong way, Gabriel."

"I won't."

Bill raised his handkerchief and sneezed. Birds in a tree took to the air in alarm. When Bill had recovered and finished wiping his nose, he sighed deeply.

"I want to find Sandy as much as you," he said, "but you have to tread carefully."

He stared out at the three fishing boats as they rounded the promontory beneath a rocky outcrop called the 'Sentinel'.

"You think I should drop it?"

Bill turned back to me. We had been back and forth over these difficult waters so many times in the past few months that I could see the signposts pointing the way.

"She was the one who did this," he said in his defence. "If she wanted us to find her she wouldn't have written that note."

I nodded.

"You're right. It's probably a wild goose chase."

Bill turned back out to sea. The three fishing boats had disappeared, and it looked as if the view didn't please him as much. A wind started running its fingers through the waters beyond the bay, and lifting the skirts of the swells. The winter was not done with us yet.

"She could have taken me to her family brothel," he said, "could have introduced me to her family – I'm not judgemental – what did I care what her family business was?"

"If these few months have taught me anything," I said, "it is that I knew very little about her."

I hadn't meant for that to sound so bitter. Bill turned to me in surprise.

"You knew her better than anyone," he said. "And you know she doesn't want to be found. Promise me you won't go chasing after her."

I smiled in lieu of making another promise I couldn't keep, and we both turned to look out to sea. The shimmering veil of wind on the water made a dash for the shore. Bill shivered and blew his nose as the chill wind struck us.

EIGHT

I couldn't sleep that night with the constant drumming of the rain on the iron roof, so I sat again on the broken deck chair at the top of the slipway outside the warehouse. I was on my third cigarette when the rain receded and I received a phone call from a number I didn't recognise.

"Is that my angelic soldier-boy?" asked Leilah in a whisper, as if she didn't want me to hear her.

"Is an angel still an angel after falling from grace?"

"There was something I didn't tell you," said Leilah.

"Only one thing?"

"One big thing," said Leilah, "about Natasha." She paused, then said, "Did you say her name was Sandy?"

I confirmed her name was Sandy and lit another cigarette. A string of lights processed across the horizon – cargo ships and cruise boats making their way in and out of harbour. Blue lights fluttered between them like butterflies caught in treacle. Police boats searching the ships.

"You still there, Angel?" asked Leilah, and when I assured her I was, said, "Can you meet me?"

We arranged to meet at an all-night bar in Long Street,

where the clientele at this hour would be mostly the women who worked the upper end of the street and their prospective customers. Leilah thought this would be amusing given the nature of her work, and my status as a paying customer.

I had half an hour to spare, so I smoked some more, and wondered again where Robyn had disappeared to. It had been only a few days since she had told me – again – that things wouldn't work between us, had packed her small bag and left me alone in the warehouse. As I watched the police boats going about their systematic searching of the cargo ships, it occurred to me that I knew exactly where Robyn would hide, because it was in her nature to put herself in harm's way. I would have to make sure I found her before anyone else did.

———

Leilah was dressed to kill, in another high-necked silk dress which covered her scar and almost extended below her crotch. Aside from the dress she wore high-heeled shoes with a fantasy of laces that spiralled up her long legs like headless snakes reaching up to nirvana. Her solemn, green eyes filled with tears when she got smoke in them from the cigarette I provided.

"I've been clean," she said, "since you came around this morning, I've not done any shit."

Her pupils were no longer mere pin-pricks and her face had a little hardness to it as if some disappointment had come to settle. I said what a good thing that was, and she smiled, but the tears stayed where they were, threatening to spill down her cheeks.

"Are you hoping to find her, Angel? My Natasha, your Sandy? Is that why you came to Pandora?

I said I was, and she looked as if she was preparing to break some bad news but didn't know how to go about it.

"You won't find her," she said.

"I won't?"

Leilah shook her head, which caused the tears to spill. She reached up a hand and palmed them away like a child.

"She's dead," she said. "Natasha is dead."

I cannot say it was a shock. Not even much of a surprise.

"You know that for certain?"

Leilah sucked on her cigarette, nodded, and wiped away more tears.

"I killed her," she said. "That's how I know."

She used the palm of her hand to wipe her nose. Her lips trembled, and she averted her eyes so that I couldn't see the toll that the performance was taking.

"No, you didn't," I said.

The performance ended as if someone had dropped the curtain. The crying continued, but now it was messy and entirely real.

"I might as well have."

"Why don't we stick with the facts instead of the might-haves?" I suggested.

She pulled a serviette from the dispenser on the bar table and used that to clean her face. Then glanced around the bar as if worried someone had seen her crying, but at this time of night nobody bothered about a working woman crying before her customer. Besides, they were mostly fumbling with each other's body parts, obscured by the pall of smoke that hung over the cracked linoleum tables.

"She saved my life," said Leilah. "I told you that, didn't I? That's a fact, we can start with that."

"You said she found the men who killed her sister."

"Only one of them," confirmed Leilah. "One of the monsters."

She finished the clean-up and gave a small, brave smile that might have been seductive if she'd had more time to hide the little girl that had crept out in the absence of any mind-altering substances.

"How did she do that?"

"She used me as bait, didn't she? She dangled me like biscuits for the dogs."

"And the dogs went for it?"

"Only later, it took us weeks. Natasha had a big plan. At first, when she arrived in hell, she said nothing about her plan. She took us away in her car, cleaned us up, and then we talked. She wanted to understand what had happened to Manda, how it all worked. Asked us about it again and again. Me and Flossie had been with Manda the night she died, and we needed to talk about it. Natasha was like our big sister – she listened to us, and she cried with us."

"Where was this, that you did your talking?"

"In Muizenberg, right near the sea. I love the sea. She rented a house just for the three of us, right by the sea."

Muizenberg was an old suburb that had developed as a holiday resort in the late 1800s for mine owners to relax and recuperate from the ardours of sending other men underground to pull the gold out. It boasted a sandy beach almost twenty kilometres long, several historic homes and many shabby, less historic homes.

"She was like my sister," said Leilah again. "Told me I had the same birthday as her father, you know that? It bound us together. I believe in star signs, and destiny, and all of that. Do you? I think Natasha did."

"The plan to find the men who killed her sister," I said,

without committing to the question of destiny. "When did that come about?"

"She always had the plan. Don't you see? But she made like it was our idea. She would make little comments, then bring us back to it when we talked, ask us again how it happened, how we ended up at the party, what we remembered about what they had said to us on the red couch."

"And it worked?"

Leilah pulled out another serviette and blew her nose into it, then gathered up the serviettes and my glass and walked to the bar, saying nothing. She returned with a fresh whisky for me and a chocolate milkshake for her, and settled back into her seat.

"Yes, it worked," she resumed. "We got special invites. Another party, very exclusive. Flossie and me agreed it looked the same, and Natasha went and had a meeting with someone to talk about it. It was the same arrangement, the same big money. They wanted three girls, and they said nothing about only two of us coming back. That's how they did it, Natasha said – they would gather the girls that were already lost. You know what I mean?"

"Girls who had fallen out of the system? No paperwork, nobody looking for them?"

Leilah nodded, and sucked at the straw of her milkshake, then looked up at me with her cheeks sucked in and her green eyes glowing. It occurred to me how young she looked; she was probably not yet twenty years old.

"Do you know how many of us lost girls there are?" she asked.

I was reminded of Sandy's father asking me the same question.

"Many," I said.

"Hundreds, thousands maybe," said Leilah. "We fell

through the holes and dropped in the gutter. Some run away from parents who couldn't care, or some parents do care, but the girls just make the wrong friends. Flossie was one of those. She broke her mother's heart, she used to say, like she was proud of it. Some boys too, but most of us are girls. We used to joke with Natasha about being her lost girls, and she'd say she was lost too."

"Did you go to the other party?"

Leilah sucked at her milkshake again and shook her head so that the straw dipped in and out and made slurping sounds.

"When Natasha found the men who organised the party, she said our work was done. That was all she needed us for; to find them. She took us to Pandora, set us up with our new lives."

"She didn't tell you anything about the men who organised the party?"

"She said it was big; they had a network, like a spider's web, for finding girls who could get lost. Like magicians, she said, they waved their wands and the girls would be gone. She'd found the apprentice and was going to find the magician."

"Your hell-hole with the red couch was a part of it?"

"Natasha said so. She made loads of notes, and was working the whole thing out like a detective."

"She wrote it down?"

"Always writing. She had pages and pages of things she wrote. We would tease her about it and she would laugh with us, but she kept her pages all together in a folder and said they would help us get our revenge on the men who had done this to us, and then she wasn't laughing anymore and we would stop too. We also wanted revenge on those men."

Leilah's chocolate milkshake ended with a slurping sound, and she used the straw to suck the last drops from the sides of the glass.

"Do you know where those notes are?" I asked.

Leilah shook her head and pushed the empty glass away. "All gone. They took them when they came to kill her."

"When who came?"

"When *they* came," repeated Leilah, and she pouted, then looked around the room as if only noticing now that it was a dive.

"Take me somewhere else, will you, Angel? All this talking you're making me do is taking the breath from me. I need some fresh air."

I paid for our drinks and on the pavement Leilah leaned against me, shivering in the frosty night wind.

"Signal Hill," she said. "There's plenty of fresh air up there, and I'll throw in a blow job for an extra hundred bucks."

She laughed, and her green eyes mocked my feigned shock. But behind the laughing eyes I could see a frightened girl reluctant to spill more of her horrors.

———

Beside the well-known, flat-topped Table Mountain, endemic feature of wall calendars and tourist guides to Cape Town, is a smaller mountain, which viewed from a particular angle resembles the head of a lion, complete with a cluster of pine trees which form the ridge of a furry eyebrow. Beneath the mane of Lion's Head is a smooth hill resembling the body of a prone lion, ending in the raised haunch of Signal Hill. From here the glittering lights of

Cape Town city can be viewed, and on a clear winter's night one can see all the way across the bay to the Hottentots Holland mountains and watch the airliners as they pick their way over the mountain peaks and line up for final approach over the Atlantic Ocean.

It is a favoured spot for parking a car and misting up the windows with physical exertions, but Leilah explained she had been joking about the blow job, or at least had been joking about expecting me to pay for it, and that she would rather snuggle together in the back seat of my car than talk anymore. So we snuggled into the back seat, and I said it would be best to get the talking over with – to just say what she had to say quickly. And so she did.

"I told Thabo," she said. "Told him everything."

"Your main man, Thabo? The pimp who let you go to jail?"

"I wanted tik, and I knew he could get me some, so I called him."

Leilah looked at me with big, green eyes, and she bit her lip. I sensed she was preparing for more histrionics.

"Let's not do any more play-acting," I said. "No more tears; just tell me what Thabo did."

"He sent men around to the house. They were his bully-men. Brutes."

"What did the men do?"

"I was there with Natasha. Flossie wasn't there yet. We'd already moved to Pandora and Natasha was closing everything up. She had asked for our help to clean. The brutes must have followed me, mustn't they?"

"What did they do?"

"They tried to kill me, and they took Natasha. They said there was a man who wanted to see her, and they hit her when she fought back, so badly she couldn't stand up. Then they dragged her out."

"What did they do to you?"

Leilah reached behind her neck and unzipped her dress. The angry scar across her neck stood out against her skin in the pale moonlight.

"They didn't know how to do it, not the way it was done to Manda. I was bleeding so much they just left me there, they thought I'd die. So did I, but Flossie found me when she came in later."

"Why did they do it?"

"Because of what I told Thabo."

"Which was what?"

"I told him about Manda, and I told him about Natasha, and the notes she was making. That's what I told him, nothing else."

"How do you know the men were sent by Thabo?"

"They wore the shirts of a club Thabo worked at. It had to be him."

"What kind of club?"

"A men's club. He calls it a 'gentleman's club', but it's just a way of arranging hookers for men who want to do special things, and don't want to be stopped by the police when they pull over by the side of Long Street. Thabo is one of their pimps."

"What did they do with Natasha?"

"That's what I asked myself all the days I was in the hospital, when they stitched my head back on."

"And what was your answer?"

"They killed her, didn't they?"

"You've seen Thabo since then?"

Leilah shook her head. We sat in silence for a few

minutes and watched the lights of an airliner come in over the brightening eastern horizon.

"Do you think you could find the monsters again?" I asked. "Could you piece it together the way you did before?"

"No. It was Natasha who did it. It took her weeks."

"But she told you a name, told you who one of them was."

"No, she didn't. She never said the name."

Leilah looked up at me with her innocent, green eyes.

"You told me that Natasha found one of them and that she told you his name. She named the devil, that's what you said this morning. Yesterday morning."

"I must have been high," said Leilah and she blinked her innocent eyes. "Why don't you call her Sandy if that was her name?"

"Because Sandy disappeared. Your Natasha is who she became. I call her by the name she chose, not the name she abandoned."

"What made her do that?" asked Leilah. "Why did she stop being Sandy? Stop being one person and become another?"

"You think I know?"

"I think I need you to hold me, Angel. That's all I think. The sun is coming up, and it's like we are the only survivors, aren't we? The world has gone to hell, but we survived."

"So far," I said. "We've survived so far."

And I held her frail body tight as the sun rose.

NINE

Benjamin looked up from the glass he was polishing and his golden eyes appeared magnified by the heavy-framed spectacles, probably an illusion caused by the way his pupils contracted when he saw me. The hand holding the cloth with which he was wiping the glass released it to flutter silently to the floor behind the bar. He placed the glass down lest he drop that too, and gave me a smile that was friendly, but frightened.

Several customers were gathered about the wooden tables, engaged in quiet conversation and enjoying the warmth of the fire that crackled against the white noise of the rain drumming on the windows.

"Don't say it," said Benjamin. "Not here, not now." He must have seen the news I'd brought written all over my face. "I'll get someone to cover for me and we'll talk privately."

Benjamin had a huge umbrella, which he opened as we stepped out of the entrance lobby. It bore the hotel insignia, and he explained it was a golfing umbrella loaned to guests who wished to risk the capricious Cape weather on the local course. The explanation was merely a means of delaying what I had to say, so I said nothing. The two of us splashed in silence along the muddy strip of sidewalk to his house. I held the umbrella as he inserted a key into the freshly painted front door, then folded it and propped it against the door frame so that it didn't drip all over the wooden floor.

The front door opened directly onto a small lounge which resembled more the cosy study of a university professor than a room for socialising or entertainment. There was a fireplace with the embers of a fire, a modest couch which faced the fireplace, a worn Persian carpet and a wall of books, the shelves reaching from floor to ceiling. At the far end of the room two sash windows provided a view of a patch of vegetable garden, some neatly pruned fruit trees and a path of stones leading down to the river.

"It's just me," said Benjamin, as if he felt I needed an explanation. The wall with the fireplace was a Mondrian collection of photographs and framed press clippings. Sandy was there, many times over, smiling at us and laughing. And a girl with the same eyes as Sandy, younger, prettier, but thinner, with hollow cheeks and a haunted look.

"Are those Sandy's articles?" I asked, indicating the press clippings.

Benjamin nodded and removed his spectacles to polish them with a handkerchief that he pulled from his waistcoat pocket.

"You should just say it, Ben," he said. "It won't get any easier by not saying it."

I had prepared a short sentence to convey my news, but Benjamin spoke again before I had the chance.

"My Sandy is dead, isn't she? You've found proof of it. That's where she's gone – she's passed on."

"I think so," I said. "Yes, I think she's dead."

"Do you know how? Who?"

"No," I admitted. "I have some ideas about how it happened and who was involved, but no certain details. I have been told by someone who was there, and suffered injuries of her own."

Benjamin replaced his spectacles and sat down heavily on the couch as if his legs had given way. He peered at the fire grate, which produced a trickle of smoke from a heap of ash.

"Shall I light a fire?" I suggested. The room was cold, the skies outside the sash windows so black with rain clouds it felt as if a bleak night was already upon us.

"There's no time," said Benjamin.

"We've got an hour. That's enough."

I found some kindling in a basket beside the fireplace, with chopped wood stacked neatly beside that.

"An hour to mourn my daughter," said Benjamin, "that's what my life has come to. Months of worry and staving off the grief, and then an hour is all I get."

"You don't need more than that," I said. "You need to be with people, get back behind your bar." But I knew that wasn't true; the barman is invisible, not someone supported by the camaraderie of his customers.

The kindling caught with little encouragement, and I found a light switch to augment the cold light trickling in through the windows. Soon the room felt a little warmer. Benjamin stared at the fire while I boiled the kettle and set about making some tea.

"Sandy didn't phone to tell you she had found her sister," I said when we were sitting side by side on the couch and were both nursing a hot mug.

Benjamin turned to me, his damp eyes surprised.

"The phone call she made to you after she disappeared," I said. "That was not when she told you Amanda had died."

"She made me promise," said Benjamin, and he turned back to the fire, raised his mug to his lips and blew steam into his glasses as if to close himself off from the world.

"Promise what?"

"That I wouldn't tell anyone I had heard from her."

"Why not?"

Benjamin turned to me, the lenses of his spectacles an opaque white with condensation. He removed them.

"She was going to go after them," he said. "She was so angry, she wanted to avenge Amanda's death."

"Do you know who she was going after?"

Benjamin took a sip of tea before answering.

"Important men, she said – prominent men who had a club of sorts. She'd found a letterhead belonging to the club. She was going to expose them, show the world what they had done."

He went silent again and studied me through the steam rising from his mug.

"Sandy said you were not a regular soldier," he said.

"I was not."

He nodded slowly, his eyes still on me, as if debating whether to continue.

"Three respected men, she said. The kind of men who think they are above the law."

"I see," I said.

"She was so angry when she called. Something terrible had happened to her, but she wouldn't tell me what it was. I told her to come and see me – I worried she might do something foolish – but she refused."

"Did you ask who the men were?"

"She wouldn't say. I begged her to share the burden of

her knowledge – that kind of thing can be a terrible burden, you know."

"But she refused that too?"

Benjamin nodded, and we both drank some tea.

"She sent me a letter, weeks after. Made me promise never to share it. But – well – given the circumstances."

Benjamin stood abruptly, crossed the room and opened a door at the far end of the wall of books. He returned a minute later with some folded pieces of paper, sat down with a sigh and unfolded them – they were a little crumpled as if they had been crushed in anger, then smoothed out again. He held them delicately, lest they fall apart in his fingers.

"Dear Father," he said and then thought better of reading the whole thing to me, and his finger moved down the margin of the handwritten letter until he found the relevant part. "The first is a judge," he read, "the others a politician, and a church leader." Benjamin looked up at me, his eyes damp behind the thick lenses. "She names the judge," he said, and looked down at the letter again. "The Honourable Francois Rousseau, a judge of the Gauteng High Court." He ran a finger down the letter, but found nothing else to read and looked back up at me.

"Just the one name?" I said. "No other details?"

"They used false names on the letterheads of the club's documents, but she thinks they were names with the same initials. It's mostly guesswork on her part. That's why she wanted me to keep quiet about it. It's all supposition. She thinks the judge called himself Frank Rose."

Benjamin handed me the second sheet, which bore an unimaginative letterhead of curvy lines that might have represented two interlocked mermaids. Beneath the tails were three names. The first was Frank Rose.

"She said it took her a long time to work out who the judge was. She was working on getting the other names."

Benjamin blinked again and looked down at the letter as if he might find something else there.

"I knew it was foolish of her. You don't interfere with people like that. But how could I have stopped her? She only sent me the letter because I had begged her on that call to share the burden of her knowledge. What could I have done?"

Benjamin's voice dried up. He reached for his mug of tea, sipped at it, and swallowed noisily.

"There was nothing you could have done," I said. "Do you think she went to that judge? Confronted him?"

Benjamin removed his spectacles again and pinched the bridge of his nose.

"His name eats at my soul," he said. "And the thought of the others – three prominent men who consider themselves above the law. What could I do? Spend my life standing beside the street under my big umbrella and getting splashed by their fancy motor cars as I watch them and think morbid thoughts? I wish now she had not sent this to me. She knew I could do nothing. And she was right about that. Some men can step up and take action, but I am not one of them."

Benjamin replaced his spectacles and laid a hand on mine.

"Another mug of tea?" he suggested.

"Of course."

I went through the open door of the kitchen and refilled the kettle.

"How did you know she didn't phone to tell me about Amanda?" Benjamin called after a minute of companionable silence.

"I found a friend of Amanda's, and she told me about meeting Sandy – but Sandy only disappeared some time after discovering what happened to Amanda."

"I warned her," said Benjamin. "When she said she was going to find out what had happened to Amanda, I told her to be careful. I knew it would only bring her trouble."

"There was no stopping her," I said. "There never was."

We finished our second cups of tea, then left the fire burning with extra logs so that Benjamin would have some warmth to return to that evening. We splashed our way back to the hotel like old friends sharing the umbrella.

"Have you forgiven her yet?" he asked when we reached the entrance to the hotel.

"No," I said, "I don't think I ever will."

"Good," he said. "I don't think forgiveness is what she would have wanted."

"Vengeance perhaps," I said, and Benjamin shrugged.

"Maybe vengeance is what we all need," he said, then he reached out his arms to embrace me. His shoulders were frail and hunched with sadness and regret.

He watched me from the porch as I struggled back through the rain to my car, and he raised a hand beneath his enormous umbrella as I tried not to splash him when I passed.

———

First is a judge.

It didn't take me long to find the address of the Honourable Justice Francois Rousseau, and that afternoon I took the two-hour flight to Johannesburg. It was a Saturday.

Sunday morning seemed a good time to pay a visit to a judge.

II

Then a Politician

TEN

The rainstorm over Cape Town on Monday taunted me by hiding the Atlantic Ocean from view, then revealing it again suddenly, but snatching it away the moment I thought the day was brightening up. Winter might have been nearly over, but the season was running encore performances and was giving us all it had.

Cape Town shelters beneath the flat-topped Table Mountain, which forces westbound traffic into a series of bottlenecks as it winds along the narrow coastal road. Heading west from the city you reach a string of luxury apartments teetering on the cliffs above the sea, strung down the coast like the pearls of a necklace. These luxury apartments are where you find the film stars, underage entrepreneurs, spuriously wealthy and other scoundrels. But before reaching this luxurious stretch of the peninsula you are squeezed into a narrow passage that leads through the less salubrious suburb of Seapoint, where the prostitutes lie in wait hoping to snare themselves a wealthy customer. And on the doorstep of Seapoint is a tranquil cove called

Three Anchor Bay, a jumble of buildings that teeter on the side of respectability.

My apartment is on the fifth floor of one of those buildings. There is never any parking within several blocks, and so by the time I unlatched the door and stepped into the apartment my clothes were thoroughly wet and I dripped all over the terracotta tiled floor as I listened for signs of Robyn.

I heard nothing but the sound of the rain, so loud that it might as well have been raining inside. I discovered why when I walked further into the apartment and found the glass door onto the balcony wide open, allowing the wind to bring the rain in and spread it across the floor. Robyn was seated with her back to me, facing the open door and the storm that entered through it. I stepped up to the door, closed it, and turned back to her. Her face was pale, her dark eyes showed no surprise or pleasure in seeing me. She was wearing a crumpled white shirt that I recognised as one of mine, a shirt she had liked to wear at night when she had stayed with me in the apartment.

"The colonel told me to find you," I said.

Robyn didn't react, but her dark eyes were steady on mine. She has a quirky beauty. Not spoilt, but enhanced by the fact that her chestnut hair was still growing out after they shaved it for the stitches when one of Breytenbach's men had tried to shoot her. She has delicate, pointed elf-like ears, and a narrow nose, with eyes that are constantly alive and amused. But today the amusement was all spent, and her eyes were full of regret. On the counter behind her was a row of empty bottles, and I wondered where she was in the cycle of her addiction. Probably coming out of a period of intense drinking – she had tidied up, arranged the bottles as evidence of her failure – and was hoping that by sheer willpower she would pull herself out of the deepening spiral she had fallen into.

"We need to go back to the warehouse," I said.

Robyn blinked, and she opened her mouth. She took a deep breath, then let it out in a sigh.

"I'm not going anywhere," she said.

"Be sensible, Robyn. It's only a matter of time before Breytenbach sends his black-suited goons over here."

"Let him."

Robyn reached a hand to the low table beside her chair and lifted her Glock 9 mm.

"You can't shoot all of them," I said. "You know he'll just send more."

Robyn looked down at her gun, as if wondering whether I was right.

"I'm tired of running," she said, her eyes still on the gun. "Let them come and get me, it's what I want." She looked back up at me and said, "I've been drinking," as if that explained everything.

"I know you have, but that's it for now. I'm taking you back."

"Why?"

"Because waiting here for BB's men will not solve anything. We're in this together, you know that. You're being selfish, and besides, self-pity doesn't suit you."

That roused a flash of anger. "Did you promise Brian you'd look after me, Ben? Is that why I cannot shake you off? You promised him, just before he stepped on that mine?"

I didn't answer. Brian came up whenever we argued and there was nothing more to say on the subject. It had been a few years since he had triggered the IED in the forests of the Congo. But as my friend and Robyn's fiancé, he continued to haunt us. Robyn looked down at her Glock and stroked it as if she was trying to soothe it after her outburst.

"Did you find her?" she asked after a moment of silence.

"Yes."

She looked up at me and knew I was lying.

"I'll get your things," I said.

Robyn closed her eyes like she was turning to stone. She knew there was no way out. Not for her, or for any of us.

———

I took the high road back to the docks because on my way to the apartment I had driven past a team of soldiers mounting their shiny aluminium pod beside the main road. Robyn sat in silence, her face drawn as if with pain, and she kept her eyes closed. The rainstorm weakened as we climbed the gorge and I caught occasional glimpses of one of the world's most beautiful coastlines, the deserted sandy beaches being scrubbed clean by an angry sea. As we descended the narrow shoulder between Table Mountain and Lion's Head, the rain stopped as abruptly as if someone had flicked a switch and the city lay before us, glistening in the late afternoon light that poked beneath the cloud.

"Did you really find her?" asked Robyn, whose eyes had opened with the sun.

"No," I said.

"Is she dead?"

"What makes you say that?"

"I can hear it in your voice, Ben."

"Yes," I said, "I think so."

Robyn released her breath in a drawn out sigh.

"I'm sorry."

We drove in silence for a few minutes.

"He wants to move the gold, doesn't he?" said Robyn suddenly.

"Yes. We need to move it – Breytenbach's goons are searching the docks. You would have had to wait a long time before they showed up at my apartment. They're too busy trying to find the gold."

"We should let them find it. They can take it back and suffer the consequences themselves."

"What consequences?"

"That gold is cursed."

"That's nonsense, Robyn."

"Think about it, Ben, all the way back to the first person who had the idea."

"The first person? You mean Chandler? Or me?"

"No, I mean Brian."

"It wasn't Brian's idea," I said. "That was nothing but a ridiculous joke."

"You told me he made you promise."

It was true that Brian had suggested we take some of Breytenbach's gold for ourselves. In the messroom on the mines in Uganda, the snores of our helicopter pilot coming through the thin wall. It was a suggestion that our captain had rejected because he swore he would never stoop as low as common thievery. But Brian had persisted and had extracted a promise of sorts from me. It was a lighthearted promise, not a serious one. And we hadn't known it was the last night of his life.

"It wasn't a promise either of us took seriously," I said.

"But that gold is cursed," said Robyn again. "You wait and see, it will bring us nothing but problems."

ELEVEN

"You're an hour late," said Chandler, who had been standing outside the warehouse. He watched us with obvious anger as we arrived on foot, having left the rental a safe distance away. His pale grey eyes studied us with displeasure.

"I found Robyn," I said, unnecessarily because she was standing a few metres from us. "And we managed to avoid the roadblocks."

Chandler turned to Robyn. I thought I detected a brief look of relief to see her standing. Or was it disappointment at the sight of her pale, drawn face?

"Robyn?" he said.

"I'm here, aren't I?" said Robyn as she took her bag and walked up to the small door in the side of the rusty, old warehouse. She yanked it open as if it had insulted her.

Chandler and I stood for a moment and were buffeted by the wind that came across the water from the twinkling lights of the Waterfront.

"She'll be okay," I said.

"I hope so, corporal. I've said it before: if one of us goes down, we all go down together."

———

A rhythmic sliding and clicking noise was echoing about the warehouse space. Fat-Boy was hunched over one of the chest of drawers in the brightly lit kitchen and was sliding a drawer open, watching it settle into position, then pushing it gently with a sausage-sized finger as if trying to determine the minimum effort required to have the drawer close again. It was a favourite activity of his. He stood and turned to face us at the sound of our footsteps. Fat-Boy looked like someone had rolled a large globule of viscous material into position and left it to droop in the middle of the bright kitchen – he was shaped like an enormous drop of water, small and pointed at the top and spherical below. His left eye was lazy and half-closed, a feature that he used to express a range of emotions from disappointment to scorn. He gave us the full range now as we approached, although his wide Xhosa nostrils flared a little at the sight of Robyn, whom he liked to call 'sex-bomb', because he was not immune to her appeal; but he did that mostly out of her hearing. Fat-Boy's real name was Stanley, but only his close friends called him that – I was not one of them – I was one of the others, obliged to use the subtly insulting, but appropriate, nickname.

"Damage anything and you pay for it, Fat-Boy," said Chandler.

"Pay with what?" countered Fat-Boy, and he gave Chandler a blast of scorn from his lazy eye. "Got nothing to pay with, have I, Colonel?"

"That's why we're all here," said Chandler and he

clapped his hands together and rubbed them as if he was about to perform some kind of hands-on healing.

Fat-Boy made a scoffing noise, but it was an act – he held Chandler in the highest regard, an attitude that sometimes verged on hero-worship. He only heckled because it brought him attention, and we all knew it.

"Briefing centre," announced Chandler, as if he was auditioning for a war movie and expected us to salute him and fall into line. Fat-Boy gazed at him as if he hadn't understood, then turned reluctantly and shuffled over to the deck chairs beside the hull of the Anna-Marie. Robyn was already there, settling into her regular chair like a cat curling itself into a ball. She was irritable and jumpy, but trying not to attract attention. Chandler stood against the rusted hull, and I took a seat in the back row.

"Our man Breytenbach," said Chandler in his military briefing voice, "has been putting the pieces together. My connection to his chief of staff tells me he believes that crates containing live animals shipped from Maputo to these docks were used to conceal the gold that he is missing."

Chandler produced a smile that was little more than a stretch of the lips into a flat line. He looked around at us, but there wasn't a significant reaction. Robyn seemed to be sinking into a meditative trance and Fat-Boy was frowning with confusion. I gave a small smile to show Chandler I was keeping up.

"He's got money on us," complained Fat-Boy. "You see that? One million bucks on each of us."

"Don't worry about that," said Chandler. "Did you recognise yourself in that picture?"

"No," admitted Fat-Boy.

"Nothing to worry about. Besides, that's one million

dollars of protection on each of us. He wants us alive so that we can tell him where we've hidden the gold."

Fat-Boy scowled and looked unconvinced.

"So!" said Chandler, doing his best to keep the momentum. "We need to move it."

"How the fuck we gonna do that?" asked Fat-Boy.

"By sea – Breytenbach is a landlubber – we're going to sneak it out to sea."

"I don't do sea," said Fat-Boy.

Chandler's smile didn't falter.

"You didn't do wild animals either Fat-Boy, but look how that turned out."

"Yeah – I got shot, the Afrikaner blew himself up, and I still ain't got no gold caps on my teeth."

Chandler sighed. He was a man who had been born to lead, and I often thought it was one of the tragedies of his life that he had ended up with this small team of misfits.

"You brought those lions in like a champion circus trainer," he said. "You're going to do just fine at sea. Now let's clear this place up in case BB's goons come snooping. Let's get to it."

And before Fat-Boy could think of any further complaints, he brought the briefing to a close with another clap of his hands.

———

It didn't take me long to dismantle the steel-frame bed Robyn and I had used. Then Fat-Boy helped me carry the pieces out to a rusted old hull outside the warehouse, which was filled with scrap metal and other junk.

"Think she can still shoot straight?" asked Fat-Boy with a jerk of his head in Robyn's direction. She was sitting at the kitchen table, packing her collection of handguns into a tog-bag, ejecting the magazines, and racking the slides of each to check the chambers were empty. "Sex-bomb," added Fat-Boy, in case I hadn't realised who he was talking about.

"Straight enough," I said. "She's been doing it since she was just a kid."

"'Cos her father raped her," said Fat-Boy. "The colonel told me about it."

"Her step-father," I said.

"The colonel says she cannot shoot to kill, though. What good is that? If those Breytenbach men come at her with their guns, she needs to kill them."

"No, she doesn't. The last thing we need is dead bodies."

I offered Fat-Boy a cigarette, and he cupped an enormous slab of a hand around the flame as I lit it.

"It's only you that thinks she's sexy," said Fat-Boy. "You know that?"

"Nonsense, I've seen your lazy eye wake up and get out of bed when it sees her."

"Too skinny," declared Fat-Boy. "I like something to hold on to."

"You're the one that calls her sex-bomb."

"That's to make you jealous. What's going on with you two, anyways? The colonel says you're not doing the dirty anymore."

"It's none of your business."

Fat-Boy gave me a big smile full of white teeth. "Dead giveaway," he said. "Actually, the colonel didn't say a thing, but your answer just told me all I need to know."

"Put it out," called Chandler as he emerged from the warehouse. "There's no smoking in my car."

"We going somewhere, Colonel?" Fat-Boy dropped his cigarette and ground it into the wet surface of the quay.

"We've got a ship's captain to go see, Fat-Boy. Angel, I want you and your girlfriend out of here by sundown, you hear me?"

"Yes, Colonel," I said, and dropped my cigarette so that I could stand at attention.

"Get inside and clear up," snapped Chandler. "What did you not understand about us needing to clear out of here?"

"Of course, Colonel," I said.

Chandler looked at me sharply, as if he knew that even though I'd said 'Colonel', I was thinking 'Captain'.

———

The warehouse seemed empty when I went back inside. I locked the door with the rusty old padlock as the sound of Chandler's Jaguar faded. Robyn had finished packing her guns and there was no sign of her. The air was thick with the dust Chandler had scattered over the kitchen to make it look unused, and I stood for a moment trying not to sneeze, then heard a metallic clicking noise from above.

A steel platform was suspended from the top beam at the pitch of the roof. It had a motor in a metal enclosure, and chains which ran through pulleys with heavy iron hooks dangling from them. I glimpsed Robyn's head between the bars of the cage. I had forgotten that she had used the cage as a storage space for her collection of weapons.

"You going to give me a hand?" she called. "Or just stand there gaping?"

I climbed the steel ladder encased with hoops that led to

a gantry fifteen metres above the floor. As I clattered along the wobbly gantry, I saw Robyn was dismantling her McMillan TAC-50, a sniper's weapon that she had bought on the black market as a gift for Brian when they announced their engagement. She looked up at me as I approached, but her hands kept busy with her routine. A finger confirmed the chamber was empty, shifted the safety into fire position, then she pulled on the trigger to within a hair of the release. Her eyes smiled at me as she gave the final squeeze, so subtle that if I'd been watching her finger, I wouldn't have seen it move. The trigger hammer gave a tiny, well-oiled click, and Robyn looked down to move the safety back into the safe position.

"Brian teach you that?" I asked. The McMillan had been his gun of choice.

Robyn laughed. It was an absurd suggestion, because by the time she met Brian she had known enough about weapons to teach him a thing or two. In fact when Brian had told me in his thick Yorkshire accent that he had found himself a "witch of a felon" I hadn't realised that he really did mean that she was a felon. But she was: she had spent three years locked away in a medium-security jail for her part in a botched bank robbery. Brian enjoyed telling that story because of the mild sense of shock that it caused, but he would immediately follow up with the explanation that she had been young and had fallen in with a bad crowd. He rarely explained that Robyn had been carrying three hand-guns, one of which was the Glock she had stolen from her step-father when she ran away from home. And he skipped the bit about her having learnt to use the Glock by shooting at photocopied print-outs of that same step-father pinned to the target. And he didn't explain that the step-father had sexually abused her from when she had been only eleven years old. He shared those details with me only when he started trying to find reasons for the difficulties that had appeared in their relationship, and the two of us had settled down with a bottle of Jack Daniels in an effort to figure it out.

"I told the colonel about the curse on the gold," said Robyn as she packed the pieces of the gun into her tog-bag.

"What did he say?"

"He said I shouldn't drink so much." She looked up and smiled. "And he said the gold had nothing to do with Brian's death."

"He's right about that."

"But that's the thing about the Midas curse. It all seems unrelated, but it's not."

"Midas curse?"

"You don't know the story of King Midas?"

"I thought he had the gift of turning anything to gold. Not a curse."

"It was a gift that became a curse. He turned his own daughter into gold and then turned his food to gold. He almost starved because of it, and he lost his only child."

"Almost starved?"

"He was granted the gift of washing himself of the curse. So he washed away the ability to turn things into gold."

"And you're saying our pile of gold is a gift that will become a curse?"

"No, I'm saying it has always been a curse."

"So we're thieves with the Midas touch?"

"Yes," said Robyn, but she was not joking – her eyes were serious. "Everything we touch turns to gold, but we'll end up starving to death."

Robyn lifted the heavy tog-bag, and the movement

caused our suspended platform to swing and the chain to the motor produced a series of musical clinks which echoed about the vast space. Then suddenly they were overwhelmed by a loud banging of metal on the corrugated iron door of our warehouse. Robyn looked up at me, but before she could say anything, the banging repeated with increased urgency.

Chandler had been right to be in a rush to clear out – and we had taken too long. Breytenbach's men had arrived.

TWELVE

The sound of the banging echoed about the warehouse like a spirit playing chase in the vast space. There was another silence for a few seconds, and then the banging came again. Robyn laid the tog-bag down gently and I heard some metallic clicks as she reassembled the McMillan. It was an overly powerful gun for the small space of the warehouse. But Robyn was not one for subtlety, and she might not have been wrong: Breytenbach's men would bring their Vektor R5s. Nevertheless, I drew my Glock from its holster – less powerful but easier and quicker to use. I preferred to be nimble, particularly when trapped on a small metal platform fifteen metres above the ground.

As the third round of bangs faded away, we heard the single sharp blow of something heavy against the door: they were trying to break open the rusted padlock. It took five blows, the last followed by the clinking of bits of the lock as they fell to the ground.

Then came the scraping of the door, and the gloomy space of the warehouse filled with a golden light that swelled as the setting sun peeked inside. The light dipped for a moment as if someone was fiddling with the fader – it flickered three times – and hard boots beat a syncopated rhythm across the floor. They stopped in unison as they encountered the kitchen. There was a pause filled with surprised murmuring, and then some barked orders in a native language. Robyn and I leaned forward to get a better look. There were three men wearing the black uniform of Breytenbach's army, and carrying the usual R5s. Two of them were starting to work their way across the warehouse floor, searching haphazardly by lifting tarpaulins, kicking at paint cans and poking warily at the shelves of shipbuilding tools. The third focused his attention on the kitchen and started using the butt of his Vektor to break the glass hood of the cooking island.

A moment later the warehouse darkened as something large filled the door frame.

"You'll not find it like that," announced a bellowing, slightly familiar voice. "What are you? A bunch of monkeys?"

"You said they hid it here," protested the man who had been attacking the cooking island.

"I said *they* were hiding here, not hiding the gold here – didn't the white man teach you English?"

I realised then why the voice sounded familiar. He spoke with the same accent as Fat-Boy – the musical lilt of the Xhosa people. Most of Breytenbach's private army had been recruited in the north, and they spoke either Zulu or Sotho. Presumably they were speaking English because it was the only language they had in common. There was a sulky silence into which soft footsteps padded. I leaned slowly to the side until I could see the shadow of the new arrival in the golden light spread across the floor. It was not the thin shadow of an able-bodied member of a private army. It appeared almost circular. I leaned a little further, and for a split second I wondered why Fat-Boy was standing there. The body shape was similar, the skin colour matched, but the scowl and the heavy jowls were not those of Fat-Boy. He was also not dressed in Fat-Boy's baggy jeans and stretched T-shirt, but looked as if he had just wrapped up a meeting of the board – a dark suit hanging open and a white cotton shirt with the collar still twisted from when he'd removed the tie. The platform Robyn and I were on swayed as our centre of gravity shifted. A chain hanging from the motor gave a small clank. Robyn grabbed at it and held it as I pulled back. The big man glanced up as I ducked out of sight.

"Where are your friends?" asked Breytenbach's man.

I could still see the shadow of the man with Fat-Boy's build and I saw the hand he held up as if to silence his companion.

"We must wait for them to come back," he said, but the shadow figure was gesturing urgently in contrast to the calm voice, pointing up to the roof.

"How do we know you've not been lying to us?" demanded Breytenbach's man in a voice that was developing a nasal whine as his anxiety mounted. He clearly didn't speak the same sign language as the big man in the suit.

"Get your men to fix that lock," said the big man, "and we wait for my friends to return." His deep voice was still calm, but his shadow gestured more urgently.

"I give the orders here – why don't you tell us where the gold is?"

"I told your boss – they've kept the location of the gold a secret from me. We need to wait for them to return. Get your men ready."

There was a silence, and then the other two members of the Breytenbach squad stepped out of the shadows and lifted their R5s to their shoulders. I guessed the big man's gestures had finally penetrated. A moment later, a burst of gunfire deafened us in the echoing space. Several bullets ricocheted off our metal platform and their impetus caused us to swing a little. The chain clanked and holes opened up in the corrugated roof above us, pencils of light piercing the dark space. The leader of Breytenbach's squad issued orders in their language, and from the shifting of the shadows on the floor it was clear he was sending his men to investigate.

"Raise your arms," he said in a pinched voice.

The circular shadow of the man in the suit raised his arms.

"You've got it wrong," said the big man, in a soothing voice which emphasised the mounting tension.

The leader gave no response. I turned to watch the ladder that provided access to the gantry and our suspended platform. A moment later, the black cap of a soldier appeared. He had his R5 slung over his shoulder, and it caught on a steel hoop and blocked his ascent. I felt Robyn's weight shift as she brought the McMillan around to point at him.

"You said it was here," said the leader, his voice rising to a shout.

"I said they were *hiding* here," said the big man slowly, as if he was speaking to a child.

The soldier climbing the ladder had backed down a few rungs in order to free his R5, and he turned to grasp the gun. Although he was entirely focused on his gun, we were in full view, and if he looked up, he would see us. Robyn didn't hesitate; she squeezed the trigger of the McMillan. There was the sharp crack of the shot, then the metallic clang of the bullet striking the metal of the ladder, and the man dropped from view. A moment later came the thump and cry of pain as he hit the floor six metres below. On his way down he had struck the second man who had been climbing behind him, and had dislodged him, so that he dangled now, one hand clinging to a rung, his legs flailing about. Our platform was swinging because Robyn had turned to find the leader, but I took careful aim and saw the burst of blood as the bullet from my Glock shattered the hand the man was dangling from.

Robyn was trying to get a line on the leader, who still had his weapon pointed at the big man, but had turned to look with amazement at the fallen figures of his two comrades. Robyn cursed as our platform swung back and hid him from view.

The leader shouted something, and as our platform swung I glimpsed the big man as he too shouted. No calm in his voice now. The leader turned back to him, and that was when the big man made his mistake. He lowered his right hand suddenly and slipped it into his jacket. The soldier reacted instinctively and squeezed the trigger of his Vektor. A single burst shook the air, followed by a silence which was broken by a shocked gurgling sound from the big man. He dropped to his knees like a noble beast being brought down. He looked at his chest. Blood was already blossoming across his cotton shirt.

Robyn had her line on the leader. She fired three shots in rapid succession. The first struck him in the arm holding his Vektor. His whole body jumped to the side from the blow and his arm flung out as if he was tossing the gun away, but the strap pulled it back to his side where the other arm instinctively grasped at it. The second shot caught him in the forearm and the Vektor fell to the floor with a loud clatter. The third shot pierced a boot, causing him to jump back and fall with a thump onto the concrete.

Our platform swung back to reveal the other two soldiers struggling at the foot of the ladder. One of them was sitting against the wall, cradling a shattered hand against his chest. The other was trailing blood from his leg as he crawled to his Vektor, which had fallen a few metres from him. I fired again and hit his other leg. He spun about on the floor like a toy windmill, and the warehouse filled with the sound of his screams.

We swung back, and the platform kicked under us. The leader had retrieved his Vektor and was using his good arm to fire at us like he was spraying water from a hose.

I put my third bullet into his forehead. His body dropped back onto the concrete floor like a sack of stones. The remaining two soldiers beneath us scampered across to the open doorway. I raised my Glock, but Robyn caught my eye and shook her head. A reflection off the water painted a sudden pattern against the far wall beyond her, and one of the fleeing soldiers fired a burst at it, which opened up more holes in the corrugated metal wall. A moment later we heard the jeep engine accelerating, tyres kicking up loose gravel, and then there was a deathly silence, broken by a gasping cough from the big man below.

He was still alive when I reached him, but there was nothing I could do to save him. He had lost a lot of blood, which formed a pool around him on the concrete floor, and it filled his lungs. His eyes were wide and confused, pleading for help. He tried to speak when I crouched beside him, so I cupped a hand under his shoulder to turn him so that his lungs could drain. But no words came out, and I knew he had only a few moments – I've seen enough death to recognise the signs. I moved my hand to his head, hoping that it might provide some comfort in those last moments. I'm not sure that it did.

———

I found the man's wallet in his jacket pocket, and inside that were some business cards. His name was Vusi Madikwe and his card proclaimed him to be an 'executive consultant'. He had no weapon inside his jacket, or anywhere else on his body.

"I didn't mean to kill him," said Robyn, who was breathing in quick gasps and looking at the dead body of the leader of Breytenbach's squad.

"You didn't," I said, pocketing the business card. "I killed him, and I meant to."

Robyn closed her mouth and calmed her breathing, staring at me as if I had said something to make her angry. For all her experience with guns, death still shook her. I reached an arm out and turned her away from the bodies.

"Breytenbach will send reinforcements. We need to get out of here now."

Robyn lifted her tog-bag and hesitated for just a moment, as if to pay her last respects to the two dead bodies we were leaving behind. Then we left the warehouse and walked up the deserted quay through the rain.

When we reached the rental, I drove us out of the docks and into the city, where I parked beside the strip of park called the Company Gardens. I was confident nobody had followed us, but we sat on a bench where I could watch the car and we took a moment to gather ourselves. I pulled the business card I had found on the big man out of my pocket and turned it over.

"Dark Bizness," I read aloud.

"Bizness with an I - Z?" asked Robyn.

"That's what it says, b-i-z-ness."

"They're a cosmetics company," said Robyn. "Make cosmetics for dark skins. They're big."

"So what was a man from a cosmetics company doing with Breytenbach's goons in our warehouse?"

"He was pretending to be Fat-Boy."

"But why?"

"Call the colonel," suggested Robyn.

"Didn't I tell you?" said Chandler on speaker-phone after I had given him a summary of the afternoon's events. "Breytenbach might as well have been handing out pamphlets announcing he's lost eighty million US dollars. That man was just the first entry in Breytenbach's treasure hunt."

"Let's hope he's also the last," said Robyn.

"Call it in," said Chandler.

"Call it in how?" I asked.

"You tell me, Angel," said Chandler. "You're the one with all the contacts."

"There will be repercussions."

"We'll face those. Right now the two of you need to fade from view. Lie low and wait for my call. I'll arrange somewhere for us to stay. Then we'll discuss your repercussions."

———

"The Angel Gabriel," proclaimed Captain Andile Dlamini, when he heard my voice. "I've been looking for you."

"You have?"

"Our girl Khanyi has five numbers for you, but she tells me none of them are working anymore."

"This is my new one," I said. "This one works."

Andile Dlamini was a wiry homicide detective I had worked with when the Department had dragged me in on a recent job. He was a dedicated policeman with integrity, as far as I could tell, a rare commodity in a country plagued with corruption and bursting at the seams with lawlessness. He seemed as good a person as any to call about the unfortunate dead bodies in our warehouse.

"What was the cause of death?" he asked, once I had explained the reason for my call.

"Gunshot wounds."

"Oh, Freddy," he said and I could hear the sucking of his breath and crackling of the tobacco, which meant that he still hadn't kicked the habit. When I had first introduced myself to Andile, it had been with the name on one of the Department's fake ID cards, because of my futile efforts to escape the attention of Breytenbach. Freddy Moss had been the name, and Andile still liked to use it occasionally, perhaps to highlight the inauspicious start to our relationship. "You didn't fire the gun that caused the gunshot wounds, did you, Freddy?"

"Not all of them."

"And you just happened to find these bodies? At the docks, is that what you said?"

"The docks," I confirmed, and gave him the location of the warehouse.

"Any witnesses who could confirm that you discovered the bodies after the occurrence of the gunshot wounds and not before them?"

"Unfortunately not," I said. "I was alone. And if you could consider this an anonymous tip-off, that would be for the best."

Andile sighed and sucked on his cigarette again.

"That's why you called me, is it? To avoid the call tracing."

"I knew you would help."

"What are you getting yourself into, Gabriel?"

"Did you say you've been looking for me?"

Andile sighed again. "There was a judge who climbed into his swimming pool recently and didn't climb out again."

"A judge?"

"Judge Rousseau." He sucked on the cigarette again.

"A swimming accident?"

Andile blew smoke into the microphone.

"You could say that."

"What does it have to do with me?"

"I need you to come in and see me."

"Could we meet somewhere?" I said.

Andile laughed at my tone of voice. "Let's meet on neutral territory," he suggested. "We'll meet at your old offices."

"The Department?" I didn't bother concealing my surprise. "What do they have to do with it?"

"Your previous employers have been helpful in my efforts to find you, Gabriel. They tell me they're expecting you to pay them a visit on other business. We could kill two birds with one stone."

"I see," I said, although I saw very little. There was a moment of silence. "How's the cracking of the nuts going?" I asked.

"None of your business."

"I've always thought you and Khanyi would be a good match," I said. "I'm on your side, you know that."

Andile and Khanyi had met on the recent job I'd done for the Department. He had been the police liaison, and the mutual attraction between them had been obvious from their first meeting. Although Andile had once described Khanyi to me as 'a tough nut to crack'. Speaking to either of them about the other was always a good way of changing the subject.

"I'll set it up for nine tomorrow morning," said Andile, with another sigh. "Get there on time and we'll keep your tip-off anonymous, how about that?"

"Sounds like a deal," I said.

"But try not to make a habit out of finding bodies with gunshot wounds, Gabriel. Khanyi warned me about you."

I laughed at his joke, but it occurred to me after he ended the call how ironic it was that Khanyi should have warned him about me. Most of the things I had done that Khanyi knew anything about had been done on her behalf. The person he should have been warned about was her.

THIRTEEN

When death came to Justice Rousseau, it did not come gently, according to the newspaper report I read that evening.

His life took some time to extinguish. The judge struggled against the knife used to cut his throat, which only brought him more pain, and deepened the incision that brought about his demise. He trailed blood across the soft carpet of the entertainment room where we had held our conversation. He trailed blood across the marble-tiled surround of his infinity pool and the immense splash that he made as he hit the water woke a slumbering girl beside the pool. The reporter described how she had watched in horror as he floated belly down and his blood spread like a blossoming flower about his naked body.

Is it possible that Justice Rousseau saw his life flash before him in those last moments as he gazed into the depths of the pool? According to the newspaper article, it had been a life that started with much promise, fuelled by a passion for justice. But I supposed his unusual appetites eventually got the better of him, although there was no mention of this in the newspapers.

I wondered whether it was the young, passionate and committed man who reached up to him from the depths of that pool to take him down. Or was it the depraved, sexual predator with an obsession for young girls who embraced him in those last few moments?

When the witness beside the pool had found sufficient clothing, had called security, had packed her minimal belongings into an overnight bag, and made a quick getaway without leaving her name, the police were called. But by then the knife – and the person who had wielded it – were both long gone. Security believed there had been a group of young girls enjoying a party with the judge, but the police were struggling to identify any of the guests and were calling for anyone who had information to come forward.

The murder of Justice Francois Rousseau was condemned as a heinous crime, and his good works were lauded. No mention was made of his unacceptable appetites, and certainly no mention was made of a secret club whose list of founding members included a Frank Rose.

But I knew that Frank Rose was only the first of three founding members of that club. The first to be listed in the club's official documentation, and – apparently – the first of them to die.

———

I arrived early the next morning at Greenmarket Square, the old cobbled heart of Cape Town on the edge of which the Department had its offices. I had dodged three roadblocks that had sprung up around the docks since dawn and I felt good enough about that to treat myself to a coffee at Giuseppe's. Greenmarket Square hosts a flea market during the day which acts like a spiderweb, trapping tourists like flies on their way in and out of the five-star hotel on the western side of the square. I was in time this morning to watch the stall holders setting out their wares, their casual banter providing a comfortable white-noise background to my anxious thoughts as I wondered what the Department had to do with Justice Rousseau, and why Andile had insisted on meeting in their offices.

I spotted Khanyi approaching me across the square as I was firing up my third cigarette. It would have been hard not to spot her because the leopard print outfit she was wearing had been made from a rare purple leopard, and it hadn't been a very big one so there was not very much of Khanyi's outfit. Khanyi was a Zulu from up north, and she had inherited all the best bits of her warrior ancestors, particularly her well-proportioned build, long muscular legs, strong mid-section and impressive upper layer. Her dramatic sense of dress extended beyond her choice of colour and paucity of material, to include tempting buttons in all the places they seemed most likely to pop.

"You still indulging in that disgusting habit?" Khanyi asked, as she sat down on the other side of my hubcap-sized table.

"Your police captain hasn't kicked it," I said, and Khanyi's already dark face darkened further.

"He's not *my* police captain," she said.

"Although I think he wants to be," I said.

Giuseppe had also spotted Khanyi's approach, and felt the need to express his Mediterranean appreciation of her beauty, which he did by pressing her against him tightly enough to see if any the buttons would pop. They didn't, and so Khanyi ordered a milky coffee, refolded her long legs and studied me with evident disappointment.

"I can't believe you're getting yourself into trouble again, Gabriel," she said. "This is the third time this winter."

"It's only the second time. That Minhoop affair was not trouble of my making. And as I remember it, you asked for my help."

Khanyi sighed.

"And we all know how that ended," she said.

We did. It had ended badly when an Afrikaans socialite walked onto a rugby field and detonated the explosives attached to his body in front of a television audience of millions. The fact he had spent the last half hour of his life in my company was not looked upon favourably by the Department.

Khanyi was blowing into the foam on her cappuccino and looking at me as if expecting me to say something. I realised she had spoken again.

"What was that?"

"Father said you shouldn't expect us to protect you."

"Protect me? Of course I don't expect that. Protect me from what?"

"The police, Captain Dlamini, all this trouble you're in."

I was about to protest again that I wasn't in any trouble when it occurred to me why we were meeting at the Department offices. Andile Dlamini was throwing me a lifeline in the form of my erstwhile employers. He didn't want to have a casual conversation about a judge who had failed to climb out of his swimming pool, but had accusations to level, and he expected my previous employers to defend me. He was likely to be disappointed. We all were.

"You can tell Fehrson I don't expect any protection," I said.

"You can tell him yourself," said Khanyi. "Captain Dlamini is already upstairs. We can go up just as soon as you've put that cigarette out."

"Oh good," I said, and made the cigarette last as long as I could.

———

"You broke into his house and threatened him," complained Andile Dlamini, after we'd all greeted each other with brisk squeezes of the hand – no smiles because of the circumstances – and had taken our seats at the vast oak table in the meeting room they called the Attic.

"I paid him a visit," I said, "I certainly didn't break anything."

"He lodged a formal complaint. The Gauteng office has a charge sheet against you."

Andile looked perpetually tired. His long, thin face stretched taut with weariness. He had told me he had given up smoking when we worked together after the Minhoop massacre, but that hadn't applied to smoking other people's cigarettes, and as he bared his teeth at me now, I confirmed it was something he was still struggling with. His teeth were tinged with yellow and his breath was mint, with an undercurrent of burnt tobacco. I took the baring of the teeth as a friendly gesture and notched up my innocent confusion.

"There must have been a misunderstanding," I said.

"You didn't threaten him?"

"Not at all."

"You realise this is a murder investigation, Gabriel?" Andile's eyes rested wearily on mine. He hadn't mentioned the dead bodies the police had cleared from the warehouse the previous evening – with a bit of luck we could avoid that unfortunate mess altogether.

"Of course I do," I said, and tried a reassuring smile, but it didn't have the intended effect. Andile sighed, and turned to Fehrson, who was sitting at the head of the table like an umpire at a tennis match.

"Perhaps," suggested Fehrson with an encouraging smile, "you should tell us what you were doing there? In the judge's house."

Fehrson had started his work with the security services back in the dark ages of the apartheid years when his masters had discovered his extraordinary ability to hold two opposing views and argue each with equal passion. It had been a useful skill for a pastor fighting in the army of the world's greatest pariah, but his masters realised it was also a skill that could be put to use in the shadowy world of intelligence. And Fehrson was living testament to the truth of that, as one of very few bastions of the apartheid era who had survived the transition to the new government.

"Of course," I said, and spread my reassuring smile around a bit. "I went to see Justice Rousseau about a woman."

"I knew it," said Khanyi quietly, her eyes on the table. "There's always a woman."

Fehrson gave her a warning glance and turned back to me.

"Captain Dlamini would appreciate your cooperation with this, young man," he said in his fake private school accent that matched the tweed suit he was wearing as if he was about to depart for a hunting weekend. He was in fact an Afrikaans man from a small rural town, but had spent most of his life behaving as an English gentleman –

behaviour I was convinced was a clever ploy for surviving the transition from the apartheid government to the democratically elected government almost thirty years ago. But Khanyi insisted I was being cynical whenever I suggested this and told me that his continued employment in state security was because he was such a good man. He was looking at me now like the paragon of all good men, his pale blue eyes kind and innocent, his white hair in quaint disarray.

"Captain Dlamini has been asked by his colleagues in Gauteng to produce a report regarding your visit to Justice Rousseau."

"I see," I said, and looked at Captain Dlamini, who was not looking enthusiastic about it.

"That is why we are all here. So if you could provide him with as much information as possible," said Fehrson, "we can all get on with more important things."

"Yes, of course."

"Truthful information," said Fehrson, in case I had not understood that aspect of his suggestion.

"Of course," I said. "Fire away with your questions, Captain."

I kept my eyes on Andile, keen to start imparting the truth. He looked back at me with his weary eyes and reached into his crumpled jacket as if to retrieve a pack of cigarettes, but then withdrew his hand empty. It was a habit of his, and I had often wondered whether he had a pack in his pocket and liked to touch it for reassurance, or whether the pocket was empty and the action was unconscious.

"Who was the woman?" asked Andile.

"She was young – little more than a girl. She'd been given a short jail sentence, but after her release from jail she disappeared."

"Disappeared? In what way did she disappear?"

"Her father filed a missing person report, but nothing came of it. They didn't find her."

"She served a jail sentence for what?"

"Solicitation. She had taken to working on the streets."

"Prostitution," said Khanyi, who had started her career with the Department as a secretarial assistant and despite her meteoric rise to power still had the minute-taker's habit of finding the most succinct word to ensure we were all talking about the same thing.

"Prostitution," I agreed.

"What would that have had to do with Justice Rousseau?" asked Andile. "He was a High Court judge. He wouldn't have been dealing with a young girl on the streets."

I wanted to suggest that Andile might be surprised by the extent to which Justice Rousseau had dealt with young girls on and off the streets, but I said: "He was sitting on the JSC, so I guess he was a judge of judges, wasn't he?"

"JSC?" asked Khanyi.

"Judicial Service Commission," explained Andile. "They investigate complaints against judicial officers." He turned back to me. "I didn't know Rousseau was sitting on the JSC. You would think it would have come up in the investigation. Are you sure about that?"

"Not sure," I admitted. "But I do know there was a complaint levelled at the judge who had sentenced the girl, and I was led to believe that Justice Rousseau was dealing with that complaint."

"What kind of complaint?"

"It was suggested that young girls were sentenced by the lower-level judge and then groomed when serving their sentence."

"Groomed?" said Andile. "Are you talking about trafficking?"

"That's right," I said.

A nasty silence descended on us for a moment.

"Justice Rousseau was allocated the responsibility for the complaint against another judge?" repeated Andile, as if he was trying to fit the pieces of a puzzle together in his head.

"I believe so."

I didn't elaborate because there were many holes in my quickly fabricated story. It is always best to stick to the truth when facing tough questions, and some of what I had said was true. It was the bits that I hadn't said that were gaping at us now as Andile tried to fit it together.

"I don't understand why it was necessary to visit the judge at his home on a Sunday morning," said Andile, unerringly spotting the biggest hole.

"I had information that I thought might be pertinent to the case."

Andile gazed at me and said nothing. He wanted to hear the pertinent information, but was too weary to explain that.

"The girl has been found," I added.

"The prostitute?" asked Khanyi. "The one that went missing?"

"Yes."

"And what did she have to say?" asked Andile.

"Nothing – she was found dead."

"I see," said Andile, although he didn't. But his sharp mind picked out the next hole. "What did all this have to do with you?"

"The complaint against the judge was brought by someone I know."

"Ah," said Andile.

"The girl's sister."

"And who is she?"

In my rushed preparation for this meeting, I had decided there was no reason not to mention Sandy, but I still had reservations. What would happen if they looked too closely into Sandy's disappearance? What would they discover about her and the things she had been doing? But I had little option, so I drew a breath and said, "A friend of mine. A journalist."

"Your journalist?" said Khanyi, who was familiar with the Sandy situation, and had after all been the one to provide me with Sandy's phone records.

"Yes," I said, "my journalist."

Although I wasn't sure that Sandy had ever been mine, or that our relationship had involved possession of one another.

"You found her then," said Khanyi, connecting the dots.

"Found her?" said Andile. "Had you lost her?"

"She disappeared," explained Khanyi.

"Like her sister?"

Fehrson made a noise like a disgruntled donkey, which turned out to be a clearing of his throat so that he could say, "Awful lot of people disappearing. Is it a family condition? Something they all suffer from?"

"It seems to be," I said, and gave my biggest smile yet to show how amusing I thought that was.

"But you found her?" insisted Khanyi. "Those phone records were useful?"

I turned to look at her. "Yes," I said.

"Phone records?" said Andile. "For the journalist who also disappeared?"

"She was trying to find her sister," I explained. "She

believed her sister had been trafficked, and my journalist didn't disappear so much as go undercover, as it were, in an attempt to find her."

"Ah – and so she is the person who discovered that her sister was dead?"

"Yes."

"I see," said Andile again, although he still didn't. His exhausted eyes gazed at me as if he had too many questions and wasn't sure which one to ask next.

"Your journalist would confirm your story, would she?" he asked, skipping past all the troublesome questions.

"I am sure she would."

"Could you arrange for us to meet with her?"

"Yes, of course," I said. There was a moment of awkwardness, like when the percussionist bangs the cymbals together at the wrong part of the song, but I think I was the only one who noticed that.

"Well then," said Andile, and he bared his teeth again, this time in a distinctly friendly way. "We'll take a break for a cigarette, shall we?"

"It would be foolish not to," I said. I had noticed him eyeing the pack of Gauloises in my jacket pocket.

"Then we'll go over it again so that I get it right for the report."

"Good idea," I said.

"It all seems above board," announced Fehrson cheerfully as we got to our feet. He always liked to have the last word at these meetings.

"We'll go through it again," insisted Andile, who would not say which side of the board we were on. "There's a lot of pressure on this – we've got politicians breathing down our necks."

"Why politicians?" asked Khanyi. "It's not a political crime, surely?"

Andile shrugged. "He was an important judge, so it's a big case. And I suppose Ndoro is looking for a cause to boost his popularity."

"Ndoro?"

"Jessop Ndoro – Minister of Education. You know what these politicians are like, scrambling around for something to put them in a good light."

"Well, I am sure we can sort it all out for them," said Fehrson confidently. "The disappearing journalist will be the key." He gave the relieved smile of a man who had avoided being asked to come to the defence of an ex-employee of dubious moral standing.

I smiled back at him to show I agreed and did my best to look confident about the disappearing journalist being the key to it all.

―――――

"Just a quick word, if you do not mind, young man," said Fehrson, as Andile took his leave with his notes tucked into a folder under his arm and his breath reeking of burnt tobacco.

"Of course, sir," I said. I would have smiled, but my cheek muscles were tired, and Fehrson certainly wasn't smiling. Neither was Khanyi.

We sat in silence for a full two minutes until the sounds of Andile's footsteps were only a distant memory. There had been a time when Khanyi would have escorted Andile off the property and returned flushed and out of breath from the heavy burden of their mutual attraction. But there had clearly been a shift in the balance of power – Andile probably had his own access card now.

"He is a good man, that police captain of Khanyisile's," said Fehrson, as if he had been reading my mind. "Coffee?"

"I would rather not, thank you," I said. The Department's chief of catering mixed a ruinous blend of brown powder with tepid water and sour milk, which I did my best to avoid.

"If you are sure," said Fehrson, but he didn't push it.

"I am," I said, and waited expectantly for the 'quick word' he had mentioned.

"Nasty business," he said, "this thing with the judge."

"Very nasty," I agreed.

"And worrying," added Khanyi.

"Very."

There was another pause. I thought I could hear the ticking of Fehrson's antique clocks that filled his office two floors below us.

"There was something you wanted to discuss?" I asked.

"We like to do things the right way," said Fehrson.

"Of course," I said, although I had seen no evidence of that when I had worked for him.

"The paperwork all in order," explained Khanyi, who would know, because she liked the paperwork. "Permission received for everything we do."

"Official sanction," said Fehrson.

"Yes," I said. "Official, of course."

"There have been times, I will not deny," confessed Fehrson, "when we have employed methods and people who operate a little beyond the law." He splayed a handful of gnarled fingers before him, as if admiring his manicure. "When exigencies demanded of course, and only within the parameters laid down by our leaders."

"I'm not interested," I said.

Fehrson looked up from his fingernails, and his blue eyes were sharp with surprise.

"Not interested in what?"

"You're about to offer me a job. But I'm not interested. I'm not looking for a job."

"Because of your recent windfall," said Fehrson, and he gave a tight smile.

"Windfall?"

"That man Breytenbach has suggested the value of the gold stolen from him is in the tens of millions."

"Goodness," I said.

"United States dollars."

I almost said "Goodness," again, but chose instead to look impressed.

"Even split four ways," said Fehrson, "that is not an amount to be sneezed at."

And there it was, finally: Fehrson's threat. Chandler had been right about their interest in the people around me. I said nothing, so we sat in a murky silence for another minute.

"It's not a job," said Khanyi eventually. "More a relationship, than a specific job."

"I'm honoured you would think of me," I said, "but honestly I have enough difficult relationships as it is."

Fehrson splayed his hand again and spoke to his fingers.

"Recent government changes have tightened the leash they hold us on. There comes a time when the dog is held so tight, he begins to question the integrity of the person holding the leash."

"You're speaking of treason," I said. "Are you suggesting I undertake operations that are not sanctioned by your masters? Or perhaps mutiny would be a better word – is that what you're planning?"

"We wanted to bounce some ideas off you," said Khanyi. "That was all."

Fehrson kept his eyes on his fingers, but Khanyi kept hers on me.

"There would be rewards," she said.

"A relationship with perks?"

"We could overlook a few of those millions, perhaps."

"That sounds generous," I said, and gave an amused smile. "If only I knew where those millions were."

Fehrson looked up at me now and they both waited as if expecting me to broaden my smile, and provide them with an enthusiastic yes.

"As touching as your desire to have a relationship with me is," I said, "I must decline the opportunity you are offering."

Khanyi looked down in disappointment, and this time it was Fehrson's eyes that stayed on me like icy needles of disdain.

"Let's hope your disappearing journalist can clear up this business with the judge," he said.

"Let's hope so," I agreed.

"And soon," said Fehrson.

"The sooner the better," I said, and did my best to keep the smile going.

I didn't need him to draw me a diagram. They had started the fire and were closing the exits. I was running out of options.

FOURTEEN

"Where on earth have you been?" asked Chandler, when I joined them on the terrace of the Twelve Apostles.

"There were two dead bodies in our warehouse," I said. "The ones you asked me to have removed?"

"There's no need to be sarcastic about it," said Chandler. "You've been gone all morning, and we have a right to know where you've been – we're all in this together. So you can get off your high horse and tell us what you've been up to."

"The police officer I called about the bodies wanted to see me," I said, taking my seat at the table Chandler had claimed for us on the edge of the hotel terrace. The crumbling stone wall alongside didn't look like it would do much to prevent us from plunging down the cliff and into the ocean if anyone gave us a push.

"About the bodies?"

"No, about another matter. I did say there would be repercussions."

"Another matter?" said Chandler, and his eyes

narrowed. I smiled at his narrowed eyes, and we sat in silence for a moment.

"To do with your journalist," said Robyn, as if she knew all about my meeting at the Department, although I hadn't mentioned it to her. Her dark eyes were steady and her face was made of stone.

"That's right," I said. "My disappearing journalist. They have been helping me find her, and the policeman wanted to discuss it, in return for the favour of recovering those bodies without dragging us into it."

Chandler nodded slowly like a toy Buddha, and it looked as if he was wondering whether he should pursue the matter, but Fat-Boy blurted: "You've missed all the shit."

"The shit?" I said.

"With the Dark Bizness guy."

"Vusi Madikwe," said Chandler. "The man they shot in our warehouse, was not merely an executive at Dark Bizness. He was the brother of Lebogang Madikwe, the man who started the company."

"It's in all the papers," said Robyn, and she pushed a folded newspaper over the table to me. The headline announced the tragic death of one of the Dark Bizness brothers, with a cheerful photograph of two equally obese men with huge grins and big cheeks in circular faces.

"Didn't I tell you Breytenbach was going to make trouble for himself searching the docks like that?" said Chandler.

"They don't know his death had anything to do with Breytenbach," I said. "Or the gold. There's no mention of the man from Breytenbach's army."

"Not yet, but we need to change that."

"We do? Isn't it better to keep Breytenbach out of it?"

"What do you think that man Vusi was doing there?"

"Looking for our gold," said Fat-Boy, who never saw the point of allowing Chandler to run repeat performances of scenes he'd already watched.

"Indeed," said Chandler, then paused as a waiter delivered my coffee to the table. "Bring us all another round," said Chandler, "but this time put some goddamn coffee beans in the machine. We've had enough of the dishwater."

The waiter said he would do his best, and Chandler sighed heavily.

"At least he didn't ask whether you wanted cream or foam," said Robyn.

"It's a travesty," said Chandler.

"He asked whether the colonel wanted cream or foam in his cappuccino," Robyn explained.

"Five stars," exclaimed Chandler incredulously. Then he realised Robyn was just riling him, and he drew a deep breath and let his anger out in another heavy sigh, then turned to look out over the calm ocean.

The luxurious Twelve Apostles Hotel was perched above the Atlantic Ocean on the road that squeezed between the sea and the range of twelve mountain peaks that formed the spine of the Cape Peninsula, providing breathtaking views of both the mountains and the sea. Chandler had arranged fake identities, so we were now posing as foreigners on a business trip. He argued that a five-star hotel would be the last place that law enforcement officials, or angry mining magnates, would look for people on the run, but I was not entirely convinced. I suspected his refined taste and penchant for fine dining were more persuasive reasons.

"We need to move it," he said, after a long regretful pause while he gazed out to sea.

"The gold," clarified Fat-Boy.

"Which is now going to be impossible," I said. "Breyten-bach's men are going to step up their search, and the police are crawling all over our warehouse. You don't think someone is going to notice us sneaking past them with three tons of gold bricks under our arms?"

"The Dark Bizness affair has provided us with an opportunity," said Chandler. "From what Robyn has told us about what happened in the warehouse, it is clear the Dark Bizness man had an arrangement with BB's goons."

"He seemed to be pretending he was one of us," I agreed. "He bore some similarity to the picture of Fat-Boy that BB has been putting out, so he was probably getting BB's men to do the dirty work of dealing with us. Goodness knows what he was planning to do when they had dealt with us."

"Dark Bizness have a warehouse in the docks," said Robyn. "They were probably going to make a deal with Breytenbach and move some of the gold there. But the death of the brother will have ruined that plan."

"So now we have Breytenbach and the biggest cosmetics company on the continent to contend with. How is that an opportunity?"

"The Dark Bizness brothers were like two peas in a pod," said Chandler. "How do you think the surviving brother will feel when he learns that one of BB's goons killed his brother?"

"He'll want revenge," said Fat-Boy.

"Damn right he will. It will escalate, and before long the local authorities will have gang warfare on their hands."

"Warfare?" I said. "Dark Bizness is a listed company – they're not a gang."

"But they do have their own army," said Chandler.

"Officially it is called their private security, but it's an army."

"They're not a normal company," said Fat-Boy.

"They are not," agreed Chandler. "And neither are they your usual peace-loving Xhosa family. Look at that picture of him with his cousin."

Beneath the article, another photograph showed the surviving brother embracing a man in green military fatigues. A caption branded this man as a cousin of the two brothers.

"They're not what you might call the peaceful type," said Chandler. "That cousin of theirs has never fought in an army, but when the brothers waved a portion of their profits in front of his nose, he decided to create an army of his own."

"An army to do what?" I asked.

"To keep all those little bottles of ointment safe," suggested Chandler, and his grey eyes shone with amusement.

"They've made enemies over the years," said Robyn. "Their early success came from skin whitening products, helping their black brethren be less black. It was very popular until that kind of thing lost its appeal."

"And it started making people angry," said Chandler. "They probably needed that army to help them overcome their history. Nothing like a bit of military action to help people forget sins of the past."

"But even if Breytenbach and the Dark Bizness crowd start fighting," I said, "how would that help us?"

"It's the perfect cover for moving our little bars. They'll be so busy fighting each other they won't notice."

"It sounds risky to me. The docks will be crawling with armed freaks wanting to shoot one another."

"It will be like old times," said Chandler, and he gave me a grim smile. I didn't think it would be anything like old times, but I said nothing about that.

"How do you suggest we tell the big brother who was to blame for the little brother's death?" I asked.

"We make friends with him," said Chandler.

"Are you suggesting he and Fat-Boy exchange Xhosa folktales, discuss ancestral memories, swap wives, that kind of thing?"

"Swap wives?" protested Fat-Boy. "Now you're being racist."

"No," said Chandler, before I could respond to Fat-Boy's allegation. "I want you and Robyn to go see him. You're a charming couple. Go and shed a few tears with him about the trauma of seeing his baby brother killed. Give him a bit of the real stuff, tell him how you held his brother's hand, his last words, all that shit."

"How would we explain our presence there?"

"Tell a little of the truth for a change," said Chandler. "Breytenbach has your name, we know that. He knows who you are. We're not giving anything away by sending you in to see this man. But we have everything to gain if he goes to war with BB."

"Then after the war starts – if it does – you want to bring the crane down?"

"We bring it down, cut our little yellow bars out of that concrete, and float them out to sea."

There was a long silence as we all considered this hare-brained scheme.

"I don't do sea," announced Fat-Boy eventually, breaking the silence.

"We could get you swimming lessons," I suggested.

Fat-Boy's lazy eye jumped open in order to see whether

I was making a racial slur. He had once told me that racial prejudice in the country had prevented him from learning to swim.

"You are racist," he said.

"I'm trying to right the wrongs that were committed against you because of your race," I said. "That doesn't mean that I'm prejudiced against you. A racist is prejudiced because of race, not because of your inability to swim."

Fat-Boy produced a sound like a jazz trumpeter warming up his lips.

"That's enough, you two," said Chandler with the weary tone he adopted whenever he struggled with the incompetence of his crew. "We have a plan, and we need to get moving. Coast guard activity has delayed our fence, but he will be in place to receive our little bars in less than a week. So let's get moving. We've got a war to start."

Chandler fixed me with his icy glare again. "And no more personal issues with the women we've lost, is that clear?"

"There is one person I need to see, Colonel," I said. "One quick meeting, and then I'm all yours."

Chandler considered me through narrowed eyes again, as if he was trying to communicate telepathically. When that failed he said, "Make it a quick meeting, then we're all hands on deck. Swimmers and non-swimmers alike."

———

Jessop Ndoro had won awards for his humanitarian work. As a politician he had expressed the humanitarian side of his nature by motivating for a change of the laws that were preventing the children of impoverished families from gaining access to the education that benefited the children of wealthy families. He had argued vociferously, had sprayed his opponents in the National Assembly with spittle because his saliva glands became overactive when he was excited, and he had become the champion of the poor. Which was a little ironic given the excessive wealth he accrued over many years of accepting bribes to award contracts to companies to deliver that education to the poor. But this irony was seldom mentioned because who wants to criticise the champion of a good cause?

He wasn't looking much like a champion as he sat in the members-only bar of the Miners Club, sweating a little with anxiety. Not from the heat, because the subtle lighting was not warming the place at all, serving only to make the opulent room feel ominous. He was wearing his dark suit and striped tie, which were both looking a little worse for wear. He had come to the bar directly from the Parliament buildings because he had agreed that meeting at his soonest convenience would be to his advantage, given that it was his own safety that we needed to discuss. From the way his tie hung askew and his collar was twisted, I surmised that the martini before him on the bar was not his first.

"What do you mean?" he said to me after we'd exchanged a handshake and I'd been served a single malt on the rocks by the barman, who then retreated discreetly to the far end of the bar. "What do you mean ... at risk?"

"I mean that I believe your life is at risk," I said. It seemed clear enough to me what that meant.

"At risk?" repeated Jessop Ndoro as if the two words might have some other meaning that would become clear if he repeated them often enough.

"In the same way – and for the same reason – as the life of Justice Francois Rousseau was at risk," I said.

"I didn't know Rousseau," he declared, and reached a shaky hand out for his martini.

"He died a few days ago. In his swimming pool. But he didn't drown – he bled to death, from a knife wound to his throat."

The hand carrying the martini wobbled and a small amount of gin, vermouth and olive juice splashed onto Jessop Ndoro's shirt.

"You're white," he protested, as if he had just noticed the colour of my skin.

"I am," I admitted.

"You said you were a journalist, Sandy something or other. But I looked the name up, and she was coloured, and a woman."

"I said it was about her, not that I was her. Do you remember her?"

"Never met her."

Jessop Ndoro gulped a little more martini than he should have. He swallowed the alcohol with an effort, and his tongue came out to clear up the traces of salt around his lips.

"I'm trying to find out what happened to her."

"What does that have to do with me?"

"I asked Justice Rousseau about her, and he also denied knowing anything."

The alcohol had reached Jessop Ndoro's stomach, and he emitted a small belch like a slimy toad sitting on a big rock.

"Why are you threatening me?" he asked.

"I'm not threatening you. I'm warning you. We both know what happened to Justice Rousseau."

"I could call the police and have you arrested." His saliva gland started over-compensating, and his voice climbed the scale. "I'm a Cabinet Minister and you are making threats on my life. I should call the police."

"You could and you should," I said. "But then you would have to explain about the club."

"What club?"

He put his martini glass down in case he would need both hands to fend me off.

"The club of which you are a founding member," I said, and sipped at my whisky while Jessop Ndoro's bloodshot eyes challenged me from the heavy bags of flesh they rested upon. "There are three founding members. The first was Justice Rousseau. The second is you."

"I don't know what you're talking about," he said, and sprayed some saliva over his distended belly in his indignation.

"Your name isn't on the club papers," I said. "But the same initials are. Do you know a James Nokwe? That seems like a foolish conceit – to use the same initials. Justice Francois Rousseau did the same thing by using the name Frank Rose."

"Would you stop talking about Rousseau? I didn't know the man."

"Didn't you? You must have met each other without the masks at some point."

"I've done nothing wrong," said Jessop Ndoro, and he reached for his martini without removing his eyes from mine, and succeeded in knocking the glass forward – it fell and shattered across the bar. The barman looked up at the sound and produced a damp cloth from nowhere as he travelled behind the bar towards us.

"Haven't you?"

The barman cleaned up the mess and provided Jessop Ndoro with a fresh martini while the humanitarian's wary eyes studied my face for clues to the depth of my knowledge.

"Nothing," he said eventually, by which time the barman was out of earshot.

"Human trafficking is considered wrong," I said.

"Trafficking?" spluttered Jessop. "What do you mean, trafficking?"

"It is the word that is used to describe the enslavement of others."

"I know what it means. I've never been involved in anything like that."

"Where do you think those girls came from?"

"Girls?"

"Young women, like the one who died at that party."

"What party?"

"The party you wore the mask to."

Jessop Ndoro's eyes sagged lower into the bags of flesh.

"I don't know what you mean," he said.

"Was it just the one party? Or were there others? That's something I haven't been able to work out."

He gazed at me as if he hadn't heard my questions.

"I want to know what you did to her," I said. "To the journalist, not the poor girl who bled to death at the party. I know what you did to her."

Jessop Ndoro stood suddenly, an anticlimactic action that involved little more than rolling his stomach forward to find support on his spindly legs, which were shorter than the legs of the barstool so that his swollen face actually dropped a little lower.

"I'm not scared by your threats," he said in a voice weak with anxiety. "I'm not scared," he repeated, a little more forcefully and with more spittle.

"You should be," I said. "Justice Rousseau is dead, and I think that you know why."

Jessop Ndoro said nothing. He turned away from me and stumbled a little as he rushed for the exit to face his fear from behind the fog of five martinis.

I finished my whisky and told the barman to put it on Jessop Ndoro's tab. If my suspicions about the circumstances of Justice Rousseau's death were correct, I wasn't sure he'd be alive long enough to settle it, but no doubt the executor of his estate would honour all outstanding debts. Debts of a financial nature, that is; I didn't expect that the other debts would ever be settled.

FIFTEEN

The head offices of the Dark Bizness cosmetics company occupied the twenty-fourth floor of Portside Tower, Cape Town's most sparkling skyscraper. Its outer walls were floor to ceiling glass, which gave one the impression of floating in an alien spacecraft above the city. The alien invasion was being planned by the amorphous mass of flesh that was Lebogang Madikwe, from his super-strength office chair that had enough levers and hydraulic arms to serve as a dentist's chair should the need arise.

Lebogang was staring out over the city, presenting us with the back of his chair and large bits of his stomach which bulged out to either side, testing the elasticity of his woven-silk Armani suit.

We sat in silence for several minutes. Robyn and I were both wearing black in honour of the situation, and Robyn looked as if she had been crying, but I think that was just an effect of having been sober for two days. The interior walls of the office were lined with individually spotlit panels with high-definition photographs of black women, their oiled skin resembling the dunes of a dark-grained desert, or a stream of molten chocolate. I noticed that there were no images from the early range of creams that Dark Bizness had offered when they promised that lightening the colour of your skin would change the course of your life. The latest range of Dark Bizness products suggested the reverse – a better life would result from a darkening of the skin.

A subtle purring sound came from Lebogang Madikwe's chair as it revolved to reveal the magnificence that was Lebogang. He was a tall man, taller than his late brother, but the same vast circumference. I was struck by the physical similarity he bore to Fat-Boy. The same large middle section, wide Xhosa nostrils in a round, bald head. But Lebogang's eyes were closer together and not nearly as generous, and the wrinkles on his face – drooping now with grief – were deeper with age and the struggles of a hard life. There wasn't a muscle with enough energy to hold the corners of his mouth up, and so it curved down like a child's drawing of sadness. He gazed at us blankly; we waited respectfully.

"You knew my brother," he said eventually, in a deep bass voice.

"We did, Mister Madikwe," said Robyn in a voice hoarse with emotion. Lebogang's eyes lingered on her.

"He would have mentioned someone like you."

"We asked him not to," I said. "In our discussions with him we asked him not to mention us to anyone."

Lebogang's eyes swung reluctantly onto me.

"Why?"

"Because of the nature of our business."

"Business?"

"The nature of it. Moving items of great value can attract unwanted attention, so we asked for his discretion."

Lebogang did not look impressed. I played out a little more line.

"Vusi," I said, hoping his younger brother hadn't gone by some nickname; Lebogang's eyes narrowed in his enormous face, and his mouth tightened. "Vusi was helping us with a problem we have in the Cape Town docks. With moving items of value."

Lebogang's eyes widened again as the penny finally dropped.

"You're with that gang!" he exclaimed in a loud voice, as if someone had twiddled the knob too much. "You're the gold gang!"

I gave a polite smile and used a bit of silence to emphasise the need for discretion.

"You killed him," he shouted. "You're the ones who killed my brother!"

I kept the smile up and shook my head.

"No," I said with as much regret as I could muster.

"We would not have come to you, Mister Madikwe," said Robyn soothingly, "if we had killed your brother."

Lebogang's eyes turned back to her, and his anger subsided a little.

"Who did?" he demanded, his voice cracking. He lowered the volume and asked again, "Who killed my brother?"

"Unfortunately your brother made a regrettable error of judgement," I said. "We asked your brother not to mention to anyone that we had an understanding. And I knew that – as a man of honour – he would keep his word. And so, we might just be the only ones who know what actually happened."

I raised a hand to block Lebogang's protests, although he made no sign of making any.

"Regrettably, your brother made friends with the wrong people."

"What wrong people?" asked Lebogang.

"The people who killed him. You see, we were not the only people your brother was communicating with about the items of value."

Realisation spread across Lebogang's broad face.

"That man Breytenbach," he said.

I gave a solemn nod, and Robyn said gravely, "Never trust a Breytenbach," as if that was a common aphorism.

"He had an arrangement with Breytenbach," I said. "An arrangement that I don't believe Breytenbach ever intended to honour."

"Breytenbach killed my brother?" asked Lebogang.

"One of his men," Robyn had a slight catch in her throat, as if a memory of the dying brother had returned to her at the mere mention of it.

Lebogang raised a dinner-plate sized hand and smashed the other fist into it. His glum face set with determination. We sat in silence as feelings of resentment built up in the mountain of a man across the table from us.

"We have a suggestion to make," I said, when I judged the time was right. Lebogang's thin eyebrows climbed up his forehead.

"The thing is, we need to retrieve our items of value, but Breytenbach's men are making that extremely hard. We would be more than happy to share some of the bounty with you, if you could see your way to dealing with Breytenbach's men. By which I mean keeping them busy while we retrieve our valuables."

"Bounty?" asked Lebogang. "How much is the bounty?"

"In our conversations with your brother – which he would not have repeated to you, being a man of such honour – he told us that Mister Breytenbach had lied to you about the value of the material we have in our possession."

"It's twenty bars," said Lebogang knowingly. "Vusi told me. More than the five bars the papers talk about."

My smile broadened, and I shook my head at Breytenbach's extraordinary audacity.

"It is a little more than that."

"Thirty?"

I shook my head again.

"Thirty-five?"

I gave a subtle nod. Lebogang's lips pursed as if to whistle, but instead he sucked in some air like he was trying to inflate.

"Three quarters of a million per bar?"

"Roughly," I said.

"If I get Breytenbach's men off your back, how many bars is that worth?"

"Well, we would like to honour the arrangement we had with your brother – twenty percent – which if you do the math is better than the offer Breytenbach was making."

Lebogang looked as if he was doing the math. His eyes glazed over for a moment, but then he said, "Thirty percent," as if it was an automatic response.

I raised an eyebrow and allowed my smile to freeze.

"I very much doubt we could do that, Mister Madikwe. We might be able to stretch it to twenty-two percent."

"Twenty-eight," said Lebogang.

I considered this for a moment.

"I will have to go back to my people with a suggestion of twenty-five percent," I said. "They might ask you to go a little extra distance for us."

"Extra distance?" he said.

"Well … our situation has worsened. As you can well imagine …"

But Lebogang was still doing the math in his head on the twenty-five percent, and so his imagination was a little clouded. I provided more detail.

"It is not a matter of simply driving the items of value out of the area. The police have the place surrounded. We cannot get near it."

"The place?"

"Our warehouse, the place where your brother …" I let the sentence tail off.

"That's where it is," said Lebogang, and the greed in him struggled with his anger so that he had to clear his throat and say it again. "That's where the gold is? In that warehouse where my brother died?"

I gave a regretful smile again, and a tiny nod of affirmation.

"He thought you were just hiding out there. Vusi was convinced you had the gold hidden somewhere else. Why didn't he tell me this?"

"He was a man of honour. We asked him not to say anything to anyone until we had dealt with the Breytenbach problem, but then of course …"

Lebogang stared at me, and I realised I had overplayed the honour line. I pushed on.

"You see our problem. When the police finish their investigation into your brother's death, the men that killed him are going to take the gold for themselves."

"Breytenbach's men," said Lebogang, as if our meaning was beginning to penetrate.

"They plan to walk in there," said Robyn bitterly. "And take the gold for themselves, trampling over your poor brother's departed spirit."

A new light had appeared behind Lebogang's eyes as Robyn's impassioned plea mingled with the results of his mathematical calculations. His voice was a little hoarse as he said, "Lebo, call me Lebo."

"Thank you, Lebo, I will."

"What do you need me to do?" he asked, a question that ended in a rasping cough because of the grief and the greed conspiring to clog his throat.

"Breytenbach's men are nothing short of a small army," I said. "We don't stand a chance against them. We need to get into the warehouse, and keep his men clear of the area."

Lebogang moved his body for the first time since the start of our discussion. Some muscles deep beneath the belly pushed his chest upwards, and he leaned forward over his desk, placed his elbows on the glass surface, and clasped his enormous fists together.

"I have an army," he said. "If they want to play war games, we'll play with them. We'll show them what war really is."

Robyn and I both smiled in unison.

"We expected nothing less of you, Lebo," I said.

"An eye for an eye," said Lebo, from whom the fire of vengeance fuelled by greed was bringing forth the orator. "My Vusi was worth ten of those men."

"Amen to that," said Robyn.

———

The first strike in the gang war that would later be christened the "Docklands War" was struck by the Dark Bizness team, although we were the only ones to know that because they didn't announce themselves before opening fire on a jeep that was patrolling through the docks with three of

Breytenbach's private security on board. They were wearing well-worn camouflage outfits and the weapons they fired were AK-47s. These two details inspired the suggestion that they were a team of mercenaries brought in from one of the trouble spots to the north of our country, sparking furious allegations that foreigners were destroying our fragile balance. One of Breytenbach's men died, one was wounded, and the third claimed to have inflicted some damage on their assailants, although this was not confirmed.

The situation escalated fast. The Breytenbach side responded by sending in reinforcements, and three more gun battles took place in the next twenty-four hours. Thirty-six hours after the first shot was fired, the army moved in, and the entire area of the Cape Town docks was declared an emergency zone.

"We'll give them eighteen hours to get it under control," said Chandler, as he placed his teacup into its saucer and glared at it as if he suspected it of being poisoned. He had given up on ordering coffee from the Twelve Apostles kitchen.

"You found a boat?" asked Robyn.

"We did," said Chandler. "Perfect for the job."

"It's barely seaworthy," I said, but Chandler laughed that off.

"Nonsense, the boat is perfect."

Chandler would not be floating out to sea in the rough collection of wooden planks we'd hired for an exorbitant rate that morning from a scoundrel who operated a salvage business in the docks.

"It hasn't left harbour for fifteen years," I pointed out.

"That's because they took his licence away," said Chandler.

"Which is another reason I am concerned about going to sea with him," I insisted.

"And I don't do sea," Fat-Boy reminded us.

"You'll be fine," said Chandler. "The Angel goes because he can steer the boat, if it comes to that. You go because we need the muscle you're hiding under all that flab. Do you expect Robyn to haul those concrete blocks around? Besides, the captain is Xhosa – you can speak the lingo with him. Honestly, you two. Nobody said this was going to be easy."

Fat-Boy pouted, and I looked out to sea. From our quiet corner of the terrace, the sea resembled a flat sheet of grey steel.

"They're forecasting a storm for tomorrow," I said.

"All the better," said Chandler, and he gave us an encouraging smile.

———

The storm was forecast to hit the shore the next evening, but there were some warm-up acts in the form of rain showers that started early in the morning and continued relentlessly through the day. Despite being an emergency zone, the docks needed to maintain some level of operation, and the soldiers posted at the west entrance were allowing workers in and out because most of the trouble was in the eastern section. They warned us not to drive too far east, and Chandler assured them we wouldn't do anything so foolish, but then drove us to the second last quay on the eastern edge – the one with seven cranes. Across the stretch of water that separated the quay from its neighbour we could see the figures of soldiers standing miserably in the rain around our warehouse, which had been identified as the central focus of the Docklands War.

"No good," proclaimed Chandler, and he sucked his teeth in a disparaging way, squinting up at the cage that held the counter-weights. The massive concrete blocks dripped the morning's rain over us.

"No good?" repeated the supervisor from beneath his broken umbrella and he peered up reluctantly through the gap where the material had pulled away from the metal rib. "You can tell that from here?" he asked doubtfully.

The supervisor, who had three missing teeth, an exhausted face, two gold earrings and a bald head upon which his hard hat perched like the top half of a peanut, had suggested that we come back for the inspection on a day that it wasn't raining. But Chandler had laughed, insisted that we weren't made of sugar, and had pushed me ahead of him into the rain with nothing but our hard hats to keep us dry.

"Tell you what," said Chandler, still peering up at the collection of dripping concrete blocks. "We can get started on this one today and look at the others later. That suit you?"

The supervisor didn't look as if that suited him at all, but the thought of inspecting the other six cranes in the midst of a rainstorm suited him less.

"They didn't know what they were doing," said Chandler cheerfully as we picked our way around the puddles back to the supervisor's brick hut. "That much is obvious. What were they? A team of amateurs?"

The supervisor didn't answer that, but Chandler wasn't really looking for an answer from him. His eyes were on me and they were laughing. The amateurs that had cast the concrete counter-weights on that crane had been Fat-Boy and me. Mostly me, because I had returned to set the one hundred and twenty gold bars into the concrete after Fat-Boy had been shot while offloading them from the crate we had concealed them in. To describe it as an amateur job was an understatement.

"We got a ship coming in early tomorrow," complained the supervisor, "and with all this trouble, the army and all ..."

"Which is why we'll get them replaced tonight," said Chandler. "Rain doesn't bother us, does it?"

I assumed that question was also aimed at me, but I didn't answer it. The rain did bother me – I was not looking forward to spending the night trying to substitute three tonnes of concrete blocks while avoiding the army patrols. Chandler's analysis of the situation held that both Breyten-bach's black-suited goons with their R5s and Dark Bizness's troops of militia with their AK-47s would stay hidden tonight. He was probably right – three men had been killed and several wounded, and if anyone understood the rhythm of war it was Chandler – but I was struggling to share his confidence in our ability to sneak the gold out while the two private armies focused their attention on one another. It seemed to me that it would be the fool in the middle, the one trying to hide the gold bars from the others, who had the lowest chance of survival.

———

The rain stopped at eighteen-hundred that evening, but the quay was little more than a series of stepping stones in the midst of the ocean because of the amount of rain that had collected. The cage of counter-weights was lowered by a bad-tempered crane operator, and Fat-Boy chewed his tongue as he operated a front-end loader to carefully remove the concrete blocks one at a time, lift them off their steel frame and lay them in neat stacks of three atop each other on a set of wooden pallets on the edge of the quay.

"Don't drop any in the water," I teased. "We'll never be able to get it back up, and it'll come out of your share."

Fat-Boy glared at me through his good eye, told me to stop being racist and assured me he knew what he was doing, although I noticed he reduced the speed he was driving at, so I suggested he speed up a bit or we would be there all night.

"You just be sure we got the right crane and the right fucking blocks," he said, and came to stand beside me as I used a knife to scrape away a section of concrete. I had set eight bars into each block, arranged in a simple grid and covered with about a centimetre of the pale concrete mix. It took a few minutes to cut away a strip of concrete, then the blade struck something harder, and Fat-Boy shone a torch into the small hole and we saw the glint of gold shining back. Fat-Boy's face split into a hundred white teeth and he gave an ecstatic sigh.

"There you are," he cried. "My little soldiers, safe and sound. We're coming for you babies, not long now, hang on in there."

A little after twenty-hundred an open-topped army vehicle came bumping over the stepping stones of the quay and a soldier asked Fat-Boy what we were doing. Another soldier pointed his Heckler and Koch MP5 in our approximate direction, in case we happened to be planning an assault on one of the warring factions with our blocks of concrete. I kept my head down and used the hard hat to shield my face. Not that I expected they had any idea what members of the 'Gold Heist Gang' looked like. They weren't much interested in me anyway – Fat-Boy distracted them enough by complaining that he was being abused by his racist foreman and suggested they give him a hand – but they laughed, turned their vehicle around and left us to it, despite not having received a clear answer to their question.

It started to rain again shortly after that, and I began to worry that the docks were so quiet. Despite Chandler's sense of the rhythm of war, it was odd that there was absolutely nothing happening. Where were Breytenbach's men? And Lebogang's militia? We had seen no sign of them. Fat-Boy suggested that the rain was keeping them away, and I wanted to agree with him, but I felt uneasy nonetheless.

At twenty-one-hundred our boat arrived. A wooden barge with cracked paint and black smoke billowing from the pipe above the ramshackle bridge. It hadn't looked seaworthy to me when Chandler and I had met with the captain the day before, so I was surprised it had made it all the way to our quay. The captain had assured us the boat could reach fifteen nautical miles from shore with no problem, even though it hadn't left the harbour confines for over fifteen years because of bureaucratic difficulties he was having with the authorities. And he had showed us a mouth that was missing most of its teeth, in a smile that was in no way reassuring. His weatherbeaten cheeks were all wrinkles, his eyes were bloodshot and the iris of his left eye had lost all its colour: he told us he was blind in that eye, but assured us that didn't affect his ability to steer his boat, even outside the harbour, and reminded us that Xhosa people had the sea in their blood. Chandler said that he thought the Xhosa were land-based people who tended to cattle as opposed to being a seafaring race with the sea in their blood. The captain, whose name, just to confuse us further about his racial heritage, was Jannie, had laughed and looked at

Chandler through his good eye with wheezing anticipation of his next joke.

Jannie poked his wizened head out of the broken perspex window of the bridge and waved to us as the wooden barge approached the edge of the quay at an alarming speed.

"Shouldn't he slow down?" asked Fat-Boy, but the barge twisted sideways and coasted gently against the quay so that the old tyres hanging from its side bumped against the edge in a chorus of muted squeaks.

"The weather not a problem?" I asked, after Jannie had fastened the lines to hold the boat in place, had greeted Fat-Boy with what sounded like an abusive string of Xhosa insults, and had exchanged a sequence of handshakes with me that left me wondering whether I had been initiated into a secret organisation.

"Weather?" said Jannie as if he wasn't familiar with the word, and he gave a cackling laugh that carried a strong smell of garlic and alcohol.

The barge had a crane mounted on the stern, which was the primary reason Chandler had chosen it; the secondary reason was the bureaucratic troubles that Jannie had endured, which had tainted his respect for officialdom. Jannie undid the ties holding the arm in place and operated the levers so that the arm unfolded and dangled a hook over the pallet of concrete weights we had arranged for him to bring as substitutes for the ones on the quay. He looped a worn set of straps around the pallet, connected them to the hook, and then pulled a lever to lift it. The boat shifted and bobbed in the water in a worrying way as the pallet lifted. But Jannie didn't seem to notice, so I kept quiet about it, and helped to guide the pallet into position on the quayside.

Jannie called out something in Xhosa to Fat-Boy as he

struggled to loop the straps beneath one of our pallets for the return trip of the loading arm. Fat-Boy hurled an answer back at him, and Jannie laughed.

"I say he's too fat," explained Jannie, "but he's a real Xhosa that one – tells me size means wealth. He must be one wealthy Xhosa." Jannie's good eye narrowed and I suspected he was looking for the opportunity to ask about these heavy blocks of pale concrete we were paying him so handsomely to take to sea, despite his bureaucratic difficulties. But he said nothing, gave me a toothless smile instead, and kept himself busy with the loading. No questions had been one of Chandler's conditions.

It took us almost two hours to transfer the concrete weights, and then Fat-Boy climbed down the iron rungs set into the side of the quay, stepped onto the boat and gave me an anxious glance as it wobbled under his weight.

"I don't do boats," explained Fat-Boy as he and Jannie went through their handshake routine. He said it in English for my benefit so that his complaint could be formally lodged. "Don't do sea nor water of any kind," he said. "Don't swim neither."

"You don't need to swim," said Jannie. "That's why we got the boat."

"What kind of Xhosa drives a boat?" said Fat-Boy, which seemed to support my thoughts about the spurious nature of Jannie's claim that the sea was in his blood. Jannie laughed at that, which didn't make me feel any better about his ability to take us out to sea and bring us safely back again. And then he rummaged about in a locker and produced two well-used life jackets.

"This thing won't make me float," protested Fat-Boy when he'd strapped it on. "You seen how big I am?"

But Jannie laughed again and said that Fat-Boy

wouldn't need to be doing any floating. We went up to the bridge to enter the first set of coordinates into the GPS. I had memorised them at Chandler's insistence: there were three separate coordinates so that we didn't sail a straight line to the ship waiting for us, in case someone followed. The bridge smelt of diesel and comprised a wheel, some engine instruments, a radio with a microphone on a cable that had been poorly repaired with electrical insulation tape, a cracked wooden counter on which stood a half-empty bottle of cheap whisky, a large-screen GPS with a damaged screen that flickered off and on, and enough standing room for me and Jannie and about half of Fat-Boy. Jannie said it would take us three hours to reach the first position, and suggested that we make ourselves comfortable below deck where he had bunks for us to rest, and a few bottles if we had any difficulty with that.

He climbed back onto the quay, untied the ropes, looped them around the bollards, and tossed the ends down to us so that we could hold the boat in position while he climbed back down. Then he cast off, gave the engine a brief boost, and spoke into his radio. The harbour master gave us permission to transit the harbour entrance, Jannie brought the engine up to a constant hum and he pointed the nose to sea with the maniacal look of a man about to break the law.

SIXTEEN

Fat-Boy stood in the cabin below deck and held onto a pole that provided the bunks with support. He swayed like an enormous beach ball as the boat rolled over the calm swells of the harbour.

"I don't do boats," he said to me angrily, then clamped his mouth shut as a wave of nausea struck him.

"It will be better up on deck," I said, and helped him up the gangway steps.

The rain strengthened its onslaught as we travelled across the outer basin of the harbour. A large tanker was squeezing through the winking lights of the outer moles, and its wake raced across the water towards us like an underwater monster. Jannie turned our boat to cut across the wake, and we bobbed up and down like a child's toy in a bathtub. Fat-Boy's eyes widened, and he clutched onto me. The two of us lurched in unsteady steps towards the wooden railing at the edge, and we grasped at it as the boat settled again and the thrumming sound of the engines picked up speed.

"Not feeling good," said Fat-Boy.

"Focus on the horizon," I recommended, but it was useless advice. The horizon was a worrying haze of thrashing waves and rain squalls when it was visible at all.

We made our way between the outer lights, and Jannie turned the boat to follow the coast. I discovered that our life jackets had straps with carabiner attachments, and clipped them onto hooks on the wooden railing.

"Feeling worse," said Fat-Boy, and this time I didn't give him any advice because I was feeling queasy myself.

Chandler called when we were fifteen minutes out of harbour. I pressed the phone to my ear but couldn't hear a thing, so I went below deck.

"I said TROUBLE," shouted Chandler, when eventually I could hear him.

"What kind of trouble?"

"A motorboat followed you out."

"Breytenbach's men?"

"The other crowd – looked like AK-47s and camo outfits."

"They'd be lucky to find us out here," I said. "It's rough."

"They'll have radar. Keep an eye out."

I made my way back on deck. Fat-Boy had his eyes closed and looked as if he was trying to do a mind over matter exercise. I said nothing about Chandler's call, but I think he guessed the content of it.

Jannie turned the lights off when we were twenty minutes out of harbour, which was what he had agreed to do. Fat-Boy and I moved to the starboard side of the boat because that way the wind came mostly from behind us, although the weather had deteriorated so much that it seemed to come from all sides. From here we occasionally glimpsed lights on shore, but they offered little in the way of comfort, particularly when the thin line of lights lurched into precarious angles.

Fat-Boy managed not to vomit until we were about an hour out of harbour, at which point he leaned over the edge without ceremony and threw up with a great heave of his shoulders. The wind caught his vomit and threw it back at us, spraying me liberally with it.

"Feel better," said Fat-Boy, and I tried to look enthusiastic about that, but as I had turned my face away from the spray of his vomit something had caught my eye. It was a gap in the string of lights on shore. A hard-edged black hole. There was something between us and those lights. I searched the water carefully, but I could see nothing besides the thrashing waves and veil of rain. Then suddenly I saw it again. The clear silhouette of a boat.

"We've got a problem," I shouted and pulled Fat-Boy down to crouch beside me, with only our heads above the rail. The silhouette disappeared then reappeared as our boats moved up and down in the heavy swell, but the outline was unmistakably that of a sleek motor boat, the sort of pleasure cruiser the wealthy load up with alcohol and girls in bikinis in the hot days of summer. It had a raised bridge area, and above that I could make out the occasional profile of two men. One of them was pointing in our direction, and looked as if he might be calling out orders. We had the benefit of the lights on shore behind them to provide the silhouette – it would be difficult for them to keep us in sight without lights behind us, and no lights on our boat.

We watched the intermittent progress of the boat for a full minute. They were slowly gaining on us, and I guessed we had about ten minutes before they would be alongside. It didn't look as if they were planning on having a conversation; the two dark profiles above the bridge of their boat both had something slung over their shoulders, something that looked very much like the barrel of an automatic weapon.

I told Fat-Boy to keep an eye on them, unclipped myself and lurched unsteadily to the bridge. Jannie turned to me with surprise as I pulled the door open.

"We've got company," I shouted over the sound of the engine, the wind and rain.

Jannie instinctively reached for the throttle, but I shook my head.

"Keep our speed up. Do you have a gun?"

Jannie nodded and reached into a compartment under the engine gauges and pulled out an old Makarov pistol which had probably made its way down the continent from Moscow during the apartheid years.

"Don't shoot it," I warned him. "They're approaching on our starboard side, and they've got bigger guns than us, you understand? Do nothing unless to defend yourself. If you shoot, they'll shoot back. Let me do the shooting."

I drew out my Glock and showed it to him. He nodded, as if he understood.

"That Koeberg ahead?"

It had occurred to me that the lights we had seen on shore were the town of Van Riebeekstrand, beyond which there was a stretch of empty scrub leading up to the Koeberg Nuclear Power Station.

"Koeberg," confirmed Jannie.

"Get close as you can to the beach, try to get into their waters."

Jannie shook his head. "No can do. They'll send out security."

"That's what we need," I said. "Set the course, then jam the wheel and join us in the stern."

"I'm the captain," he protested. "I stay here."

"They'll attack the wheelhouse – safer outside."

He shook his head again and brandished the Makarov.
"Safer here," he said.

There was no time to argue about it. I went back out into the foul weather and made my way down the edge of the boat to Fat-Boy, who was still crouched in the same position, his eyes fixed on the dark shape of the approaching motor boat.

I unclipped Fat-Boy's carabiner and helped him to the stern of the boat, where I clipped us both onto the mount of the loading arm, and then lay flat beneath the arm, gaining a little cover from the low stacks of concrete blocks which were arranged like a miniature city around it. Jannie adjusted our course, and we drew nearer to the shore, watching as the motorboat slowly gained on us. The two men on the raised bridge of the boat shifted restlessly as they drew nearer, watching for any signs that we had noticed them. Jannie turned his head a few times. But I doubt they could see that, and he did the right thing by keeping our speed and bearing constant. If they thought they had lost the element of surprise and it turned into a chase or a shootout, we wouldn't have a chance against their faster boat and bigger weapons. Our only chance was to attract the attention of the power station security; I reasoned we could claim any number of mechanical or navigational failures and take refuge within the no-go area around the power station. Our concrete blocks would not attract much attention.

But our pursuers were not about to let us reach the safety of the power station. With a surge of speed, the boat accelerated towards us and drew alongside as the rain intensified. There was a minute in which they disappeared from view as their lower profile craft was hidden. Then a coil of rope leapt out of the sky and a heavy grappling hook struck the wooden deck of our boat and skittered across it before jumping overboard again. Another minute of waiting before the hook leapt out at us again, and this time it caught on the steps leading up to the bridge where I could make out the profile of Jannie holding his old Russian pistol before him. I cursed myself for leaving him in there, and not insisting that we tie up the wheel and let the boat continue on its course.

The two men came over the ledge, somersaulting head first, their AK-47s held between locked elbows as they'd been trained to do. I had less than a second to take aim and fire at the one closest to us. His body twisted with the blow of the bullet. I fired again. He crumpled to the deck, and his weapon bounced away from him. The wind had muffled the sound of the shots, so his partner probably didn't know he'd been hit and kept rolling across the deck until he struck the base of the wheelhouse. He disappeared from my view just as I was taking aim, but I kept my gun on the spot I had last seen him, waiting for him to sit up. There was a pause, and then came the shout of a man's voice. A silence, and then a repeat of the shout. I guessed he was calling to his colleague who was lying slumped against the railing they had jumped over. The shout came again, a thin noise under the barrage of wind and rain. Again, there was no answer.

That is when Jannie made his mistake. The sounds of the Makarov shots seemed distant because of the strength of the wind, but I could see his hand poking through the broken perspex window at the back of the bridge and it was jerking with the recoil of the shots. I couldn't see for a moment what he was firing at, but then realised the head of a third person had appeared over the ledge, probably in response to the shouting. The head ducked down again as

Jannie's shots went wide, and a moment later the bridge exploded in a shower of splinters. The man taking shelter beneath it had opened fire and was showering the rickety structure with bullets. I still couldn't see him and watched helplessly as the bridge tore apart, bits of wood and perspex flying off into the storm.

Our boat lurched to the side as whatever Jannie had wedged into the wheel to hold us on course was ripped away. We started heading directly towards the deserted stretch of sandy beach that was a part of the secure zone around the power station. The third man chose that moment to leap over the edge and onto our boat. I was ready for him and fired three shots, one of which missed its mark, but the other two struck home and he collapsed onto the deck. The man who had destroyed the bridge called out again, a desperate cry as he sought the support of his comrades. There was no reply from the slumped figures on the deck. The boat heaved suddenly to the other side as we took a swell broadside, and the two unconscious or dead men slid across the deck. The grappling hook that was holding the motor boat against our side lost its hold on the broken structure of what had been the wheelhouse, and it too slipped across the deck, snagging on one man's legs, and dragging him towards us.

I had only a few seconds to make a decision. I judged the odds to be severely stacked against us. Two other men had appeared on the bridge of the motorboat; the man who had destroyed the wheelhouse was still under cover, whereas we were exposed at the stern with very little cover, had only my Glock with four bullets in the magazine, and nowhere to go. The grappling hook ripped free of the man's leg and disappeared over the side. But already another hook was snagging the remnants of the wheelhouse. I made the decision.

"We jump," I said to Fat-Boy, whose eyes stretched wide and his mouth opened to protest, but there was no time.

I released our carabiners from the loading arm and linked them together. The boat lurched again, as if it was trying to shake us free. We were getting close to shore and had probably caught on a sandbank. We took three steps, my hands pushing at Fat-Boy's heavy back, and jumped. I looked back and glimpsed a man taking aim with his AK-47, and the shuddering of his hands as he fired, then we were in the icy water, my breath was punched out of me and I swallowed mouthfuls of it before I gained the surface, only to be struck down again by a wave which punched the side of my head. I came up and gasped for breath, but drew in nothing but water as I was pulled under again, kicked and struggled to get back to the surface, then realised the reason I wasn't moving was the tugging weight on the end of the strap attached to my life jacket, the panicked tugs of Fat-Boy flailing about below me.

My lungs were bursting for air to the extent that conscious thought was being driven from my mind, but I grabbed hold of the strap and pulled myself down to where Fat-Boy was struggling. His arm struck me as he thrashed about. I caught it, found his neck, wrapped my elbow around it, and held him tight. There was nothing but black water everywhere; I knew from training that you let science take over and allow the buoyancy of your body to show the way. Not a simple thing to do when every muscle is screaming to get air into your lungs, but I kept still for a moment, squeezing too hard on Fat-Boy's neck to keep him still too. An agonising moment, and then a sense of orientation returned, and I kicked with my feet. Then our heads were above water – I gasped a mouthful of the salty water and air, and heard Fat-Boy spluttering – then we were under again. I kicked and gained the surface. Took a mouthful of air, then another of water, then coughed and my lungs burned as if I'd breathed in hot coals. Fat-Boy was going into spasm. I could feel the way his heavy bulk contracted beneath my arm. It would have been better for both of us if he lost consciousness, but we kept our heads above water for long enough to get some air into his lungs and the spasms subsided.

I twisted around in the water, completely disoriented. The swell appeared huge. Wind caught the tops and spewed jets of foam into the air. I turned about, hoping to see something that would orientate me. Then a heaving swell lifted us and from the crest I glimpsed the lights of Koeberg. We dropped as the swell moved past, but I had a bearing, and I kicked and dragged Fat-Boy in the direction of the shore.

It took twenty minutes of hard effort, then the swell started catching on the rising sea floor and we were tossed and tumbled the last fifty metres until eventually the two of us crawled up onto the sandy beach like an eight-legged monster climbing out of the sea.

SEVENTEEN

"He tried to kill me," said Fat-Boy for the third time. "Angel – he strangled me in the water."

Chandler said nothing but shovelled some egg into his mouth and chewed thoughtfully, his eyes on the plate before him. He had not taken the news that we had abandoned the barge with our gold on it very well. His usual optimistic determination had collapsed into a sullen silence, and the burden of his disappointment weighed heavily on us all.

"This was when you swam ashore?" asked Chandler.

"Yes Colonel. He strangled me."

"The sea was rough," I pointed out. "And Fat-Boy is not an experienced swimmer."

Fat-Boy's breathing had been coming in shallow gasps by the time we reached the beach, so I removed the life jacket, unbuttoned his overalls, and ripped his T-shirt from him, then waited while he vomited and recovered his breath. We found Koeberg Nuclear Power Station on high alert when we came to a watchtower at the northern end of the beach. The boats had skirted the restricted zone and the motorboat captain claimed, in radio messages, that they had salvaged a stricken boat that had drifted off course, but power station security was keeping a close watch nonetheless. We confirmed the falsehood of the stricken boat, claiming to have fallen overboard, and the power station medical officer gave us a clean bill of health. He allowed me to use the telephone in his office to call Chandler, who was just finishing the job of replacing the concrete weights we had left on the quay. Our golden barge and the motorboat with Dark Bizness militia had long since disappeared. Now we were at our secluded table on the edge of the Twelve Apostles' terrace, freshly clothed and facing up to our failure.

"You had your Glock," said Chandler, and he looked up at me.

"They had AK-47s. We were sitting ducks."

Chandler nodded, and his grey eyes studied me. "I want to believe you did the right thing, Corporal," he said eventually. "Better alive without the gold than dead on that boat with it, is what I want to think."

"He tried to kill me," said Fat Boy again.

"Perhaps he did," said Chandler, his eyes still on me. "Better luck next time, Corporal."

I caught a glimmer of a smile. Then he brought his hands together with a loud clap that made Robyn jump. "Not all is lost," he announced. "We will turn this to our advantage."

"How we gonna do that?" asked Fat-Boy suspiciously.

"We'll improvise," said Chandler. "Isn't that what we're best at, Robyn?"

"We've certainly had a lot of experience at improvising," said Robyn coldly.

"What's that tone?" said Chandler. "You need to be

with us on this, not being sarcastic and sitting on the sidelines being sulky – spit it out."

"It's nothing," said Robyn. "I am with you, don't worry."

"I do worry though," said Chandler. "I know you well enough to worry when I hear that tone in your voice. Tell us what's on your mind."

Robyn sighed and studied her uneaten breakfast.

"It's cursed," she said.

Chandler and Fat-Boy looked at her as if expecting something more.

"Cursed?" said Fat-Boy. "What the fuck you mean?"

"It brings bad luck," she said. "Every effort of ours to get that gold has met with disaster."

"I see," said Chandler, and he tilted his head to better consider this suggestion. "And because it's cursed, you propose allowing the Dark Bizness crooks to sail into the sunset with it?"

Robyn said nothing.

"Like fuck they do that," said Fat-Boy. "You and me go get it, Colonel. If the lovebirds are too scared."

Chandler's eyes turned to me.

"We're not too scared to do anything," I said.

"How many times must we fail?" Robyn blurted angrily, her eyes on me. "How long do we keep fooling ourselves? Until one of us doesn't make it back?" There was a breathless pause, then she said, "I want nothing more to do with it."

Chandler raised a hand as if to give himself a moment to understand what she had just said.

"Are you saying you want out?" he asked.

"Yes, I want out, Colonel. You have always said the door was open. Now I'm walking out of it."

"Why don't you take some time to think about it?"

Robyn shook her head. "I've had time. I've made my decision."

Chandler stared at her, and for a full minute none of us spoke. Then he sighed heavily, pushed his chair back and stood up.

"All of us, or none of us," he announced. "That's how it has always been. It's over."

"Like fuck it's over," said Fat-Boy. "We'll find that ship and get our gold back. We can do it, Colonel, we can still do it."

"No hard feelings, Fat-Boy," said Chandler. "It is all of us or none of us, that's how it needs to be. It's time to end this."

"The fuck?" said Fat-Boy. He turned to Robyn and said again, "The fuck?"

Chandler picked up his card-key from the table.

"There will be other opportunities," he said. "We'll work together again. And it will be all of us, or none of us."

And he walked away from the table, crossed the stone-paved terrace and passed through the French doors into the hotel.

Fat-Boy repeated his last words on the subject a few more times. Then Robyn stood up and – without saying another word to either of us – followed Chandler into the hotel.

"You and me," said Fat-Boy, "we find that boat, Angel. Just you and me."

"If you say so, Fat-Boy," I said. I was feeling exhausted and could think of doing nothing but lying down and sleeping. "But only if I don't succeed at killing you first."

Fat-Boy looked at me, and he opened his lazy eye a little wider.

"I'll tell you one thing, Angel," he said. "That's the last

time you touch me. What the fuck were you doing undressing me on the beach? I don't care what happens – your lily-white fingers don't touch this black body of mine again. Ever."

———

Captain Andile Dlamini had given up smoking about the same time I had, several months ago. Since giving up he had smoked at least as many cigarettes as me, but he told me he felt optimistic that the accrued guilt would soon turn him into a smoker who had not only given up, but who would also not sneak the occasional cigarette several times a day. I didn't share his optimism, but perhaps that was because of the obsessive way that I saw him sucking at a cigarette now. The Cape Town Homicide division of the South African Police Service announces at entrances to the building that it is proud to host smoke-free offices, so Andile and his colleagues kept the windows open, even in winter, as they smoked their way towards solving a small portion of the crimes that made Cape Town one of the top ten murder capitals of the world.

"Where is she?" asked Andile, as he blew a cloud of smoke at the ceiling. "When you said it was about that journalist of yours, I thought you were bringing her in with you to explain why you terrorised that judge."

"I didn't terrorise him, Andile."

"Well, if you didn't bring your journalist in to confirm your story, why are you here?"

"I need a little help finding her so that I can bring her in."

"She's disappeared again?"

"Not again, strictly speaking. I might have exaggerated a little when I said I had found her."

Andile clasped his hand over his mouth, and the tip of his cigarette turned almost white.

"Exaggerated?" he said, without bothering to blow the smoke out first. "You mean you didn't find her? You *almost* found her?"

"You could describe it like that."

He sighed.

"I don't think you realise the severity of your situation, Gabriel. You are the prime suspect in the murder of a prominent member of the justice system. Having 'almost found' the person who could support your story is not a good defence."

"Which is why I need your help," I said.

Andile sighed again, creating a small cloud of smoke that hid us from the view of his colleagues.

"What kind of help?"

"There was a young woman treated in hospital a few months ago for a knife wound to the throat."

"Which hospital?"

"I don't know. She was the victim of an attack in Muizenberg. Surely there would have been a report about it?"

"This woman your disappearing journalist?"

"No, she was a colleague of hers."

"I see," said Andile. He took another gasping draught of his cigarette. "Knife wound to the throat?"

"It was a nasty wound which they stitched up, she spent several days in hospital."

"I'll take a look," he said, and cleared piles of paper away from the keyboard of an ancient computer. He hit some keys, then hit them harder when nothing happened, and finally switched the computer on, which produced better results.

"That man you found in the docks," he said as he typed, "the one with the gunshot wound to the chest. Know who he was?"

"No idea," I said.

"Big businessman, a founder of Dark Bizness."

"Really?"

Andile tapped some keys and scowled at the computer screen.

"Have you got a cold?" he said, when I sneezed.

"Think I might be getting one."

My swim with Fat-Boy in the freezing waters of the Atlantic was taking its toll. I had caught a few hours of sleep the previous day, and then checked out of the Twelve Apostles because Chandler had instructed us to scatter. But sitting around wondering what to do with my life had been little fun, and so I had come to see Andile despite the heavy cold.

"I've got one here," said Andile. "Knife wound, throat, young woman, Muizenberg. April this year you said?"

"Sounds about right."

"It lists her occupation as sex worker."

"That's the one."

Andile turned to me and demonstrated how flexible he could be in his smoking habits by inhaling a lungful of smoke and blowing it over me, all without using his hands.

"What do you want to know about her?" he asked.

"I want to know if another woman checked into a hospital or was involved in a crime of any sort that day or within a few days afterwards."

"Should I check the morgues as well?"

"You probably should."

"And this would be your journalist?"

"Yes. She was with the young woman when she had her throat slit."

Andile turned back to the computer, tapped at the keyboard, and peered through the haze of smoke for several minutes.

"Dark Bizness," he said after a long pause, "that's who that man was. The one you stumbled across in the docks. And a member of Breytenbach's private security outfit. Gang warfare has flared up, you will have seen it in the news."

"I must have missed it," I said. "Gang warfare at the docks? That's incredible."

"Please tell me you're not involved, Gabriel."

"I don't have a gang. Gangs aren't really my thing."

"Word on the street is that the Dark Bizness crowd are fighting it out with Breytenbach's security."

"The gold mining man?" I said, to demonstrate my ignorance.

"The same," said Andile. "The one who claims all that gold was stolen from him."

"And they're starting a war over a few bars of gold?"

Andile turned to me and removed the cigarette from his mouth in order to stub it out. Then he gave me the intense stare that usually preceded tough questions. I liked Andile and sometimes thought that we could be friends. I appreciated his passion for what he did – his obsessive determination to pursue justice – and it didn't bother me that we were on different sides of the law. Although that was probably why our friendship had not developed past the occasional sharing of cigarettes.

"It was more than a few bars," he said. "Khanyi has told me you are well aware of that."

"Has she? How's that going, with Khanyi?"

I offered him another cigarette, as was appropriate if we were going to talk relationships. He took the cigarette and then cupped his hands around mine as I lit it for him.

"Khanyi is very focused on her career," he said eventually.

"That's just nonsense. I've seen the way she is around you. I always put in a good word for you, you should know that."

"I'm not sure that helps, Gabriel. Khanyi might not consider a good word from you as a recommendation. In fact, she has confided that both she and Major Fehrson are concerned about the path your life has taken since leaving their employ."

"That's very kind of them."

"Khanyi told me you were a soldier, quite respectable a short while ago. British army, is that right?"

"Never respectable," I admitted, "and between you and me it all ended rather badly."

"Yes, she told me that, too. Post-traumatic stress, she said."

Andile clutched at his face as if he regretted mentioning that, but he was only sucking on his cigarette.

"Something about a terrorist ambush in the Congo. You were posted to gold mines in Uganda?"

"That's right."

"Not Breytenbach's gold mine, was it? He owns a gold mine up there."

"Does he? What a coincidence."

"Do you know the broken window theory, Gabriel?"

"Find the people who are breaking the windows and you stop them from doing worse?"

"That's right. Smaller crimes lead to bigger crimes; larceny will lead eventually to homicide."

"In my experience it can also work the other way. Homicide could lead to larceny."

Andile inhaled again. The cigarette crackled, and his eyes narrowed.

"If you are in trouble, Gabriel, you should come clean before things escalate."

"I'll be sure to do that, Captain. Thank you."

"Khanyi has told me she is concerned about you."

"You and Khanyi should really find something else to talk about on your dates."

Andile nodded, as if allowing me that small joke at his expense.

"Did you find anything?" I asked, indicating the computer. I guessed all of this was simply a preamble to some big revelation.

"Nothing," he said, and turned back to the computer to demonstrate. "There are several clearly unrelated cases, but nothing that could be connected to your young sex worker. How would you describe the race of your journalist?"

"I would describe it as a medium toffee."

"Coloured or Indian toffee?"

"Coloured would be what it says in her ID."

Andile shook his head and scrolled through a list on his screen.

"I'm now weeks after the wounded sex worker, and there is nothing."

I waited. I knew he would not have subjected me to the broken windows speech if he hadn't found something.

"Except for this," he said eventually, after I failed to respond.

"What is that?"

"No woman, so it's not your disappearing journalist."

"Ah," I said.

"Two men, died in a fire in their car."

"Burnt to death?"

"Their car burned, with them inside it."

"How is that related to the girl in hospital?"

"It was a few days after they released her from the hospital and just up the coast in the Strand."

"It seems a tenuous connection."

"There is also the manner of their death."

"They didn't burn to death?"

"Wounds to their throats, it says here," said Andile, and he pointed his cigarette at the screen but looked at me. "Knife wounds to the throat," he said again, in case I hadn't understood the first time.

"That's interesting. What can you tell me about those men?"

He turned back to the screen.

"Local scumbags, in and out of prison, drugs, car hijacking, they did whatever came their way. Had recently turned their lives around and discovered religion – they both joined that big church, the House of God."

"Isn't it called the House of Our Lord?"

"That's the one. But according to this report they couldn't shake off their past – the deaths were put down to infighting, Cape Flats gangs, vengeance for past betrayals, that kind of thing." He turned back to me. "No mention of a disappearing journalist, or a wounded sex worker."

Andile was silent for a moment, then he said, "You will bring her in to me when you find her, Gabriel, won't you? The Gauteng boys are baying for your blood, and I'm holding them off on the basis that you will bring this journalist of yours in to explain what you were doing threatening that judge. You can be grateful none of your DNA showed up at his house, but I know enough of your background to not be surprised by that."

"My military training didn't include instruction in covering up DNA evidence," I said.

"Nevertheless, try not to stumble across any more people with gunshot wounds. And try not to visit people who end up dying from knife wounds to the throat."

"I'll do my best," I said.

"I'm also concerned about the trend developing here, Gabriel. Deeply concerned. I don't like it."

"Trend?"

"The number of people you come into contact with who disappear, or die."

"It is deeply concerning," I agreed, and left him with the last two cigarettes in the pack. Kicking the smoking habit when deeply concerning things are happening is pretty damn hard, I know from experience.

EIGHTEEN

"Where are you, Gabriel?" asked Khanyi when I returned her call.

"I'm right here."

Khanyi sighed. "I've been trying to get hold of you, but you never answer."

"That story has a happy ending though, because you've got a hold of me now."

"This your new number?"

"It is one of them."

"Father is deeply concerned about you."

"That is very kind of him, but you can tell him I'm in fighting good health."

"Sounds like you've got a cold."

"Was there a reason you were trying to get hold of me, Khanyi, or was it just the annual health check?"

"Captain Dlamini says you threatened a government minister."

"Does he?"

"Don't play games, Gabriel. I'm trying to help you. It

would be in your interest to stop playing the fool and listen to what I have to say."

She paused. I demonstrated my willingness to listen by saying, "Which is?"

"You need to give yourself up."

"To the police?"

"Yes. Give yourself up to the police."

"Why would I do that?"

"They have a warrant for your arrest – that's why Father's concerned. It would be better if you gave yourself up instead of running from the police and waiting for them to catch up with you. It would be an indication of your innocence."

"Is it those parking tickets? I can explain that."

"Of course it's not the parking tickets. But seeing as you bring them up – you realise those have been coming to the Department? You didn't hire a car using one of our IDs, did you? In any case, you should be thanking me for all the trouble I've gone to, Gabriel, not making jokes. The warrant is for two murders."

"Two?"

"And what happened to your journalist? Captain Dlamini says you went to see him, but there was no journalist. Now another man is dead, and Captain Dlamini says he can't hold them off any longer."

"Who is the other man?"

"A member of the Cabinet – Minister of Education I think – Jessop Ndoro. Captain Dlamini says if you'd been there an hour later you'd be locked up in a cell by now. The warrant came through just after you left."

"You seem to know an awful lot about what Captain Dlamini is saying. How are things going with him? You two seeing much of each other?"

There was a click and then a disappointing silence. Khanyi had ended the call, and I hadn't even had the chance to thank her.

I went out onto the small terrace of the apartment I had broken into the night before. It belonged to a neighbour of mine whom I'd overheard talking about a business trip that would take him out of town for several weeks. If he hadn't meant to include me in the conversation, he shouldn't have spoken into his phone with so much volume. And I did not think he'd mind my staying in his apartment. I'd even done him the favour of watering the indoor plants. In any case, I didn't intend staying long because it was risky, given the proximity to my own apartment. But I hadn't been able to think of anywhere else to go – and Breytenbach's men were being kept busy in the docks, so I didn't think it likely they would come looking for me. But now that the police had a warrant for my arrest, they'd be ringing at my doorbell before too long and doing searches of the neighbourhood. I lit a cigarette and thought over my options again. The warehouse at the docks was out of the question; they were still in a state of emergency. Going to another hotel would mean using an identity that the Department didn't have on their list, and I'd run out of those. The identity I'd used at the Twelve Apostles was not available because Chandler had insisted on collecting our documents before we parted ways. I would also need to abandon the rental car, which the Department were no doubt tracking as well. I had reached the point of my last resort: calling Chandler and asking for him to arrange somewhere else to hide, when my phone rang. It was one of the numbers I had for Fat-Boy.

"Where are you?" he asked.

"I'm right here." I had a sense of déjà vu.

"I been busy, Angel," he said, and paused, as if expecting me to congratulate him.

"Busy doing what?"

"I found the boat," he said in a breathless voice. "Found the fucker, Angel, I found it."

"Did you?"

"I did." Fat-Boy's voice had gone flat with disappointment at my reaction.

"And the heavy stuff? That still on it?"

"No, Angel, that's gone."

"The captain? Did you find Jannie?"

"Coast guard did. He was dead. They found the boat floating out to sea and towed it back. There's been police crawling all over it. The locals here say they removed his body."

"But no concrete blocks?"

"Why would the police take the blocks?"

"Because of what was inside them."

"No, they didn't take the blocks. There were no blocks when they found the boat."

"The locals where? Where is it?"

"You wanna see it? We'll go there together."

I didn't see any point in going to look at an empty boat – except for the fact that I wouldn't here when the police came knocking.

"Where is it?" I asked again.

"Saldanha Bay."

Saldanha was an industrial harbour a couple of hours' drive up the west coast.

"You got wheels?"

"Sure I do."

"Then I'm in. Let's go see the empty boat."

"Are you in trouble, Angel?"

"Of course not."

"You never ask me for a ride."

"I've had problems with my rental."

"Sounds to me like you're in trouble, Angel. You can tell me, you know that."

"I'm not in any trouble."

"Is it that journalist chick of yours? Sex-bomb told me she's dead and now there's all kinds of shit coming your way."

"I'll get the rental fixed and see you up there."

"No need to be so touchy," said Fat-Boy. "I'm here for you, brother. I'll pick you up in an hour."

———

The humanitarian politician Jessop Ndoro's death had been a more dramatic one than that of Justice Francois Rousseau, if the newspapers I found while waiting for Fat-Boy to meet me were to be believed.

Unlike Justice Rousseau, he did not speed up his death by drowning, but he wasted most of his extra minutes trying to get back to his feet after his legs collapsed at the glass wall that offered a picture-postcard view of Cape Town and Table Mountain over the bay. The mountain would have glistened across those waters on a better evening because of the huge floodlights that lit the flat face of the mountain, but on the occasion of Jessop Ndoro's death the sea was troubled by an angry westerly wind and the tablecloth cloud had spilt into the city and the lights had been turned off. It occurred to me that the fact he had died on the night of the storm meant I had an alibi to prove my innocence. But explaining what I had been doing with Fat-Boy on board a barge loaded with heavy concrete blocks and a couple of corpses, might prove difficult.

Jessop Ndoro had apparently held his hand up to the wound in his neck in a vain effort to stem the flow of blood, then as his limbs weakened and his life drained from him, that hand had instead been used to try to climb the glass wall, leaving pathetic streaks of sticky blood like arcane symbols painted on the glass, as if he was trying to send a final message. If he had, it was a message that nobody understood. Some journalists suggested he had painted the sign of the Christian cross in an effort to pass in the good graces of his God, but that took a stretch of the imagination.

The newspaper articles were lyrical in their remembrance of Jessop Ndoro's concern for the education of those who could not afford it. None mentioned his preference for young sexual partners, nor his role in founding a club that arranged the availability of those young sexual partners, nor the occasion that he had donned a mask and witnessed an underage girl succumb to a death not dissimilar to the one that came to him. His three wives and a small tribe of sexual partners were kept silent with the promise of compensation from his extensive estate, and I expected that those who were not yet adult would receive their compensation first – the government couldn't afford another scandal.

And an insignificant tab at the Miners Club in Heerengracht Street had probably interested the police, who had no doubt already worked out who the man was that had ordered the whisky, a drink that Jessop Ndoro never consumed. And further deduced that the same man had caused Jessop Ndoro to phone his lawyer and complain that he was receiving threats on his life from members of the public.

———

Fat-Boy's wheels were a blue 1970s Volkswagen camper van which had last passed a roadworthy test in the previous century. But the exterior was polished, the windows were tinted and there was a foam mattress in the back which Fat-Boy said would be big enough for the both of us as long as I didn't mind him snoring. The van was also fitted with a powerful sub-woofer, which meant that we could feel the Xhosa rap music as it vibrated our hearts as well as hear it, and it left my ears ringing after Fat-Boy turned it off. The front seat was a long bench with a crater-like depression behind the steering wheel, which had been moulded by Fat-Boy's rear end over many years. He filled the driver's side of the vehicle like a loaf of bread that has risen too much and threatens to break open the oven door. His right hand drooped over the wheel, his left rested on the gear stick, and his stomach held the lower end of the steering wheel in position. He had an unnerving habit of turning to face me when I spoke, relying on his peripheral vision to ensure that we stayed on the road, which we didn't do as much as I would have liked.

We took the small coastal road because we were less likely to encounter roadblocks and Fat-Boy preferred a route that required him to keep his hand on the steering wheel, which was something he forgot to do when the road was too straight. He turned the music off after half an hour because he wanted to tell me how he had found the boat. It had taken him three days, most of which had been spent sitting in bars and drinking beers with local fishermen up the west coast, a pub crawl that had culminated in his discovery of the boat anchored outside the main harbour at Saldanha Bay.

"Just floating there, man, it's what these boat people do. They drop a heavy fucking anchor and then they sit there. There's hundreds of boats floating out there. I spotted ours 'cos the driving hut up front is all shot to shit, and there's the crane thing on the back."

"And no sign of the gold?"

"All gone," said Fat-Boy, and he scowled at the road and swung the steering wheel around a bit to get us back onto it. "No concrete, no gold, nothing – boat was empty when the coast guard found it. They towed it back in and left it there while they figure out who it belongs to. The locals say it will be sold off at auction. The cops think it's a gang thing, blaming some trouble he got into with smuggling cigarettes. I took a look at it, couldn't see too well from where I was, but our gold is gone, that's for sure."

"You didn't make it too obvious, did you, Fat-Boy? The police must be watching it – probably the Dark Bizness people too."

"Course not. There's a great campsite above the bay. That's where I've set up."

"Set up what?"

"You and me gonna camp there."

"Why?"

"'Cos we're gonna find our gold."

"By watching an empty boat? What will that achieve? We know who has the gold – Lebogang Madikwe. Staring at the empty boat won't bring it back."

"You should call him Lebo. Only a whitey would call him Lebogang."

There was a pause in conversation as Fat-Boy pretended to focus on the driving while he came up with a response to my pessimism. Eventually he said, "You're the brains, Angel. I'm the muscle. You figure out how we get it back."

Our outside wheels left the tar and started spitting loose gravel at the undercarriage. Fat-Boy over-corrected and we swung towards an oncoming car, which flashed its lights and hooted angrily as it tore past.

"Stupid fucker," said Fat-Boy. "You see that? He was going way too fast."

We settled back into our lane and Fat-Boy glowered at the road ahead.

"Is it that journalist of yours, Angel?" he asked, when we'd settled into a steady cruise. "The one that went AWOL? Is she the reason you're on the run?"

"I'm not on the run."

"I knew it was that journalist chick." Fat-Boy handed control over to his stomach and turned to me. "Sex-bomb told me you're in deep shit 'cos of her being dead."

"Robyn said nothing of the sort. She knows nothing about it."

"She's sharp, sex-bomb is. Knows stuff you don't tell her – she's got that gift. Why you two not doing it anymore? Is it 'cos you don't like her drinking?"

"It's got nothing to do with that."

"You should let her drink, man. She's never gonna come back to you if you stop her from doing her shit."

"Perhaps I don't want her back. Did that occur to you?"

"Don't give me that," Fat-Boy said with a shake of his head. "You got her right here." He lifted a hand off the gear lever and placed it on his chest. "Right here, I can see it. You want her back, course you do."

He kept his hand on his chest but turned back to the road in time to prevent another head-on collision with a car that had been flashing its lights and hooting.

"Too fast, you fucker," Fat-Boy shouted as the car howled past us.

"'Sides," he continued when we were back on an even keel. "Sex-bomb says you got enough problems, what with all the people you and the colonel killed. Fucked you up proper, she says."

"When did you and Robyn find the time to have all these discussions?"

"I gotta lot of time for sex-bomb; she saved my life, you know that?"

His lazy eye opened up to make sure that I understood the intensity of his feelings.

"I thought that was me," I said.

"Saved my life?" said Fat-Boy incredulously, then blew air between his rubbery lips to produce a scornful sound. "All you done, Angel, is nearly kill me several times."

We drove in silence for a while, then he said, "You figure out why your journalist went AWOL?"

"She got involved with things she should have stayed out of."

"Things? What things?"

"If you must know, human trafficking, prostitution, that kind of thing."

Fat-Boy gave a low whistle. "Fuck," he said, dragging the word out as long as his breath allowed. "She did that shit?"

"She was investigating it."

"But she's dead now?"

"Yes, she is dead."

"All that shit about going AWOL was just you stirring up some sympathy?"

"No, she disappeared and then later she died."

Fat-Boy turned to me again so that he could watch my eyes as I answered his next question.

"Did you kill her, Angel?"

"No, Fat-Boy. I didn't kill her."

"You coulda killed her and then acted all innocent with your stories of her going AWOL."

"I could have," I agreed.

"Sex-bomb says you never can tell with you, 'cos you've killed so many people."

Another car horn blared past us, but Fat-Boy needed to keep looking me in the eye to see if I was being open and honest with him.

"Sex-bomb is a fount of information," I said and kept looking at the road myself, hoping Fat-Boy might follow my example. He did eventually, with an unconvinced grunt.

"Gotta lot of time for sex-bomb," he said again, when he'd adjusted our course and our van had regained the road. "Speaks the truth, she does."

He turned to me again.

"I don't mind if you killed her, Angel. I don't mind about that shit."

"Thank you, Fat-Boy," I said. "That means a lot to me."

And I kept my eyes on the road.

NINETEEN

The campsite that overlooked Saldanha Bay was little more than a section of hill on an outcrop of rock where patches of scrub had been cut back to accommodate tents and camper vans. We were the only ones foolhardy enough to brave the icy weather, so we had the campsite to ourselves. Fat-Boy had selected an open patch on the front edge that offered a panorama across the Atlantic Ocean, the quaint town of Saldanha, and the busy port below, which he told me was used to transport iron ore from the mines in Sishen eight hundred and sixty kilometres away. He knew this interesting detail because the white people had killed several of his relatives by forcing them to build the railway line that connected Sishen to Saldanha.

"Forced labour?" I asked.

"Killed them," said Fat-Boy.

"I didn't know the railway lines of South Africa were built by slaves."

"My mother's uncle's cousin worked himself to death on that railway line."

"But it was a job, wasn't it? Paid employment? Or was it slave labour?"

"What's the difference? Building that railway line for the white people killed him."

"I thought you said there were several of them."

"You saying there weren't?"

We set aside our differences of opinion around the possible enslavement of Fat-Boy's ancestors and offloaded two folding deck chairs so as to take stock of the situation. Fat-Boy retrieved cold beers from the camping fridge in the back, and we looked out over the bay with the assistance of a pair of binoculars that looked as if they'd been abandoned after a failed operation in the Angolan war forty years ago. One of the lenses was cracked, but they were good enough for me to see our barge lying at anchor. The damaged wheelhouse didn't look too bad at this distance. I remembered it seeming to explode into splinters, but from across the bay it merely looked a little crooked, although the windows were no more than gaping holes. There was nothing on deck at all, except for the furled loading arm. No dead bodies, and no stacks of gold bars embedded in blocks of concrete.

"What next?" asked Fat-Boy, after we had taken it in turns to peer at the boat through the good lens and neither of us had seen anything that suggested a course of action.

"Dinner?" I proposed. The sun had dropped below the far edge of the sea and it was getting too dark to see much on the water.

"Got some sausage," said Fat-Boy, and he pulled a gas camping stove from a compartment beneath the foam mattress, unfolded a small table and in a few minutes had the boerewors sausage sizzling in a pan.

"You got a plan yet?" asked Fat-Boy after we'd opened

another beer each and he'd arranged his deck chair so that he could cook the sausage while remaining seated.

"I don't," I admitted.

Fat-Boy poked at the sausage, which retaliated with a spurt of boiling fat that produced a small cloud of steam.

"I thought you were the one with the ideas."

"Is that why you brought me out here? To have ideas?"

"You don't believe that voodoo shit," said Fat-Boy. "Sex-bomb and her shit about the gold being cursed. You and me don't believe it. We gotta show the colonel it's just a load of crap."

"By having ideas?"

Fat-Boy studied my face for a minute and closed his lazy eye to better see whether I was being disrespectful.

"We're gonna get the gold back, Angel, that's why we're here. We're gonna get it back."

"There will be other jobs," I said. "The colonel is right – we need to move on."

Fat-Boy rejected that idea with a trumpeting of his lips.

"There's only one job that counts," he said. "That's this job. That's what the colonel always says. You think he buys that curse shit?"

"It's not about the curse. It's his philosophy – united we stand, divided we fall. Without Robyn we are not united."

Fat-Boy shook his head and tutted dismissively.

"It's a test, Angel – he's testing us – he wants us to find the gold for him and prove ourselves."

"That wasn't the feeling I got."

"You don't know him as well as I do," said Fat-Boy. He switched off the gas and allowed the sausage to sizzle in the pool of fat in the pan. His look challenged me to contradict his assertion, and when I didn't he said, "You were in the army with him, is all."

I didn't rise to the challenge of Fat-Boy's resentment of my history with Chandler.

"Sex-bomb says you were killers," he said after a pause. "In the army – trained killers."

"We were soldiers. All soldiers are called upon to kill when necessary."

"Assassins, that's what sex-bomb says. You were assassins. You and the colonel and her boyfriend, the one who had the idea for the gold."

"Brian didn't have the idea for the gold. He joked about it; that was all. I'm surprised she even mentioned him."

"Why? Sex-bomb tells me everything, Angel. She and me and the colonel are tight. No secrets kind of tight."

I didn't rise to that challenge either – my status as an outsider to their tight-knit group was another theme that Fat-Boy liked to dwell upon.

"How did you meet the colonel and Robyn?" I asked instead.

Fat-Boy had two hot dog rolls which he sliced open with a folding knife, then he cut the sausage in half and placed one half in each roll.

"Ketchup?" he said. "Mustard?"

I nodded to both, and he squirted some tomato sauce and mustard into each, wrapped them with paper towel, then handed me one and took a huge bite of the other. It occurred to me that this camping trip of his had been more thoroughly planned than I had thought.

"Sex-bomb found me," he said through a mouthful of sausage. "Colonel needed someone good with computers, and I know computers, don't I?"

"You do."

"I'd had a bit of trouble, and sex-bomb said she knew someone who could help."

"What kind of trouble?"

Fat-Boy took another monster bite of his hot dog and chewed it thoroughly with his eyes on me, as if wondering whether I was to be trusted.

"I worked at a bank," he said when he had finished chewing, swallowed and washed the sausage down with some beer.

"You were doing something with computers at the bank?"

"I created a detour for some of the money," said Fat-Boy. "My ma was ill with the cancer – I needed the money more than they did, the fuckers."

"And the bank found out about the detour – that was the trouble you were in?"

Fat-Boy shook his head. "Never did, but they would have. Sex-bomb and the colonel found out about it, and told me to put all the money back before the bank locked me up."

"You did that? Put it back?"

"When the colonel says something, I do it, Angel. I learnt that lesson a long time ago. Colonel is the *man*, there's no one above the colonel."

"And your mother?"

"He took care of her, gave her everything she could need. Checked her into a care home. Cotton sheets, full-time nurses, good food, best doctors, she had everything those last months."

Fat-Boy wiped at his eyes with the paper towel from his hot dog and cleared his throat with a sound like a diesel engine starting up.

"Like the sausage?" he said.

"Delicious."

Fat-Boy wiped his eyes again.

"We need a good idea," he said, and looked out over the bay as if he might find one there. It was a beautifully clear night. The sea was flat and black and the moon was spilling its light onto the horizon. I noticed a small cluster of lights in the distance, halfway across the bay towards the town of Langebaan.

"That one of the iron ore ships?" I asked. "Looks a bit off course."

"It's a yacht," said Fat-Boy. "Big fuck-off yacht."

"You sure? It looks too big to be a yacht."

"It's only ninety metres long. The big ones are well over a hundred."

"You can tell that by looking at it?" I asked.

"Course not – it's owned by a brother isn't it?"

"Is it?"

Fat-Boy heaved himself out of his chair and fetched another couple of beers from the fridge. I looked at the glistening lights of the yacht in the middle of the bay and could make out several levels to it, with rows of lights on each. I picked up the binoculars and took a closer look. It was very much like a miniature cruise ship, with a strong, sleek prow, and elegant lines like smooth waves leading the eye to a glowing swimming pool and helicopter pad at the stern.

"Which brother is it?" I asked Fat-Boy, although I had guessed the answer, and was beginning to realise the extent of Fat-Boy's careful planning of our camping trip.

"It's the Dark Maiden," said Fat-Boy. "The brother is Lebo Madikwe, the one you keep calling Lebogang."

I studied the boat again through the binoculars. The decks seemed deserted, but I could make out the shadowy forms of several men standing at a distance from each other. They were not being sociable, and nor were they enjoying the view – they were sentries watching for trouble.

"What is your idea?" I said.

"Had myself some dinner at the yacht club last night," said Fat-Boy, then waited for my reaction.

"Did you?"

"It was a private function, but I told them I'd lost my invite."

"A good dinner?" I was getting an uncomfortable feeling. Fat-Boy on the loose was a worrying thought.

"The best," said Fat-Boy, and he took a gulp of beer.

"What kind of private function?"

"There was a funeral in the afternoon, and they were doing a sort of party afterwards."

"You didn't, Fat-Boy. Tell me you didn't gatecrash Vusi Madikwe's wake."

"Course not."

Fat-Boy gulped at his beer again; my sense of discomfort increased.

"Billy Mabele did," said Fat-Boy.

I could think of nothing to say for a moment, but Fat-Boy saw the concern on my face. He pouted with irritation.

"The colonel let me keep the clothes, the cards, the jewelry, everything. He trusts me, the colonel does."

Fat-Boy finished his beer and struggled to his feet again to fetch another. Billy Mabele was a fake identity Chandler had created for Fat-Boy to play for the Van Rensburg family when we were helping them to transport some lions and an assortment of weapons down from Maputo. Billy Mabele had posed convincingly as an arms dealer and wildlife smuggler. The lions had made it all the way to Cape Town, along with the weapons and the gold bars, but it had been a narrow victory. Fat-Boy had overplayed his character to the point that the rest of us were convinced the Van Rensburgs would call our bluff. They eventually did, but by then they had other things to worry about.

"You don't think I can do it, Angel?" said Fat-Boy as he collapsed back into his chair with another beer.

"What is it you want to do?"

"They've been cutting it out of the concrete. I watched them yesterday, throwing bags of concrete chips over the side of their yacht. They're cleaning it all up for us, polishing it, and making a big pile of our gold in that floating whore house. What do you think Lebo's going to do with it? Stare at it?"

"He's going to sell it," I said.

"Course he is." Fat-Boy's cheeks rose into a self-satisfied smirk. "He's gonna sell it to me."

––––––

We drank more beers and Fat-Boy explained his plan. In his reprisal of the role of Billy Mabele, he intended to extend Billy's criminal activities to include that of a fence. In this case, he would be fencing bars of gold.

"You didn't suggest this to Lebo at last night's dinner?" I said.

"Am I a fool, Angel? I told him how much I loved his brother. He told me how much I reminded him of his brother, and that was all."

"No mention of gold bars or fences?"

Fat-Boy blew a scoffing riff with his lips.

"Gave him my card is all."

"Those cards the colonel made? Just the name, no number?"

"Planted the seed is all. I've learnt how to do this shit, Angel. Learnt from the best, haven't I?"

"Why are you telling me about it? Why didn't you call the colonel up?"

"The colonel won't listen to me, will he?"

"I'm sure he will."

Fat-Boy shook his head and took some more beer.

"Need you to convince him. Go talk your war stories and convince him."

"Convince him of what?"

Fat-Boy looked at me. "What do you think? Of me, Angel."

I said nothing for a moment.

"Forget it," said Fat-Boy. "Should have known you wouldn't help. I'll just do it on my own."

"I'll speak to him," I said, before Fat-Boy's resentment turned violent.

Fat-Boy's eyes narrowed to check that statement for authenticity. Then he raised his bottle as if proposing a toast. He clambered to his feet to fetch more beers and insisted on enveloping me in a bear-sized embrace to make our new union official.

We finished our beers in companionable silence, then cleared up camp and Fat-Boy stripped down to his boxer shorts, which were a pink cheetah print design and were mostly concealed by the bulbous flesh of his stomach so it appeared as if he wasn't wearing anything at all. He clambered onto the foam mattress, leaving a sliver of space for me to squeeze into, and unfolded a feather duvet to keep us warm.

"Did you kill that chick, Angel?" he asked as he rolled himself up in the duvet and pulled it off me. "That journalist, did you kill her? You can tell me, I don't mind if you did."

"I didn't kill her, Fat-Boy," I said.

"Who did?"

"I'm not sure."

"Don't give me that shit. You've been creeping around like you're playing the big detective. You think I'm stupid, Angel? You know who it was."

"I think it was one of three men she was investigating."

"What three men?"

"Three important men, high up in society."

"What do you mean, high in society? Like big businessmen?"

"One's a judge, one a politician, and the third is a church leader."

"It was the church guy. It's always the ones who go to church who turn out to be rotten."

"Perhaps. But they were all rotten in their own way."

"Take it from me," said Fat-Boy. "Those church people are the worst."

And a few minutes later his snores were shaking the camper van as if they were being played through the amplifier's sub-woofer. I climbed out and had a cigarette in the deck chair, gazing out at the glistening lights of the Dark Maiden in the middle of the bay. Fat-Boy could have been right about the church leader. And, although I only had initials to go by, I had a good idea which church leader it was that Sandy had suspected. He was the third and last person who might be able to tell me what had happened to her, and I didn't have a good feeling about what he might have to say.

III

Third, a Church Leader

TWENTY

Johannes Stephanus Erasmus was no stranger to hardship, as the numerous newspaper and magazine articles about this paragon of Christian virtue liked to remind us. The youngest of seven children, he had grown up in a family that struggled to afford clothes and food, and Johannes, who preferred to be called Stephanus or JS, for reasons known only to himself, had spent much of his youth begging for food on the back streets of Brixton, a suburb of crowded apartment buildings near central Johannesburg. That had been over fifty years ago, in the early days of apartheid, a government system that had saved his family from sinking below the breadline by providing his father with sheltered employment on the railways. This provided the family with a small trickle of money, an absent father, and an opportunity for the mother to augment the family income with a host of paying lovers, most of whom were angry and violent. They occasionally expressed their anger against the dirty, underfed and under-clothed children, rendering JS Erasmus's childhood not only miserable, but perilous.

Many years later, as a man of God, JS expressed gratitude to the apartheid government for saving him from a life of misery by providing social services which removed him and two of his siblings from the family unit and found foster homes for them. They had done this after the tragic death of another of his siblings, a seminal moment in the life of JS, and the start of his path towards righteousness. It was while staying with his third foster family, at fourteen, that JS had found God, who had presented Himself to JS by means of a blinding flash of light in the middle of the night. He had called upon JS to dedicate his life to Him. JS had answered the call and despite his troubles, and his multitude of sins, had been welcomed into the House of Our Lord, although JS had only named his church years later when he decided to make money out of his religious experience. He had founded the church that was to become the largest and most profitable church in the country.

The House of Our Lord was in fact many houses: huge warehouse structures where JS Erasmus and his apprentices, whom he liked to call novitiates, would orate. Their passionate pleas for goodness and generosity were displayed on huge screens so that even the latecomers squeezed into the back of the auditorium could feel the power of their message. Musical bands would play modern hymns on their electric guitars and vast crowds of enthusiastic followers would sing along and get caught up in the emotion of the experience to such a degree that they would occasionally find themselves speaking in tongues. Even when not moved to speak in tongues they were obliged to pay a tithe to the House of Our Lord, and as the potential protection offered by the House had such a strong appeal to many business owners and entrepreneurs, the tithe system was working well in the favour of God, or at least His House, and certainly to the benefit of JS himself, who was now one of the wealthiest men in South Africa. No doubt the business owners hoped that their contributions to God would protect their fragile businesses as the country collapsed in flames about them, but as far as I could tell the only person who was really protected by their generous tithes was JS Erasmus himself.

That protection took the form of a fifteen-foot wall topped with high-voltage fencing, which wrapped around his extensive property in the foothills of the Hottentots Holland mountains. In the hundred acre estate were a small forest of oak trees, a lake with a wooden rowing boat, a tennis court, a twenty-three bedroom mansion, and an orchard of fruit trees. An apiary produced honey that was gifted to senior members of the House of Our Lord every year in a ceremony that had been dubbed the 'Anointment of Our Lord' by the envious media, who were granted only mysterious glimpses of the holy members praying at dawn.

Entrance to the property, if you wanted to avoid electrocution and mauling by killer dogs, was through a pair of huge steel gates set into the fifteen-foot wall, behind a boom and a set of retractable spikes. A camera lens stared at me insolently, and the sullen face of a uniformed guard flickered onto the small screen below it. His finger hesitated over the button that would release the boiling oil from the parapets as he determined whether I was going to be a difficult customer. I smiled and gave him my name and he confirmed with the secretary at the big house that I had an appointment, and it all ended on a positive note with the retraction of the spikes and reluctant opening of the enormous gates.

The drive up to the main house was almost a kilometre

through the oak tree forest and around the lake. I passed a small team of men jogging beside the road – the leader raised his hand in greeting, or perhaps as a benediction as I passed. I guessed they were part of his team of novitiates, all clean-shaven, athletic and glowing with the happiness Our Lord promised, according to JS Erasmus. The drive swung around in a great circle about a fountain before the Cape Dutch mansion which housed JS Erasmus, his two young daughters from his third marriage, their nanny, the constant stream of novitiates and a small army of household staff, one of whom was standing at the top of the stairs ready to brief me about the terms, conditions and protocol of entering the House of their Lord.

I parked my rusty Fiat off to the side of the grand staircase so as not to spoil my entrance, and the young man at the top of the stairs allowed me to squeeze his limp, fleshy hand in greeting. The whole of him was limp and fleshy and he wore thick spectacles through which his eyes peered anxiously. He was wearing a long, brown robe, like a monk's tunic, pinched about the middle with a length of rope. He had the softer, more friendly features of the people of one of the smaller southern African tribes who had been defeated by the fearsome Zulus. He smiled nervously, blinked and withdrew his hand as if I'd crushed the bones when shaking it.

"The Master was not clear about the nature of your business," he said, and his smile broadened.

"The master?" I said.

"Father Erasmus. Our Master. He was not clear."

"Just a quick conversation," I said, and increased my smile to match his. "It's a magnificent place – just the family stay here?"

"We are all one family in the House of Our Lord," he said, and the smile slipped a little.

"Wonderful," I said, "a very lucky family."

"Those who know God's love don't need luck," he said, then asked, "What is the nature of your business here?" His smile lost its grip and dropped off his face.

"It's personal."

"We have no secrets here, Mister Gabriel. As the Master's personal secretary I share in all of his concerns, even the personal ones."

"I'm not sure you would share this concern. It had to do with a young woman."

"I see," said the round man, and he wet his lips as he considered a response to that. JS Erasmus had survived more than his fair share of accusations of inappropriate behaviour with young women. He had even admitted to his philandering ways in a televised confession when he announced his divorce from his third wife, and had begged for the forgiveness of the South African people – after revealing that God had already forgiven him in a beneficent gesture which should be an example to us all. His third wife had also forgiven him – but I suspected that was because of the Ferrari that he had given her in the divorce settlement. Ultimately, Father Erasmus had turned the difficulty of his philandering ways to his advantage, as the televised confession and plea for forgiveness went viral and gave the House of Our Lord a boost in membership and commensurate increase in tithes.

"Which young woman would that be?" asked the round man in tacit acknowledgement that there were many candidates. His mouth twisted a little, as if the smile was trying to climb back up.

"A journalist has been asking questions about a young woman who died some months ago."

"Journalists should direct their enquiries to the press office."

"Except that in this case I believe there is also a potential threat to your master's safety."

"His safety?" said the man, and the smile reappeared because of the absurdity of there being any danger behind the walls and electric fences.

"I am concerned for his safety," I confirmed, and didn't share in the smile lest he think I was joking.

"Very well," said the round man, as if he had concluded that I was nothing but a harmless fool. "You will need this."

He lifted a white circular object he had been holding in a limp hand and offered it to me. It was made of canvas and trailed a bunch of black netting beneath it like the stings of a jellyfish. He poked his other hand into it and popped up the central portion of the disk to convert it into a wide-brimmed hat from the edges of which hung the netting.

"For the bees," he said. "You wouldn't want to get stung while expressing your concern for the Master's safety."

It was a beekeeper's hat, and I carried it with me as the round man led the way back down the stairs, crunched across the gravel and then took a path that followed a hedge into an orchard.

"Pear, apple, prune, cherry, orange, quince, and lemon," he said as we proceeded between the trees. A man in brown robes was raking up leaves and the round man raised his hand in the same gesture the jogger had made earlier. The man with the rake raised his hand in return and watched us as we passed him.

"Brother Isaiah is undergoing a period of silence," confided the round man. "The gardens provide us with the opportunity to engage with God's creation, and access His love through our silence."

"He is one of the novitiates?" I asked.

"Not yet. There is too much sin in his heart."

"Does he get to keep trying after engaging with God's creation? Or is the sin more of a permanent stain?"

"God forgives all our sins, no matter how bad they might seem to us. In His eyes they can be forgiven, thanks to His endless grace."

"That's a relief," I said. "Speaking personally."

I glanced back at the man with the rake, whose eyes were still fixed on me from beneath a pronounced forehead, which made him look like an example of primitive man. I wondered whether they supplied all the novitiates with handguns, because I could make out the outline of the shoulder harness he was wearing beneath the robes. Perhaps only the novitiates with too much sin in their hearts were provided with weapons and forced to stay silent in order to focus their minds on protecting their master.

We reached the edge of the apiary, which comprised about thirty wooden boxes arranged haphazardly in the dappled shade of eucalyptus trees. Standing in the centre of the boxes, resplendent in a full-body, white beekeeper suit, complete with hood and a black net visor was a man holding a frame of honeycomb before his face and scrutinising it, apparently oblivious to the cloud of bees that swirled about him.

"Our Master," announced the round man reverently, and he held up a hand to prevent me from getting too close. "You will want to wear your hat," he reminded me.

I pulled the hat on and felt foolish as we stood silently, waiting for the man in the suit to notice us. He lowered the frame and squeezed the accordion-style grip of the smoker so that a cloud of smoke emitted from the spout. Then he gently inserted the frame back into the hive he was standing beside. He swung around and looked at us for a beat, the smoker still producing puffs of smoke as his hand sporadically pumped it. The round man raised his hand in their style of greeting, which suddenly reminded of me of an old science fiction movie and I wondered whether that had been the inspiration for it.

The beekeeper raised a gloved hand to return the greeting and then beckoned with it.

"You may approach our Master," said the round man in case I had not understood their arcane gestures, and I stepped forward in order to do so.

———

Johannes Stephanus Erasmus responded to my suggestion with a dismissive laugh. There was none of the reluctance of the late Justice Francois Rousseau, and none of the shaking fear of the late Jessop Ndoro MP. Just a brazen, arrogant laugh.

"I have nothing to fear," he said and looked up at the sky, through the cloud of bees that surrounded us, to remind me that his God was still watching over him. "Our Father sees everything I do, and his forgiveness is complete. No ..." He looked back down at me. "I have nothing to fear."

"Justice Rousseau and MP Ndoro have both died," I pointed out.

JS Erasmus laughed again and reached into the hive between us with a metal grasping tool in his gloved hand. He pumped smoke at the crawling mass of bees, which buzzed angrily and sought refuge deeper in the hive. The tool gripped the top of a frame and he tugged at it to break the propolis seals, then pulled it out. It was dripping with bees, which crawled frenetically over the surface, as if the frame itself was alive.

"Spring is nearly here," said the church leader, "abnormally early this year. Normally I wouldn't open these hives for many weeks, but look at this." He held the frame up for me to see more clearly. I saw nothing except for a mass of bees.

"Drones," he said. "They've started making the drones already."

"Is that a good thing?"

"Good? Bad? It's God's will, that's what it is. God's bounty will be great this year."

"Because of the drones?"

"The drones are these big bees, you see them? Bigger than the others, and fewer." He held the frame closer to my face, and I tried to make out the bigger bees, although they all looked much the same size to me. Then I spotted a slightly larger bee that was not moving as frenetically as the others, like someone standing lost in a busy thoroughfare.

"That one there?" I asked. "Not moving as much as the others?"

"That's a drone. They are the male bees. The rest of the hive is female, a matriarchal society. The queen lays the eggs and the workers are all female. But in early spring they raise some big fat drones that do nothing but eat the honey. That's how we know that spring is coming early."

"The drones don't do any work?"

"Not unless you call their pursuit of the new queen work. They chase her up into the sky, and the strongest, or fastest, gets to impregnate her."

"Only one succeeds?"

"Only one. Then he, and all the rest, suffer the fate of

all men. They are cast out from the hive, denied food, and left to die."

"Is that the fate of all men?"

"Unless you are a man who knows how to make use of your innate God-given power."

He looked at me in the way that a man who has discovered how to make use of his innate God-given power looks at a man who hasn't.

"I'm not sure that I am," I admitted.

"That's because you are blind to it," said Father Erasmus. He puffed smoke into the hive to clear bees away from the space left by the frame, and gingerly replaced it, careful not to crush any bees. "Just as that judge and the politician were blind to it. Human drones – that is what most men are."

Although his face was partially obscured by the black veil, I could make out the sharp cheekbones, pointed nose, and thin lips in the ruggedly handsome face which had adorned so many magazine covers. There was a fascination to him. I could sense it now. He was charismatic, imbued with a confidence that drew people towards him. But there was more than charisma and confidence. It was easy to see why he was described by entranced journalists as the 'Hypnotist of the Church', but it was also a little frightening.

"You are blind to it," he said, still speaking about the fate of man, "because you have been deceived by the feminist narrative; women that want us to apologise for being men, take everything we have built away from us, because of their absurd demands for equality. We are taught to love our mothers, but honour our fathers. Then our mothers take that love and twist the knife that it becomes in our hearts."

"Not all of our mothers," I suggested.

He looked up at me again, his pale blue eyes cold and angry.

"We should be grateful for those who do – they open our eyes to the truth."

"About the fate of all men?"

"Women need to be controlled," said the man who guided the most powerful church in the country. "That is the truth, and they need us to control them."

"But sometimes that control goes too far, doesn't it? And the women get hurt – some of them don't survive the control."

His cold eyes stayed on me, and the hand with the smoker stopped its constant pulsing. We stared at each other for a moment.

"Why did you come to see me?" he asked, his voice cold and threatening. "Aside from your absurd suggestion that my life is in danger."

"I know about your club," I said. "And the young girls that you traffic; one girl in particular who didn't survive what you, Justice Rousseau and Minister Ndoro did to her."

I could see the surprise wash over him – the sudden dilation of the pupils, the way his mouth opened as if to say something – but no words came out. The rhythm of the hand pumping the smoker faltered, but then he recovered quickly. JS Erasmus laughed another nasty, arrogant, humourless laugh.

"There was someone who tried this before you," he said, when he had finished laughing. "Did you know that?"

I expressed surprise through the veil of my beekeeper's hat.

"A journalist, she was full of anger like you, but didn't have the gall to confront me in person – I would have been happy to meet her – but she sneaked around in the way women do, planning to trap me. What is the word they use? Ensnarement? Or is it entrapment? She used a lot of big words, speaking of sin, penance, atonement, retribution. But those are my words, and I am their master."

"What did you do to her?" I asked.

The hand on the smoker gave an involuntary squeeze, and a puff of smoke came between us. It took only a moment for JS Erasmus to realise his mistake, but instead of retreating into denials he gave another humourless laugh.

"You don't want to know," he said.

"Actually, I do want to know what you did to her. Did you send those men to take her from the house in Muizenberg? They were members of your congregation, members of the House of your Lord."

The church leader said nothing. His mouth smiled, but his eyes were cold.

"And did you order those men to be killed, too? Did you send more members of your flock out to cut their throats and set fire to their car?"

"It is you," said Father Erasmus in a quietly menacing voice, and the hand pumped more smoke between us. "You killed the judge and the politician, and now you threaten me. Why are you doing it? Is it vengeance? What is it you want?"

"I want to know what you did to the journalist."

Father Erasmus kept his eyes on me, but he raised the hand that was not holding the smoker and a moment later I heard the rustling approach of his round secretary.

"Take him away," said Father Erasmus. "Make sure he leaves the property."

"Of course, Father," said the secretary.

The cold blue eyes were still on me. He lowered his hand and resumed the pumping of the smoker.

"She died," he said. "The journalist died. You should have considered that before you came here and sullied the House of Our Lord with your threats."

"It's not a threat," I said. "It is a warning."

"Take him," said the church leader, and I felt the limp hand of his secretary grasp at my arm. I shook it off, but turned and walked away from the leader of the House of Our Lord, pulling the absurd hat from my head. The secretary scurried after me.

———

"You have deceived us," said the round secretary as we made our way back through the orchard. "If I'd known you were going to upset our Master, I would never have allowed it. You said you were concerned, but now you have upset him. It is most deceptive."

"Are your novitiates all men?" I asked.

"They are," said the secretary, and almost added something, but then closed his mouth with irritation. He would not give explanations to someone who had sullied the House of their Lord.

"Any women on the staff?"

"A few. The cooks, the nanny."

"How long have they been with you?"

"What business is it of yours?"

"With that great big wall of yours, the electric fence and all those cameras, the greatest threat to the life of your master will come from inside these walls."

"You think the women are a threat?" he scoffed. "That's absurd. They love our Master, as do we all. The House of Our Lord is a house of love."

I said nothing more about it. We reached the edge of the

orchard and crunched across the gravel to my car. The round secretary didn't want to offer me his limp hand, but I held mine out and so he allowed me to squeeze it again, then he went to stand at the top of the stairs to watch me drive off and ensure that I kept driving until I was out of sight.

TWENTY-ONE

W hile speaking with the paragon of Christian virtue, I had missed a call from Bill. I felt a momentary pang of guilt because I had not spoken to him since the dinner at which he had suggested that I stop searching for Sandy. I called back and greeted him cheerfully, but that did not ease the anxiety in his voice.

"The police were here," he said. "Looking for you."

"Were they?"

"A skinny policeman," protested Bill, "from homicide. What's happened? What have you been doing, Gabriel? They said two people have been murdered."

"Shall I come around?" I suggested. "We could sit down and talk about it."

A pause as Bill considered this.

"How about Fisherman's?" he said.

"Fisherman's would be great."

The Fisherman's Wharf was a restaurant in Hout Bay harbour, set on the edge of the sea and renowned for its fresh fish.

"Tonight?"

"Eight o'clock," I said. "See you there."

Bill ended the call, and I reflected on the fact that he had suggested meeting at a restaurant. In all the time I had known Bill, we had not once met at a restaurant. It had always been at his house, with a new dish he had created, and bottles of his favourite wine. But I supposed that when the person you are meeting is wanted for double homicide, even if they are someone one might call a friend, a restaurant is a more appropriate place to meet.

———

The Fisherman's Wharf is a weathered, unprepossessing building that squats, as its name implies, on the edge of a working wharf against which the boats of fishermen were tied that evening. Several of the fishermen stood about on the wharf, while others sat on wooden stools repairing their nets or perched on bollards, whiling away the evening with chatter. The restaurant was on the first floor of the building, above the fresh fish market which was closing as I arrived, a young Korean man winding down the metal shutters, although that made little difference to the pervasive smell of fish emanating from inside.

Bill had booked a table at the far end of the restaurant, largely hidden from the view of other diners by the assortment of lobster pots, fishing nets, rowing oars and other paraphernalia that hung from the ceiling. The table was beside a window that looked over the sea and was opened enough to allow the chatter of the fishermen below to seep in.

The turn in the weather observed by JS Erasmus seemed to be lasting, and the evening had the feel of early spring, although an occasional gust came in over the water to remind us that winter wasn't over yet.

Bill was occupying one side of the table like a sumo wrestler preparing to consume his daily ration. He ordered the calamari for both of us; he had seen them bringing it in that afternoon and it looked good enough for our consumption. To accompany the calamari, he ordered a bottle of Chardonnay, which he insisted they allow him to feel with a fleshy palm to confirm it was sufficiently chilled. He flapped the menu in his hands to cool himself because he was overheating in his lime green linen suit and wool shirt with thermal under-vest. Then he unbuttoned his collar, loosened the tie, and gazed at me with apprehension.

"Who died?" he asked. "That homicide detective wouldn't say a damn thing, except there were two of them."

"A judge," I said, "and a politician."

"Was it Judge Rousseau?"

I nodded.

"And the politician?"

"Ndoro."

Bill took a sip of his wine and used his tongue to guide it on a tour across all the taste sensors. Then he removed his spectacles, ran a sweaty hand through his hair and squared his shoulders.

"Why do the police want to talk to you about it?"

"Because I saw both men shortly before they died."

A gust of icy air came in through the window and caught a tuft of Bill's hair, which bounced up and then flopped back onto his forehead as if expressing surprise.

"Why?" he asked.

I told Bill about the house in Muizenberg, and the letter Sandy had written to her father. And the three founders of a private club whom she accused of killing her sister. Bill listened intently and said nothing. Our waitress arrived with the calamari which she placed before us without ceremony, then pulled the bottle from the ice bucket.

"Don't you dare," said Bill, his eyes closed as he breathed in the aroma of the calamari. "We'll pour our own wine." He opened his eyes and fixed the waitress with a stare. "We apportion quantity according to body weight, which is the correct approach, not according to favouritism, which would be your approach."

The waitress opened her mouth to say something, but thought better of it when Bill closed his eyes again and inhaled deeply to gauge the quality of the calamari.

"Service here is shocking," he said before the waitress was out of earshot, "but the quality of the food makes up for it."

He opened his eyes, raised his knife and fork, then held them in his fists beside his plate like he was waiting for a signal to start.

"Do you think Sandy disappeared in order to do this?" he asked. "To set up a house of call-girls and find the men who killed her sister?"

"No, I think she did that while still living with me. Do you remember all the research trips she did in those last few months?"

Bill took a mouthful of calamari, which he chewed upon as he pondered this.

"So what happened? Why did she stage her disappearance?"

"I don't think she staged it, Bill. A girl she had taken in spoke to a man who'd been her pimp. He was connected somehow to the men Sandy was trying to find. They sent men to the house in Muizenberg, tried to kill one of the girls, and took Sandy away with them."

"Took her away?"

"I think that is when she disappeared. It wasn't staged at all."

Bill poured us more wine, carefully apportioning it according to body weight.

"Her clothes were collected from the apartment," he said. "And she wrote me that note, remember?"

"I think they did that. The people who took her. Think about it. Because of those two things there has been no investigation into her disappearance."

"You mean they forced her to write that note? I can't see her doing that."

Bill's gaze held mine. Then he looked down at his plate of calamari, and placed his cutlery to the side.

"You think they killed her, don't you?"

"I think we need to consider the possibility."

Bill said nothing. He took another mouthful of calamari, but looked as if he was struggling to swallow it. The murmuring chatter of the fishermen filled the silence between us. Then Bill reached for his spectacles and put them on, shoved them against the bridge of his nose with a heavy finger and looked at me through them as if he was trying to see me properly.

"Who killed those two men?" he asked. "The judge and the politician."

"I am not the only person who read the letter Sandy wrote to her father, or knew about her suspicions of those men."

"You think her father did it?"

"Not her father, no."

"Don't take this the wrong way, Gabriel, but I can understand why the murder squad are looking for you."

"You can?"

"Yes. You are the person most likely to have killed those men."

"Do you think so?"

"You have a vengeful temperament, and I know what you did in the British army – Sandy told me you are no stranger to killing."

"I suppose so."

"You said three men. Who is the third?"

"He's a man of the church."

Bill lifted his glass to his lips and waited for me to say more.

"JS Erasmus," I said.

Bill put the glass down again.

"Tell me you haven't been to see him too, Gabriel."

"Shouldn't I have?"

"Oh god, Gabriel. That man Erasmus lives in a fortified castle, doesn't he? Bristling with security and cameras. I saw something about it in an article about him. If anything happens to him, it'll be caught on camera."

"I expect it will."

Bill pushed his calamari aside and took a sip of wine.

"Why are you warning me about the cameras?" I asked.

Bill swallowed the wine and gave me a momentary glance of consternation, as if wondering whether that was a confession.

"I've lost one friend already to this whole business," he said. "I wouldn't want to lose another."

Which was the first time that Bill had called me a friend.

TWENTY-TWO

The newspaper article about the obese and obscenely wealthy Billy Mabele, a hitherto unknown criminal kingpin who bore no relationship to the notorious arms dealer Richard Mabele, and who was being questioned by the police in connection with the notorious 'gold heist', appeared on the fourth page of the Sunday Times. It was entirely unremarkable and went unnoticed by most of the world.

"That's the way we want it," said Chandler, after we had taken it in turns to read the article and not been impressed.

"They said I was obese," complained Fat-Boy.

"That's because you are," said Chandler. "They had to say something that was true. And didn't you say obesity signifies wealth in your culture?"

"Bigness," said Fat-Boy, "not obesity."

"It was too vague," said Robyn. "It will never work."

We were on the Oasis terrace of the five-star Mount Nelson hotel, enjoying breakfast, which Chandler insisted was the most important meal of the day. I thought he might also have chosen to meet early because it was the most likely time to find Robyn sober, although in the few days since we had last seen each other she seemed to have regained some strength and looked refreshed, confident and entirely sober, which was a little irritating. Robyn, Chandler and I were reprising our roles as high-flying hotel executives, because Chandler hadn't wanted to burn another full set of identities, and he was confident he could run these a bit further.

"It was purposefully vague," said Chandler. "That was how we briefed the writer. The important points are all in there. It makes it very clear that Mabele is suspected of being the fence the heist gang were intending to sell the gold to. It makes it clear he is of Xhosa heritage and is in the market for precious metals."

"That business of Mabele expressing frustration when the journalist called was too subtle," said Robyn.

"You think so? You might be right. I'll concede that one."

"The Dark Bizness people will not link the frustration to the fact that they now have the gold. That Mabele let slip he was frustrated by delays in a big transaction won't translate in their minds as confirmation that he is the fence. He could have been talking about delays on some other business."

"It's subliminal," said Chandler. "That's what the writer said. Hint about the gold, talk about the gold, then infer about nothing in particular and they will fill in the blank ... so we get an inference about the gold. Remember, they are the only people, aside from us, that know that we no longer have the gold. I think that little detail about Mabele's frustration will have a ring of truth for them."

"Is *our* fence frustrated?" asked Robyn.

Chandler gave her a smile.

"Now you're crossing the line between fact and fiction, Robyn. Our fence is not in the least frustrated, but that's because I haven't been keeping him up to date with all our minor setbacks. He will wait patiently for my call, even if it takes many weeks."

"It's been picked up anyway," said Fat-Boy, who had a tiny laptop beside his plate of waffles and was using a sausage-sized finger to scroll through on-line news sites.

"I told you it would be," said Chandler. "It won't take long for our little fabrication to spread. And then it is just a matter of time before one of Lebogang Madikwe's minions shows it to the boss, and he'll be calling up this magnificent hotel to see if the journalist was right about you staying here while concluding other business."

"You should call him Lebo," said Fat-Boy. "Only white people call him Lebogang."

"I am white," Chandler pointed out.

"And if one of Lebo's minions doesn't call?" asked Robyn.

"Then we send Billy Mabele to him," said Chandler.

"God forbid," said Robyn.

There was a small silence.

"And while we wait, we enjoy the luxury of the Mount Nelson," said Chandler.

"It's too expensive," said Fat-Boy who was still smarting from the punitive condition that Chandler had placed upon executing this plan of his: that the costs be taken from his share of our expected bounty.

"A man such as Billy Mabele does not stay anywhere but a five-star hotel," said Chandler. "You cannot expect to be taken seriously in some two-star dive. When Lebogang comes knocking, you need to be the part, not just playing the role."

"I've done it before," said Fat-Boy.

"And you did splendidly," agreed Chandler. "Although we can be relieved that only two of the people who witnessed your first performance are still alive, and they are not the sort of people Lebogang Madikwe would have on speed dial."

"Whatever you do," I said, "don't tell that absurd story about your mother and the British kings."

"William the Conqueror?" said Fat-Boy. "There's nothing absurd about it, he'll love that story. Didn't the Afrikaners love it?"

"The Afrikaners lapped it up," said Chandler, "but the Angel is right. You need to be sharper on this one. Lebogang Madikwe did not become the successful businessman he is by being a fool."

"You don't trust me, do you, Colonel? You trust the Angel because he's an old army buddy, but you don't trust the people who have stuck by your side through the bad times. Is it because we never saluted you? Is that the problem?"

Fat-Boy grasped the edge of the table, hoisted himself to his feet, and performed a mock salute. People at neighbouring tables turned to look.

"Settle down, Fat-Boy," said Chandler. "I trust you implicitly. Stop playing the fool, will you? You're making a spectacle of yourself."

"I salute you, Colonel," said Fat-Boy in a loud voice the way he'd seen it done in the movies, attracting more attention from the other guests.

Chandler rose to his feet, looked at the sorry sight of Fat-Boy's drooping salute, then saluted him back. The two of them sat down again, and there was scattered applause from the tables about us, who appreciated that they had witnessed a ceremonial bonding moment.

"I'm not saluting you," said Robyn.

"I don't expect you to," said Chandler. "It is this kind of thing that we need to avoid, Fat-Boy. Do you see that? What happens if the Dark Bizness folk ask around at the hotel about your activities? Do you want them hearing that you saluted some old white guy at breakfast one morning?"

"I'm gonna work it into the character of Billy," said Fat-Boy, feeling more cheerful now. "I think I'll make you a lower level secretary, Colonel, and as Billy the Conqueror I insist my secretaries salute me at our morning briefings."

Fat-Boy's eyes settled on me. "In fact," he said. "I think the Angel should salute me too."

He started rising to his feet again.

"Let's all stay in our seats, shall we?" said Chandler. "We need to avoid causing a scene."

Fat-Boy subsided again with some reluctance.

"Besides which," said Chandler, "Angel might not be working with us on this – which brings us to the next point on our agenda." He turned to me. "What have you been getting up to, Angel?"

"I'm the next point on the agenda?" I said.

"You're all over the news, haven't you seen?"

"What do you mean, all over the news?"

"Last night's *Crime Watch*. They had an ugly mugshot of you – been splashing it all over the place. Find it for us, will you, Fat-Boy?"

Fat-Boy applied his finger to the screen of his laptop. Chandler's grey eyes held steady on me.

"What have you done, Corporal?" he said. "If your personal problems are going to jeopardise our operation, it might be time for you to fill us in."

"It's a misunderstanding," I said. "There have been two deaths, of prominent people – a judge and a politician. The police think I'm mixed up in it."

"You need to disabuse them of that opinion. We cannot have your ugly face all over the media if we're trying to keep a low profile."

"Of course, Colonel," I said.

"Mixed up how?" asked Robyn.

"There's a connection to Sandy, the journalist."

"That journalist of yours," said Chandler, "has been nothing but trouble."

"Considered armed and dangerous," said Fat-Boy, reading from his laptop. "Do not approach ... call the crime-stop number." He turned the computer so that we could see the screen. A file photograph of my face filled it, one that had been taken for my access card to the Department's offices. No doubt Khanyi had rallied around to help the homicide squad where she could. I looked up to find Chandler's eyes still on me, and for a moment I experienced the dislocation in time I often felt when looking into his eyes – my shoulders up against the cold steel fuselage of the plane wreck in the Kivu, Brian's blood spattered over Chandler's face, his fists locked onto my webbing, holding me back.

"Sort it out, will you, Angel?" he said.

"Of course, Colonel."

"Let us know if there is anything you need."

"Best to keep you out of it, Colonel."

Chandler shook his head. "No. Better together, Corporal, always better together. United we stand."

I got to my feet. "But it would be best if I leave this hotel," I said. "So as not to draw attention to your activities."

"Sit down," said Chandler. "Drop the heroics, and stay here – a five-star hotel is not an awful place to hide. The over-fed, over-rich guests can't see past their own egos, and the staff is taken care of. My man at the desk will alert me if there is any trouble. Just stay out of everyone's way, Angel. Shut yourself up in your room, and let's make certain the Dark Bizness people don't see you again."

"Of course," I said, and sat down.

Chandler turned to Robyn and Fat-Boy. "You two okay with this?"

They both nodded, although Robyn avoided my eyes. Chandler raised a glass of orange juice in a toast.

"Together again," he said. "And long may it last."

Fat-Boy downed his orange juice and slammed the glass onto the table as if he was taking part in a drinking game.

"Never thought I'd have a cold-blooded killer as a friend," he said.

There was a moment's silence.

"Thank you, Fat-Boy," I said.

And I meant it. Not that I enjoyed being called a cold-blooded killer, but Fat-Boy was the second person in the space of a week who had called me a friend.

———

My room at the Mount Nelson hotel was a small one on the fourth floor, with a four-poster bed and a mahogany writing desk from which I could see the Company Gardens – a strip of green that poked itself into the concrete heart of the city. It was these Gardens, according to the brochure on the writing table, that we had to thank for the presence of Cape Town city – they were the original vegetable gardens established in the 1600s to provide sustenance to ships passing around the tip of Africa on their way to trade spices in the east. Beneath the gardens, Adderley Street ran straight as an arrow down to the Foreshore area, and beyond that was the glimmering sea.

Andile answered my call on the third ring.

"You coming in?" he asked.

"Things must be going better with Khanyi," I said. "Is she less focused on her career now that she's sharing photographs of ex-employees with you?"

"You're a wanted man, Gabriel. The name Jessop Ndoro mean anything to you?"

"Sure it does. I had a drink with Jessop not long ago."

"We know that. You wouldn't know how he hurt his throat?"

"Also a knife wound?" I asked.

Andile sighed.

"We can trace this call," he said. "Why don't you just come in and talk with me?"

"I'm sure you could trace it, but I won't still be standing here in a week's time when you've had all the paperwork approved."

"Let's clear this up now, Gabriel. You are the common link between these men. Why don't you tell me what's going on?"

"If I could prove I wasn't there at the time either of those men were killed, would that clear it up?"

"It might."

"And the people who would back me up – would you give them some kind of indemnity?"

"What do you mean, back you up?"

"People who were with me at the time of the killings."

"By indemnity you mean a handshake, and then let them walk out the door without checking they've paid their taxes?"

"That's what I mean."

"You're being naïve, Gabriel. If someone makes a sworn statement in connection with a homicide investigation, they get the full service. You know that. And even if these shady friends of yours come forward, there's such a thing as aiding and abetting. Come in and talk with us yourself, Gabriel."

"There are a few things I need to do first."

I heard the clicking of a cigarette lighter, and then the buffeting of Andile's breath on the microphone as he exhaled.

"Like going to confession? You found religion recently, Gabriel?"

"Did I ever lose it?"

"That man Erasmus has more security than God himself. Whoever it is you're aiding and abetting would do well to consider that."

I said nothing. I hadn't used a fake identity to gain entrance to the House of Our Lord, because I'd run out of them. And I figured the Department and their friends in the homicide squad would know soon enough about my visit to the church leader. The last thing I wanted to do was blow one of the identities Chandler had created for me, and lead them all back to the team at the Mount Nelson.

"I know about the security," I said. "I was there recently."

I could hear the crackling of the tip of Andile's cigarette, and then the sighing exhale.

"You're going to have a lot of explaining to do when I find you," he said.

"I'll be sure to bring several packs of cigarettes," I said, and ended the call. I doubted he was tracing my location, but one doesn't want to take foolish risks.

TWENTY-THREE

W hen evading arrest because of the suspicion of having committed double culpable homicide there are worse places to be than the Mount Nelson hotel, which the brochure on my writing table described as an 'inviting hotel nestled at the foot of Table Mountain, painted pink for peace in 1918'. I wasn't sure that painting it pink had contributed much towards world peace, but it was still a fairly virulent pink, and I supposed the management was hoping for the best, despite everything that had happened in the past century. Within the pink walls, according to the brochure, the magic of a bygone era awaits. I didn't know about the magic either, but the place certainly did feel pretty old-fashioned, what with all the pastel colours and wallpaper which dated from the prohibition years.

I settled into a comfortable routine of late mornings, brief stints in the gym, and afternoons in the lounge racing to complete the tour of whisky samples from around the world, while keeping an eye on Fat-Boy in case of inconsistencies in the character of Billy Mabele. There were none that I could see, although Billy Mabele's routine was remarkably simple for a criminal kingpin. He wedged himself into a two-seater couch early in the afternoon with a pile of newspapers and was provided with a stream of rich food and beer through the day, avoided looking in my direction, and made occasional loud phone calls in Xhosa despite the irritated glances of foreign tourists. The highlight of his day seemed to be the twice daily meeting with his private secretary, which started and ended with a sloppy salute.

As it happened, we didn't need to send Fat-Boy out to find Lebogang Madikwe, because Lebogang Madikwe found him. It took him only three days to contact Billy Mabele, and he did it through an intermediary: his cousin, Justice Mkwekwe, who called the Mount Nelson hotel as we had hoped and simply asked to be put through to Billy Mabele. Billy insisted on taking the call in his room, and Justice Mkwekwe was put on hold for the ten minutes that it took Billy to extricate himself from the couch, roll along the corridor and ride the elevator up to the third floor.

Chandler and I sat quietly in his room with him and listened to the brief musical conversation.

"Have they bitten?" asked Chandler.

"More of a nibble," said Fat-Boy.

"You said no?"

"Course I did, Colonel, you didn't hear me?"

"You were speaking Xhosa," Chandler pointed out.

"Told him I wasn't interested. Told him I didn't know a Lebo Madikwe. I knew, and loved, a Vusi Madikwe, may he rest in peace."

"He mentioned the gold?"

"No, he did not mention the gold. Said they had something I'd be interested in."

"And you said?"

"That nothing of theirs would be of any interest to me. I

237

loved the brother Vusi, and I mourn him, but I have no interest in anything of Lebo's"

"Good," said Chandler. "You know what to say on the next call?"

Fat-Boy glared at him. "Who wrote the script, Colonel? Whose idea was this?"

"Full credit is due to you, Fat-Boy, but we need to play this carefully. You both saw the picture of him pressing flesh with his new best friend."

"They're not friends," said Fat-Boy. "It was the end to the Docklands War, that's all. Lebo would never be friends with that BB creep."

"Nevertheless," said Chandler. "We need to proceed with caution."

That morning's newspaper had announced a cessation of hostility in the Docklands War, accompanied by a surprising photograph of Lebogang Madikwe shaking hands with Riaan 'BB' Breytenbach and celebrating their resolution of 'temporary financial discord', which Chandler had pointed out was nonsense when he had visited my room at six that morning. There had been nothing financial about their discord. The photograph and the article beneath it bothered him deeply.

"Breytenbach is a racist pig," said Fat-Boy. "I am just about family. Nothing to worry about, Colonel."

"You'll ask him about it?"

"Course I will. Nothing to worry about."

"Alright then," said Chandler. "Sounds like we're back in business." He calmed his nerves by beaming at us both. "We'll upgrade," he announced. "Billy and his secretary will take the Presidential Suite."

Fat-Boy groaned. "I'm not taking him into my bedroom, Colonel, we don't need the Presidential Suite."

"You certainly will take him into your bedroom, Fat-Boy. When it comes time to arrange the finer details, we need him in a private space. Cannot have tourists wandering through frame while we're doing it."

"You'll like the Presidential Suite," I said. "Entrance hall, plush bedroom, dining area, large lounge, wet bar and balcony making up a spacious haven."

"Stop winding Fat-Boy up, Angel," said Chandler, "and for God's sake stop quoting that damned brochure at us."

"It's all I have to read."

"So turn on the goddamn TV."

"And look at my face all over the news?"

Chandler sighed.

"What's a wet bar?" asked Fat-Boy.

"It's a bar with a kitchen sink in it," said Chandler, and he got to his feet. "No wonder Robyn's retreated to her room. You two are driving us mad. I'm going downstairs to arrange the suite. Pack your underwear, Fat-Boy, we'll move this afternoon."

He left the room and probably would have slammed the door if the Mount Nelson hadn't been thoughtful enough to provide slam-proof doors.

"Those men," said Fat-Boy after a minute of silence. "You said there was a judge who was killed, and someone else?"

"A politician."

"The police think you did it?"

"It would seem so."

"You told me about a judge and a politician, that night in Saldanha."

"Did I?"

"And you said there was a third one, a church man."

"I'd had too many beers."

Fat-Boy had been gazing at the flowery wallpaper vaguely. His eyes moved to me now to ask his last question.

"Is the church man going to die too, Angel?"

"I doubt it," I said. "He seems like the kind of man who can look after himself."

———

"The three-cup trick," announced Chandler. We were arranged before him on the luxurious soft furnishings of the Presidential Suite. "The three-cup trick has been used to fleece the gullible of their hard-earned cash for centuries. Some sources claim it dates back to ancient Egypt."

Fat-Boy sighed loudly.

"Can we skip the history lesson, Colonel? If you're gonna start showing slides of the pyramids, we're gonna have to open up that wet bar."

"You need to understand this, Fat-Boy," said Chandler. "We'll open the bar just as soon as you understand our plan of action. Now, what do I have here?"

"Three cups," said Robyn, ever the star student.

"Indeed. And under one of them I place a ball."

Chandler held up an ice cube, which he placed under one of the coffee mugs, then he shuffled the mugs about on the countertop with the practised skill of a confidence trickster.

"Now," he fixed his gaze on Fat-Boy. "Where is the ball?"

"How the fuck should I know?"

"Take a guess."

"That one in the middle."

"Are you sure?"

"I just told you I got no idea, Colonel. Course I'm not sure."

"Let me give you a clue."

Chandler lifted the mug on his right. The melting ice cube was revealed.

"Let's try again," said Chandler, and he replaced the mug, using it to flick the ice cube off the counter. It fell to the tiled floor at his feet with a clatter.

"You dropped it, Colonel," pointed out Fat-Boy.

"Dropped what?"

Chandler shuffled the mugs again.

"Now where is it?" he asked.

"It's on the floor," said Fat-Boy. "I already told you, you dropped it."

Chandler sighed.

"The point is this," he said. "The gold is the ball, or in this case the ice." He stooped to retrieve the block of ice and placed it under a mug. "We load the gold into a vehicle in order to transport it to a location." He shuffled the mugs again.

"What location?" asked Robyn.

"Doesn't matter. Somewhere private, somewhere the mark will feel comfortable. The Dark Bizness warehouse would suit our purposes."

"What purposes?" I asked.

"To perform an inspection, nothing more. Billy Mabele will not buy a pile of gold without first ensuring it's the real deal. He'll get his gold man," Chandler pointed at himself, "to do a spot check. That is only natural and is expected by the mark. But it achieves something else."

Chandler lifted a cup to reveal the ice cube.

"It shows him where the ball is," said Robyn.

"Exactly." Chandler replaced the mug over the ice cube

and moved the other mugs to the side so that our focus was on the mug with the ice. "And having inspected the gold, it goes into escrow – we get a third-party security company to keep it locked up to make sure the mark doesn't switch it out for a pile of lead, and the mark keeps eyes on it. Billy Mabele transfers the money – that only takes a few hours – and the security company delivers the gold to him. They could sail the valuable stuff fifteen nautical miles out to sea. That way the transfer takes place in international waters where nobody can do a thing to stop it."

"I don't do sea," said Fat-Boy. "Almost died the last time. I'm not doing it again."

"You won't need to," said Chandler with a smile. "Because we don't care if they sail it out to sea. It won't get to that stage of the transaction because Billy Mabele won't be transferring any money, will he? Therefore the gold will not be sent to sea. It will remain locked up in the third-party security safes. When the penny drops and Lebogang Madikwe realises he will not ever be paid, he will open up the safes where the gold has been locked away, and will find ..." Chandler lifted the mug under which he'd placed the ice cube, "... nothing."

The ice cube was no longer there.

"How d'you do that?" demanded Fat-Boy, impressed despite himself.

Chandler gave another thin smile. He lifted another mug to reveal the ice cube.

"A magician should never reveal his secret," he said. "But seeing as you are going to have to perform this trick yourself ..."

"The ice that fell to the floor was not the original block of ice," said Robyn before Chandler could reveal his secret.

"Exactly." Chandler beamed at her.

Fat-Boy looked confused. "We'd better start practising," he said. "Gonna need a bunch of ice. Whaddaya say we open up the wet bar and get ourselves some ice?"

———

Lebogang Madikwe called Billy Mabele in person later in the day because he realised Billy was a man who didn't like to deal through underlings. Billy Mabele said that he was indeed a man who didn't like to deal through underlings, even if they were called Justice. Lebogang Madikwe suggested lunch and Billy proposed the Lord Nelson Restaurant, which we had reconnoitred earlier. It was all very straightforward. Nobody mentioned gold, frustrated fences, or barges hijacked at sea.

Chandler booked a table at the Lord Nelson Restaurant, and pre-ordered five ostrich meat burgers because Fat-Boy didn't see the point of having a burger that could be consumed with a single bite. Chandler also arranged a lunch of his own with a retired Rhodesian soldier he had fought beside before my time.

"Isn't he a retired Zimbabwean soldier?" I asked. "Don't we call Rhodesia Zimbabwe now?"

"We do," said Chandler, "but he was a soldier in the Rhodesian army, not the Zimbabwean one. The Rhodesian army lost the war – you don't start wearing the other team's jersey just because they hold the trophy."

The Rhodesian soldier was co-founder of a specialist transport company called Fidelity Cash Delivery. Chandler wanted to remind his friend over lunch of the good old days when they had fought beside one another, and ask him what the possibilities were of us borrowing one of his armoured vehicles – which were used to transport cash around the country, and were the closest thing you could get to a military tank without needing the resources of a national treasury. Chandler had decided that we needed one for Fat-Boy's plan and his three-cup trick to work.

Robyn and I had been instructed to keep out of sight of Lebogang and his entourage, and so we worked on some details in my small room while Billy and Lebogang took their lunch. Robyn had two different coloured markers, and she was drawing routes on a large-scale plan of the docks. We had marked several potential routes, all of which started at the only quay on the outskirts of the yacht club long enough to accommodate the ninety-metre yacht that Fat-Boy and I had seen floating in Saldanha Bay. The routes ended at the Dark Bizness warehouse, two kilometres from the yacht club, although the distance varied, depending on which of the circuitous routes was chosen.

"You're in trouble," said Robyn when we'd finished marking the routes. She looked up at me, her eyes flashing with what seemed like anger. "Aren't you, Ben?"

"Of course not," I said.

She shook her head with irritation.

"Stop," she said, holding up a hand as if about to direct traffic. "Stop with all the sarcasm, and the jokes and your usual bullshit. I know what you were doing when those two men were killed. I sat down and took a close look at it. You were with us – it wasn't hard to figure it out – even Fat-Boy's conviction that you killed them was shaken."

She paused, and her anger stepped up a notch.

"Why don't you tell the police? You could end all this nonsense in a few minutes."

"It would achieve nothing."

"Nothing? You wouldn't be facing murder charges, for one thing. You wouldn't be running from the police."

"But what would the repercussions be for you? How many skeletons do you think the police would dig out of Chandler's closet? And Fat-Boy's? Let alone the nonsense you've got up to over the years."

"That's a bullshit excuse. We can look after ourselves. What's the reason you're letting this drag on?"

"I'm not letting anything drag."

"You know who did it, don't you? You know who killed those men, but you're keeping quiet about it."

I didn't answer immediately, and the tightly wound spring of Robyn's anger snapped.

"Stop protecting everyone, Ben! The person doing this is not worth protecting – all they're doing is using you – don't you see that? They're hiding behind you. Because who better to hide behind than a known killer?"

I still said nothing. Robyn looked back down at the plan with a sigh.

"The police must know enough about what you did in the army," she said. "If they know only half of what Brian told me, they know enough."

She grabbed a different colour marker and started drawing angry question marks over the smaller alleys. I resumed my measurement of the routes and filled in the details of each with the careful precision Chandler expected.

"Sometimes you surprise me," she said after a long silence, her attention still fully on the road map. "You know you've been set up for this, don't you? You've been framed."

She looked up at me again, and the fire had faded from her eyes.

"But you're going to let them get away with it, aren't you, Ben? You're being careless, allowing the police to track you, so they will pin the blame on you. And in the end you will be the one who will pay the price."

"Don't be absurd, Robyn. I'm not a martyr."

Robyn smiled.

"Denial of martyrdom is the mark of a true martyr. You should remember that the next time you decide to martyr yourself."

TWENTY-FOUR

Fat-Boy, playing the role of Billy Mabele with enthusiasm, invited Lebogang Madikwe to share his concerns over their ten ostrich burgers (Lebogang had concurred with him about portion size and considered the five burgers a selfish pre-order on Billy Mabele's part). Lebogang Madikwe told Billy about the items of value that were in his possession and wondered aloud how such items of value might become the property of someone rather like Billy. Billy in turn explained if those items of value were to find their way to him, he would have his metals expert verify their value, and that it would be a good idea to then hold them in a sealed vehicle until some form of financial exchange could be made, after which they would be taken to sea and become the property of himself.

"You like the sea?" Lebogang had asked him.

"I don't do sea," responded Billy. "What kind of Xhosa does sea?"

Lebogang suggested Billy didn't have a big enough boat and explained that the only reason he went to sea was because he had a particularly big boat.

At which point they had ordered their third beer, loosened their belts to accommodate for them, and Lebogang had confessed that he was not experienced in the manner of transporting these particular items of value. He asked for Billy Mabele's recommendation. Billy mentioned armoured cash transport vehicles, dropped the name of a reliable company, and suggested they meet the next day to discuss the details in the Presidential Suite, which had a wet bar that would be open for their pleasure. Lebogang said that suited him, although he was not in a rush – he would need five days to get the items of value ready. Billy was magnanimous and suggested three days. They had ordered a fourth beer each and asked for the dessert menu.

Over dessert Lebogang had told Billy Mabele how much he reminded him of his late brother, and Billy Mabele had commiserated with him over his recent loss, a few tears had been shed, more beer had been ordered, and the two men had emerged from their lunch on unsteady feet with an arm each about the other's shoulders, and the promise of mutually beneficial business ahead.

Even Chandler had to admit that Fat-Boy had delivered a consummate performance.

"We are magicians," Chandler reminded us in the briefing before the meeting of the titans in the Presidential Suite the next day.

"I thought we were crooks," said Fat-Boy.

"Magicians pull off their tricks by misdirection. They get their audience to focus on the right hand while the left hand is doing the mischief."

"I don't get it," said Fat-Boy.

"We need Lebo to focus on the wrong thing," said Robyn.

"Exactly," said Chandler. "He needs to be entirely

focused on the logistics of the handover so that he doesn't worry about the inspection. Tell me you understand the process."

"The handover is when he takes the gold out to sea, after we pay him for it."

"That's right. Of course he won't do the handover, because we won't pay him. And the inspection?"

"Where I bring my gold man in to check the gold is real."

"Full marks. Emphasise that the handover is his call. Let him focus on that. Give him free rein. He can do it in whatever way he wants. International waters, but you are happy to be told the exact manner of it."

"I thought we didn't care about the handover? We're not paying him; there won't be a handover. Why do we care about the handover?"

"We don't," said Chandler, and he sighed.

"We get him to focus on the handover so that he doesn't pay attention to what happens at the inspection," said Robyn.

"Correct. He will be so worried about the handover," emphasised Chandler, "that he won't notice what we're doing on the way to the inspection."

"Is that wet bar wet, Angel?" asked Fat-Boy, looking over at me with desperation. "All stocked up and ready to go?"

"Fully stocked," I confirmed.

"I don't think you're paying attention, Fat-Boy," protested Chandler.

"I'm getting into my role, Colonel. This is how Billy Mabele likes to roll. He starts the day with a beer. I'll take my first one now, Angel."

I passed Fat-Boy a bottle of beer from the fridge. He

popped the cap off the bottle by holding it against the writing desk that had been in the original hotel when it was built in 1899, and delivered a swift downward blow with his powerful left fist. Chandler winced. The desk was only slightly splintered in the process. Fat-Boy licked a finger and rubbed the gash of splintered wood with it.

"Why does he need five days to get the gold to us?" I asked.

"He's got it on a boat," said Fat-Boy. "You know he has. We saw his big fuck-off boat. Boats move real slow, Angel. Didn't you know that?"

"We could do that trip in a sailboat in twelve hours. That big boat of his could do it in a quarter of the time. I don't understand why he needs five days."

Fat-Boy shrugged. "If it makes you happy I'll give him two days."

"We need more time than that," said Chandler. "Don't push too hard, he'll get suspicious."

"My homeboy Lebo isn't suspicious," said Fat-Boy. "He's taken to me like a brother."

"Don't be so sure – he didn't get to where he is by being gullible. Hit me with questions, Fat-Boy. What are his objections going to be?"

Fat-Boy took a deep draught of his beer and belched.

"I'll handle it, Colonel, don't worry."

"Suggest the Fidelity truck as an afterthought. Don't push it. Mention you've used them, but leave it at that."

"You've told me all this, Colonel, I'll be fine."

"One false move and your homeboy will walk out of here, Fat-Boy. Let's do this properly."

Fat-Boy took another draught of beer and belched again.

"I make the first bit seem easy," he said.

"That's right. Getting the gold onto land and into their warehouse is the easy bit. Laugh it off, make it seem simple. Nothing to worry about. It will be his men with the Fidelity truck, eyes on it all the way to their warehouse. What are his questions?"

"What if he doesn't want to use his warehouse?"

"Be open to any suggestion he has. We can always change location, but remind him about the roadblocks. He doesn't want to leave the docks with that gold in the back of the truck."

"What if he wants his men to ride in the truck with the gold?"

"No can do, it's not even an option. No discussion – tell him the back is air tight. Does he want his men dying of asphyxiation?"

"What if he wants to use one of his own trucks?"

"Laugh at the suggestion. Is he going to risk all that gold in a tin can truck that carries bottles of women's ointments? The Fidelity trucks are like military tanks. They are giant safes on wheels, that's what you tell him. Once the gold is loaded into the truck, it is safe. Those beasts can withstand mortar attacks; you can throw grenades at them."

Fat-Boy drank some more beer.

"I've got it, Colonel, it's gonna to be easy as pie."

"Play it carefully, Fat-Boy. Don't be overconfident."

Fat-Boy blew through his lips so they flapped in the wind to show what he thought of that.

"We need a few days, but not more than a week," said Chandler. "Don't give him too long to snoop around and ask questions or try to dig up more of your background. It's pretty thin."

"I'll give him two days," said Fat-Boy. "Let's get this show on the road."

"Two days is not enough. Five days is what we need."

Which was why we had two days for our preparations. The meeting between the two men went surprisingly well. Lebogang arrived on time, and the two muscle-bound men he had brought with him for protection were given fizzy drinks from the wet bar and waited in the corridor while Lebogang and Billy bonded in the comfort of the Presidential Suite. Lebogang was reminded afresh of how much Billy Mabele resembled his younger brother, and Billy Mabele's eyes watered at the thought of Lebogang's brother's demise. The wet bar turned out to have an inadequate supply of beer, but room service promptly refreshed that supply. Billy explained to Lebogang that the handover of the gold was entirely in his hands. He mentioned the need for a secure vehicle in passing and laughed at the suggestion that one of the Dark Bizness delivery vans would serve the purpose. He warned Lebogang of the dangers of people throwing grenades, and told a surprisingly moving story of the Fidelity Cash Delivery driver who had survived two separate cash heists in which he had bravely fought to defend the cash that they were transporting – it had been Billy's cash – only to be crushed to death by the truck when he forgot to engage the parking brake.

Lebogang left the Presidential Suite two hours and six beers later and was supported all the way to his Mercedes Benz by his protection.

Chandler was furious because we needed more than two days, but Fat-Boy said that was how black men rolled, and that the old white fogeys would just have to speed up. Chandler pointed out that the only thing Fat-Boy rolled was his substantial stomach, from the sauna to the jacuzzi and back again, with intermittent stops at the bar for refreshment. While Chandler, Robyn and I would do all the work.

Or more accurately, as I pointed out, Chandler would instruct Robyn and me, who were the only ones who ever actually did anything.

———

A Fidelity Cash Delivery representative visited the Dark Bizness offices the next morning, arriving punctually at ten-hundred, presumably with a glossy brochure of their Bulu-gaya armoured cash delivery vehicles under his arm, and departed a mere twenty-eight minutes later. Fidelity Cash Delivery had twenty-three identical vehicles in their fleet, manufactured locally and designed in response to the rash of cash-in-transit heists which had horrified the South African public with their brutality: the gangs behind the heists had known no bounds in their violent efforts to break open the inadequate shells of the imported vehicles, pelting them with semi-automatic gunfire, throwing grenades at them, setting them alight and even dropping them off bridges, usually with the driver and passenger trapped inside and unable to use their own weapons, because bullet-proof glass works both ways. The designers at Bulugaya responded to the demand for something stronger by creating monstrous vehicles that looked like the unfortunate result of a breeding experiment between a military tank and a Mars rover. Their steel bodies were three inches thick; the windows were no more than menacing reflective slits, with the barrels of built-in AK-74 rifles bristling beside them. GP-25 grenade launchers could be fitted onto the AK-74s should the need arise. The tyres of the vehicles could with-stand direct gunfire, and in the event of loss of pressure in the tyre the wheel rims had protruding spikes that would provide an uncomfortable, but effective, ride out of trouble.

Robyn and I were given a guided tour of one of these vehicles when we visited the Fidelity Cash Delivery showroom that afternoon. The rentals representative, a snivelling man who combed his thinning hair over the bald top of his head, pulled his eyes away from Robyn's taut top, which was being pushed forward by the wire-framed bra she was wearing for the purpose of distracting him, and assured me that the vehicles were entirely identical, before returning his gaze to Robyn's top.

"Except for the arrangement of the security boxes in the back," I suggested, but he dragged his eyes away again to assure me they were identical in every sense.

"What if we need to make changes to our booking?" I asked. "You know the movie business, the creatives are always changing their minds about something."

"You would phone us," said the rentals representative. "The girls upstairs will make the changes, or if it's a small change, they'll just do it on the booking sheet."

"I see. And where are those booking sheets kept?"

The rentals representative frowned. Robyn took a deep breath, as though my peculiar questions were driving her to distraction. She let the breath out in a heavy sigh, all of which did interesting things to the surface tension of her thin blouse, which distracted the rentals representative sufficiently for him to provide me with an answer.

"Manager's cubicle," he said, pointing across the football-field of a room with the top of his bald head while keeping his eyes on Robyn in case she did any more breathing exercises.

We climbed into the back of the truck with him and he showed us the rows of boxes of varying sizes in burnished steel with keyhole locks like the boxes of a bank vault, which were fixed to the back wall. The sides comprised larger boxes with black matte finish and bold black numbers on shiny aluminium tags. These larger boxes were of greater interest to us, there being thirty-six of them, each with enough capacity to hold a single smart Mactwinbox which the representative assured us was the best way to transport our cash safely because at the press of a button the cash could be destroyed, thus deterring thieves. Vandals not interested in keeping the cash for themselves could be deterred by the gas that would be released into the rear compartment of the truck and which damaged the nerves – in a few unfortunate cases that nerve damage had proved fatal. I knew that a Mactwinbox was a little larger than four London Good Delivery bars of gold because Chandler and I had done the math after his lunch with the Rhodesian co-founder of Fidelity Cash Delivery. So I agreed with the representative that the side boxes were the more interesting ones. Encouraged by this, the representative demonstrated the remote locking process for the side boxes, and showed us how the boxes could all be locked down in case of emergency, so nobody could get inside them, not even with a welding torch or a bomb. Then he jangled some keys anxiously and told me, after a surreptitious glance at Robyn's breasts, that they allowed no one but authorised drivers behind the wheel of their Bulugaya trucks, which is why he was confused by the instruction he had received from his boss to allow us a test drive.

"We're making a movie," I explained. "We're not going to be using the truck for anything but a bit of play-acting."

"She the actress?" he asked me, but looked at Robyn, who kept her shoulders back, pushed her chest forward and declared that she was the actress, and needed to ensure that she could drive the truck.

"You don't use stunt drivers?" asked the man, but it

wasn't a question that was going to impede his climbing into the passenger seat of the truck to watch Robyn drive it. The truck started with a roar, then settled to a low growl as Robyn figured out all the levers with the assistance of the rentals representative, whose hair had flopped off the top of his head in all the excitement.

Robyn closed the door, then showed off a little by double clutching as she shifted from first into second gear and the monstrous truck crawled towards the louvre door, which rolled open as she approached it. The truck crouched at the entrance as the afternoon sun sneaked in below the louvres. Tyres squeaked on the tiled floor as she pulled off. A startlingly bright indicator flashed, and then they were gone. The louvred door rolled closed again and plunged the vast room into gloom as I walked across to the manager's glass cubicle in the corner. A man was sitting there with his feet up on the desk, his hands folded neatly across his abdomen and his chin resting on his chest. I knocked politely on the glass and he awoke with a start, then glared at me.

"You have a booking for the day after tomorrow," I said. "Dark Bizness is the company. It's a pickup in the docks."

"What if I do?" said the man, as he shuffled some papers that his feet had been resting upon across the desk. His hair was an explosion of tightly curled dreadlocks, which were trussed up with an elasticized band in the yellow, green, and black of the ANC flag. His chin had a straggle of patchy hair.

"I need to make a minor change to the location," I said, trying not to stare at the nascent beard. I gave a small, regretful smile. "Not a big change, it's just around the corner. We're not able to get the yacht into the usual spot, so we have to move it."

"And who are you?" asked the man.

"I'm with Dark Bizness," I said and produced the card we had printed that morning with the Dark Bizness logo and a name I'd already forgotten. The man took the card and tested it with his thumb to see if it had hidden compartments.

"Why are you here?" he asked. "They do those changes upstairs."

"It's such an insignificant change they told me to come down here and make it on the booking sheet."

The man with the hairy chin looked at me. I looked back at him. In the history of Fidelity Cash Delivery this situation had not previously arisen, and hairy chin was probably searching his marijuana-soaked mind for some reference from his inadequate training as to what to do.

"Just a tiny change," I said, and kept the smile going.

Hairy chin looked down at his papers and used a stained finger to page through a bunch of them in a cardboard folder. He found one that grabbed his interest and pulled it out.

"Yacht club," he said.

"That's the one. Cannot get the yacht in, so we're doing the load around the corner. Still in the docks."

Hairy chin picked up a pen.

"Address?" he said.

"I have GPS coordinates."

"If that's what floats your boat."

Writing the string of digits onto the booking sheet took us some time, and then we both checked them to be sure.

"Those cardboard boxes," I said. "The pre-folded ones we saw in the brochure, the ones that fit into the side lockers, and that seal when you close them. Did the boss order some of those?"

Hairy chin looked down at the booking sheet and shook his head.

"Could you add them? We'll need thirty, perhaps a few extra in case something goes wrong."

"If it floats your boat," he said, and marked the booking sheet.

"What's the time set for?" I asked.

"Early," he said, and looked up at me. "You need to change that too?" His eyes narrowed with the beginnings of suspicion.

"Depends how early," I said.

"Six-thirty."

"Perfect," I said, "that's perfect."

I could feel his eyes on my back as I walked across the vast room and disappeared into the gloom.

"That actress of yours," said the rentals representative when he climbed out of the cab, his hair still hanging lopsidedly like a piece of him was peeling off, "she sure can drive."

"She's not really mine," I said, "but I know what you mean. You should see her doing it in uniform. That is truly convincing."

The rental representative realised his hair was peeling off, and so he flattened it back over his bald head with a practised move of the hand, and wet his lips at the thought of what Robyn might be capable of in uniform.

"You get customers requesting particular drivers?" I asked. "Like wanting a woman or a man, you know: being specific."

The rentals representative had been watching Robyn walk over to us, but he looked back at me with some suspicion. "Sometimes," he said. "More often a man than a woman."

"Unless they like women in uniforms," I suggested and smiled to show how well I understood that kind of thing.

"I suppose so," he said.

"I guess they just call the girls upstairs?"

"Yes. They call the girls upstairs."

"Speaking of uniforms, we'll need a couple of your staff uniforms – do you provide them yourselves, or is that a separate company?"

Regretfully, for the rentals representative, that was a separate company, but he provided us with the details.

"Could you throw in some of those pre-folded self-sealing cardboard boxes? We'll need about thirty of them. We'll collect them tomorrow if we can, that way we can get everything packed up ahead of time."

"Sure can," said the representative, and his eyes lingered for a last moment on Robyn's upper portion as he marked the details on the booking sheet.

"You should wear that bra more often," I said to Robyn as we left him to his paperwork and squeaked our rubber-soled shoes across the tiled floor to the exits. "There would be no limit to what you could achieve."

"How do you think I snared you?" she said.

"My interest in you runs deeper than your breasts."

"Does it?" she said, and smiled at me as she pulled her shoulders back.

TWENTY-FIVE

At oh-six-thirty on the appointed day, Robyn brought the monstrous truck to a halt at the far end of the Nkwenya wharf. We were both wearing the full uniform of the Fidelity Cash Delivery driver-and-stooge pairs that risked their lives every day to carry other people's cash around. Our uniforms included the excessive helmets worn when valuable things needed to be carried through marauding crowds, so there was slim chance that anyone would recognise us. We had provided our own weapons and substituted the standard issue Berettas with our preferred Glocks, but otherwise we looked pretty damn convincing, and I knew the rentals representative would have been impressed if he had been there to witness the sight of Robyn driving his armoured vehicle in full uniform.

A Dark Bizness minion who carried an AK-47 over his shoulder like it was a satchel, greeted us at the entrance to the yacht club. He explained that his boss required that we remain in the vehicle while he and his colleagues did the loading, and we said that suited us fine. Robyn climbed out of the cab and opened up the back to show him how to fold the cardboard boxes that would fit perfectly into the side compartments and how to seal them. He said that the boss had not mentioned cardboard boxes, and she said we strongly recommended that they should place their items of value into the boxes and seal them to avoid damage. He countered by stating that their items could not be damaged, but Robyn won the round by suggesting what his boss would do to him if by chance there was any damage, such as when a passing vandal tossed a grenade under the truck. At which point he capitulated, explained where the new Nkwenya wharf for obscenely opulent yachts was situated, and then walked ahead of us to ensure that security booms were lifted and nothing impeded our path.

Robyn turned the truck around so that the rear end faced the sleek contours of the huge Dark Maiden yacht, then she remotely unlocked the rear doors. We tilted our seats as far back as they would go, and settled in to witness the rays of sunlight dribbling down the face of Table Mountain like someone was spilling luminous pink paint from the heavy cloud settling over the top of it.

Three Dark Bizness minions had been charged with transferring the gold from the yacht into the armoured truck, and it took them a while to figure out how to do it. There was a good deal of banging and cursing from the back of the truck as they discovered how heavy four London Good Delivery bars are when packed into a cardboard box, but eventually they figured out that carrying the bars individually in a relay style was the best way of doing things and they settled into a comfortable routine.

Chandler called to check on our progress when we were about ten minutes into the loading, and I told him we looked to be on track to finish in about an hour.

"Any sign of the big boy?" asked Chandler.

"None yet."

"I'll get Fat-Boy onto him. We don't want him climbing into the truck to salivate over his gold at the other end."

Chandler called back five minutes later.

"All arranged," he said. "Fat-Boy's speaking to him now. We'll test the group call. You doing this through that helmet of yours?"

"I am," I said. "They're damn uncomfortable." Our helmets had built-in headphones and a microphone with Bluetooth links to our phones. Chandler connected Robyn to the call.

"I'm testing it's all working," he said.

"We tested it yesterday," said Robyn. "Three times."

"The devil is in the details," said Chandler, then ended the call before Robyn could tell him not to sweat the small stuff, which was their standard routine.

"Don't sweat the small stuff," Robyn said to me.

"That's right," I said. "Keep an open mind and be ready to adapt to changing circumstances."

I knew how important these little routines were to her. Like the checklists a pilot runs through before take-off, they prepared our minds. She lifted the visor of her helmet so that I could see her eyes, and I marvelled at their clarity.

"You nervous?" she asked.

I lifted my own visor so that she could see my calm sincerity.

"Not a bit," I said. "What could possibly go wrong?"

———

Lebogang Madikwe arrived in his stretched Mercedes Benz twenty minutes later. He carried his stomach before him like an enormous balloon that he was struggling to get his arms around. I watched him proceed down the wharf towards us, a bodyguard to each side, and was struck again by the physical similarity he bore to Fat-Boy. Lebogang passed right by my narrow slit of a window, but he didn't look in – his attention, and that of his bodyguards – was drawn inexorably to the glinting bars being loaded into the back of the truck. He shouted something in Xhosa, and the loading process halted. There followed a stream of Xhosa with its surprising pops and clicks as he probably criticised what they were doing and maybe scolded them for sealing the gold into cardboard boxes where he couldn't see it. Then the truck rocked on its suspension as he climbed up into the rear compartment, and there was a profound silence as he took in the sight of the boxes and the gold bars being packed.

I phoned Chandler and told him the big boy had arrived and was inspecting the gold.

"Good," said Chandler. "Let him indulge himself. You all set?"

"Just about, loading the last of it now. The roadblock ready?"

"They've ripped the tar up, and are busy digging a great dirty hole in the road."

"Less than an hour to go," I said.

"We'll be ready," said Chandler, and ended the call. Some people like to end their phone conversations with a closing comment, good wishes, or a reference to the next contact, but Chandler was not one of those people. He preferred a cliff-hanger.

"What's up?" asked Robyn. "You're not usually this nervous."

"Do you think that man has bought Fat-Boy's act?" I asked.

"He's loading the gold into the truck, isn't he? It wouldn't have gone this far if he didn't believe him. What's wrong?"

"It's been too easy."

"Things don't need to be hard, Ben. Sometimes good things are easy."

She smiled at me, and despite myself, I wished it were true.

TWENTY-SIX

It took the underlings only another half an hour to complete the loading process under the watchful eye of Lebogang who, having been mesmerised by his glittering bounty, stood on the wharf like an enlarged beach ball and gazed greedily at his men as they worked.

The truck shook as the rear doors were closed, and then a lackey banged on Robyn's door. She closed her visor, opened a narrow slit of window and looked down at him.

"You can lock it?" he said. "There's no lock on the door."

"Sure can," she said, and pressed a button on the dashboard. Three loud beeps sounded.

"Follow us," said the lackey, and he pointed to a black Mercedes Benz, which was doing an eight-point turn on the wharf ahead of us.

"No problem," said Robyn, and she closed the window as the first heavy drops of rain struck. The man ducked his head down and jogged up to the Mercedes. By the time he reached the car, it was coming down in sheets.

"You know where the windscreen wipers are?" I asked

as Robyn started the engine with a roar. She didn't answer, but flicked a switch and the wipers cleared the front windscreen, their motor making a high-pitched whine.

"This will work in our favour," I said, and Robyn nodded. I realised her adrenalin was up, and could feel the familiar tingling in my fingers that announced the start of the main act.

I called Chandler and told him we were rolling. He started shouting instructions to his team before I ended the call. We were at the top end of the wharf when he called back and connected Robyn to the call.

"The big boy behind or in front?" he asked.

"Behind," I said, and checked in the side mirror that the stretched Mercedes was following us, two rings of LED lights glittering through the curtain of rain.

"Couldn't be better timing," said Chandler. "The rain will work in our favour."

I smiled at that and whispered to Robyn about my being little more than an echo of Chandler. Robyn didn't smile. She stared ahead at the road, then twisted her head from one side to the other to ease the tension in her neck.

Chandler kept the call open, and I announced each of the landmarks we had identified on the route. Robyn handled the truck with her usual steady confidence. She kept up with the lead car on the first straight stretch out of the yacht club, then fell back as if the truck was struggling to maintain speed. The lead car took a few seconds to notice that we were falling back, which is what we wanted, and as it slowed down to allow us to catch up Robyn tapped the brake to surprise the car behind us, then accelerated again, easing her foot at the last moment so that we nearly rammed into the back of the car ahead, which gave that driver a nasty surprise and he accelerated away. Both cars gave us a little more space after that.

The first of the road workers was in position eight hundred metres along the straight. He was waving his flag lazily and had his revolving sign turned to the stop position. There was a barrier across the road, and a queue of five vehicles waiting to continue in the opposite direction to us. The lead car slowed to a stop. A hand emerged from the window as the passenger remonstrated with the road worker. He dipped his head to reply and pointed with his flag at the blue arrow and detour sign. Then he made us wait a full three minutes until Chandler gave the call on the radio and he swung his sign around to the go position. The car in front of us swung across the empty lane and bounced down the small alleyway that would lead us to the maze of broken streets, alleys and dead-ends that ran between the industrial warehouses clustered around the docks. The tar was broken and patchy on these roads, and the car ahead kept slowing to crawl around potholes, then sped up again and raced ahead on the sections of good road. That was exactly what we wanted, and Robyn played it perfectly, bouncing like a ping-pong ball between the two cars, gradually expanding the distance in which we were held. Neither of the drivers seemed to notice, and the driver in front was clearly allowing his frustration to cloud his judgement as he accelerated ever more angrily away from the bad spots.

There were two more turns to make, each of them clearly signposted, with a miserably wet flag-waver showing us the way. Robyn's body tensed as we made the next turn. Then she took a deep breath and let it out steadily, like she was breathing into an alcohol tester. Her body relaxed, she eased off on the speed and I called the distance to Chandler. We had five hundred metres to go.

At two hundred metres, the dirty yellow of the road grader glowed through the haze. Behind it was our hired pantechnicon, already flashing its lights with mock frustration at the slow progress of the grader. Robyn lifted her foot from the accelerator and our speed dropped.

"First car ready to come through," I said. "Clear the way."

The indicator light of the car ahead of us was flashing impatiently and I could see the cluster of road workers rush with uncharacteristic enthusiasm into the open, getting drenched by the rain as they moved the barriers off the road. They cleared the lane, and the car made the turn, accelerating through the flooded potholes and splashing the road workers. Robyn slowed to a stop, our indicator ticking loudly. I watched the car ahead pass the eighty-metre mark where a truck with a fifteen-metre trailer reversed into the tiny road and wedged itself across it so that our lead car was hidden from view. Robyn waited like a nervous driver as the grader approached, the rhythmic clicking of our indicator filling the anxious silence. The grader was a critical thirty seconds late, but the driver was doing what we had rehearsed, slowing down as if he was going to turn, but not indicating.

"They'll stay in their car," I said. "Won't get out because of the rain. Anyway, they know their big boss is behind us."

Robyn didn't reply, she was focused on the approaching grader. It crawled towards us, still not indicating. Then Robyn kicked the accelerator pedal, and we lurched forward as if she had lost patience, and we crossed in front of the grader, our rear fender missing it by inches. Robyn lifted her foot, and we slowed to a crawl. The Mercedes Benz behind us flashed its lights, throwing a line of sparks through the rain like a warning shot. Robyn turned on her hazard lights to acknowledge them, and we crept forwards at a slow walking pace as if we were waiting for them to make the turn and catch up. The long trailer was still wedged across the road ahead, and we were now only in sight of the car behind us. I watched the progress of the grader in the side mirror. It seemed to have developed engine trouble. The huge pantechnicon behind it was flashing its lights and blaring its horn as we'd rehearsed. It couldn't pass the grader because of Lebogang's Mercedes waiting to turn. Robyn watched the screen with the rear-facing camera, and I watched in the side mirror. The grader ground to a halt a little beyond our road. The pantechnicon stopped behind it, entirely blocking the sight line of Lebogang and his driver.

"Go," I said, but Robyn had already kicked the accelerator and turned the wheel. Our truck bucked like a horse leaving the gates, and in three seconds we had bounced through the open gateway of a warehouse and taken the gaping entrance of the building like we were planning on driving through and bursting out the other side. Robyn jammed her foot on the brakes and we aquaplaned across the smooth concrete floor and twisted to the side as she lost directional control. I flung my door open and leapt out before the truck shuddered to a standstill. I sprinted across to the chain that would lower the door in manual override and yanked at it with all my strength. The gears were well oiled, we'd made sure of that. The door slid downward with a whump. As it dropped, I caught a glimpse through the rain of Chandler in the warehouse across the road. An identical Fidelity Cash Delivery vehicle was reversing out of his warehouse, hazard lights also flashing. They would take less than ten seconds to back out and turn in the direction we had been travelling.

Our warehouse had been plunged into darkness when the door closed. Robyn killed the lights of the truck, then the engine died and the sound of the rain drumming on the iron roof swelled to fill the space, accompanied by the clicking and hissing sounds of the hot engine.

Chandler's voice called for the grader to move on, and I could hear the double-click acknowledgement on the radio. Then silence, and then the growl of a large truck engine passing. The truck that had wedged itself behind the lead car had cleared the road on Chandler's cue.

This was the critical moment. If the FCD truck sitting between the two cars looked different in any way, or if one of the men in the front car had stepped out despite the rain to look around the truck that had been blocking their view, this was when we would know about it. The men in both cars had AK-47s with them and I didn't doubt they would use them.

Robyn came up beside me, her Glock held low. The silence extended. Nobody came through the door. Nothing but silence in our headphones. We waited for Chandler's word. He had sight of the road because there was no need for him to close his warehouse door: the fewer moving parts, the better.

We waited the full two minutes Chandler had specified. Then he spoke into his radio, calling a wrap on the road-works and repeating the wind-down details. Robyn lowered her weapon, and I returned mine to its holster. Robyn smiled, and I felt the adrenalin ease, although we weren't done yet.

"You going to make me stand out here in the rain?" asked Chandler's voice in our headphones.

I unlocked the small pedestrian door, and he stepped

inside, remarkably dry beneath a standard issue black umbrella. I closed the door behind him. He folded the umbrella and pulled his phone out of his grey linen jacket pocket and ended our call. We removed our helmets, and both took deep breaths. Chandler's eyes were twinkling, and his mouth was stretched in the way it did when he was pleased.

"Didn't notice a thing," he said. "I told you this rain would work in our favour."

"Let's get a box out," I said. "Fat-Boy will be here any minute."

Robyn unlocked the rear doors of the truck, then disarmed and unbolted the side compartments. She and Chandler climbed into the back, while I opened the roller door for Fat-Boy.

The rain was still falling, although it looked as if it was easing. Fat-Boy pulled his hired BMW in and I did a quick check for anyone taking an interest in what we were doing. There was nobody out in the rain, and only a few cars in the street passed by as fast as the potholed road allowed. I dropped the door again.

Fat-Boy popped the trunk and pulled the trolley with the scale out. Robyn and Chandler carried one of the cardboard boxes down together and slid it into the locker beneath the scale. The scale itself was light and didn't need the trolley to support it. But four London Good Delivery bars weigh forty-eight kilograms, and it would have looked very odd for Chandler to arrive with a portable scale that he struggled to lift out of the car.

"Can't we just show him one bar?" said Fat-Boy who was looking resplendent in an off-white bespoke suit that was imitation *Ermenegildo Zegna* all the way down to the embroidered gold-thread initials.

"You know we can't," said Chandler, as he locked the compartment beneath the scale and pocketed the key.

Fat-Boy pouted at us while we lifted the trolley back into the trunk. Then he climbed into the passenger seat. Chandler settled behind the wheel. I opened the roller door, and they drove off towards the Dark Bizness warehouse. They would take the direct route, ignoring the fake diversion signs we had posted, and would arrive less than two minutes after the other FCD truck with its entourage of Lebogang and his underlings.

———

Chandler called us again a minute later and reminded us not to move until he gave the all-clear. I confirmed and muted my microphone. Robyn turned the truck around and we sat in the murky dark of the empty warehouse and waited.

"You see that uniform on Robs?" we heard Fat-Boy ask Chandler.

"I did," said Chandler.

"Damn," said Fat-Boy. "Is she a sex-bomb, or what?"

"Robyn can hear you," said Chandler. "I've opened the call to them."

"I know that," said Fat-Boy. "D'you think I would talk behind her back?" There was a pause, then he shouted, "You're looking damn sexy, Robsy."

Robyn shook her head. But I could see a glimmer of teeth in the dim glow of the dashboard instruments because we'd exchanged our helmets for single ear-buds.

"Tell Fat-Boy he needs to focus," she said. "And later we'll have a conversation about harassment."

"I'm not frightened," said Fat-Boy, when Chandler had relayed this message.

Chandler declared everything looked normal when they arrived at the Dark Bizness warehouse. The two Mercedes Benz vehicles were parked beside the FCD truck in the large space that had been cleared for the inspection. The rear doors of the truck were open. Lebogang and his minions were standing outside, looking up at it. Everything seemed completely normal. Chandler gave the command for us to move.

Robyn started our truck, and I rolled the door open again. We could hear car doors slamming through our ear-buds, then a distant call of greeting from Fat-Boy. The sounds of Chandler lifting the trolley from the trunk of the Mercedes, then the voices of Fat-Boy and Lebogang increased in volume as Chandler approached them, the wheels of the trolley squeaking under the weight of the gold bars.

"He hasn't touched it," announced Fat-Boy. "Can you believe it? My man Lebo listened to me and hasn't even touched the stuff."

"You told me not to," said Lebogang in his rich baritone. "You told me your man would want to choose one for a spot check."

"Better that way," said Chandler.

"This is Colchester," said Fat-Boy. "Colonel Colchester. He fought in the war."

"Which war?" asked Lebogang.

"There were several," said Chandler with reserve.

"Collie is my gold man," said Fat-Boy. "And my diamond man, pretty much my everything man. I insist we salute each other whenever we get together for a meeting, with him being military and all. Look at this."

There was a solemn silence – presumably Fat-Boy and Chandler were saluting each other.

"The colonel will be furious," said Robyn, as I climbed back into the truck. "He told him to drop that shit about the saluting."

"Perhaps that's Fat-Boy's secret," I said, checking my microphone was muted. "He gets away with all this play acting exactly because it is so over the top."

"Let's hope he does get away with it," said Robyn. Despite her earlier assurance that good things could be easy, I sensed she shared my growing concern that something was not right. She turned onto the road for the yacht club. The saluting performance had drawn no audible reaction from Lebogang. We heard nothing but a potentially awkward silence.

"Get up there, Collie," said Fat-Boy in a mocking voice. "Stop flapping your arms about. My man Lebo doesn't care if you're a war hero. Take your trolley, Collie, and let's look at my brother Lebo's shiny stuff."

The squeaking of the trolley wheel resumed and Fat-Boy's volume faded a little as he said, "We need to weigh it, you understand Lebo, make sure you haven't got yourselves a bunch of lead bars or some other shit that they've painted gold and shiny to fool you."

A grunt from Lebogang.

The sounds of Chandler's effort as he lifted the trolley into the back of the truck came next. Then Fat-Boy called out.

"Choose one of those boxes at random, Collie, I don't want you taking the first one you see."

"Ask the driver to unlock number twenty-three," called Chandler, and there was a silence as they sent an underling to relay that message.

"Told the drivers to stay in the vehicle," we heard Lebo-gang say distantly, "like you said Billy. Told them to stay up front. We don't want them seeing what we've got back here. I was surprised to see the driver's a woman."

"Is she?" said Fat-Boy. "In uniform?"

"Yes. They are both in uniform."

There was another silence. Robyn and I pulled up to the yacht club entrance and Robyn explained to security that we were back for the second load, and helped him find the record of our initial entry, which saved him the trouble of having to fill in the details again.

"That's it," called Chandler, and we heard him press the release button on one of the side compartments. It would be the one they'd left empty when they loaded the truck with the boxes we'd filled with plaster and chunks of lead the night before.

Robyn turned away from Nkwenya wharf, but nobody seemed to notice. And we rolled slowly towards the low-slung structures that housed the lock-up storerooms used by yacht owners for the detritus that yachts inevitably gather.

"Let's get up there and take a look," said Fat-Boy.

"I'd be surprised if they both fit," I said.

"It'll be a squeeze," agreed Robyn, and she gave a tight smile.

"Only way to open these boxes," said Fat-Boy. "Isn't that right, Collie?"

"With a knife, Mister Mabele, that's correct. They are tamper-proof, see? Have to throw it away after you open it. Which is why you should leave the boxes sealed. Usually the transport people provide an extra box or two so we can repack this one."

"Look at that," interrupted Fat-Boy in an awestruck voice. "There it is. Beautiful. There is no other word for it."

A silence ensued. Robyn found our lock-up and reversed the truck up to the door while I unlocked it.

"Let's see how much this baby weighs," said Chandler. Another long silence with an occasional beep as he calibrated the digital scale.

Robyn unlocked the rear door of our truck and released the side compartments. I brought the motorised loader up into position, and the two of us started unloading the remaining twenty-nine boxes. It would be some time before we could take the gold back out to sea, and Chandler had reasoned this was the safest place to store it. No additional security records involving an FCD van, no exposure to searches when leaving the docks, and convenient for loading onto a boat when the time came.

"That doesn't look quite right," said Chandler.

"What d'you mean, Collie? It's not gold?"

"Well, it's marked as ninety-nine point eight purity, and the weight should be ... no, sorry, my mistake. Let's recalibrate." Further beeps ensued. The tension was palpable.

Robyn and I unloaded and stacked four boxes before Chandler spoke again.

"There we go ... perfect," he exclaimed, and Fat-Boy gave a whoop.

"It's the real shit?" asked Fat-Boy. "That what you saying, Collie?"

"Ninety-nine point eight percent pure gold," said Chandler.

"Looks like you got yourself some good shit here, Lebo," said Fat-Boy. "Check the others, Collie."

"The other boxes, Mister Mabele?"

"Of course not the other boxes, you idiot. My brother needs the other boxes sealed and locked up tight in this truck. Cannot have a pile of shiny golden bars sitting around while you wait for the money to come through, can you, Lebo? A pile like that could stretch the concept of trust in your men further than you'd want to."

"It's not my men I mistrust," said Lebogang. "You seen those metal things they carry? Your war hero knows what they do even if you don't, Billy. If you wanna take the boxes without paying for them, you'll have to send an army, not a couple of drivers."

"Just weigh the other three bars we've got here, Collie," said Fat-Boy. His facetiously confident tone had dropped a notch.

There were a few more beeps and Chandler muttered "Good ... that's good ... that one too." Then he said, "Looks like we got a full house here, Mister Mabele. You've got some pure London Good Delivery gold bars here."

Fat-Boy whooped again and there was the sound of something soft being hit, which I guessed was Lebogang's round shoulder receiving an embrace from Fat-Boy.

"Pack those bars up, Collie," said Fat-Boy. "My brother Lebo and I need to go have a talk, where the children can't hear us, don't we Lebo?"

"I want to do it," said Lebo in a breathless voice.

"You can't be bothering yourself with that shit, Lebo. The packing and carrying is for the workers, we've got bigger things to deal with."

"I want to. I want to touch it again, feel the weight of it."

There was a silence and some shuffling sounds. Robyn and I paused in our labours.

"Something is wrong," said Robyn. "You think he's noticed it's not the same truck?"

"Maybe he just wants to hold it. Fat-Boy's like that, enjoys looking at it and holding it in his hands."

"It's a good feeling," said Fat-Boy, as if he'd heard what I'd said. "You're right, brother Lebo, feels good."

"It's what destroyed our country, Billy, this heavy, shiny metal. It destroyed our land, you know that?"

"I thought it was the white people that did that," said Fat-Boy, and Lebogang laughed, although his laughter, like the tone of their banter, sounded strained.

"Not suspicious," said Robyn hopefully, "just greedy."

The conclusion of the packing of the gold was heralded by satisfied sighs and grunts from Lebogang and Fat-Boy, and then Fat-Boy instructed Chandler to return the box to its compartment.

"No need," said Lebogang, and he called something out in Xhosa.

"You need to wait for the money transfer to come through," protested Fat-Boy. "Don't send the truck off now. Is that man taking photographs? No photos, Lebo, what are you playing at?"

"There's been a change of plan," said Lebogang. "We're taking the gold out to sea now. Someone's waiting for it. Let's me and you go have that talk." It was a simple suggestion, but a menacing one.

"Photos?" I said. Robyn shrugged.

I unmuted my microphone. "All good?" I asked, but there was only the sound of the trolley wheel, which didn't squeak so much as Chandler rolled it back and lifted it into the trunk of the car. He said nothing, not even a whisper.

A moment later we heard the FCD truck start up, and the beeping as it reversed out of the warehouse. Robyn and I hastened the offloading of our boxes, pushing the loader to its limit, my anxiety increasing with each passing minute. Then we locked the storeroom with a flimsy padlock that wouldn't withstand a blow from a carpenter's hammer, so as not to attract attention, and climbed back into our armoured truck. Robyn started the engine in silence, and we rolled to the end of the alley between the lock-ups. We had placed spare clothing in lockers at the yacht club, and the plan was to change now and disappear. But we needed the go-ahead from Chandler. And there had still been no word or sound from him. It would have been comforting to know whether he still had Fat-Boy in sight, or whether they'd disappeared into some room where Lebogang was pulling out Fat-Boy's fingernails. But I guessed Chandler would not risk being seen speaking.

"Photos?" I said again.

"Why has he sent the truck off without waiting for payment?" asked Robyn. The two of us looked at each other for a moment. Then Robyn turned the wheel in the other direction and gunned the engine so that we bounced down the narrow track back towards the yacht club entrance.

Finally, Chandler spoke.

"We have a problem," he said, his voice sounding calm.

Then the sound of Lebogang's deep voice came softly through the ear-buds. It was soft because he was standing a long way from Chandler, but the fury in his voice was not muted. A moment later came the sound of a fist hitting bone and a grunt of pain. Then several more blows.

It sounded like Chandler was not fighting back. I knew that he was not armed and could win any punching match against Lebogang. But you don't demonstrate your fighting skills before a team of poorly trained soldiers holding automatic weapons if you want to survive. There were the sounds of more punches, then a booming crack on the microphone as Chandler hit the floor and his ear-bud was shaken loose.

Then Lebogang was calling out instructions in Xhosa,

and there came the sounds of men exerting themselves. Were they carrying Chandler? Or tying him up?

Then Lebogang's voice, close to the microphone and full of malice. "Your fat friend has changed sides. You understand? Me and him are keeping the gold for ourselves. Find your other friends and start running. Run far away. You hear me?"

The sound of a slap.

"You hear me? If we see any of you again, my men will shoot first and ask questions later. You hear me?"

An indistinct mumble from Chandler. Then the sounds of feet running, what might have been Fat-Boy's distant voice calling out. Doors slamming, and engines starting.

"Still there, Angel?" Chandler's voice was a little muffled.

"On our way," I said, and our truck lurched forwards as the booms at the entrance to the yacht club opened and Robyn flattened the accelerator.

TWENTY-SEVEN

Chandler had been tied up. He was lying in a crumpled heap in the centre of the deserted warehouse. For a moment I thought he was unconscious, but he writhed and twisted as we ran up to him, trying to pick at the knots binding his feet with hands tied behind his back. I cut the ropes and the cloth that had been used to gag his mouth.

"He left men outside?" he asked, spitting more blood over his linen suit. "Tell me he posted men around the warehouse."

"Not one," I said. "Gates were open, we walked right in."

"The place is deserted," confirmed Robyn.

I helped him to his feet, but he pushed me away.

"It was just a few punches, Angel. I'm not a goddamn cripple." He stretched as if to realign the vertebrae. "What do you think that man's playing at?"

I shrugged. In the few minutes it had taken us to reach the Dark Bizness warehouse, I'd asked myself that question many times, but not come up with an answer.

"He saw us coming, didn't he?" I said.

"But why take the gold back? And what's he doing with our big boy? Did you hear him? Why that business about 'changing sides'?"

"Fat-Boy would never betray us," said Robyn. "That was sheer nonsense. He said it so we wouldn't go after him to get Fat-Boy back."

Chandler nodded, his eyes flickering from one to the other of us, as if he might find some answers if he looked hard enough.

"Robyn takes the truck," he said, "Angel and I take the BM. We'll rendezvous at the gold. If Fat-Boy's given anything away, we'll find them there."

"He won't have," said Robyn.

"In which case we'll go from there and get our boy back."

Robyn nodded, turned sharply and strode back to the truck.

"From the beginning, you think?" Chandler asked me as we reached the BMW. "That first evening when Fat-Boy gatecrashed the brother's wake? You think he saw us coming then?"

"Probably. It's the only thing that makes any sense."

"Robyn!"

Robyn was already climbing into the truck. She paused and turned back to us. Fat-Boy had been absolutely right about the way she looked in that uniform.

"We're going to get our boy back, you hear me?"

"I hear you, Colonel," said Robyn.

"Questions later. We've got to act fast if we're to get him back."

"Yessir," said Robyn, and she swung herself up into the driver's seat.

———

"What do you think, corporal?" asked Chandler, as we followed the FCD truck through the wet streets back to the lock-up. "How do the three of us fight our way through dozens of trigger-happy, wannabe soldiers, find our boy on that floating gin palace, then get him out again?"

"There's only one way," I said, after giving it some thought. "It has to be the Greek way."

"Greek? You mean we make ourselves a Trojan Horse? That Dark Maiden yacht is our city of Troy?"

I nodded.

"And the Trojan Horse is what?"

"That will be one of us."

"But once we get inside, how do we get back out?"

"We use the contents of that armoured truck. We know what's really inside it. When he discovers we've taken the gold, that will be our bargaining chip."

"Are you suggesting we give back the gold?"

"Yes. The gold in exchange for Fat-Boy."

"It sounds risky to me," said Chandler, but without conviction. He knew it was our only option. He looked at himself in the visor mirror, cleaning the blood off his face with a handkerchief. One blow had cut open his cheek badly enough to need stitches, and had been high enough that he would have a black eye in a few hours.

"You want to go in?" he asked. "Or shall I?"

"I'll go in, Colonel."

Chandler turned to me. I rarely called him Colonel when we were alone.

"OK, Corporal," he said. "But play it safe. We'll get only one shot at this."

———

The morning's rain had left everything soggy, with puddles of water in the access way between the rows of lock-ups. The clouds hadn't given all they had to give, and they hung low overhead, pressing down like they were going to smother us.

We abandoned the vehicles in the yacht club parking, split up and approached from different directions, carefully on foot. There was hardly any sound, only the lazy chiming of yachts' main sheets against their masts. The area around our lock-up was deserted. Fat-Boy had not betrayed the location of the gold. Chandler stopped outside the lock-up and waited for us to join him. He looked up at the heavy clouds, as if he was expecting something to fly out of them. The cut on his cheek had opened up again, and blood dripped onto his jacket.

"Run through it again," he said to the sky, after I'd explained our makeshift plan to Robyn.

"I understand it," said Robyn. "But I'm going in with Ben."

"No, you are not," said Chandler, and he gave up on the sky and turned his gaze to her.

"It will be more convincing that way, and those soldiers will be less likely to rough me up. They'll keep their distance. It's basic human instinct."

"Don't be so sure. They're not a gentlemen's club."

"And I can shoot," said Robyn. "You'll need me if the big guy doesn't like the bargain you want to make with him."

Chandler drew a breath and let it out in a sigh.

"You shoot better than most, Robyn, I won't deny you

that. But you've never shot with the intent to kill. If things go bad, we're going to have shoot to kill."

"I understand. I can do that, Colonel," said Robyn, and she held his gaze to show him how much she meant it.

Chandler gave a reluctant nod of agreement.

"Alright then. You go in together."

"I won't let you down," said Robyn.

Chandler nodded again, but he didn't look entirely convinced.

"Let me do something about that cut on your cheek," said Robyn. "We can't have you bleeding all over their nice yacht."

She went off to fetch the first aid kit from the FCD truck.

"We're a bunch of amateur clowns, aren't we?" said Chandler, watching her go. "And the biggest clown of all is me."

"Perhaps we are clowns," I said. "But the difference between us and other clowns, Colonel, is that there is nothing funny about some of the things we can do."

He turned to me.

"So let's do those things, Corporal. And let's do them soon."

———

The Nkwenya wharf was strangely silent. The Dark Maiden looked as though she was preparing for departure, but there was no swarming activity. Instead, there was an ominous sense of expectation. A few sailors were busy on deck, engaged in checking machines and positioning levers, as if the Dark Maiden was an autonomous machine that was going to be sailing herself out to sea. At the far end of the wharf, out of sight of anyone on land, the FCD truck was being offloaded, each of the sealed boxes carried by two soldiers apiece. They were being loaded onto a smaller craft that looked like a fishing vessel well past its expiry date.

A heightened level of preparedness was expressed in the soldiers standing along the quay, holding their AK-47s ready, and staring ahead like they were awaiting inspection. They were wearing full combat uniform, including field helmets. That seemed unnecessary, but it was an encouraging sign for us – an over-dressed soldier is often an under-trained soldier. Several of them also wore dark glasses despite the gloomy weather, which worked in our favour – our plan required that Chandler disguise himself as one of them.

"It's a mixed crowd," said Chandler with some relief.

He'd been concerned that the Dark Bizness militia might be an entirely black team, and as Robyn pointed out, a uniform would not conceal the colour of his skin.

"Let's take a closer look at that boat they're loading the boxes onto," said Chandler. "Now is as good a time as any to get their attention."

We were riding a small dinghy that we had taken from the club's main wharf, where sailors of yachts at anchor left them tied with a slip knot to a bollard when they came ashore. I turned the dinghy and started heading towards the FCD truck as if we were intending to get involved in the offloading process.

It didn't take them long to notice us. A soldier pointed and called out to his comrades, one of whom stepped up to the edge of the quay and shouted something. We kept approaching and the pointing soldier raised his weapon to get our attention.

"Hold it here," said Chandler, and I cut the motor.

We drifted closer to the quay and I could hear some words from the soldier shouting at us. "Private!" he called several times in more than one language. "Keep away!"

Our momentum died, and we bobbed up and down a stone's throw from the quay's edge. The shouting soldier turned to the one waving his gun, who stopped waving, turned smartly on his heels and disappeared from our view towards the Dark Maiden.

"Looks like that's done it," said Chandler. "Back out a little, we don't want them testing the range on their AKs."

I engaged the motor again, and we backed away slowly. The soldier that had been shouting at us watched in confused silence. Others had joined him, and they raised their weapons in case they needed to open fire. Then the spherical form of Lebogang appeared in the company of two soldiers on an upper deck of the yacht. They gestured at us, and Lebogang stood absolutely still for a moment.

"Now," said Chandler, and I swung the boat about and headed to the berth we had agreed upon at the far end of an adjacent jetty. As we passed out of sight of Lebogang, we heard him utter a bellowing command that sent a burst of energy through the soldiers on the dockside. They turned and started sprinting down the quay.

Chandler and I leapt onto the jetty, leaving Robyn to moor the dinghy, and the two of us jogged along our hastily planned route, giving the soldiers a tantalising glimpse of us before we disappeared into a cluster of yachts mounted on rusted supports like a junkyard of crippled boats.

We split up when we reached cover, and I took a moment to catch my breath beneath an old fifty-foot sloop with a broken mast. The sounds of the soldiers' boots announced their arrival and expressed their confusion as they faced the labyrinth of broken yachts, oil drums, pipes, and other junk. A moment later they spread out to form a line, as one would to search open ground. But this was not open ground, and they assumed we had fled as far as we could into the chaotic jumble of the yard, instead of remaining in the exposed outskirts. Chandler and I had planned a simple pincer move on a narrow track that ran between a low shed and a thirty-foot catamaran to the side of the yard. I heard a clattering as Chandler threw something against the shed to attract attention and saw a soldier gesture to a colleague to move towards the sound. The two of them were on the edge of the line, which kept moving onward, leaving them dangling behind. They found the entrance to the narrow path and hesitated. For a moment it looked as if both of them were going to enter the blind passage, but their training won out, and one of them stayed at the entrance with his gun raised, covering the other.

The rest of the soldiers moved ahead, intending to surround us and contain us in the area, which would have been a good plan if we had moved deeper into the yard. But they left us, and the two soldiers we had distracted, outside the ring they were forming. I crept silently around my yacht and approached from behind the soldier at the entrance to the path. He was scanning back and forth with the nervous movements of a man whose training hasn't covered the impact of adrenalin. His focus was on the one thing he understood – his comrade moving down the narrow path ahead of him, so he didn't notice my approach.

I waited a beat to give the other soldier time to reach nearer to where Chandler was waiting, then I made a scuffling noise and immediately stopped moving and raised my arms before he'd even noticed me. He swung about sharply at the sound, and the surprise caused him to jerk his AK-47 upwards, but he didn't squeeze the trigger. I stood quite still, a few metres from him, my arms raised.

He called out with a voice cracked by tension and a minute later two other soldiers arrived, breathing hard, their weapons up, fingers twitching on the triggers. I kept still as the new arrivals grabbed at my elbows and brought my hands behind me. One of them used zip-ties to bind my hands, the other patted me down and found the empty holster. That didn't seem to surprise him. They turned me about roughly, then pushed me ahead of them towards the Nkwenya wharf and the Dark Maiden. The remaining soldiers were calling out aloud to one another now. Having caught one of us they had abandoned all stealth, and sounded confident they would trap Chandler, despite all the noise they were making. Their shouts faded as we moved away from the scrapyard, my escorts breathing heavily under the weight of their full kit.

It was a slow walk back to the Nkwenya wharf, picking our way over the pipes and potholes. As we approached the Dark Maiden, there came a triumphant call from behind us and my escorts stopped me with the butt of an AK-47 in my chest. I stared ahead as the soldiers who had called out joined us with an excited babble of conversation. Then I turned to see Robyn, her hands behind her back, escorted by three Dark Bizness soldiers. She didn't look at me, but kept her eyes on the ground before her as if all the fighting spirit had gone.

"Just one of you left," jeered a soldier, and he prodded me with his AK-47, pushing me on towards the Dark Maiden.

TWENTY-EIGHT

We climbed the stairs of the gangway into the Dark Maiden, where our escorts engaged in a heated debate about which of them would have the honour of presenting us to their leader. Robyn kept her eyes down and I feigned disinterest as I took in the splendour of the Dark Maiden, which felt more like a five-star hotel than a yacht. Nautically themed artworks lined the bulkheads, recessed lighting filled in for the inadequate winter sun leaking through the portholes, and the pale oak decking looked freshly polished. The movement of the boat in the water was barely noticeable. There was an inaudible murmur and hardly detectable tremor under our feet from the distant engines. Eventually three of the soldiers were chosen to present us to the big boss, including a mute one who had arrived with Robyn and had somehow attached the rope that bound her hands to the webbing of his uniform, which he demonstrated with a silent mime. The others turned back to join their colleagues in the search for Chandler, and the winning escorts used their boots to push us ahead of them along the passageway and up a flight of spiral stairs.

The stateroom on the second level of the Dark Maiden had a deep-pile carpet with a pattern that started out by replicating the oak decking, then twisted in a fantasy of lines that swirled across one another in a rush to get past the low couches, card tables with *Jacobsen Swan* chairs, and bulbous columns of glowing translucent glass, to reach the far end of the room where a full-wall aquarium was filled with bright tropical fish and exotic coral.

Lebogang Madikwe was standing before the aquarium, his back to us, his head tilted up as if he was admiring the fish. It looked like a pose designed to express his indifference to our presence, which he did not acknowledge. He stood in this manner for several minutes, and the five of us waited patiently, Robyn, myself and our three guards. One soldier, unaware of the subtleties of Lebogang's body language, gave a soft cough. Lebogang's head twitched with irritation.

"Never underestimate the allure of gold," he announced to the fish tank as if he was about to embark upon a lecture on the subject. Then after a long pause, during which there was no response to his announcement, he added, "They say that, don't they?"

The silence extended. We were probably all wondering who Lebogang expected to answer his question. And so I did, with a question of my own.

"Do they?" I said. "I thought it was the evil of gold we need to be careful of underestimating."

Lebogang turned to face me, a look of amusement on his round face.

"I told that old man to run and hide," he said. "But you couldn't resist coming back for the gold, could you? Couldn't resist its allure."

He looked from me to Robyn with smug satisfaction. "It

will be the death of you, that shiny metal, you realise that? You will all die because of it."

Robyn said nothing. She kept staring at the carpet.

"What were you hoping to do?" asked Lebogang with a false laugh. "Jump on the boat and stow away with the gold?"

He gave another laugh and there ensued a heavy silence.

"Well?" he demanded of Robyn.

She finally looked up at him.

"They also say," she said, her voice hoarse with exhaustion, or perhaps despair. "That you should never underestimate your enemies."

Lebogang opened his mouth with mock surprise.

"Oh ... have I underestimated you? Should I have expected more of you? Should I have sent more of my men to chase after you? Taken greater precautions to prevent you from taking my gold from me? Oh, but wait ..." He gave a sneering laugh. "You didn't take my gold, did you?"

"Or perhaps we did," said Robyn. "And you should have realised that we did not come back for the gold."

Lebogang opened his mouth and produced a great rumbling laugh.

"But you haven't taken it! What are you babbling on about? If you didn't come back for the gold, then what were you doing floating about on that little boat?"

"We came for our friend."

"What nonsense," he said. But he didn't manage another laugh, and I thought I detected the stirring of some uncertainty behind his brave facade. "Your friend is with me now. Didn't the old man tell you? Us Xhosa people, we stick together."

"In which case," I said. "I am sure he has told you that

those boxes your men are loading onto that boat don't contain any gold."

Lebogang swivelled his small eyes onto me and considered me with scorn. But the glimmer of uncertainty grew into doubt, and it spread across his face. He couldn't hide it from us. He reached into the pocket of his silk jacket, which could have been the inspiration for the imitation suit Fat-Boy had been wearing, and pulled out a small mobile phone, pressed a button and said something to the phone, keeping his eyes on me. We heard the faint buzzing of a call being connected, then a click and a deep grunt. Lebogang spoke a few musical words, then ended the call.

We stood in silence for several minutes. Lebogang glared at me as if he was trying to read my mind. A soldier behind us shifted his weight and his boots squeaked.

Then the door behind us burst open with a bang. Heavy boots stamped across the carpet, as if they were a new pair of boots being worn in. The bearer of the boots gave us a wide berth and came to a halt beside Lebogang. It was the cousin, Justice Mkwekwe, the family resemblance clear in his facial features, but Justice was of lesser girth, and clearly fancied himself as having a military bearing. He was wearing the green fatigues of the Dark Bizness militia with three stars on the epaulets, and carried an AK-47 over his shoulder.

He spoke rapidly in Xhosa to Lebogang, his deep voice resonant but filled with anxious urgency. Lebogang asked a question in disbelief, gave us a confused glance, and Justice provided what sounded like a definitive, if angry, answer. Then Lebogang turned to me. There was surprise and anger scrawled across his face now.

"Plaster?" he demanded. "And lead? You replaced my gold with lumps of lead?"

"Bring our friend to us," I said. "And we'll tell you where the gold is."

"Do you really think you're going to walk off this ship?" Lebogang's voice climbed a tone or two.

"If you want to see the gold again," I said. "That is exactly what we will do."

"But I have a better idea," declared Lebogang, his anger rising quickly. "I'll cut your limbs off one at a time and let's see who breaks first." He swung round to his cousin and shouted at him, "Fetch the fat one!"

Justice hesitated only a moment, then swivelled on his shiny new boots and stamped his way out of the room. We stood in silence again. The restless soldier shifted his weight back onto the other foot, and his boot squeaked again. The coughing soldier coughed. Only the mute one who had tied himself to Robyn was completely silent and still.

There was something bothering me. I watched Lebogang, but his eyes avoided mine and they settled on Robyn. Something about the angry outburst bothered me. There had been a sense of drama to it, as if Lebogang was playing some lines for us, but laughing on the inside. Then, as I watched him look at Robyn, he gave the glimmer of a smile. It was a strange gloating smile, as if he'd just thought of something nasty he could do to her. It took me a moment to work out why it troubled me, but then I realised – his burst of anger had been forced. There was no genuine anger, but a surprised amusement that he had covered with the pretence of anger. And this smile was the smile of a man who was about to get away with something. It was not the smile of a man who has just discovered he has lost tens of millions of dollars.

The door opened again, and the stamping steps of the cousin were accompanied by the sound of feet shuffling across the soft carpet. Fat-Boy's hands were tied behind him, and his legs were bound to hobble him. His head was covered with something that looked like a pillowcase, blotched with patches of blood and held with a drawstring through Fat-Boy's mouth, presumably to gag him.

Lebogang gave a curt order. Justice loosened the drawstring, pulled the pillowcase off Fat-Boy's head like he was revealing a surprise, then tossed it to the floor. He said something to Lebogang, as if he was announcing Fat-Boy's arrival at our little gathering. Then he swivelled about and stamped out of the room again.

Fat-Boy had been punched several times. He had suffered a nosebleed and a split lip, which had trickled blood down the front of his imitation *Zegna* silk jacket. He looked at me without surprise, the glum expression of an admonished child. I gave him a small but encouraging smile. He didn't return it.

"Your friends," announced Lebogang with the false glee of a man who is about to enjoy a good taunting. "Your *friends*," he repeated with extra emphasis, "think that I'm going to let you walk off this boat like free men, despite your efforts to deceive me."

There was no response from Fat-Boy, who had looked from me to Robyn, and now gazed at the brightly coloured fish in the aquarium behind Lebogang as if he had seen nothing like them before.

"But, sadly for you," continued Lebogang, "that is not the way this will go. You know what the penalty is for cheating a Xhosa." Then, noticing Fat-Boy's distraction, he raised his voice and shouted something at him in their language.

Fat-Boy turned to me.

"They opened the boxes, Angel," he said. "They know we switched the boxes."

His lazy eye drooped, and a trickle of blood oozed from his swollen lip and dripped down his chin.

"But they're still loading them, Angel. Still loading those boxes full of that lead shit onto that boat. Why are they doing that?"

"Explain the penalty," shouted Lebogang. "The penalty for deceiving amaXhosa."

"Is this your rescue plan?" Fat-Boy asked.

"We didn't have much time," I admitted, and tried smiling encouragingly again, but from the look on Fat-Boy's face it didn't work as intended.

"The penalty," bellowed Lebogang, "is death!"

Suddenly, the small things that had been bothering me fell into place like pieces of a puzzle. I realised why Lebogang's anger was feigned, even now, as he bellowed his hollow threats at us. I realised why he had given Robyn a gloating smile, why he didn't care that we had taken his gold, and why his men were loading boxes of plaster and lead onto an old boat. Our rescue plan had failed. I knew it in that moment. We had come into the enemy's lair hoping to bargain our way out of it, only to discover that we had nothing to bargain with.

I turned to the mute soldier standing immobile beside Robyn. He was wearing full combat kit, reflective sunglasses hiding his eyes and most of his face. The arms and legs of the uniform were too short, as if it had shrunk in the wash. But the sides of the jacket drooped on his thin frame as if it had been stretched, or been made for a man with a very different build. It was not his uniform. Because he was not a member of the Dark Bizness militia at all. I couldn't see his eyes behind the glasses, but I knew the pale grey eyes were watching me. He was no doubt also realising the extent of our failure and trying to figure out our next move. Because the mute soldier was Chandler, our Trojan Horse. He had detached the rope that bound him to Robyn, and her hands were now not bound at all, although she held them behind her as if they were. Now that we were reunited with Fat-Boy, the time had come for us to move, time for me to give the word. I glanced at Fat-Boy, who did not know the plan, but I didn't think it would take him long to catch up once the fireworks started. I turned back to Chandler.

"Now," I said.

He swung around to the soldier standing between us and swung his AK-47 by its barrel, striking the side of the soldier's head like he was trying for a home run. The soldier staggered backwards and dropped his weapon. It made no sound as it fell to the soft carpet. Chandler leapt onto the stumbling figure, hammering at him with his fists. I crouched low to bring my centre of gravity down and then twisted around in a poor imitation of a Capoeira cartwheel move. With my hands bound behind my back, I rolled onto my shoulders, and my legs caught the soldier standing behind me with a double blow across his chest. He lurched back in his surprise, and grappled at the fire selector of his AK-47, which was a foolish thing to do because it lost him time. My feet found the floor again, and I rolled through the move and used the momentum to spring off the soft carpet and raised my head into his chin. His head snapped back-wards, and I guessed the nerve clusters beneath his jaw were lighting up. He dropped, and I landed clumsily on his legs, rolled over and brought a knee onto his diaphragm. His body twisted as I drove the air out of him, and he rolled to the side as his muscles spasmed.

Out of the corner of my eye I glimpsed Fat-Boy gliding across the carpet towards Lebogang who stood frozen by surprise. He turned as Fat-Boy charged towards him, his head low. Fat-Boy's solid skull struck Lebogang on the cheek. The two of them staggered backwards and Lebogang's head made a resounding bang against the glass wall of the aquarium. For a moment I thought he might have cracked it, but there was no rush of water, only the squeaking sound of Lebogang's bald head sliding down the glass.

I flung a glance at Chandler. He was using the zip-ties to bind the hands of the soldier he'd overpowered. The soldier beneath me struggled to shake me off, but I used his movement to flip him over and held him to the floor with my knees. Chandler came over, caught his flailing hands, and bound them together with a tie, then caught the legs and bound them too.

I glanced up to see how Fat-Boy was faring and saw Robyn. She had her Glock in both hands, staring down it with a killer gaze. She opened her mouth and uttered a cry that might have been a command. I looked to where she was pointing her Glock. Lebogang had an arm around Fat-Boy's neck, holding him before him like an enormous rag doll. Fat-Boy's eyes goggled at us and spluttered as Lebogang throttled him. In his other hand, Lebogang held a pistol, the barrel at Fat-Boy's temple. He was pushing so hard that he'd drawn blood.

"Drop it," shouted Robyn again, her hand holding the Glock steady.

"You going to shoot your friend?" jeered Lebogang between gasping breaths.

"Do it, Robsy." Fat-Boy's voice was only a hoarse whisper. "Do it," he begged her.

Robyn was perhaps five metres from the two of them, and she could see only a sliver of Lebogang beyond Fat-Boy. But she could have done it, I knew she could. I'd seen her shoot. It was a shot well within her capabilities. But she did nothing.

"Shoot him," wheezed Fat-Boy.

Lebogang sneered. "Put your gun down," he ordered Robyn.

Robyn didn't move. We'd lost our advantage. Lebogang started making an indistinct sound that might have been the beginnings of a laugh. His attention was still entirely on Robyn and her gun.

I covered the distance to Lebogang and Fat-Boy in less than a second. I launched myself like I was diving off a cliff, and leapt for their feet. I struck just below the knee, and both Fat-Boy and Lebogang toppled onto me. There was a deafening bang. I wasn't sure whether Robyn had taken the shot or whether Lebogang's finger had squeezed the trigger as he dropped. The sound of glass cracking behind me answered that one. Lebogang's bullet had gone wide and shattered one of the bulbous columns. Lebogang squirmed to the side and rolled off me, reaching for his gun, which he had dropped as he fell. I kicked at it and sent it spinning away. Fat-Boy was sprawled on the carpet beside Lebogang. They both had blood streaks down the front of their silk jackets now, and it felt like I was seeing double as they struggled side by side on the carpet.

Chandler was behind me, cutting through the zip-ties that bound my hands. Then he had a knee on Lebogang's chest. Lebogang cried out, but a punch from Chandler cut the cry short. I grabbed at Lebogang's legs and the two of us rolled him over. Chandler bound his hands, and I bound his ankles. Lebogang cried out again with more force. I grabbed the pillowcase that had been over Fat-Boy's head, and forced it over Lebogang, then pulled the drawstring tight to gag him. Lebogang's cry became an indistinct mumble.

I helped Fat-Boy to his feet and Chandler cut the zip-ties binding his hands. Robyn was still training the Glock on Lebogang, her face white and drawn. Then Chandler and I checked the ties on the two soldiers, who were alive but not conscious. Lebogang got himself onto his knees, moaning like a stricken animal.

"You're my prisoners," said Chandler to us. "Got it? I'll escort you off the boat."

I nodded, Fat-Boy grunted, and Robyn tucked her Glock back inside the waistband of her FCD uniform.

"Take these." Chandler gave us each a zip-tie. "Make it look real. Now go."

We turned to the door. Robyn in the lead, then Fat-Boy, me, and Chandler covering us with his AK-47. Robyn was only a few metres from the door when it swung open suddenly. I grabbed at Fat-Boy and pulled him down to the floor with me. Behind us Chandler dropped to the other side. But Robyn stopped in her tracks and stood immobile as the door revealed the person beyond.

Justice Mkwekwe had returned.

TWENTY-NINE

Justice's eyes widened with shock as he looked from Robyn to the kneeling, hooded figure of Lebogang, and back to Robyn. He grabbed at his AK-47 and swung it around to firing position. Robyn was backing away, her arms raised. Justice looked again towards Lebogang, and then he saw the prone figures of the two soldiers. In that moment, Lebogang suddenly reared up onto his feet, bellowing through his gag like a wounded animal. He hopped towards the door on his hobbled feet, his bound hands behind him, the pillowcase over his head.

Justice did not hesitate. His right hand pressed the fire selector of his AK-47 down to the semi-automatic position, and he brought his finger back to the trigger moments before the monstrous form of Lebogang reached him. He squeezed it. Not once, but three times in rapid succession.

The 7.62 mm round fired from an AK-47 can pass through human flesh without doing much damage, unless the bullet twists and yaws. Two of the bullets to pass through Lebogang probably failed to yaw, but the third did, and the damage it caused to his heart would have killed him before his huge body hit the floor. Justice squeezed the trigger a fourth time, and this bullet flew over the collapsing body and struck the wall of the aquarium, which produced a loud crack, and then split suddenly into a thousand shards, pouring water, fish and coral over the floor. This spectacle provided a momentary distraction for Justice, but when he turned from the aquarium to look around the room, the AK-47 was raised and ready to fire again. He swung around to choose which of us to shoot first.

And then he saw Fat-Boy for the first time. The shock rippled across his face as he realised that the man he had shot was his cousin.

Fat-Boy, crouched beside me, raised his hands and stood up very slowly. Justice lifted the AK-47 to his shoulder as if looking through the sights would deliver a more fitting punishment. There was a breathless pause filled with the gurgling sound of water trickling from the aquarium.

Then Robyn called out. She had her Glock in her hands and was pointing it at Justice.

Justice ignored her. He drew a breath, and his finger tightened on the trigger of his gun. In the momentary pause before the trigger engaged, Robyn squeezed the trigger of her Glock. His head whipped back and the AK-47 fell from his grasp. He dropped to the floor beside his cousin.

Fat-Boy let out a choking gasp. Chandler and I were silent. Robyn lowered her Glock, looked down at the two bodies on the floor, and closed her eyes for a moment. Then she looked up at me, her dark eyes filled with tears.

Chandler gave her a few seconds.

Then he said, "Get moving," and stepped over the bodies as he herded us out of the room.

We closed the door behind us, and walked with heads down, shuffling our feet even though they weren't bound. Chandler walked behind, covering us with his AK-47. We shuffled down the spiral stairs and along the gangway, where we encountered the first two Dark Bizness soldiers running towards us. Chandler shouted at them to hurry and to call the medics. The sight of his uniform seemed to allay any doubts they might have had, and they ran on.

We continued down the gangway and onto the quay. A handful of soldiers watched us approach from the far end. Chandler called out to them to return to the yacht. They didn't think to ask questions, and set off at a jog spurred on by the urgency in his voice. At the entrance to the quay, where it joined the main dock, we descended some rough concrete steps that led to the floating wooden jetty where Robyn had tied up the dinghy. It was low tide, and the jetty was several metres lower than the Nkwenya wharf, which provided some cover. Chandler sent me out because Robyn seemed to have been struck dumb, wrestling with her inner demons. The wooden planks of the jetty shifted and clattered as I stepped on them. There was an ominous silence from the hulking concrete wharf above me, as if the Dark Bizness militia were paralysed by the shocking sight of their dead leaders. It didn't take me long to reach the dinghy. I climbed in, started the motor, and returned to fetch the others.

"Didn't I tell you?" Fat-Boy said to me, after we had chugged our way back past the still-silent Dark Maiden and reached the safety of the yacht basin.

"Tell me what?"

"Saved my life," said Fat-Boy, gazing adoringly at Robyn.

"You did the right thing," said Chandler to Robyn, who had not spoken a single word. She seemed not to hear him and gazed steadfastly out to sea.

"What were they doing?" asked Chandler, his eyes on Fat-Boy. "What were they doing to you? Why did they take you with them?"

"They were loading those boxes onto an old boat," said Fat-Boy. "Getting ready to sail them out to sea."

"Why?"

"You think I know, Colonel?"

"I don't understand what they were planning to do with you."

"They said I was going out to sea with the boxes. I told them I don't do sea, but then they put that bag over my head."

"You were there when they discovered the boxes didn't have the gold in them?" I asked. "What happened?"

"There was a lot of shouting. Then they took the bag off my face so they could hit me again."

"But they kept loading the boxes?" I asked.

"Kept right on loading them."

"What were they playing at?" asked Chandler angrily.

"We need to look at that gold, Colonel," I said.

"What do you mean?"

"Ben's right," said Robyn, turning from the horizon to face us with her damp eyes. "They've been playing us."

"Playing us how?"

"They figured out how to do the one thing we've not been able to do."

"Which is?"

"Let's look at the gold, Colonel," said Robyn. "I have a feeling it's not what we think it is."

———

By the time we had reached the far end of the yacht club, we could hear distant sirens approaching. We climbed ashore, tied up the dinghy, and made our way to the lock-up. Robyn unlocked it, and then I cut open one of the boxes and used the knife to scrape the soft gold.

There was only a thin layer of it. Beneath was a silver metal.

"Tungsten," said Chandler with disgust. "The same weight, but a fraction of the cost. All these bars would come to less than five hundred dollars."

"Now we know why he wanted five days," I said. "Can't have been easy finding someone to make this number of fake bars in the time he had."

The four of us gazed down at our pile of useless metal.

"But why was he sending them to sea?" asked Chandler. "And what did he want with Fat-Boy?"

"He wanted to lose them," said Robyn. "Lose the gold, and Fat-Boy at sea."

Chandler looked up at her.

"Lose them at sea," he said, testing the idea by repeating it. Then a look of realisation spread across his face. "You're right. He figured out how to do the one thing we could not."

A feeble amount of afternoon light was trickling in through the door, making Robyn's face no more than a blur in the gloom.

"I need light," said Chandler, his voice tight with anger. "Light and air, goddamn it."

He turned from us furiously and strode outside.

"I don't understand," said Fat-Boy. "Why lose the fake bars?"

"What has been our biggest problem?" asked Robyn. "Ever since we first laid eyes on the gold."

"Breytenbach," said Fat-Boy.

"Exactly. You said there was someone taking photos at the warehouse, when the colonel was pretending to inspect the gold?"

"Like a tourist," agreed Fat-Boy. "Snapping pictures of us."

"He wanted a record of the whole thing," said Robyn.

"For what?"

"To show Breytenbach. Why else?"

"You'll have to run that by me again," said Fat-Boy.

"I think he told Breytenbach that we were selling the gold to him."

"But he would never convince Breytenbach with fake bars."

"I don't think he intended to. Breytenbach wouldn't know they were fake if they were lost at sea. Something was going to happen to that old boat with the boxes of fake gold."

As we turned to look at our pile of fake bars, I went over it again in my mind. Robyn was right. It was the only way to make sense of what Lebogang had done. He had intended to show Breytenbach the evidence of the carefully repli-cated gold bars being weighed on the scale that Chandler had rigged so he could look like an expert. Perhaps some fake paperwork about the deal he had negotiated to buy the gold from us. Then would come the photographs, video, or news report of whatever disaster he had planned at sea.

"Lost at sea," said Fat-Boy. "With me. Now you under-stand ... that's why I don't do sea."

The rain was pelting down in great billowing waves when we joined Chandler outside. He was standing looking up at the sky as he had earlier, but this time his eyes were closed and he was allowing the rain to wash the blood from his face like he was taking a shower. The sound of sirens had stopped now. There was only the sound of the wind, the rain, and the angry clanging of the yachts' sheets against their masts.

"If Breytenbach thought the gold was lost at sea," he said to the sky, "it would take him years to salvage it. If not decades. At an exorbitant cost. And by the time BB discovered it was fake, if he ever did, Madikwe would have disappeared. Didn't I say we should be careful of underestimating him?"

"But where is the real gold?" asked Fat-Boy.

"I imagine the only people who could tell us that," said Chandler, turning away from the rain, "are the two people lying dead on that yacht."

"We're better off without it," said Robyn.

Fat-Boy opened his mouth to protest, but Chandler spoke before he could.

"No time for all that now, Fat-Boy. They'll be starting a search at any moment. We must part ways here, and now. Use the yacht club facilities to change. Ten minutes apiece. Angel and Robyn up first, then Fat-Boy. I'll go last. You remember your locker numbers?"

We nodded in unison.

"Change and then disappear. If you need help with that, you call me. You know the number. You understand?"

He studied each of us in turn, and we each nodded. Then we performed secret handshakes with Fat-Boy, a

Mediterranean embrace with Chandler, a kiss on the cheek with Robyn, and turned to go our separate ways.

"And for God's sake, Angel," Chandler called, as I turned to walk to the clubhouse, "sort out your nonsense with the police."

"Roger that, Colonel," I said.

And I had every intention of doing just that. Because of all the confusing puzzle pieces that had been chasing around my mind the past week, I realised there was one piece that stood out above all others.

The piece with the two dead men sitting in a burning car. Dead from the knife wounds to their throats.

THIRTY

The sun had all but given up on bleeding into the horizon by the time I trespassed again on the balcony of my neighbour's apartment, lit a cigarette, and dialled Leilah's number.

"You're psychic," she said, after a bit of heavy breathing into the microphone as she moved away from the sounds of laughing colleagues and found a quiet spot to talk.

"I am?"

"I've been thinking about you all day."

"Good thoughts?"

"The best kinds of thoughts," she said, and sighed as if her emotions were getting the better of her.

"Are you free?" I asked. "Can we meet?"

"I'm available." She gave a small, musical laugh. "I'm never free, soldier-boy. If it's tonight you want me it will have to be here at Pandora – I'm on duty, aren't I?"

"Tonight is good," I said.

"Shall I put you down for the whole night?"

"No. There's something I want to talk about. It won't take very long."

"You do too much talking. Isn't it enough with the talking? Why don't we move our relationship to the next level?"

"I'm not sure you'll want to, after we've had our talk."

"Words don't frighten me, Angel. Do they frighten you?"

"More than anything."

"You sound stressed, Angel. Have you had a hard day?"

"I've had worse."

Leilah put me down for the full night and announced that she would take a bath. Would I prefer the scent of lavender, eucalyptus or rose? I chose lavender, and she promised to be smelling of it by the time I arrived, then reminded me that her customers were obliged to pay in advance – even her favourite customers.

———

Leilah's teddy bear was still looking disgruntled atop the pile of pillows in the icy wind coming through the open window. Leilah was draped in a diaphanous robe, her green eyes glowing, and smelling, as promised, of lavender.

"I've been clean," she said, after greeting me with a lingering kiss, her bright eyes gazing into mine as if we were lovers reunited after a long separation.

I said what a good thing that was and told her I had not been clean in the slightest. She gave a light laugh and pushed me into the armchair, then straddled my lap as if she was about to perform a lap dance, although the effect was disconcerting – a young girl seeking solace on the lap of her father. She tucked her lower lip under her teeth and looked at me solemnly.

"It's because of you I'm clean," she said.

"The only thing I did was choose the lavender."

"No, silly, you know what I mean. Talking to you has lifted a weight from me, like I was carrying around a heavy bag of shit. Now I've given it to you and it's all gone."

"All of it? Or is there more you need to unburden?"

Leilah chewed on her lip and dipped her face to give me more of the little girl effect.

"What more do you want me to say?" she asked, as if I was demanding too much.

"What about the two men who died?"

Leilah kept her face down, her lip pinched in her teeth, and looked at me through her eyelashes.

"Which two men?" she asked, eventually.

"They were in a car which was burnt; but they did not die in the fire. The police say they were already dead when the fuel tank ignited."

Leilah's cool green eyes gazed into mine.

"It was a few days after you left the hospital," I said, to jog her memory. "That's when they burned."

Leilah stood up, went over to the bed and reached a hand up to take the seductive pose she'd struck on my previous visit. But after a moment the hand dropped back down, and she slumped onto the bed, causing an avalanche of pillows to fall to the floor and her grumpy teddy bear to tumble after them.

"Are you with the police, after all, soldier-boy?" she said eventually, and her lower lip trembled. "Have you come to arrest me? All your stories about Natasha were just a trick?"

"I'm not with the police. But they are not far behind. Let me help you, Leilah."

She took a deep breath and let it out in a jagged sigh.

"Shall we cut the histrionics?" I said. "Just tell me what happened – without the performance."

She glared at me. The lower lip stopped trembling, and her mouth clamped tight.

"The two men," I prompted. "When you left hospital, what happened?"

"I only helped a bit," she said. "I didn't do all of it."

"You killed one of the men, not both?"

"I didn't kill either of them. I helped burn them afterwards, that's all I did."

"Helped who?"

"Natasha. She cut their throats."

I said nothing for a moment. Leilah waited – as I drew the obvious conclusion and put all the pieces together – her eyes steady.

"Natasha is alive," I said, after a long pause.

Leilah nodded, then rushed to explain.

"When I woke up in the hospital, the first thing I did was I called her. But her phone was off. It was off for days. I told the police, but they said there was nobody called Natasha, that I'd done too much tik, I was confused. They thought I was making up stories about one of the other lost girls they couldn't care less about. So they did nothing. I kept calling her, every few hours. I thought she'd been killed and her body thrown onto one of those rubbish dumps where they find body parts."

She went silent, then wiped her nose with the back of her hand.

"But she hadn't?" I prompted. "She hadn't been killed. And she did answer your call?"

"She said she'd killed them. Cut their throats like the monsters had done to her sister, like she thought they'd done to me." Her hand reached up to hover over the scar across her throat. "They forced her to watch as they slit my throat.

Did I tell you? She was sure I was dead; couldn't believe it was me when I called."

"It must have been a surprise for her to hear your voice."

"She broke down and cried."

"And the phone, why had it been off for days?"

"The battery died. They'd tossed it into a corner of the shack where the beasts took her."

"What shack?"

"In the township. They wanted to have their fun with her before they killed her. Tied her up and threw her into a back room, then they raped her. They gave her water and bits of food to keep her alive – only just alive though."

Leilah watched me carefully to see how I was taking her story. From the look on her face, I guessed she didn't think I was taking it particularly well.

"Let's smoke," she said, and went to stand at the window, where she shivered in the cold air. I suggested she put more clothing on when I joined her there, but she snuggled up to me and said I was keeping her warm enough.

"One man carried a knife," she resumed when we had our cigarettes alight. "The knife he used on me. One day while he was raping her, she got hold of it. She killed him while he was still on her. Then she cut the rope they'd tied her with and waited for the other man to come back from the shebeen. He'd been out drinking, and didn't even see her until after she'd sliced his throat."

Leilah's hand touched her scar, and she ran a finger along it gingerly.

"She laid the bodies down on the bed in the back, then she panicked. Didn't know what to do, didn't know where she was, she'd eaten nothing but bits of bread for days, and there were two dead men on the bed. She stayed in the shack and screamed. That's what she told me. She screamed and screamed, but she must have done it without making any noise because nobody came. And there were lots of shacks around there. People would have come if she'd made a noise. She found her phone and the spare battery. Turned it on and then didn't know what to do. She called her father, but couldn't tell him what she'd done. She wanted to call her boyfriend, but said she couldn't."

Leilah twisted under my arm to look at me.

"Was that you, Angel?"

"It was."

"I called the next morning," continued Leilah, "after she'd spent the night looking at the bodies of those men she'd killed."

She paused and sucked on her cigarette.

"I borrowed a car from a friend. Natasha went out and looked at the names of the streets near the shack – she had to walk a way because there in Gugulethu the street names aren't so good. But she found some, and I found the place on the map. I went to her, still with my bandages and the stitches in my neck. We waited until after the middle of the night, about three o'clock. The men had parked their car up against the shack. Natasha and I carried the bodies out and put them in the back."

Leilah finished her cigarette and flicked the butt out of the window.

"It's cold," she said, as if she had only just noticed. She shivered, then announced: "I'm taking a bath."

"You just had one."

"This one is to warm me up."

She left me to finish my cigarette and a moment later the sound of running water came from the en-suite bathroom.

"You want bubbles?" she called, but by the time I had

disposed of my cigarette and reached the bathroom she was already kneeling beside the Victorian free-standing bathtub, frothing the water with childlike glee.

"Natasha drove the car with the dead men to one of those deserted beaches on the Strand," she said, as she frothed the bubbles. "Where the sand dunes blow over the car parks and you can do anything in a car there, nobody will see you. It was my idea, I've been taken there often."

She stood up and shook her robe from her like she was shrugging off an extra skin. Then she climbed into the bath, lay back, and closed her eyes. I settled onto the closed toilet seat, which had a fluffy pink cover on it, and waited for her to continue.

"I followed Natasha. I don't know what we would have done if we'd been stopped. We hadn't even thought about that. We just drove. Natasha was different, she'd changed. It was like something had broken inside her. When I looked at her, it was like I was looking at a stranger. I couldn't see the Natasha I knew."

Leilah opened her eyes and two perfect tears rolled out, travelled down her cheeks and dripped into the foamy bath.

"I loved her, soldier-boy, you know that? I loved the Natasha I'd known before. I would do anything for her. Anything."

She gazed at me through her tears. I said nothing.

"We put the bodies in the front seats, then poured petrol over them; tried throwing matches at the car but they went out. Then I lit a cigarette and threw that. It made such a big flame our eyebrows burnt off. We were lucky we didn't catch fire ourselves, everything smelt of petrol, and we'd got it all over ourselves. But we didn't catch fire – we got into my car and drove away."

"Where did you go?"

"I brought her here. The dragon lady's got a good heart. She let Natasha stay a few days while she got her strength."

"And then? When she had recovered her strength, where did she go?"

"She went to find the monsters who killed her sister. She had heard the men who cut my throat and raped her talking on the phone to someone who'd paid them to kill us. A funny name, like one of those Bible names, Jeremiah or Isaiah. They even said he came from a church and they called him the prophet. Natasha was good at digging around, asking questions, and finding people."

"And she found this prophet, Isaiah?" I asked, thinking of the scowling face of the novitiate with the prominent forehead and too much sin in his heart.

"She found him, but he didn't recognise her or know who she was. Can you believe that? When Thabo told him people were digging around, he must have described me to them. But he didn't even know what Natasha looked like. Besides, Natasha said the prophet was nothing more than a servant of a bigger devil."

"And she found that bigger devil?"

Leilah dipped her chin into the bubbles, then looked up at me with a sad smile, a white goatee dripping from her chin.

"She's still looking," she said, and allowed her eyes to fill with tears again.

"Are you sure about that?"

"Still looking," repeated Leilah.

"But she found some of the devils, didn't she? You told me she named one of them. It was a judge, wasn't it? Justice Francois Rousseau."

"I know nothing about a judge," said Leilah, and she shivered as if the water had grown suddenly cold.

"And the politician?" I asked. "Tell me about Jessop Ndoro."

"I don't know anything about a politician."

Leilah sighed and lowered herself into the bubbles, as if she could hide from me.

I stood up and pulled a huge fluffy towel off the heated rail.

"Get out," I said. "I've had enough of your games."

"I don't know about them. I've told you everything," she protested, and the tears spilt down her cheeks.

"When you've got some clothes on, you can tell me about the judge and the politician. Get out of that bath."

Leilah heard the anger in my voice and climbed out of the bath, then stood dripping before me. She didn't take the towel that I held out to her, but opened her arms as if to offer herself to me.

"You don't like what you see?" she asked. "Other men do. Or is that the problem? You think I'm used goods?"

"I think you're a young girl who's spent so much of her life lying to everyone that you cannot distinguish truth from fantasy."

"That's not true," said Leilah, and she cried silently, her eyes on mine like great pools of aggrieved innocence. Then she grabbed at the towel with defiance and dried her face with it. She wrapped the towel around herself and strode back to the bedroom.

―――――

Leilah had her see-through robe on again when I joined her at the window.

"You'll catch your death of cold," I said.

"It would be your fault. You can make the speech at my

funeral and tell them it's because you hated me so much you did nothing to keep me warm."

I opened my arms, and she snuggled against me.

"I'm a Virgo," she said. "On the cusp of Leo, but I've got Chiron in Virgo."

"That sounds bad."

"It is. You know about Chiron?"

"Not as much as I should."

"He is the wounded healer – given the power of healing, but could not heal himself. That's why Chiron is so tragic."

"And you've got him in Virgo?"

"My birth sign, that's why I need to be loved. It's my gift and my curse. I heal others with my love, but I cannot heal myself. It's my destiny to spend my life searching for love. No one will ever love me as I love them."

The two of us stood in silence for a few minutes at the open window, Leilah shivering with each gust of chilled air. Eventually, she sighed.

"Natasha wanted to ask questions," she said, "but the judge didn't give her a chance. He booked a night with me, through Natasha. It was her idea – not to get revenge on them, but to reach them. He refused to talk to her when she tried before. She called him up, told him she was a journalist, wanted to ask him some questions. But he wouldn't talk to her, so she laid a trap with me as the bait. When we arrived, he was surprised there were two of us, but then he realised we'd tricked him. Natasha asked him to confess and tell her who the others were, but suddenly he got nasty. He said he'd been warned that she was after him. He had a knife in a pocket of the disgusting robe he was wearing. He pulled it out and cut Natasha badly. He wanted to kill her.

But I ..." Leilah paused, and swallowed as if the words stuck in her throat. "I helped to hold him down."

The nasty thought that had occurred to me earlier as I stood on my neighbour's balcony beneath the bleeding sky twisted again at the back of my mind. If the judge had not been warned, would he have carried the knife that was used to kill him?

"And the politician?" I asked.

"Natasha knew his initials, because she had some kind of official papers. She mentioned a name to the judge before things got nasty, when he was still denying he knew anything. He laughed about it, and said Natasha would do better to speak to a man called Ndoro. But when we went to see Ndoro he had also been warned – he didn't have a knife, but he was angry. Natasha had kept the judge's knife. She attacked him before he'd done anything much. Natasha has changed, Angel, I told you. She's not the person I knew before. I think she went there planning to kill him, not talk or ask questions."

Leilah shivered and snuggled closer for more warmth.

"And the third man?" I asked. "The man from the church."

"I told Natasha I couldn't do it again. I couldn't help her kill anyone else. She said she didn't need me, anyway. I look in the newspapers every day because I don't think she's planning to ask that church man questions either. I think she's just waiting to kill him."

"Tell me where she is, Leilah. We must stop her."

"No, Angel. We mustn't stop her. We need to let her do it. You know what those men did."

"We need to take her to get help, before she gets near that church man," I insisted. "For her sake, not his. He has security who won't hold back. They'll do anything to protect him."

"But you are too late," said Leilah, and she turned her green eyes onto me. "She's already near him. Don't stop her now, Angel. Those men deserved to die, and he deserves it too."

Leilah moved closer, and her lips brushed against my cheek. "Besides," she whispered, "you've warned him, haven't you? Like you warned the others. You've done everything you can. Now come and lie with me, Angel. Will you do that? Just lie with me and hold me. Talking about those men has made me cold again. I need you to keep me warm."

The teddy bear glared at me from its position on the floor as I lay beside Leilah and kept her warm until her breathing settled into the slow, steady rhythm of sleep. I climbed out of the bed, positioned the teddy bear in my place, and allowed myself a cigarette at the window to gather my thoughts.

After the cigarette, I left Leilah a note and let myself out of her room. The lights in the hallway were dim, and the soft carpet dulled the sound of my tread. It was almost two o'clock in the morning, but death, like time, waits for no man.

THIRTY-ONE

I f there was one thing I had learnt from Chandler during the second iteration of our relationship – the one that developed while conducting criminal activities together, as opposed to the first iteration in which we had defended the rights of the citizens of her Majesty's government by killing other people – if there was one thing I had learnt, it was that the simplest approach was usually the most effective. And the simplest approach to gaining access to a property guarded by the most advanced security systems available at the southern tip of the African continent, was not to arm oneself with semi-automatic weapons, dress in black and attempt to vault the electrified fences, but to be invited onto the premises and welcomed as someone they wished to see. Which is why at oh six hundred hours, only four hours after creeping out of Leilah's bedroom, I was sporting a dull grey tracksuit, and jogging at a leisurely pace around the outskirts of the fortress that was the House of Our Lord.

The sun was only just warming the horizon, so I didn't think there was much chance of my being recognised, but the hooded tracksuit top would conceal my face from the scrutiny of the guards who had recently taken over from the night shift, and were probably watching me with interest as they finished up their cornflakes in front of all their screens. I also didn't think that they would have been alarmed when I suddenly turned and crossed the road at the point where the stripe of new tar showed clearly the path of the optical fibre cable that provided the complex with its connection to the outside world. It had not been hard to establish which service provider the House of Our Lord used because they had boasted on their website of their pride at connecting Our Lord with the rest of the world. An early call to their 24-hour service centre had been very informative. I had been told not to worry about the cable being damaged by road workers, because the cables were protected within steel tubing, the only vulnerable spots being the junction boxes, accessed by small plastic covers with the helpful insignia of the company which distinguished them from the many other subterranean mysteries that littered our sidewalks.

I jogged around a corner, away from the prying cameras of the House of Our Lord, and identified an emblazoned access point a little further down the quiet sidewalk. I stooped to tie my shoelaces, prised the cover open, and exposed the splitter that lay beneath. I didn't need to use the knife I had brought along because the splitter could be simply unscrewed once the sealing tab had been broken. I was back on my feet in less than a minute and made my way to the unmarked panel van I had stolen an hour earlier.

I called the helpful 24-hour support again and reported what had looked to me like an act of vandalism as I was taking my morning jog, and gave the exact location of the access point. They thanked me, and assured me a technician would be there before lunchtime, which would give me more than enough time.

I changed into my dock-worker overalls, which were not entirely appropriate for an internet cable technician, but were the nearest thing I had to the clothes that someone providing a technical service might wear, and then I gave the administrative people at the House of Our Lord half an hour to discover and report the loss of their high-speed connection to the outside world, and to get all hot under the collar about the poor service they were being provided.

I pulled up to the gates of the House of Our Lord a little after oh seven hundred hours. The cameras buzzed with interest and swung on their pivots to get a better look at my unmarked panel van as I approached. I kept my peaked cap low over my face and held an arbitrary identification card up to the camera to block my nose and mouth. I explained I had been in the area, and that I was ready to fix their internet problems if they would be so kind as to open their gates. The security guard was not keen to be that kind, because he had nothing about it on his list of approved visitors. But after a heated consultation with someone at the main house, the gates buzzed, and they welcomed me onto the property.

Once inside, I pulled to the side of the road, stopped the van, switched on the hazards, and climbed out. I waved towards the window of the security hut, and a moment later a security guard stepped out with an angry scowl on his face. I explained to him that their internet cable passed through a trench under the ground, and that I would have to check it all the way to the main house to find the problem, and would therefore not be arriving at the main house for some time. He shrugged. I gave him an encouraging smile, and climbed back into my van.

Security systems, even advanced ones, are mostly a waste of money. That was something else I had learnt from Chandler in the pursuit of our criminal activities. Because the problem with all security systems, no matter how expensive they are, is in distinguishing between those who should be allowed in and those who should not. In obvious situations, such as a man dressed in camouflage, wearing a balaclava, and carrying an automatic weapon, it is not difficult to make the distinction. The difficulty arises on the subtler distinctions, such as when deliveries are made to the house, as in the case of the delivery of gas bottles for the kitchens, which occurred at oh eight thirty that morning at the House of Our Lord. The sweaty, obese driver of the truck that bore the gas bottles onto the property was pleased to see a worker provided by the House to help him with the arduous task of rolling the heavy gas bottles inside. It was probably the first time the staff had provided such thoughtful service, but he would not complain about it. And the kitchen worker who opened the back door to allow the gas bottles in was not surprised to see that the man delivering the gas had brought someone along to help, and was too busy peeling potatoes to stand there and make sure that they both left the premises.

The gas delivery man left me in the storeroom to arrange the gas canisters more neatly against the wall. I found an empty box which looked as if it had held vegetables, lifted it onto my shoulders and set out to explore the House of Our Lord. I wandered back into the kitchens, where three cooks were cleaning up after the breakfast service. They didn't challenge my right to walk through the kitchens with an empty box on my shoulder, and were very helpful in providing directions to the laundry when I explained it was my first day on the job.

The laundry was occupied by a single woman in her

late sixties with glasses made from the bases of wine bottles, and the beginnings of a beard sprouting from her chin. She was happy to provide me with a full novitiate outfit, although she grumbled about the request not being submitted in the usual way and insisted that I sign a scrap of paper to the effect that I absolved her of all blame. Having done this, I confessed I was feeling confused on my first day and had already forgotten how to get back to the main office. She laughed, revealing that her teeth were in no better condition than her eyes, and told me it was one floor up and on the other side of the building. I admitted I had thought that was the Master's private section, and didn't want to wander where I was not welcome, but she reminded me that the Master occupied the second floor of the west wing, and that there was someone on watch there who would prevent my accidentally wandering into the Master's private zone, because after breakfast he returned there to spend time with his daughters.

She then explained where the bathrooms were on this lower level, I thanked her again, and changed into the novitiate clothes in a stall of the bathrooms. I packed my dockworker overalls into the cistern of the old-fashioned toilet because I didn't want the kitchen staff raising alarms. Then I made my way to the second floor of the west wing.

Brother Isaiah – whom I had last seen raking up leaves in the orchard beside the apiary – was on guard duty upstairs. He was sitting at a desk, wearing the same brown robes that I was. I guessed that his period of silence during which he had engaged with God's creation had gone some way towards cleansing the sin that had weighed so heavily upon his heart. He looked up at me, and a glimmer of recognition flitted across his face. But it didn't linger. I raised my hand in an imitation of the science fiction salute I had seen them all give one another on my previous visit and hoped that the master had not watched any new movies and changed the protocol. Brother Isaiah returned the gesture and then narrowed his eyes slightly as a way of asking me what I wanted. I noticed his robes were a little bunched at the left shoulder, as they had been in the orchard, by the strap of his handgun holster.

"Our father," I said, fighting the feeling that I was about to lead a group prayer, "has asked me to wait for him here."

"Wait for him?" said Brother Isaiah, and his pronounced forehead wrinkled as he attempted to process that, his sinful eyes narrowing further.

"Until he is ready for me," I said, by way of clarification.

"Ready for you?" said Brother Isaiah, who was not turning out to be a talented conversationalist.

I gave a nod and then made a temple out of my fingers and turned to place my shoulders against the wall and bowed my head as if I was about to pray silently.

"Father is at morning study," said Brother Isaiah, coming up with something original to add to the conversation.

"Of course," I said, and bowed my head again as if that was an end to the conversation.

"Do I know you?" asked Brother Isaiah, who was not entirely buying my performance.

"You do not," I said, and a long silence ensued during which Brother Isaiah studied me from beneath his Neanderthal brow and I gazed at the patterned carpet.

Brother Isaiah had still not dredged my face from his memories, which were perhaps buried even deeper than had been his sin, when we both heard the sudden chiming of a young girl's laugh. It was a surprisingly joyful sound that echoed down the hushed corridor that Brother Isaiah was protecting, and I looked up to see who had produced it. The corridor was empty – it was a long corridor of dark wooden flooring with a patterned carpet stretched down the centre. There were five doors on each side of the corridor, all the same dark wood, all closed. A door at the far end opened and a beam of early morning sun sprang out of it, followed by a girl of about three years old, who laughed again as she trotted with small uncertain steps, her blonde curls bouncing with joy. Close behind her another girl followed, a few years older, with long, auburn hair that looked as if it had just been brushed, and which flowed about her shoulders like a viscous fluid. She was chasing after the younger girl, reaching out with both hands as if to grab her, but taking small steps as she ran to prolong the game. Brother Isaiah and I watched the two girls approach. Then a woman appeared behind them, silhouetted for a moment against the dazzling beam of sunlight. A slender body in a yellow spring dress, the details filling in slowly as she walked towards us.

A part of me had expected to see her, but the shock of surprise struck me like a physical blow, and I felt myself sag against the wall for a moment. Except that her hair was shorter, she was as I remembered her: the high cheekbones, her pointed nose, and full lips. Her eyes created the illusion of sadness, an illusion that was shattered when she opened her mouth to smile, which she did now as the girls' happiness spread down the corridor. The smile started with a curl of the edges of her lips, then spread up to her golden eyes. She lifted a hand in acknowledgement of Brother Isaiah, who had risen to his feet and was stooping down, preparing to catch the young girl barrelling down the corridor towards us. She hadn't seen me yet, and the smile grew into a laugh as the girl was swept up by Brother Isaiah with a squeal of delight from the girl. I stepped away from the wall and stood behind the kneeling figure of Brother Isaiah, and I saw the questioning glimmer of a frown. Then the blink of her golden eyes, the faltering step and the laugh and the smile dropped from her face. She stopped dead in the centre of the corridor, and her hand dropped against her side. She stared at me, and I stared back.

The little girl stopped squealing and the older girl's laugh died as if the tension between us was silencing everything in its path. Brother Isaiah stood and looked from her to me and back again. The two girls turned back to her, then rushed to stand at her side, and turned to face me as if I was threatening them all.

"Hello, Sandy," I said.

Sandy said nothing. Brother Isaiah reached under his robe and pulled out a Sig Sauer, which he pointed vaguely in my direction and his great brow wrinkled.

"Is there a problem, ma'am?" he asked. He was looking at me, so he hadn't seen Sandy close her eyes, as if she thought she could make me disappear. "He's waiting for the Father," he explained, and the pistol wobbled in a way that revealed his lack of experience at handling it.

Sandy opened her eyes, and two tears rolled down her cheeks.

"There's no problem, Brother," she said, and the sound of her voice was another painful jab. "No problem at all," she said.

"Do you know this Brother?" asked Brother Isaiah.

"I do," said Sandy, and there was a long pause. Brother Isaiah glanced at her anxiously, but might not have noticed the tears which glistened on her cheeks because she smiled at him, and her smile was dazzling. "Would you mind watching the girls for a few minutes? This man has come to see me."

"He's waiting for the Father," said Brother Isaiah again, and the gun wobbled with confusion.

"I know he is," said Sandy, and she raised the smile again, which calmed Brother Isaiah enough for him to lower his gun. "Could you ask the Father to join us in the break-fast room when he comes up from study?"

Brother Isaiah said that he could, and he returned his gun to its holster. Sandy stooped and whispered something to the two girls, who then trotted back up the corridor and each took one of Brother Isaiah's hands.

"Come along, Ben," said Sandy, and she turned and walked down the corridor to the sunlit room.

THIRTY-TWO

S andy was already standing with her back to me at one of the huge sash windows, her face tilted up to receive the sun, which was doing its best under trying circumstances. Her eyes were closed, her face turned slightly so that I could be reminded of the profile I had loved to see in the mornings of another life long ago: the long lashes, the high cheekbones, the delicate cheeks.

"Leilah is such a poor liar," she said. "I knew you wouldn't believe her."

"She mixed her lies with a lot of truth," I said.

Sandy turned to face me, her eyes more golden than ever; the sun providing highlights on her cheek.

"I learnt that from you," she said. "Don't make it up – isn't that what you always said? Make it all true, but leave the harder truths out."

"I heard some of the harder truths last night," I said.

Sandy smiled her sad smile. The lips curled and her eyes shared the sadness, but then amusement flipped it over and the sadness fled.

"I thought she might tell you the full story. She wants you to stop me. That's why she told you."

"Yes," I said. "I think so. She is struggling with the burden of having helped you kill those men."

"But you won't stop me, will you?"

"Won't I?"

"When the judge told me about you going to see him, it was such a surprise. Did Leilah say it was because of you he carried a knife with him and tried to kill us with it? But you are not to blame for his death, you must know that. Nor is Leilah to blame, for holding him down. No, the blame is all mine. I think it was inevitable that I would do it."

"Or perhaps some of the blame was his," I said. "Was Amanda the only one? Or were there other girls?"

"There were others. Many others. These men developed a taste for it. Isn't it true that when a lion develops a taste for human flesh, it must be killed? That there is no other way of stopping it?"

I didn't provide an answer to her question, and we were silent for a moment.

"You always told me that killing leaves a mark," said Sandy. "And I have realised you were right. I couldn't come back from it – from that first time, after killing those two men in the shack."

"Why didn't you try?" I asked. "Why didn't you come to me and ask for help?"

"I did. Didn't you know that?"

"You collected your clothes."

"No, I came back to you, came back to our apartment. I stood in the lounge and I wept. That was all I could do. I climbed into our bed and smelt you there, and I wept some more. It was pathetic. I couldn't stay. I knew then what had happened to me, Ben. Something inside me died the night I killed those men. I knew you were out looking for me, talking to the police, pushing for justice, fighting for what was right in the way you always did, and I realised then what had happened to me."

"You can get help. People who've been through that kind of trauma can be helped."

Sandy shook her head and gave another sad smile.

"I know you speak from experience, Ben, but everyone's struggle is different. I thought I was fine, I really did, that all I needed was a bit of time to recover. I didn't mean to leave forever, just for a short while. I thought that I would expose those men for what they had done, and that would be my path to recovery – isn't that what they call it? The path to recovery, like it's a simple, straight line you walk along."

"It's not a path you should walk alone."

"Isn't it? You walk it alone, don't you? You are still trying to recover. I know you are. Besides, I was not alone. I had Leilah."

"And you lost your way?"

"Yes. When the judge pulled out his knife."

Sandy paused, and her eyes studied me.

"Do you understand, Ben?"

We stood in silence as she searched me for a sign of understanding, or perhaps a sign of anger, even of forgiveness.

"I took my clothes," she said, when I gave no answer. "Because I knew the police would stop searching for me."

"And you hoped I would too."

"I needed time," she said, and her eyes filled suddenly with tears. "You are still angry with me, aren't you? Is that why you're here? Or have you come to save a monster's life?"

"Bill is the one who's angry."

Sandy blinked, and the tears spilt from her eyes.

"I know what damage I have caused, how much hurt."

She hesitated, then smiled, and there was maybe a little joy in it.

"You do understand."

I didn't confirm that I understood, but neither did I deny it.

"And you do want to stop me," she said. "That is why you're here."

"You will deprive those two girls of their father. Is that what you want?"

"A monster is not a father."

"Don't be so sure. Fathers come in all forms. Would you take their father away as yours was taken from you?"

She blinked again, spilt more tears.

"That's where you started," she said. "I didn't understand how you found Leilah, but it was through my father, wasn't it?"

"He is a good man," I said.

"He is. Hurting him has been another sacrifice in order to stop this evil."

"No, it hasn't. Sacrifice is when you pay the price, not volunteer others to pay on your behalf."

"You don't think I've paid the price?"

I didn't answer that. The sun passed behind a cloud and the golden rim to Sandy's cheeks disappeared as the room was plunged into a sudden gloom.

"This man is a monster, Ben – as was the judge and that politician. This one was given the chance to redeem himself with the gift of fatherhood. But he didn't. They are monsters, and they believe nobody can stop them. Who was it said the world won't be destroyed by those who do evil, but by those who stand by and watch? Should I have done that? Stood by and watched them, like everyone else, and not done anything?"

"You've sent your message," I said. "Why not show your grace? Allow him to live and change his ways."

Sandy shook her head.

"No. Because he won't. There will be no changing of his ways."

We fell to silence again, and the sun made a weak attempt at getting back into the room, but failed.

"Can I ask you something?" said Sandy.

I didn't say whether she could, but she asked anyway.

"Who were you protecting when you said nothing to the police? I've seen your name all over the news. They have you as the person who's been doing this, and you've said nothing. Did you think it was Leilah? Or did you know it was me? Leilah says you believed her when she told you I was dead."

"Leilah is a poor liar," I said.

The door to the room opened abruptly, as if someone was expecting to discover us in a compromising position. It was flung so hard that it swung all the way to smash against the wall with a bang. Sandy jumped at the sudden sound. I turned to see Johannes Stephanus Erasmus standing in the open doorway, wearing his black robes with the white cleric's collar, his dark hair carefully parted, his pale blue eyes burning with an icy rage.

"What is this?" he demanded of the room.

Neither Sandy nor I provided an answer. He clenched his jaw and breathed out through his nose like a bull snorting before it charges. Then he stepped into the room and closed the door behind him with measured movements, as if he was struggling to keep his anger in check.

"Why don't you lock the door behind you?" said Sandy. "Like you do when those young women come to visit."

JS turned to her and blinked with surprise.

"You will address me as Father," he said. "What is going on? Who is this man?"

"I will not address you as Father," said Sandy. "Never again."

JS blinked again. "This is the man who threatened me," he said. "Do you know him?"

"I do know him," said Sandy. "He is a good man – one of the best – a man I loved deeply. And now he might be the only man who stands between you and your death."

"My death? What do you mean, woman? Are you saying he's going to try to kill me?" He turned his furious eyes onto me. "Just let him try."

"Not him," said Sandy. "Me. I am going to kill you."

JS uttered a contemptuous laugh, then closed his mouth and his lips trembled with anger. He took a few steps further into the room, and gave the laugh again, forced and unconvincing.

"Do you know who I am?" asked Sandy. "Have you ever asked yourself who I am?"

"I know who you are," he said dismissively, but didn't prove it.

"No, you don't. Brother Isaiah probably never told you that the two men he sent to kill me failed."

"What two men?"

"Brother Isaiah paid two men to kill me, but they didn't succeed. Was that something he kept quiet from you?"

JS Erasmus swallowed and found no words to say.

"That is who I am," said Sandy. "I am the woman you thought you had killed. The sister of one of the girls you did kill. At a party at which you wore a mask on your face, alongside the judge and the politician. Together, you men of power raped her and you killed her. And today I am going to kill you."

"How are you going to do that?" asked JS, in a voice that was stretching a little thin across his anxious throat.

"With this," said Sandy, and she brought her hands before her to show him the surgical scalpel she was holding. The stainless steel handle glinted as the sun tried to make a return from behind the cloud, but failed again.

JS laughed for a third time with weakening conviction. "You're going to kill me with that?" he scoffed.

"It's a knife that belonged to Judge Rousseau," said Sandy. "It's so sharp that it will slice through your neck like a hot knife through butter. The skin just peels away. That's what it did with the neck of Rousseau, and the neck of Jessop Ndoro."

JS Erasmus turned to me.

"What are you doing? Are you going to stand there, insulting the robes of my church, and do nothing while this pathetic woman threatens me?"

"You should leave, Ben," said Sandy. "Leave me to finish this, and lock the door behind you."

But I did not leave, and I did not lock the door, which was something I would regret later. Instead, I stood still. There comes a moment in any situation where the smallest thing could tip the balance and cause an avalanche of events. I sensed we were approaching such a tipping point now and wanted to be ready in case the avalanche went the wrong way. Sandy was not focusing on me or whether I was leaving or locking the door. Her eyes were on JS Erasmus.

"I understand you," she said to him. "Because I come from a family that services men – a long line of prostitutes – that's what we are, a long, long line. But now it is time for you to pay for the service my family and others like us have provided."

JS was watching her with increasing trepidation. It might have been that he realised she was going to use the knife, or perhaps his sins were finally coming back to him. It looked as if he was feeling his grip on reality slip. He kept his eyes on Sandy, but shouted suddenly at the top of his voice, a desperate cry for help. The surprise of his sudden call deprived me for a moment of hearing the words, but then he shouted again: "Brother Isaiah!"

That sudden shout tipped the balance. The silence that followed it was a brief suspension of time, a pause before everything that ensued.

Sandy leapt across the space between them like an animal launching at its prey. JS Erasmus held up his hands to block her strike, but all he blocked was the hand without the knife, which she used to swipe aside his flailing arms and clear the path to his neck. The hand with the scalpel plunged forwards and upwards and a burst of blood sprayed into her face as she pressed the blade deep into the side of his neck. The carotid artery is only a few centimetres below the surface at its shallowest point, and by sheer chance Sandy found that point.

JS Erasmus staggered backwards, his head tilted back, driven by the momentum of Sandy's leap. He dropped to his knees, and Sandy fell onto him. I moved towards the door, hearing the rush of heavy steps approach down the corridor. A moment later the door burst open, kicked by Brother Isaiah, who was pointing his Sig Sauer uncertainly before him. The barrel wobbled, and I swung my foot to kick at it, aware of Sandy's head coming up to look at him. His eyes were wide and frightened as he took in the sight of his master on his knees, and the blood on Sandy's face. The

Sig bounced in his hand as he squeezed the trigger, firing a single shot before my foot connected, breaking his fingers and flinging the gun across the room. Brother Isaiah turned his huge forehead to me with dazed confusion and I punched him on his nose, breaking it with a nasty crunch and a spurt of blood. His eyes opened wider, and he pulled back a hand to punch me in return, but he was wide open and no fighter, despite all the sin in his heart, and my next punch connected with his jawbone halfway between the chin and the ear. I struck him so hard that I cracked the bone. The two nerve clusters beneath his ear would have delivered a shock to his brain stem that caused such an over-load that he lost consciousness before he hit the ground.

Sandy had been struck in the chest. The force of the bullet had pushed her backwards, and she was lying in a crumpled heap, her eyes staring up at the ceiling, and her mouth moving as if she was trying to say something.

JS Erasmus had fallen to his side, a pool of blood spreading beneath him. I didn't spare time for him, but knelt beside Sandy and gently lifted her so that I could feel for the wound. It was in the centre of the chest and blood was seeping out of the exit wound on her back. I held her as tightly as I could.

"I said you wouldn't stop me," she whispered.

"Don't speak. Save your energy."

"Nothing to save," said Sandy. "It's too late."

"No, it's never too late."

But I knew it was. I have seen too many people die, and the fear was fading now from her golden eyes.

"I understand," said Sandy, her breath losing its force, her voice only a whisper.

"Understand what?"

"Why you said nothing. Don't take the blame, Ben."

Her warm blood was trickling through my fingers, and her eyes flickered like a candle blown by the wind.

"Don't take the blame for their deaths."

"Don't talk," I said, but she kept whispering even though her breath was all but gone.

"Sometimes," she coughed and blood came out of her mouth and trickled down her cheek. "Good men must stand aside and do nothing in order to triumph over evil."

The flickering of her eyes slowed, then stopped. They stayed open, and I looked into them as her life expired. There was the slight sigh of the last gasp as it left her body. Then she drooped in my arms. I closed her eyes and lay her gently on the floor.

The lifeless eyes of Johannes Stephanus Erasmus gazed up at me as I stepped over him to reach the sash window. I tugged at the handles and the window slid upwards. There was a four-metre drop to the garden below, a well-tended garden with a lawn that came right up to a narrow gravel path that skirted the building. I could hear the sounds of footsteps approaching down the corridor, and I considered making the jump.

But instead, I returned to Sandy's side.

THIRTY-THREE

In Pollsmoor Prison they provided me with accommodation of my own. That was probably for my own safety, not because of the danger I posed to those around me, although I did wonder.

And then I waited.

I sat in silence, stared at the chipped plaster wall and listened to the sounds of despair that were the white noise of one of the most notorious prisons in the world.

I had a lot of time to think about the mistakes I had made, the things I could have said to Sandy, to Robyn, and even to Fat-Boy and to Chandler. I replayed Sandy's last moments several times and thought of the things I could have expressed, but then let it all go. Familiar enough with the dark spiral of regret and recrimination that the death of someone close can cause, I have learnt many of the ways of fighting my way back out of that deepening spiral, but a prison cell is not the optimum place to fight that battle. By the third day of my incarceration, I had slipped further down into the dark chasm than I liked to admit. Things that Robyn had said to me about her own struggles came back, and I was grateful for the rungs of support they provided. I was mulling over that, and the two women in my life and what we each did for one another, and didn't do, when three guards arrived at my cell door. They fitted me with handcuffs and leg-irons which trailed chains across the floor as I shuffled between them towards what they euphemistically called a 'meeting' room.

"You got a meeting with your lawyer," said one of the guards, as if he was trying to cheer me up by telling me about the treat that awaited.

"I don't have a lawyer," I said.

He pursed his lips and raised his eyebrows, which was as far as he was going to go towards resolving that existential puzzle.

My lawyer had a black eye and a nasty cut on his cheek that had required stitches. But he was dressed in an Armani suit, with a pink silk tie and his cropped white hair and military bearing made up for the flesh wounds and presented a fairly convincing display of legality.

He was standing behind a wounded chair on the other side of a perspex screen in a row of interview booths. A guard stood behind him with the look of a man who would not be listening in on our conversation.

We sat down together like the choreographed move in an old etiquette movie and reached for our handsets. He looked at me and concern spread across his face as he took in my diminished state. He said nothing for a beat, so I spoke first.

"What happened to your eye?" I said.

"Good job," said Chandler, ignoring my insolence, "with the whole keeping a low profile thing. Sorting out your issues with the police, and all that."

"You should not have come here," I said.

"Fat-Boy cannot believe you killed the woman as well. But Robyn says she was your journalist, and you might not have killed her."

"You should not be here," I said again.

"They've been denying you legal representation, wouldn't let me see you until now. Seventy-two hours!"

"There is a reason for that. They have been waiting."

"Waiting for what?"

"For you."

Chandler said nothing.

"They have asked me no questions, there have been no interrogations, not even a standard arraignment. There is a reason, Colonel, that you are the first person I have seen."

I closed my mouth and cursed myself – I had called him Colonel.

"Colchester," said Chandler, who also realised my slip. "Colonel Colchester."

He would have had to present identification to be here, but it appalled me that he should have played that card again.

"Colonel," I said. "I am relying on your knowledge of the law to understand their reason for waiting. Please act accordingly, and quickly. I hope it is not too late."

Chandler nodded and I could see the cogs turning as he realised the implications of what I was saying. I let the guard know we were finished and avoided further eye contact with Chandler lest I interrupt his thoughts. As I shuffled back down the corridor, I hoped the cogs would turn fast enough. Because if I was right about the reason the police had not interrogated me over the murder of JS Erasmus, and had stretched the delay to the seventy-two-hour limit, then it seemed likely that someone was now paging with interest through Chandler's old army files – making connections to me, perhaps to Robyn and to Fat-Boy; drawing neat little organograms of heist team structures. And if I was right, Chandler's arrival here today had provided them with the last piece of a complicated puzzle they had been trying to solve. And that would mean that it would not just be me paying the price of my sins.

———

My second social engagement occurred less than an hour later, which seemed like an ominous confirmation of my suspicions. I was fitted with all the chains again, and guided down the corridor to a different meeting room. The same guard walked beside me, but he didn't raise any further existential questions and made no effort to cheer me up.

Captain Andile Dlamini was sitting on a wobbly chair at a stained wooden table. I shuffled in, while his weary eyes watched me as if refusing to believe the evidence of my depravity. He wasn't looking much better himself. It didn't look as if he had slept since I had last seen him, and he was obviously too tired to return my smile. The guards left us alone because Andile had that kind of clout, and then Andile stared at me for a good minute before saying anything.

"What on earth were you doing?" he asked. "Were you trying to stop her, or were you there to help her?"

I opened my mouth to reply, but he held up a hand of nicotine-stained fingers.

"Don't," he said. "Spare me the sales pitch, Gabriel. It would be hurtful to have to endure any more lies."

We sat in silence for another full minute as if we were

mourning something – perhaps the end of a promising friendship – then he looked up at me, his eyes red with exhaustion.

"At least your disappearing journalist reappeared," he said.

"She did," I said, "yes."

"You were trying to persuade her to come in and speak with me? When you visited her at the religious leader's fortress?"

"I was. But she didn't think it was a good idea."

Andile had a folder on the table before him. He flipped it open and stared at a bunch of handwritten pages as if he was mustering the energy to read them to me.

"We had men there," said Andile. "In the house."

"I thought you might," I said.

"Recognised you when you came through the gate."

"Did they?"

"Then they lost you. They were out in the gardens while you were inside."

I did my best to look regretful about that.

"You are lucky they reached you before those men in the dresses."

"I think they prefer the term 'robes'."

"The whole thing raises some questions," said Andile, "about other members of the church, and how many of them knew what their leader was up to."

"Sounds like a good thing," I said. "There are many questions that should be raised about what was happening in that church."

Andile held up his hand again to stop me from getting ahead of myself, and his eyes scanned the handwritten notes. He looked up after a pause.

"There is someone who has come forward," he said. "Since your arrest."

"Ah yes?" I fervently hoped that someone would not turn out to be the foolish Colonel Colchester. He had been using that false identity for way too long.

"Yes," said Andile, and his eyes held mine to see whether they would give anything away. They didn't. He looked back down at the handwritten notes and I looked at them more closely. I realised with a rush of relief that it was Sandy's handwriting. Perhaps the reason they had delayed pressing charges against me was not that they were waiting for Chandler to wander in.

"Claims to be the father of your journalist. Identified the body for us, and further claims that he knows you."

He looked back up at me.

"He does," I said.

"Thought his daughter had died some time ago, it seems. Provided us with some notes that she made. Helped us work out what had been going on."

Andile dried up at that and seemed to wait for a response. I didn't provide one.

"Nasty business the whole thing. Trafficking of underage girls, luring them in with drugs, a party where they killed a girl – it's hard to believe."

"Very nasty," I agreed.

"We will reduce the charges against you to 'aiding and abetting'. Carries a lower sentence, might even be suspended. You'll be released in a couple of hours. Someone has paid your bail."

"Someone?" I said.

Andile sighed with some regret.

"You have friends in high places. Why don't you go and

see your ex-employers, Gabriel. They wield more influence than you realise."

"The Department paid my bail?"

"I'm only suggesting you see them because we have a personal relationship, and I feel you deserve a nudge in the right direction."

"Did it take you seventy-two hours to decide to reduce my charges? Or has there been another reason for the delay?"

"Speak to them, Gabriel. That's all I will say about it."

"Thank you," I said, and I meant it.

He called for the guards to take me away, and we sat in silence as we waited.

"It wasn't my doing, Gabriel," he said, as I stood to leave. "Your lawyer should have been more circumspect, instead of arriving here and showing his face to all the cameras."

He sounded genuinely regretful.

"I kept telling him that," I said, and followed the guard back to my cell, full of my own regret.

———

"We are very pleased of course," said Fehrson, "very pleased indeed."

He bared his long teeth and receding gums in what might have been a smile.

"Of course we are," he repeated in case the inevitability of their pleasure had not been clear.

Khanyi joined him in his smile.

"There was a delay," I said, "of the full seventy-two hours."

Khanyi shook her head in sympathy and Fehrson tut-tutted.

"A law unto themselves," said Fehrson. "The police these days, shocking what this country has come to."

He gave a dip of the head in silent regret. Belinda, the nearly spherical chief of catering for the Department, announced her arrival in the Attic with a series of loud puffing sounds like a steam train letting off excess steam.

"Coffee," announced Fehrson, as if the murky brown water Belinda brewed was something to celebrate.

"The milk was sour," said Belinda. "I added powdered creamer."

"Sounds wonderful," said Fehrson, but he didn't keep the enthusiastic smile up for long when faced with the white lumps that floated at the top of his mug.

We waited until Belinda had huffed and puffed her way back down the spiral staircase and then I spoilt the celebratory mood by saying, "Could we stop with all the pretence, and get straight to the point?"

Khanyi looked up from the mug she had been squinting at as she blew the white lumps to clear them.

"What point?" she said.

"We all know the reason for the seventy-two hour delay. I expect that you have identified the man who came to see me by now. What is it you want from me?"

"Want from you?" asked Khanyi, but she placed her coffee mug back onto the table in case she needed both hands for the next bit.

"There are four of us," I said. "I suppose you have established that by now and have already identified the others. What is it you want?"

"Must you insist on speaking in riddles, my boy?" asked Fehrson, and in his irritation took a sip from his mug, then winced and placed it onto the table and glared at me as if it was my fault.

"You've traced them," I said, "haven't you? You know Chandler was my captain when I served in the British army, and I expect you know about his associates, and some of what we have been up to recently."

Khanyi glanced at Fehrson, but he was staring regretfully at the whirlpool of lumps in his coffee as he made a loud clattering sound, stirring it with a teaspoon.

"Your police captain suggested we meet here," I continued, "when he had questions about that judge, because he described it as neutral territory. But that was nonsense, wasn't it Khanyi?"

Khanyi opened her mouth to provide another denial, but I spoke before she had a chance.

"There was a reason for your keen interest in the police investigation into my activities. And it has not been hard to guess who posted my bail."

Neither Khanyi nor Fehrson said anything. They both looked up at me with clear eyes and innocent expressions, but I was not fooled.

"Before you deny it," I said. "Allow me to make a proposal. If I must sell my soul to the devil, let me at least name my price."

"The devil?" said Fehrson, and he tried to produce a laugh.

"What price?" asked Khanyi flatly.

"Indemnity. Not for me, but my colleagues."

Khanyi said nothing. Fehrson reached for his cup of coffee and raised it to his lips, before remembering his earlier regret, and lowered it again.

"You would want it in writing?" he asked. "This indemnity?"

"I would," I said.

"I will let Khanyisile take care of the paperwork," said Fehrson, and he raised his mug towards me as if he was about to propose a toast. "You always were a cunning devil, young man. Your colleagues must be grateful they have you on their side."

"Not at all. My colleagues regret the day I joined their side," I said. And I meant it.

THIRTY-FOUR

Chandler drove us to the airport in his custom Jaguar XJ220, with matte bronze finish and surround sound. It felt like we were floating along the highway in a bubble, with Yo-yo Ma and a fifty-piece orchestra stuffed into the trunk. We finished the Adagio movement of Elgar's cello concerto and Chandler switched it off. We drove in silence for a few minutes.

"Know why the cello does that to you?" asked Chandler.

"Does what?"

"Stirs up the emotions more than any other instrument – you know why?"

"I don't."

"It is the instrument that is closest to the human voice. Evokes the sense of a fellow human desperately trying to express themselves, but with no words, no meaning, only the pure sound. It's the sound of desperation that evokes the emotion."

"You're making that up," I said.

We drove in silence for a few minutes.

"What did your government goons want?" he asked, eventually. "It was them that paid your bail, wasn't it?"

"They wanted nothing."

He took his eyes off the road in order to study me.

"They never want nothing, Angel. Don't lie to me."

"Did it for old time's sake," I said.

Chandler turned back to the road.

"You're with us now, Angel, on our side of the line. Remember that. If you need anything, you come to me, not to those snivelling white-washers."

"I won't forget," I said.

Chandler switched the player on again, and the first jaunty chords of the fourth movement sprang out at us. Then a breathless pause and the cello's plaintive tone evoked so much emotion in Chandler that his grasp on the steering wheel wobbled.

"Desperation," said Chandler, "that's what it is. The sound of desperation."

———

Fat-Boy was waiting for us at the entrance to the hangar. We performed a series of complex handshakes, and he pulled me in close, pressed me up against his belly, and squeezed hard.

"The colonel says you didn't kill those men," he said in a tone that made it clear he hadn't believed the colonel.

"I didn't," I said.

"Want to tell us what this is all about, Fat-Boy?" asked Chandler.

"We'll be about an hour," said Fat-Boy, and he indicated the Cessna-182 standing behind him. A youthful boy with a peaked cap was holding a phial of fuel up to the sky.

"That child the pilot?" asked Chandler.

"He's got a licence," said Fat-Boy.

"One he bought off the black market? Or did he do the test?"

"He's my aunt's nephew," said Fat-Boy, as if that answered the question.

"All set, Uncle Stan," called the youth.

Fat-Boy swung his arm wide in a gesture that invited us to climb aboard.

"Grab yourselves a headset," he said, "we've got shit to talk about."

Chandler sat up front beside the pilot and I noticed his hands hovering beneath the dual controls as we accelerated down the runway in case he needed to take over. But the young pilot lifted neatly into the crosswind and kept us straight until five hundred feet, then turned onto a westerly bearing, and Chandler relaxed.

"Three times," said Fat-Boy into his headset microphone so that the words nearly burst my eardrums. "That's how I knew."

"What did you know?" I asked.

"Where it was," said Fat-Boy in his gloating voice. "How many times do you think those Dark Bizness slave-labourers carried that gold?"

"Three times?"

Fat-Boy glared at me through his good eye.

"Not counting the time it was in the concrete," said Fat-Boy, dissatisfied with my answer. "They used a crane for that. I mean with their hands."

"Twice?"

Fat-Boy shook his head.

"Three times," he said.

"That's what I said the first time."

"Why three times?" asked Chandler irritably.

"That's what I asked the man guarding me in that little room on that boat. He got guard duty 'cos he refused to carry those boxes again."

"Little cabin," said Chandler. "Rooms on boats are called cabins."

"No, Colonel, this was a room."

"What did the man say?"

"*Kathathu* is what he said. It means three times. He was an angry Xhosa, that one. Said they had to carry those bars *kathathu*, not *kabini*."

"I don't understand," I admitted.

"Remember that other boat?" said Fat-Boy. "The one you pushed me off? With the captain with one eye that got killed."

"I remember it," I said.

"When I asked him why three times he said: first onto this big ship, then onto that old boat, then into the truck."

"Why onto the old boat?"

"That's what I wondered. Then afterwards I realised – if the bars they loaded into our truck were fake bars, they must've loaded the real bars somewhere they thought nobody would look. That's why three times. Didn't I tell you that old boat was going to be auctioned off?"

"You did."

"Don't tell me you bought the goddamn boat, Fat-Boy," said Chandler.

"I didn't," said Fat-Boy. "But it turns out Lebo Madikwe did."

———

Fat-Boy's nephew landed without incident on the dirt strip at Langebaan, and then another of his relatives, presumably from the branch of his family that had not been killed when building the railway line, drove us to the harbour and took us out to the barge in a small dinghy.

The wheelhouse was still leaning at a crooked angle, splintered wood scattered across the deck. Fat-Boy led the way down below.

There was an old tarpaulin lying over what could have been a pile of bricks. Fat-Boy pulled the tarpaulin off, and our gold glimmered in the dim murk.

"One hundred and twenty bars," said Fat-Boy. "I counted them."

Chandler turned to me.

"I will leave it to you," he said, "to tell Robyn that her curse has returned."

———

"I knew they were wrong," said Bill and he blew his nose on a bright purple handkerchief before clarifying, "about it being you who killed those men."

"Thank you, Bill," I said. "There was a moment when I thought even you might suspect me."

Bill's eyes were full of tears, and he blinked in preparation to deny his suspicion. But I smiled to show I was only teasing. "It was a beautiful speech," I said.

"I got a bit emotional," he complained, and wiped his eyes.

"We all did. That's what memorial services are for."

"I like Robyn," he said. "She's very kind."

We both looked over to where Robyn was supporting Tannie Sara.

"She is," I agreed, and Robyn looked up as if she knew we were speaking about her.

There had been a small group at Sandy's memorial service, and afterwards a handful of us stood around her grave, while the wind played tug of war with our scarves and pressed the priest's robes up against him in an inappropriately intimate fashion as he finished the final prayer. Bill had made a very moving speech and Leilah had clung to me and wept, leaving my shoulder so damp that it was now growing cold in the icy wind at the grave. Benjamin stood on the other side of Sandy's last resting place, his lips moving in a silent prayer of his own. Then he turned from the grave and, with Leilah on his arm, led the way to his house where we were going to celebrate Sandy's life in what he had described as a non-denominational wake.

Bill and I trailed a little behind Tannie Sara, who walked with Robyn's support, and was trying to find her sunglasses in an enormous bag that hung over her shoulder. She found the glasses, at least three sizes too big for her face, and used them to cover her red eyes. Then she found a tissue to wipe the tears that fell beneath them.

"For a short while I did," admitted Bill when we were halfway down the hill. "Just for a short while, I thought it was possible that you killed those men. You seemed so angry, so vengeful."

"You didn't try to stop me," I said.

"Why would I stop you? I was also angry. I believed you were doing it for all of us."

We continued in silence to Benjamin's house. The fire was still burning, and I helped him warm the mulled wine. Then we stood before the wall of photographs of Sandy and her sister and proposed toasts to them both.

———

Robyn and I walked to the foot of Benjamin's garden and we stood together on the bank of the river.

"I'm so glad you wanted me to be here," said Robyn.

"Sandy has been a part of your life. Of course you should be here."

She leaned up against me, and I put an arm around her and held her close.

"Our lives are going to change now, aren't they?" she said.

"In what way?"

"In a good way."

"What do you mean?"

"We've done enough running, and trying to escape. Things are going to swing back in our favour."

"I hope so."

"Now that we've shaken the curse," said Robyn, and she looked up at me with her dark eyes, as if she was asking a question.

"Exactly," I said. "Now that we've shaken it."

The sky was clear, and the light of the moon shone off her face.

"Unless the curse has returned," I said. "Then we might be in trouble."

Robyn shook her head and smiled.

"It's nonsense, all of that, isn't it? There is no curse."

"I thought you were convinced about it."

Robyn laughed, as if the idea was absurd. We stood in silence for a moment and listened to the sound of frogs in the river and laughter from the house.

"Fat-Boy has found the gold, hasn't he?" asked Robyn, her eyes still on mine.

I nodded. "Fat-Boy and the colonel have been frightened to tell you."

I looked into her eyes and realised that she had tricked me.

"You are convinced it's cursed, aren't you?"

"Of course it is. We're not just in trouble, Ben, we're in deep, deep trouble."

But she smiled, and then she kissed me.

When we returned to Sandy's wake, Tannie Sara was wearing her sunglasses again because she didn't want us to see that she was still crying, although the streaks of mascara were a bit of a giveaway. She had asked Benjamin for his forgiveness – he had given it – and the two of them were standing arm in arm and laughing at Leilah who insisted that she would give Bill a special discount if he ever found himself at Pandora. Bill was blushing and drinking his mulled wine too fast. I helped myself to more wine, Robyn fixed herself some sparkling water with elderflower cordial, and the six of us laughed and cried all night.

It was a night I wanted to last forever.

ALSO BY DAVID HICKSON

Have you read them all?

Treasonous – *The Gabriel Series – Book One*

A journalist's dead body is pulled from the waters of Cape Town harbour, and disillusioned ex-assassin Ben Gabriel wonders whether he died because of questions he was asking about the new president. Gabriel knows that sometimes it takes one killer to stop another, and will do anything to discover the truth, even if that means stepping outside the law.

Murderous – *The Gabriel Series – Book Two*

When a massacre in a small country church shatters an Afrikaans farming community, the message that this is "only the beginning" sparks the fear of genocide. The Department asks Ben Gabriel to apply his unconventional approach to discover the truth behind the massacre – a task made more difficult by the intensive search to find a large number of gold bars stolen from one of the country's most powerful men.

Vengeful – *The Gabriel Series – Book Three*

A series of prominent members of South African society are being brutally murdered. When the police discover that a certain Ben Gabriel recently visited each of them, he becomes a hunted man. And when Gabriel is linked to a multi-million dollar gold heist, his life becomes even more complicated.

Culpable – *The Gabriel Series – Book Four*

A foreign chemist is on the run and Gabriel needs to find him before he betrays the country and sells his deadly secrets. But who is the chemist running from? And why are members of the gold heist gang being targeted? Is someone looking for the stolen gold, or are they trying to stop Gabriel?

ENJOY THIS BOOK?

YOU CAN MAKE A BIG DIFFERENCE

Reviews are the most powerful tools at my disposal when it comes to getting attention for my books. Much as I'd like to, I don't have the financial muscle of a big publishing house. I can't take out full page ads in newspapers or put posters on the subway. (Not yet anyway!)

But I do have something much more powerful and effective than that, and it's something those publishers would kill to get their hands on.

A committed and loyal bunch of readers.

Honest reviews of my books help bring them to the attention of other readers.

If you've enjoyed this book I would be very grateful if you could spend just five minutes leaving a review (it can be as short as you like) on the book's Amazon page, on Good-Reads, BookBub and everywhere else.

Thank you so much!

WANT TO READ MORE?

If you have enjoyed this story then I know you will love reading a short novella called **_Decisive_** which tells the story of a mission Ben Gabriel is sent on by the Department to assassinate someone ... but who?

If you join my Readers' Club I will send you the novella (as a free eBook), as well as provide updates about new books in the series and special Readers' Club deals.

Join the club and get your free novella on my website: www.davidhickson.com

I look forward to welcoming you to the club!

ABOUT THE AUTHOR

David Hickson is an award-winning filmmaker and writer from South Africa. His work has included internationally released feature films, television series and live entertainment television shows.

David travelled to Italy several years ago, an adventure that he and his family, including two young troublemakers and an assortment of spoilt and demanding domestic animals, are still enjoying. He loves walking and cycling in the hills of Italy, drinking the local wine, and telling stories that entertain and stir the emotions of his readers.

For more books and updates:
www.davidhickson.com

Made in the USA
Columbia, SC
06 January 2022

53709934R00221